BREAKING THE RULES

CRYSTAL KASWELL

COPYRIGHT

This is a work of fiction. Similarities to real people, places, or events are entirely coincidental.

ALSO BY CRYSTAL KASWELL

Sinful Serenade

Sing Your Heart Out - Miles

Strum Your Heart Out - Drew

Rock Your Heart Out - Tom

Play Your Heart Out - Pete

Sinful Ever After – series sequel

Dangerous Noise

Dangerous Kiss - Ethan

Dangerous Crush – Kit

Dangerous Rock – Joel

Dangerous Fling – Mal

Dangerous Encore - series sequel

Inked Hearts

Tempting - Brendon

Playing - Walker

Pretend You're Mine - Ryan

Hating You, Loving You - Dean

Breaking the Rules - Hunter

Losing It - Wes - coming early 2019

More coming in 2019

Standalones

Broken - Trent & Delilah

Dirty Rich

Sign up for the Crystal Kaswell mailing list

EMMA

There's something wrong with my brother.

The house is spotless.

No dishes in the sink.

No papers on the dining table.

No pillows strewn over the black leather couch.

The only sign of life is the *tap tap tap* of the shower upstairs.

"Brendon." I kick off my work flats. Move across the living room. Up the stairs. "Can we talk?" I swallow the nerves that climb into my throat.

I need to stay cool and collected.

So he believes my version of events.

If my brother finds out what really happened…

That's not an option.

The shower turns off.

I take a deep breath. Exhale slowly.

I'm convincing my brother this isn't a big deal. Period. End of story.

"Hello?" A low, deep voice fills the hallway.

It's familiar.

But it's not my brother's.

That's definitely not my brother.

That's…

Uh…

Fuck.

I try to make eye contact, but I can't.

He's dripping wet.

Naked.

Huge.

"Emma?" The familiar voice asks.

Something clicks in my head.

That's him.

He's wearing way fewer clothes, yeah, but I'd recognize those blue eyes anywhere.

Hunter.

Hunter is naked in my brother's house.

Hunter is naked in my brother's house and I'm staring at his cock.

I should stop.

Really, I should.

But he's so…

"Fuck. Sorry." He turns and marches into the bedroom.

My eyes stay fixed on his tan skin.

I try to look at something else—his sandy hair or the lights in the bathroom or the beige carpet—but I can't.

He's so naked.

And I'm so into it.

"You okay?" He steps into the hallway.

Finally, my eyes obey my command. They trace a line up his long, lean torso. The dreamcatcher tattoo on his shoulder. The strong chin. The piercing blue eyes.

They're so fucking intense.

"Emma?" he asks again. With extra concern. "Are you okay?" His voice drops to something closer to a whisper.

It's not even remotely close to a *baby, I want you whisper*, but that's still where my head goes.

He's wearing a towel.

Only a towel.

And he's wet.

I…

He…

God, he's beautiful.

"What are you doing here?" I press my palm against the doorframe. Dig my toes into the carpet.

"Brendon didn't explain?"

"No."

"I'm staying here for a few weeks."

I just barely nod.

"And I'm filling in at Inked Hearts. While he's in New Jersey."

"Oh." Of course the one guy who makes me blush is filling in at Inked Hearts. Of course he's house sitting the one time I want to stay here. "That's great."

"You sure?" he asks.

"Yeah." I try to find something to say. Fail. It's weird. Unlike me. I hold my own around guys. Even half-naked ones. But after *that*… Fuck, I don't know anymore. "You'll fit in."

"You work the front desk?"

"Yeah. Sometimes." I take a step backward. Suck a breath through my teeth. Hunter is still wearing a towel. My brain is still struggling to function. It's still screaming *Hunter. Towel. Wet.*

It's a cavewoman who can barely put words together.

Though there's a certain flow to *Hunter. Towel. Wet.*

It's poetic.

"I should get dressed." He nods to the office.

3

"Right." I press my lips together. He's so... This is so... I'm so not doing this. "I should... um... I'll see you later."

He nods *sure*, turns, and disappears into the office.

I press my bedroom door closed.

Then I slide to the ground and I die of embarrassment.

HUNTER

This is not the time to be hard.

And that is not the woman to be hard over.

But Emma isn't the gawky kid who used to look at me with doe eyes.

She's all legs and energy.

I drape my towel over the couch.

Crouch over my suitcase. Find a clean pair of boxers. Jeans. A black t-shirt.

This room is mine for as long as I want it.

Brendon was welcoming.

He's the only person who gave a shit about helping me piece my life back together.

He asked one thing in return: look out for his little sister.

And here I am, still hard.

But, God damn, the way she stared.

It's different now.

It's been forever.

That must be it.

Because it sure as hell can't be that I want Emma Kane.

That's out of the question.

I repeat the explanation to myself as I dress, but it doesn't stick.

This is my self-destructive streak acting up.

Lusting after the one woman I'm not supposed to touch—

That certainly sounds like me.

I pull out my cell. Consider texting Brendon. Decide against it.

What am I going to say? *Sorry, I gave your sister a show. But damn was she into it. Would you mind if I took this back to her room and fucked her senseless?*

That isn't happening.

Even if everything was different, Emma is a good kid.

I'm not.

I push my suitcase aside. Sit on the leather couch I'm currently using as a bed. Open my sketchbook to the sleeve I'm doing tomorrow morning.

It takes forever, but, eventually, I concentrate on the gig I need to ace.

Then Emma knocks on my door and all my focus scatters.

"Hey. Hunter. I, uh, Brendon's only stopping by to grab his stuff. And he's got another two hours at the shop first." Her voice is soft. Nervous. "So, um, I… I'll just be downstairs. Studying."

"Sure."

"You mind if I play some music?"

"Go for it."

"Thanks." Her footsteps move down the hallway. Then the stairs.

The house quiets. Then it booms with a heavy guitar riff.

It's familiar.

One of Chase's favorites.

It tugs at something in my gut. Some place that's still empty.

Someplace that's always been empty.

There wasn't one reason why I spiraled into self-destruction.

It was all these little things. Mom mentally bailing on us. Dad checking out with her. My inability to connect. Or understand. Or feel anything stronger than this dull ache that got bigger and bigger until it threatened to consume me.

Fuck, I can't get into this now.

I need to get through this gig.

To survive Emma downstairs.

To find an anonymous fuck to drown my thoughts.

That isn't happening—it's too close to everything.

Right now, work is the only distraction I have.

It has to be enough.

I slip my sketchbook into my backpack. Sling it over my shoulder. Head downstairs.

Emma's sitting on the couch. Her long legs are spread over the leather. Her white tank top is low on her chest. Her lips are *fuck me* red.

It's not what she's saying.

She isn't saying anything.

She's minding her own fucking business.

I need to do the same.

"Hey." She looks up from her textbook. "I, uh—"

"I gotta—" I reach for an explanation that isn't *I have to run away from you because I don't trust myself.* Find nothing. "I'm gonna grab dinner."

"For yourself?" She looks up at me expectantly.

I guess it is a dick move, grabbing dinner for myself when she's here. "What do you want?"

"Something good."

"Specifically?"

"Pasta." Her attention shifts to her textbook. "See you later."

"Yeah." I force myself to turn away from her as I cross the living room and slip into my shoes.

But even as I step outside, I can feel her stare.

7

It's still doing shit to me.

It can't.

I may not be in control of much, but I'm in control of this.

I'm not reacting to Emma Kane.

Even if it kills me.

EMMA

My brother steps inside the house with a heavy sigh. Not an *I'm tired* sigh or even *damn, it's been a long day.*

That sigh is pure *what the fuck did you do now?*

"Kay said something happened." He runs his hand through his dark hair. That *I'm so beyond tired of your shit* gesture.

No. That's his thing.

I think.

I can't read him as well as I used to.

I bite my tongue to keep from blurting out a defensive answer. I need tact. I need to include just enough of the truth to make this plausible. "It's not a big deal."

"Really?"

"Yeah. You can see that."

He shakes his head. "You don't give me enough credit."

"I give you too much credit."

He moves into the kitchen and grabs something from a high shelf. "I only have half an hour, Em."

"We need to find a new place."

"Why?" He pulls open the freezer door. Places exactly two ice cubes in his glass. But he doesn't go for the whiskey the way he usually does. He fills the glass with water. "What did you do?"

"Maybe your angel did something."

He steps into the main room and shoots me a *really* look.

Yeah, that's not exactly a believable argument. Kaylee, my room-mate slash best friend, is Brendon's girlfriend. And she really is an angel. Straight As. Perfect work attendance. Closet full of cardigans.

It's weird, him dating her.

Especially since he's my dad as much as he's my brother—our parents died when I was a kid.

It's bullshit, that he still acts all *my house, my rules* when he's dating a girl two months younger than I am.

But that isn't changing in the next half an hour.

Convincing Brendon this is normal is a bigger concern.

No more defensiveness.

"Management has been giving us attitude about the noise complaints." I sell my story with all the conviction I can muster.

He stares back at me.

"They didn't warn us. It was suddenly 'oh, you're playing your music too loud. You're throwing too many parties.'"

Brendon's brow furrows, but he presses on. He motions to the Bluetooth speaker on the table, the one blasting Bayside. "This the shit you've been playing?"

"If you want me to turn it down, just ask."

He moves to the table and hits the pause button.

The room falls silent.

Way too silent.

I can hear the hum of the refrigerator.

The cars outside.

Laughter.

Footsteps.

Waves.

Wind.

The noise isn't so bad.

But the thoughts that are suddenly loud enough?

I can't stomach that.

Brendon takes another step toward me. "What did you do, Em?"

"I just told you."

"There's no way you're being asked to leave because you have bad taste in music."

"Your girlfriend has the same taste."

He motions *kinda.*

I fight my smile.

He's teasing me.

Yeah, he's digging for holes in my story like an expert police interrogator.

But he's doing it because he cares.

He wants this to be easy.

If I make it easy, he'll believe me.

"I threw a few too many parties. Pissed off too many neighbors. Technically, we can stay. But I don't want to fight management." I press my lips into a smile. But that's not right. A frown is closer.

His dark eyes bore into mine.

They're so much like Mom's eyes.

Like mine.

"You threw two parties last year," he says.

"That you know about." I shrug as if this isn't a big deal.

His stare intensifies.

It's a classic Brendon stare. *I know best. I know everything. I'm waiting for you to figure it out.*

But he doesn't have time today.

He has to pick up Kaylee and fly to New Jersey.

He finishes his glass of water and sets it on the table. "What's your plan?"

"I'll find a new place. Kay can check it out when you're back."

"Until then?"

"I'll stay here for a while."

"It's that bad?"

"Yeah." It's worse. I cross my fingers behind my back. Pray he'll accept this as being about the eardrum blasting volume of my music and nothing else. "I just have to get my stuff. I… uh… I'll do it tomorrow."

"You okay?"

"Great." I try to smile. Fail. Fuck. I'm giving too much away. And I can't. I can't talk about this. I can't even think about it.

"Em, what happened?"

"I told you. The super is a dick. And I want to stay here." I hug my text book to my chest. "Go. Finish packing. Pick up your angel. Join the mile high club. I have to study."

"All right."

Once again, he stares through me.

He waits for me to break.

He's good at it. Usually.

But this time, I'm sticking with my cover story.

The super is a dick about music. Period. The end.

If Brendon finds out…

That ends someplace ugly.

"Does Kay know what really happened?" he asks.

"I told you what really happened."

He folds his arms.

"Don't put this on her." I swallow hard. She doesn't know either. She suspects, sure, but she doesn't know.

"Em…" His voice gets soft. Caring. He wants to know. To make sure nothing bad happened.

His concern means a lot.

Really, it does.

But I can't take it today.

I can barely stomach this.

Two more minutes of selling this story.

Then I can lock myself in my room.

Scream as loudly as I want.

Run as far away from this as I want.

He moves closer. "You promise you're okay?"

"Yeah." I force a smile. "I'm good. Really."

"I told Hunter he could stay here. But—"

No. It's good. I've known Hunter long time. He's a trouble-maker yeah, but he's always looked out for me. "I'll cook. He'll clean."

"You sure?" Concern drips into his voice.

It's weird. How can he trust his friend to stay here but not trust him alone with me?

Either he's more over-protective than I thought.

Or there's something about Hunter I don't know.

"Go easy on him," Brendon says.

I raise a brow. "Easy how?"

"Don't fuck with him."

"Okay." I'm not promising that. Not if Hunter is anything like he was at Brendon's birthday party. All drunk and difficult and teasing.

"Don't fuck him."

"What?" Where the hell did that come from?

"He's not in the headspace for it."

"Are you his shrink?"

"Trust me for once."

Okay…

"He used to babysit you." He crosses to the stairs.

"No one ever babysat me."

"Still. He's almost ten years older."

"Am I supposed to stay away for him or for me?"

"Just be his friend."

There is something up.

But I'm not going to get greedy and dig.

I sold Brendon my story. That's good enough for tonight.

Right on cue, the front door opens.

Hunter steps inside with a takeout bag curled under his arm. His blue eyes flit from Brendon to me.

"What did you get?" I turn to Hunter. Ignore my brother's stare.

"Glass noodles and green curry," Hunter says.

"Thanks." I meant Italian pasta, but noodles are noodles.

"You bought her dinner?" Brendon asks.

Hunter nods.

"I got that." My brother reaches for his wallet.

Hunter shakes his head. "No way in hell."

Brendon nods *fair enough*. "Em is gonna stay here for a while."

Concern fills Hunter's blue eyes. "Should I—"

"No. She needs someone around to look out for her." Brendon turns back to me.

"What about Hunter?" I mean, he's not in the headspace for casual sex. And I'm not supposed to fuck with him. "Should I look out for him too?"

"Yeah." Brendon's voice is serious. "You should. You good for that?"

"Oh?" I bite my lip.

"Yeah." Brendon looks between us. "Keep each other honest."

"Sure." I offer Hunter my best *awesome that we're roomies* smile. It's not good. It's more of an *oh my God, I saw you naked an hour ago* blush.

He smiles back. Drops the bag on the kitchen table. "I'm gonna shower."

"But you—" I zip my lips. No commentary on his recent shower. No need to put that idea in Brendon's head.

"Start without me." Hunter motions to the food then crosses the living room and moves up the stairs.

Brendon waits until the bathroom door shuts to move close enough to whisper. "Seriously, Em. Don't."

"Don't what?"

"I saw the look." His gaze flits to the upstairs. "Don't fuck with him. He's been through a lot."

"A lot meaning…"

"I won't ask about the apartment again," he says.

He doesn't have to add *don't ask what the deal is with Hunter.*

I get the message loud and clear.

The tortured bad boy has a secret.

And it's none of my business.

4

HUNTER

H onestly, I'm not sure why Brendon trusts me with his kid sister.

Or why he's willing to help me.

But I'm earning that trust.

Whatever it takes.

I text him a promise I'll keep an eye on Em.

He texts back something about helping her with clearing out her old apartment and finding a new place.

And a thanks.

Fuck, it feels good.

Him caring. Expecting help from me. Believing I'm a worthwhile guy.

I'm not used to it.

I need to deserve it.

If that means helping Emma without touching her—

I can do that.

For a while, I turn my attention to my sketchbook. But it doesn't distract from the questions swirling around my head.

It's too close. Too personal.

When I draw, my subconscious takes over.

All that shit stirring inside me, the shit I don't want to face, is right there.

On the paper.

I'm not sure what this means—a bottle in the shape of the heart, broken on the floor, bleeding whiskey like it's blood—but I know what it means about me.

Footsteps move up the stairs. The hallway light turns off.

Emma moves back downstairs.

Yeah, she's a smoking hot woman with a smart mouth and perfect tits.

But she's also my new roommate.

I need to get over how much I want her.

I close my sketchbook and move into the hallway.

She stops halfway down the stairs. Turns back to me with irritation in her dark eyes. "You don't have to spy."

"I'm not." I'm not a good liar. Not sober. The words are awkward on my tongue.

Disbelief spreads over her face.

Yeah, I'm obvious. But I can still spin this. "You finish studying?"

"Yes, Dad, thanks."

"Usually, I save the daddy shit until date three."

She fights a smile. "Gross."

"Don't knock it till you try it."

Emma laughs as she moves down the stairs. "You are not into that."

"You sure?" I follow her to the living room.

She grabs the remote and plops onto the couch. Her eyes fix on me. They study me.

Her eyes are lighter than Brendon's, but they have the same intensity.

"Mostly." She taps the remote a few times. The DVD menu loads. *Hercules.*

A Disney cartoon.

Not what I expected.

"Why?" I ask.

"Why am I sure you're not into the Daddy thing?"

I nod.

She tilts her head to one side, studying me. "It's a vibe."

"That's it?"

"That's it." Her eyes flit to the TV then back to me. "Are you gonna stand there?"

"Yeah."

"Don't. It's weird." She pats the spot next to hers. "Sit down and watch the movie or go back to your room."

"What if I want to stand here and watch the movie?"

"Then I'll blast Bayside all night."

"What if I like shitty emo music?"

"Then you wouldn't enjoy something as quality as Bayside."

I chuckle. "You're the one using it as a threat."

"Used to Brendon's reactions."

Truth be told, I enjoy that particular style of music. But it makes me think of my older brother. And that's a minefield. "I have better taste."

"That's setting the bar low."

My chuckle gets louder. Heartier. Fuck, there is something about her. This spark. She's always had it. But it's different now.

Or maybe it's that I'm different now.

She grabs a chocolate bar from the table, unwraps it, breaks off a square. "I'm going to say thanks for dinner, then we're even. You stop spying. I stop spying."

It's a smart offer.

She's a sharp kid, trying to blackmail me into backing off.

But it's obvious she's bluffing.

"And if I report every detail?" I move down the stairs. Take a seat on the couch next to her.

She turns to me with a glare. "You won't."

I shrug *won't I?* But it's not nearly as casual and aloof as it should be. I no longer know how to pull off casual and aloof.

"He warned me not to fuck with you."

"Oh?" This time, I'm better at playing cool. I keep my voice disaffected. I lean back on the couch, shrug my shoulders, spread my legs.

"Yeah. But he told you to keep an eye on me."

"And?"

"Don't you find that strange?"

No. But I can't exactly explain the why to her.

"He even told me not to fuck you."

My balls tighten. That sounds too good on her lips. It's putting too many ideas in my head.

"I didn't float the idea or anything. But he had to add it." She breaks her square of chocolate in half and sets a piece on her tongue. "Here's my question."

"Yeah?"

"Is that for me or you?"

My shrug is stiff. Awkward. I can do babysitter. I can do watchful older brother. I can't do honest conversations.

"Supposedly, you're not in the headspace for casual sex."

"I'm not."

"Because?"

Because I haven't fucked someone sober since I was her age. "Why are you here?"

"Trouble with management. No big deal." There's something in her voice.

It's a lie.

But I'm not pushing it.

I can't afford her pushing back.

"What about you?" she asks.

"Needed a place to crash."

"Your old one?"

"Long story."

"Mhmm." She turns her attention back to the TV.

I have no response to that.

I should probably come up with a plausible explanation.

But it's hard to concentrate with her this close.

"It's been awhile since I've had a roommate." Not counting rehab. "I'll try not to step on your toes."

"Except for when you're babysitting?"

"I'll keep an eye. That's it."

"Right."

"You can do the same."

"I will."

"Good."

"Good." She breaks another square from her bar of chocolate and hands it to me. "Now be quiet or go upstairs."

My fingers brush hers as I take the chocolate.

It sends an electric current though me.

It's a tiny thing. Almost imperceptible. The kind of shit I was too trashed to notice.

But it's there.

And, fuck, being able to feel it—

It's everything.

5

HUNTER

Dean's light eyes brighten as I step into the shop.

The tall tattoo artist is all smiles and fucking with people. He always has been.

I've known him since high school.

And now I'm working for him.

Fuck, it's weird.

He nods a hello then looks to his suite.

"Hmm?" Chloe steps into the main room. She folds her arms over her chest. Taps her combat boots together.

She's his apprentice.

And—I don't have the details, but there's something between them.

They've known each other since high school.

Hated and wanted each other in equal measure.

They would make a cute couple.

He's a foot taller than her. He's bright and cheery down to his white t-shirt and his checkered Vans.

Whereas she dresses exclusively in black.

"I looked at you. That enough to make you miserable, sunshine?" he teases.

Her eyes narrow. *Of course it is.* She turns back to me. "Hunter, it's nice to see you again." Her tone shifts to something pleasant. The irritation falls off her face as she extends her hand.

I shake. "You too, Chloe." We just barely knew each other in high school, but I stopped by last week to sign my paperwork.

"Chloe Grace Lee," Dean adds. "She knows karate—"

"Aikido," she corrects.

"Don't fuck with her or she'll fuck you up." Dean lets out a hearty chuckle.

It's a sweet warning, though it's obviously not the case. He's already fucking with her.

She's biting back, yeah.

But considering his lack of bruising, I'm pretty sure she isn't fucking him up.

"Shit, you can cut the sexual tension with a knife, huh?" Dean winks at Chloe.

She stifles a smile.

Her eyes light up.

They stare like they're waiting to rip each other's clothes off.

It's bizarre.

And, this time, I'm pretty sure it's not my inability to communicate sober.

More their inability to hide their desire to bang.

"You're borrowing Brendon's suite for now." Chloe motions to the suite in the middle of the room. "Not that it's officially his. Now that you're working here—"

"I'm just filling in," I say.

She looks back to Dean.

He nods.

I'm not sure what the hell it means, but it conveys something to her.

She turns back to me with a smile. A big, bright smile that

24

lights up her eyes.

She's expecting something from me.

But I haven't got a clue what it is.

"Been awhile, huh?" I ask.

"Yeah." She looks from Dean to me. "How have you been?"

I study her expression. It's earnest. Chloe was always the earnest type.

Except with Dean. The two of them traded barbs like it was going out of style.

She must not know what a mess I made of my life.

Better to keep it that way.

"All right," I say. "How about you?"

"I'm here." She looks back to Dean then raises her voice. "It's horrible torture, being here, but at least I'm learning."

"Oh yeah? You want to quit?" Dean teases.

She flips him off. "Fuck off, dick face."

He blows her a kiss. "You know I take that as a compliment."

She makes a show of rolling her eyes. "He's under some delusion that by calling him dick face, I'm saying his dick is beautiful."

"And?" I ask.

"I've seen better." She steps into the suite and points out where everything is. "You have a few appointments; the stuff Brendon couldn't move. And you can take walk-ins. We usually get a few."

"Thanks." I find a spot for my backpack then pull out my sketchbook. "Good seeing you again."

She nods. "You too." She plays with the pocket of her black jeans. "Let me know if you need anything. And Dean..." She lowers her voice to whisper. "Sometimes, he's okay. I'm sure he'll help if you need it." She turns and moves back to the desk.

Dean whispers something.

She laughs.

It's funny. Familiar. Like high school.

Like I didn't spend the last eight years fucking up my life.

MY ELEVEN O'CLOCK STEPS INTO THE SHOP WITH A NERVOUS SMILE. Stephanie. Instantly recognizable from her Instagram, mostly shots of her hot pink hair or an outfit showing off her massive tits.

She's hot.

My body gets it.

But it's not like it was with Emma yesterday.

The guy I used to be wants to fuck Stephanie.

He wants to sweet talk, to flirt all through her ink, to let his fingers linger on her skin.

He doesn't care that she's nervous and vulnerable.

That guy is still there, at the back of my head.

He still wants to get wasted and take her home.

But the guy I'm trying to be—

He knows better.

"Hey, Hunter." Her red lips press into a smile. "You look just like your pictures." She opens her arms for a hug.

I accept it.

She squeezes tightly.

It's the closest I've been to someone in months.

It should feel good having a hot woman's body pressed against mine.

But it doesn't.

It's too much.

Too intimate.

Too demanding of something deep inside me.

She releases me with a smile.

I motion to the coffee machine and the water cooler next to it. "You want something to drink?"

"Coffee's probably a bad idea. With all the nerves?"

I nod. I've already had too much. I'm shaking. It's a cliché, trading an addiction to booze for one to caffeine and sugar, but that's 'cause it works. "How about a decaf?"

"Decaf?" Her brow furrows. "Is there a point?"

"Water?"

She nods. "Thank you."

I motion to the suite. "Take a seat. I'll bring it over."

She does.

I fill two cups with water. Chloe and Dean look up from whatever they're doing at the front desk to watch me.

They whisper like best friends trading gossip.

Or lovers.

Hard to tell.

I'm not sure what they know.

Brendon is a quiet guy. I trust him to keep secrets. But it's not hard to put the pieces together.

Last time they saw me, I was drunk and wild.

Now...

I'm not sure what the hell I am, but I'm not that guy.

My fingers brush Stephanie's.

She looks up at me with a smile. It's somewhere between *I'm so excited about this* and *I want to fuck you senseless*.

It's the mix of adrenaline and dopamine that comes with ink.

It's that I'm a hot tattoo artist about to mark her body.

It's not about *me*.

She finishes her water in three gulps, then hands the cup back to me. "Am I supposed to be ready?"

"I still get nervous too."

"Really?" Her eyes go wide as she studies the sleeve on my left arm. "After all that?"

Sometimes. But it's not the needle on my skin that scares me. It's having my hands on the gun.

I've done this buzzed a lot more than I've done this sober.

I need this job.

I need to be as good as I was.

"That's part of the thrill." I finish my water. "The rush is addicting."

She nods *true* and looks to the tattoo on her forearm—the lyrics to a song. I don't recognize them, but they're familiar. Something I've seen before. And not just on her Instagram.

"You ready?"

She nods *yeah*.

"Then let's start." I wash my hands. Don gloves. Play with a few temporary tattoos until we find the perfect placement.

It's all normal. Easy. Familiar.

Then I clean her up.

Get her in the chair, facedown—this is going on her shoulder blade—and tape the stencil to her skin.

My heart thuds against my chest.

My limbs get airy.

There's something about the gun. Something more than that Spider-man quote about great power and great responsibility.

Lightness spreads through my torso and chest as I turn on the gun.

This is an easy design. A simple stencil. Chloe's been apprenticing for a month and she could probably do it.

I can do this.

I've been doing this for nearly a decade.

So what if this is my first time accepting a paying client sober?

I suck a breath through my nose. "You ready?"

"I think so."

"Take a deep breath."

She does.

"Slow exhale."

She does that too.

"Stay like that, Steph. Okay?"

She giggles at the nickname. "Okay."

This is it. I need to let routine take over. Flirt. Tease. Work. "On three."

She nods.

"One, two." I bring the gun to her skin. Turn it on. "Three."

She yelps as the needle hits her skin.

I freeze. Turn it off. "You okay?"

"Yeah. Totally. Keep going."

"Sure." I'm not sure which of us is more scared, but I'm the one who has to deal. My nerves are only going to make hers worse. It's part of my job to walk her through this. The biggest part, even. "Tell me about this tattoo."

"Yeah?"

I turn the gun on.

Her breath gets shallow, but I still bring the needle to her skin.

"This will be fast. I promise." I bring the gun closer.

She nods. "Go."

Again, she yelps as the needle hits her skin. Her fingers dig into the teal vinyl. Her toes tap the shiny tile floor. "It's the lyrics to a song."

"What do you like about it?"

"Huh?"

I finish tracing the first letter and move to the second. My shoulders and back tense. Sweat drips to my brow. I'm not used to this position. I'm not used to this, period.

"What do you mean?"

"The song must be special. Or you wouldn't want the lyrics on your skin forever."

"Yeah." She grunts as I finish the second letter. "Is it going to hurt more or less as you move to the right?"

"Both. Closer to bone hurts more. You need a break?"

"No. Just conversation."

"I'm waiting."

"Oh. Yeah. It's just… kinda personal."

"But you want the whole world to see it?"

"It's on my back."

"You live in Southern California."

She laughs.

"I saw your Instagram, Steph. I know you show off."

Her laugh gets bigger. Heartier.

I have to pull the gun away, so it won't stutter.

"Am I that bad?" Her voice gets bouncy. Coquettish.

She's flirting.

I can flirt back.

Hell, I should. That's the easiest way to relax her.

But I can't bring myself to compliment her tits.

It feels wrong.

She saves me from finding a response. "I guess... it means something to me. But you know how it is. Most people don't look closer. They think about how they love the band or the song. But... God this sounds stupid."

"It doesn't."

"Did you ever feel like no one understands you?"

For the last decade. "What gave it away?"

She laughs. "Something about you."

"Where you at that party where I stood up and started singing Linkin Park?" I tease.

Her laugh gets louder. "I wish. I'd love to see you do *In The End*."

"How about *Crawling?*"

Again, she laughs. "How about you sing it with me?"

"You want the main vocals or the backing vocals?"

"Which gets you on stage?" She makes eye contact through the mirror. "You seem more like the backup type."

"Why do you say that?"

"There's a steadiness to you. Like you don't want attention."

"I might be convinced."

"I know a place that does karaoke Tuesdays. No cover. Strong drinks."

And there's that hitch.

At some point, I'm going to have to face the fact that everyone wants to combine alcohol with... everything.

But not yet.

Right now, I just need to get through this.

"I have a card in my wallet. I'll leave it at the counter," she says.

"Thanks."

"I... Uh... I guess everyone feels like that sometimes. Like no one understands them. But this song... when I was a teenager, I felt like no one would ever get how fucked-up my head was. But this song did. It was the only thing that made me feel like someone would understand."

It hits me right in the gut.

She's honest and vulnerable and she's offering that to me.

I should reach out.

Say *me too. I'm still fucked-up. I've been fucked-up since I can remember. I thought it was cool, when I was a kid. I thought there was something beautiful about embracing my misery. About drowning everything I felt under a bottle of bourbon. But when I got over the idea of beautiful damage and realized I wasn't having fun anymore, I couldn't handle that. I couldn't handle shit.*

So I drank more.

It was the only way to make everything easier.

Now that I'm sober, everything is so fucking hard again.

And I don't remember what the point of it is.

When does it get easier?

I want to understand it.

I want someone else to understand it.

To understand me.

I say none of that.

Stephanie is brave as hell, laying herself bare like this.

I'm not there yet.

31

I'm not even close to there yet.

"Is that stupid?" she asks.

"No." It's really not. "Everybody wants to be understood."

"And to understand someone else."

"Yeah."

"Why can't it always be this easy?" she asks.

"This is easy?" I finish another letter.

"Painful. But easy."

"It's the same with other people, isn't it?"

"Yeah, I guess it is. Simple. But painful." She bites her tongue.

"Halfway there."

"Thank God."

My laugh is soft.

Stephanie is sweet.

If things were different, if I was the kind of person who could handle intimacy—I'd run into her fucking arms.

But I'm not.

I can't.

I can barely handle this.

I bring up the band's first album.

Stephanie starts gushing about her favorite song.

I lose myself in finishing this work.

For the first time in forever, I'm on steady ground.

This is where I'm supposed to be.

What I'm supposed to do.

The reason why I need to hold my shit together.

For a while, I feel good. I check her out. Make it through my second client. Shoot the shit with Dean.

Then Emma steps into the store and shoots me that look that's equal parts *leave me the fuck alone* and *I want to see you naked again.*

And the ground falls out from under me.

6

HUNTER

Dean explains the shop mantra as Emma settles into her seat behind the counter.

Cute girl checks customers out. Flirts to increase the line of the tip. Takes home a small percentage of said tip on top of her salary for the trouble.

He explains it loudly, to irritate Chloe, which he does.

She rolls her eyes and stomps to the office.

He follows her.

I focus on a mock-up for an old client. Natasha. She'd get something once a year. Wake up one day inspired, beg me to squeeze her in, gush over what I whipped up in a few hours.

When inspiration struck this morning, she went into Blacklist Tattoo looking for me. Heard that I'd moved on.

I guess that's that.

Chase made it clear I wasn't welcome when he issued that ultimatum.

Time and sobriety haven't done shit to heal this.

I'm not sure anything is going to heal this.

I snap a picture of the mock-up. Send it to Natasha.

The shop is quiet. There's always noise—rock music, the hum of the tattoo gun, soft grunts—but there's no conversation.

Emma is sitting at the counter, copying notes onto a clean sheet of paper.

She looks up from her text book.

Catches me staring.

Blushes.

Because she wants me.

Or because her story about playing shitty music too loudly is bullshit.

Or because she's terrified I'll report to her brother.

Or maybe all of the above.

I want to repay the debt I owe Brendon.

But there's something else too. Something about her. Something besides her long legs and her soft lips.

Fuck, I need to get over that.

I'm helping her as a favor.

I'm not getting involved.

That's best for both of us.

Natasha sends notes on the design.

I make changes and send another snapshot.

We go through a few rounds of refinement.

As Dean and Chloe finish with their client. Run to the backroom. Get into a huge fight that has her storming out.

As Emma flirts with a walk-in.

The poor sucker wants his girlfriend's name.

I should refuse—people always regret this shit—but there's something about the look in his eyes. It almost makes me believe in love.

Eventually, my three o'clock arrives.

He goes straight to the desk.

I meet him there.

"Hey." Emma forces her red lips into a smile. "You must be John."

He nods. "And you?"

"Emma." She bats her eyelashes. Giggles loudly. "You're in great hands. I bet you'll end up with something amazing." Her cheeks flush as she looks to me. "Hunter is talented. If you can get past him thinking he's always right."

"Not sure I can," the guy says.

Emma's fake laugh is awkward. Forced.

Her brow furrows.

Her lips curl into a frown.

The realization that she's failing to flirt spreads all over her face. "Well, let me know if you need anything. Water. Or coffee." This time, she pulls off the smile.

"Yeah." My client is oblivious to her clumsiness. He's buying the flirting hook, line, and sinker.

He gives her a long once over.

His tongue slides over his lips.

His gaze shifts to her chest.

My fingers curl into fists.

My jaw cricks.

What the fuck does he think he's doing?

I shake my head. Shrug the tension from my shoulders.

Yeah, I'm keeping an eye on Emma.

But that's all it is.

One friend looking out for another.

After I finish with this guy, she flirts through checkout. Packs her stuff.

Argues with me about the two of us walking home together.

Relents with a smile.

An *I want to fuck you* smile.

I tell my body to cool it.

But my head still fills with thoughts of stripping her naked and driving inside her.

35

"So..." Emma presses her palms against her dark jeans. "Any word from Mr. Brooding Bad Boy?"

I stop at the crosswalk. Hit the button. It's a gorgeous day. The sunset streaks the sky orange. The air is cool and crisp. It even smells like fall. "Mr. Brooding Bad Boy?"

"Brendon."

I can't help but chuckle.

"Don't laugh. You're giving him a run for his money."

"Oh?"

She nods.

"Your type?"

"Yeah. Just like how you're into the daddy stuff." She shakes her head, but a smile still spreads over her red lips.

"Glad you accepted it instead of kink shaming me."

She makes a show of rolling her eyes. "I know it's been a while since we've hung out one-on-one, but I don't remember you being this annoying."

"I was. You've forgotten."

She stifles a laugh. "I still remember that time you came over to console Brendon after his girlfriend dumped him."

Fuck, I forgot about that. He barely dated. But there was one girl in high school he adored. They wrote punk lyrics together and dyed each other's hair red.

He didn't pull it off.

And, fuck, I was out of my depth with honest conversations about relationships.

"You two stayed up late drinking something you stole from your parents' liquor cabinet. Then you threw up all over my rug."

"How is your rug?"

The light switches to green. Emma looks both ways and steps into the crosswalk. "It never recovered."

"Fuck, how will I make that up to you?"

"Hmm... it's almost like you could stop babysitting me."

"But I couldn't." I've failed Brendon enough times—I sure as hell didn't help him get over his breakup. It's not happening again.

She groans in agony.

"Am I that bad?"

"It's all relative." She steps onto the sidewalk. This is the last main street before we move into the neighborhood, but this entire area is swarmed with cars. It's a mix of shops, houses, beach.

The Kane place is right on the beach in Venice Beach. No doubt it's worth multiple millions now. Brendon and Emma's parents had money.

All our parents did. It was five-figure tuition or scholarship to attend our fancy high school. And none of us were the scholarship type.

"Relative to Mr. Brooding Bad Boy," I say.

"If you follow all his orders, you're basically him."

"But I won't complain when you blast emo music."

"Thank God I have that."

My lips curl into a smile. It's weird talking with Emma.

Familiar but different.

I've seen her a dozen times in the last few years. But it's always been quick things. Her and Brendon at my birthday party. Or me at his. Or...

Well, it's always been parties.

And I've always been too busy drinking and starting shit to really talk to her.

"All right, you're babysitting me," she says.

I nod.

"So I guess we can talk."

"Horrible."

"I know, right?" She makes a show of groaning.

I can't help but laugh. She's vibrant. Bright. Full of life.

"This was your first day at Inked Hearts, huh?" she asks.

"Yeah."

"Why is it Brendon recruited you?"

"It's not obvious?" I motion to my face.

She laughs. "Yeah, that must be it. Your beauty. How could I not see that?"

I try my best easy shrug.

Her laugh gets louder. Heartier. "You should stop with that. The shrugs don't suit you."

"No?"

"No." She takes another sip. "They make you look more uncomfortable."

"That doesn't fool me."

"What doesn't?" She turns the corner. Walks past the house next to hers. Then to hers.

"You turning it around. It's not gonna get me so disoriented I forget you're going to your old place to get your stuff."

"No idea what you're talking about."

"Hate to break it to you, but Brendon briefed me."

She bites her tongue. "Brendon assigned you as my bodyguard?"

"Basically."

Frustration flares in her expression. It shutters that spark. Drains the bounciness from her voice. "Asshole."

I'm not sure if she's talking about me or him.

We both deserve it.

I'm putting what he's asking before what she wants.

"May I accompany you, Em?" I ask.

Her eyes narrow. "What if I say no?"

I stare back. *You know what happens if you say no.*

"It's not a request if you're coming either way."

"I'll help. It will go faster."

"Whatever." She moves to the door. Unlocks it. Steps inside.

I follow. "I'll wait here."

She shoots me a *really* look, then she marches up the stairs.

It takes a few minutes for her to grab suitcases and make her way to me.

She moves outside. To her car.

Stares at me like I'm the devil.

Like I've betrayed the intimacy we've built in the last twenty-four hours.

It twists something in my gut.

I'm capable of building trust with someone.

Of reaching out.

Understanding.

But I'm fucking it up again.

Classic Hunter Keating destructive shit.

I slide into the passenger seat. Turn the music to something she likes.

She shoots me a *nice try* look, but she still taps her fingers along with the beat.

This car is her. Bright red and messy.

It's a sedan, yeah, but it still screams with personality.

"I'm sorry your brother is over-protective." Fuck, I don't know how to get through to her. Only that I want to.

"No, you're not."

"You can pretend I'm not here."

"Whatever." She pulls out of the parking space. Turns onto a local street.

For a moment, there's nothing in the car but the breathy groan of the singer.

Then she looks to me. "Maybe we were never best friends. But you were always honest with me."

That's true enough. I nod. "Yeah."

"So don't dress up this bullshit with a bow. You're babysitting me because Brendon asked."

"I am."

"Why?"

39

"I owe him."

"For what?"

"Helping me out."

She rolls her eyes. "That's not an answer."

"What's the real reason why you're moving out of your apartment?"

"I told you. Noise complaint."

"Maybe we were never best friends, but you were always honest with me." I throw her words back at her.

It's the wrong thing to do.

Her eyes turn down.

Her lips curl into a frown.

Her brow furrows.

"You're an asshole," she says.

"No argument there."

Her gaze shifts to the street.

"But I'm still coming with you."

7

HUNTER

"**I**f you're going to be here, help." Emma points to the overflowing bookshelf in the corner.

"All right."

"DVDs only."

"Sure." I move to the shelf. Stack a dozen Disney movies on the dining table.

Then a collection of frothy romantic comedies.

It doesn't seem like Emma.

She's a lot of things.

But light and easy aren't among them.

She moves into the bedroom as I arrange the movies in her bright red suitcase.

I've never been all that neat—certainly not as neat as her brother—but since I got clean, I've learned to appreciate the merits of putting things in their place.

Like the line between me and Emma.

It's a fat thing that screams *you're here to look out for her. Don't get invested.*

Usually, that's easy.

Usually, I avoid connection as much as possible.

But there's something about her.

She moves into the main room with a dozen dresses folded over her arm.

Her dark eyes flit around the room.

Fix on me.

"You really want to help?" she asks.

"Yeah." I need to feel useful. Like I have a purpose. Or my head fills with thoughts of bourbon and numbness and I forget the point of this sobriety thing.

She motions to the kitchen. "Pack the coffee."

"Your brother has a ton."

"Dark roast." Her nose scrunches in distaste. "If I wanted burnt coffee, I'd go to Starbucks."

"I have good shit."

"So do I." Again, she motions to the kitchen.

I move into it. Find the coffee on a high shelf, behind a mug labeled *Please Wait, Sarcasm is Loading.*

I chuckle.

"What?" She turns to me. Watches me pull the mug and two bags of beans from the shelf. "Oh."

"Suits you."

"And your mug says *Babysit Harder*?"

"I was thinking Carpe Diem."

Her laugh cuts through the tension. "You're… you're kidding right."

I arch a brow.

"It's just so…"

"Obvious?"

"Yeah." Her lips curl into a smile. "Does it really?"

"Don't have a sassy mug."

"Maybe you need one."

"Maybe." I meet her at the dining table. Stack her coffee and her mug neatly.

Her fingers brush mine as she grabs the mug. "Thanks."

"Sure."

She looks up at me. Her eyes fill with something, some hint of apology, then she blinks and the vulnerability is gone. She's all fire again. "Can you wrap this in the dish towel?"

"Sure."

"Thanks." She sets the mug on the table. Turns. Moves into her bedroom.

I wrap the mug. Nestle it in the skirt of a short red dress. It's pure Emma. Stylish. Sexy. Bold.

For a moment, my eyelids flutter closed. I see her in that dress. See her pulling it up her thighs, parting her legs, motioning *come here*.

Then I blink and she's there. Crouching over the suitcase. Arranging another pile of clothes. Jeans. T-shirt. Sleek black panties.

Fuck.

My cock stirs.

It's been a long time since a woman has worn something to impress me.

No. The women I fuck aren't trying to impress *me*. It's empty sex. I'm a warm body, nothing more. There's no connection there. No intimacy. Nothing but two people exchanging orgasms.

This—

This is the most intimate thing I've done outside of rehab in a long fucking time.

Emma looks to me and raises a brow. "Do you need more coffee or something?"

"Always." I need a drink.

That's out of the question.

Which means I need to sort out my shit.

After we finish this.

Emma can't know I'm reacting to her.

I can't do shit about the thoughts flitting through my head.

"You have more of that?" I motion to the jeans she's folding.

"Yeah. Everything in the second drawer."

I nod. Rise. Move into her bedroom.

It's a small place with a big bed. Crimson comforter. White sheets. Desk covered in lyrics.

But the rest of the room is empty.

The plain white walls show signs of a former life. There are poster mounts and hooks stuck in the corners, but whatever they were holding is gone.

Like she tore her room apart.

I want to know what the fuck it means.

I want to know more about her.

What the hell is wrong with me?

There are a million girls I can date. I'm not getting attached to the one who's off limits.

I pull out the second drawer. Bring it into the main room.

Emma isn't crouching over the suitcase anymore.

She's at the door.

And there's a tall guy with her.

He's got dark hair, thick glasses, and an air of intellectual superiority.

"Are you really leaving?" he asks.

"Yeah." Emma turns to me. Studies my expression.

She's asking for something.

I'm not sure what it is.

Only that this guy shouldn't be here.

He follows her gaze. "Am I finally meeting the great Brendon?"

"No, um…" She stumbles over her words.

"I'm Hunter." I hold my position. Stare him down. There's something about his posture. Something I don't like.

"Vinnie." He offers his hand.

I stay put.

He nods *no problem* and turns to Emma. "What happened?" His voice is sweet. Sincere. Like he's dying for her to pour her heart out.

"Noise complaint." Emma takes a step backward. Folds her arms over her chest.

"Not everyone appreciates emo music as much as you do," he says.

Her laugh is impossibly fake.

"I liked it. It was special. Like you," he says.

Is he a shitty player or just an asshole?

I can't tell.

She's curling into herself. Getting smaller. Slower. Stiller.

"Thanks. We, um, we have to get packing." Her voice is quiet. Low. Free of her usual confidence.

"You have my number." His lips curl into a half-smile. "I'll call you. Make sure you settle in okay."

"That's okay." She takes another step backward. "We have it covered."

He looks to me. "You and Hunter?"

"Yeah." She clears her throat. "We're actually really busy, so—"

"You're Emma's neighbor?" I jump in.

He nods. "I thought we met." He tilts his head to one side, trying to place me. "You look familiar."

No, I've never seen this asshole before.

But I know this type of guy.

He's a coward.

All it takes is a threat from a bigger guy and he'll back off.

Those years of drunken stupidity bought me a fair amount of wisdom.

"No." I step forward. Offer my hand. "Just got out."

His brow furrows with confusion as he shakes.

"Yeah." I move into his space. He's the same height as I am, but he's wiry. "I was in the joint for assault. It was a bullshit collar, but you know what cops are like."

"You were in jail?" His eyes go wide.

"They say a year goes by fast, but it doesn't," I say.

"Right." Disbelief spreads over his expression. He looks to Emma for a clue.

She nods, going along with my story.

She wants to scare this guy off.

Fuck, I don't like the implications.

But I can think about that when he's gone.

"Nice to finally meet you." I shove him playfully. Well, faux playfully. It's too hard.

He feels it. Cringes. Shrugs it off.

"Heard a lot about you."

"Yeah… You too."

"Always good to hear someone's taking care of my girl," I say.

His gaze goes back to Emma. He stares like she ripped his heart out. Like she's a bitch for lying. "Of course," he recovers. "I've always wanted to meet Emma's boyfriend."

She clears her throat. "Yeah. Vinnie has been a really close friend. I should have told you more about him, but I know you get jealous."

I shrug, playing my role. "Fuck, can you blame me?" I turn back to Emma. Blow her a kiss. "You know guys don't give a shit a woman's taken. And one as gorgeous as mine—"

She presses her lips into a smile. "You don't mean that, baby."

"I do." I shoot her *fuck me* eyes. "I'll show you how much when we get home."

"You're living together?" he asks.

"Fuck yeah. Paradise after a year in the joint. We got a lot of time to make up for too," I say.

"Right." He smiles to hide his confusion, but he doesn't sell it.

I turn back to Vinnie. Smile through my teeth. So he knows

I'm not going to let him touch Emma. "Thanks for treating my girl right, Vinnie. What goes around comes around."

"Yeah. Sure." His eyes meet Emma's. They ask for something. For something she isn't giving.

She clears her throat. "We, um, we have to meet Brendon at... uh... the karate dojo. So we better finish this. I'd hate for you to miss your martial arts practice."

I nod. She's overselling it.

But it's working well enough.

Vinnie nods goodbye and backs away.

I close and lock the door.

But, still, Emma stays on edge.

She turns to the table. Moves a pair of jeans from her dresser drawer to her suitcase with shaky hands.

"Em—"

"Don't call me that."

"What the hell happened with that guy?"

"Nothing."

"Bullshit."

"It wasn't a big deal."

Bullshit it wasn't.

But pushing isn't going to help.

Her dark eyes are streaked with fear.

Her entire body is shaking.

She had to deal with one asshole already.

I'm not adding to that.

No matter how desperate I am to know what happened.

To make Vinnie pay for whatever he did to scare her like this.

"All right," I say.

She stares into my eyes, assessing my intentions. She must not buy me dropping it, because she continues. "It really wasn't a big deal. Just awkwardness."

"I get it."

"We hooked up and it wasn't very fun and he didn't take the hint that I wasn't interested."

"It happens."

"It is what happened."

I nod. "All right."

"It is."

It's clearly not.

I want to know.

But I want to soothe her more.

I want to promise her everything is going to be okay.

I can't remember the last time I felt like that.

I'm not sure I've ever felt like that.

WE MAKE SMALL TALK AS WE FINISH PACKING. IT'S AWKWARD. Tense. Filled with all the shit we're not saying.

She knows I don't believe her.

She knows I'm dropping it.

She doesn't trust my reasons.

When we get home, she practically runs to her room. Locks herself in it.

I give her some time to cool down, then I carry her red suitcase up the stairs. Knock on the door.

"Yeah?" The defensiveness drops from her voice. She isn't hard edges and locked walls. She's a scared, vulnerable girl who needs understanding.

I want to be the kind of guy who can offer that.

I want to be the person she needs.

"Your suitcase." There's something I need to say. Some way I make this better.

But I don't know what the fuck it is.

I settle for what I can handle. "You hungry? I'll order something."

"No. I'll cook." The handle turns. She pulls the door open. Steps into the hallway. "Thanks." Her fingers wrap around the handle. Her eyes stay on the floor. "But later."

I nod.

"I, um… I'm going to take a walk first."

"You want company?"

"You're actually asking?"

"Yeah."

"No. I want to be alone. If that's allowed."

"Don't see a rule against it."

"There are rules?"

"Not exactly." Brendon didn't have to spell it out. I get that Emma is off limits. That a guy like me needs to stay the fuck away from a girl like her.

"Who made these rules?"

"There's a code."

"Guy code?" She rolls her eyes, but her heart isn't in it.

"Something like that."

"What are the rules of guy code?"

I've been out of the loop a while, but I'm pretty sure *don't touch your friend's kid sister* is at the top of the list. "You okay?"

"No. I'm not okay with a bullshit set of rules about how men can tell other men not to touch certain women. Are you?"

No. "Wasn't planning on touching you."

"Whatever."

"Your brother is just looking out for you."

"I though nobody made the rules."

"You know what I mean."

She shrugs *I guess,* but there's no give in her expression. She's still sure it's bullshit. She's just done discussing it. "Guess I'll see you for dinner."

"Until then."

She shuts the door.

A moment later, a thrashing rock song fills her room. It's loud, but not eardrum bursting.

Not enough for a noise compliant.

That's not why she's leaving her apartment.

I want the truth.

Not for the sake of it.

To help her.

Soothe her.

Connect with her.

I have to earn her trust.

To let her in.

How the fuck do I do that?

8

EMMA

"I don't understand why I need to learn this." I stare at my Art History text book.

The impressionism chapter recap.

There are a dozen questions I can use as practice.

But they might as well be in another language.

I'm so out of my depths here.

"You gonna be one of those tech people who constantly complains about how useless the humanities are?" Hunter glances at me from his spot in the kitchen. He's fixing a cup of coffee. Two actually.

With a pour over.

It's some fancy contraption straight out of a sci-fi movie.

Don't get me wrong.

I'm not a coffee newb.

I've seen these long necked kettles, the hourglass shaped cups, the cone filters.

But I've never seen a civilian use one.

"Em?" He repeats his question for the ten millionth time tonight.

I'm in the clouds.

Ever since I saw Vinnie hanging in the doorframe, I've been floating away from the moment.

I guess it's some sort of Pavlovian response.

Vinnie equals disassociation.

Though, it's not really Pavlovian if the conditioned response happened one time.

Or is it?

Thankfully, Psych 101 is in my rearview mirror.

I don't need to know that.

Whereas the subtle difference between Van Gogh and Monet—

That's of utmost importance.

"No." I read question three again. Eight images of paintings. I'm supposed to name the title and artist. The first is easy. Monet. W*ater Lilies.* "I'm going to own a boutique."

"Oh."

"What do you mean *oh*?"

"That would suit you."

I stare up at Hunter for some clue to his intention. Is he teasing or serious? I can't tell with him.

He's Brendon's spy.

But I think he's trying.

He did thank me for dinner. Then compliment my pesto penne again and again.

And now he's fixing coffee.

He's not all bad.

"You don't take orders," he says.

"Why should I?"

"Besides my daddy fetish?"

"If you keep joking about that, I'm going to reverse my ruling."

"Good." His lips curl into a smile that lights up his blue eyes.

He is teasing.

And serious.

Not about the kink.

About wanting me to believe it.

Wanting me to find him repulsive.

Which is kind of ridiculous.

He spends God knows how much time at the gym perfecting his biceps. He wants every other woman on the planet to gawk. And I'm supposed to see his perfect ass and think *damn, I don't want to touch that.*

"I think the lady doth protest too much," I say.

"You're quoting Shakespeare?"

"Yeah." Okay, I stole that one from Kaylee. She was quoting Shakespeare nonstop last semester, during her British literature class. "He has good shit."

"You've read *Hamlet?*"

"I did go to high school, yes."

"Then you know what I'm getting at."

"The dirty talk, yeah." My cheeks flush. "Ophelia knows how to get what's hers."

"Yeah."

"Are we allowed to talk about this?" I mean to sound teasing. To push him. Remind him what a hypocrite he is. Instead, my voice wavers. I stumble over the words. I'm still stiff and awkward when it comes to sex.

"As much as we're allowed to look at what's on page two hundred twenty-three." He sets the pot of water on the counter. Pulls two mugs from a high shelf.

He already has the lay of the land.

"How long have you been here?" I ask.

"A few days."

"Oh." My fingers slide over the pages as I flip to 223. It's weird,

Hunter being comfortable here. Like he knows the house better than I do.

"You gonna look?"

"Timing is everything." It's a painting I haven't seen before. *L'Origine du monde* by Gustave Courbet. A woman, from her breasts to her knees, her legs spread, her cunt on full display.

It's practically pornography.

It's certainly erotica.

Fuck, this is in a museum and it's as erotic as anything in a dirty magazine.

No wonder all the guys at the shop got into art.

I'd be into art too if I was a horny teenage boy.

"How did you know?" I ask.

"Had the same book in high school."

"But Brendon—" Lost all the shit he had in high school after Mom kicked him out. "Never mind. Wait. Why did you have this memorized?"

"I was fourteen at the time."

"The Internet existed."

Hunter's laugh is big. Hearty.

The biggest laugh I've heard from him.

His shoulders relax. His eyes brighten. His fingers dig into his soft cotton t-shirt.

At least, it looks soft.

It looks touchable.

He looks touchable.

I want to run my fingers over the fabric. To press the cotton into his skin. Feel the hard muscles beneath it.

I want to toss that t-shirt aside.

Run my fingers over his chest and stomach.

Soak up his warmth and hardness.

Until he is hard and I'm—

Fuck.

I clear my throat.

Which does nothing to hide my blush.

I…

I can't remember the last time I thought about touching a guy. Since *that*, I haven't. And now he…

I did see him naked.

I've had a crush on him since the day he taught me the f-word. But it's more than that.

I want this guy, the one standing in the kitchen, fixing coffee, laughing about dirty art.

The obnoxious babysitter who's actually trying.

Who is going to stick with that whole *no way am I touching you; you're basically your brother's property; I could never violate that.*

"You there?" he asks.

"Yeah."

"Or you fantasizing about Gustave?"

"You memorized the artist's name?"

"I learned shit in high school."

"Yeah, I can see that." I shake my head. "What bullshit."

"Oh?" He brings our mugs of coffee to the counter, places one next to me, the other in front of the seat opposite mine.

"Yeah. Guys get to gawk at beaver. What do women get?"

"You've never seen *David*?"

"I've seen him."

"And?"

"I've seen better."

Hunter shakes his head as he moves into the kitchen to grab cream and sugar. "Better than a statue that's served as an example of the perfect male specimen for centuries?"

"Yeah."

"Better how?" He slides into the seat opposite mine.

"You really want to know?"

"Yeah. If David doesn't do it for you, who does?"

"Don't you think he's a bit… ahem?" I motion to my crotch.

His lips spread into a smile. "Really?"

"Yeah."

"Guy could be a grower."

"Still. It's a statue, not a cast. The artist could have given him a bit more."

"You know men." Hunter chuckles. "They want to look good. Artist probably wanted women looking at David then thinking *damn, my man is loaded*."

"Probably."

"The artist being…" He motions for me to finish the question.

"Not an impressionist. Not necessary for this test."

"Em, really?"

"Did you think I'd ask for your help if I was prepared and informed?" My brow furrows. It's not too late to call Chloe and beg for her assistance. But she lives on the other side of the Valley. And she and Dean got into that huge fight…

I can't bother her with something this trivial.

I have to accept Hunter's help.

Or fuck up this test.

And I'm not fucking up this test.

"Michelangelo," Hunter says.

"Good for him."

"It was. The ladies were knocking down his door."

"'Cause he looked so huge compared to his sculpture?"

He nods. "Exactly."

"That's ridiculous."

"But plausible."

It kind of is, actually.

And funny.

Joking with him…

It feels good.

And… fluttery.

My chest is light.

My limbs too.

I wrap my fingers around my coffee cup to ground myself.

It helps.

And, fuck, this is amazing.

"Thanks." I take another sip. Swallow hard. "You're gifted."

"Coffee and tattoos."

"Is that how you got into it?" I motion to the dirty painting. "Love of *art*?"

Again, he laughs.

Again, his eyes brighten.

My stomach flutters.

The air gets warmer. Sharper. More electric.

"No. My brother Chase. He was artsy and I thought he was the coolest dude in the world. Wanted to be exactly like him."

"Now?"

"Chase is a tattoo artist too." Joy fades from his face the second he says his brother's name.

It's not rocket science.

His brother is a tattoo artist.

He's from Los Angeles.

But he's staying here and working at Inked Hearts. Not staying with his brother, working at his shop.

There's a story there too.

But his expression is a brick wall. He doesn't want me to know.

Usually, I turn around when I hit a wall.

I don't try to dig deeper. Unless it's Kaylee, and, even then, I give her space.

But I want to know.

I want to know why Hunter is here.

Why he's shouldering all this baggage.

"Older?" I pick an innocuous question. One that might tempt him to answer.

"Yeah."

"You had two brothers, right?"

He nods. "One older. One younger."

"Both hot?"

"Yeah. Why?"

"Well, you're good looking, but your personality is atrocious. I was thinking maybe one of them might be as beautiful inside as out."

"They might. But I'm not gonna introduce you."

"Because they're not the kind of guys I should date?"

"You're too young."

"But one is younger."

"Not that much younger."

"Does it get tiring holding up the patriarchy?"

He flexes his bicep. "How do you think I got these guns?"

I can't help but laugh.

He's being annoying and over protective, but it's kind of sweet.

I'm not supposed to like this.

I'm not supposed to need it.

For nineteen years, I've hated having an army of guys treating me like a kid who needed protection.

Suddenly wanting that…

It means something changed.

And that's not okay.

I need to prove nothing has changed.

But what the hell does that mean?

I used to date, but it wasn't to make a point. It was because it was fun. Because a cute guy asked. Because I had a free Saturday night when Kaylee was working.

Now, all I do is work and study.

Hunter…

Maybe we can't date.

But we can be friends.

And that's progress.

I think.

Either way, it's a concern for tomorrow.

First step, ace test.

Second step, figure out my shit.

I take another sip of coffee. Let the caffeine wake my brain. Inspire a great devotion to mastering impressionism.

It inspires a devotion to caffeine.

But that's close enough.

"When's the last time you studied?" I lean back in my chair. Force myself to look Hunter in the eyes.

"You want my help or not?"

"So far you've provided none."

"What do you call that?" He motions to my coffee.

"I can make coffee."

"That good?"

No, but I'm not admitting that. "Clock's ticking."

"You have flash cards?"

"Yeah. Of course."

He motions *give me.*

I do.

He motions to my stack of pens. *Can I take one?*

I nod.

He picks up a black pen. Looks at the chapter notes. Draws a perfect approximation of Water Lilies.

Okay, maybe it isn't perfect. But considering it's black on white paper, it's close.

It's badass, actually.

"What's on this test?" he asks.

"I'm not sure. The professor said that we'll be fine as long as we've done the reading and paid attention."

"Have you?"

"Yeah, but professors always say that."

"What is it you don't get?"

"It all looks the same. I can memorize which is which, yeah.

But if you showed me a painting I hadn't seen, I couldn't tell you if it was Van Gogh or Monet or Renoir."

"Really?"

"Yeah." I fold my arms over my chest reflexively. Deep breath. Slow exhale. This isn't a time to be defensive. He's helping. He's trying. I do appreciate that. "Art isn't a big thing to me."

"You want to own a boutique."

"Yeah…"

"Fashion is art."

"Yeah, but it's democratized."

"Thousand-dollar purses are democratic?"

"Hell yeah. Go America."

Again, his chuckle fills the room. It's low. Hearty.

Hot as hell.

It hits me somewhere deep.

Makes my chest warm.

Makes my sex ache.

"Fashion is as elitist now as paintings were in the Renaissance. Only the rich and famous can afford a fancy designer outfit," he says.

"No. They can buy a wallet or a small hand bag. You aren't up with the times. Luxury has been scaled down. I was just reading this book—"

"Huh?"

"What? I can't read?"

"No. Just—"

"You really don't know me at all, Hunter. Don't tell me what I can do."

"Methinks the lady doth protest too much." He copies my Shakespearean insult.

I flip him off.

He laughs.

Again, my chest warms.

God, this feels good.

I need more of it.

I need to keep him up all night.

"My boutique is going to support local, indie designers. And maybe some of that cheap stuff that's made in China. Girl has to have margins."

He nods. "She does."

"I've learned some stuff working at Inked Hearts."

"Is that why you do it?"

"Yeah."

"You want to learn more?"

My heart thuds against my chest. Do I want to learn more about running the business? Why doesn't he ask if I'd like more coffee? Or chocolate? Or a Disney movie marathon?

I'm dying to learn.

But Brendon and Ryan are the only guys who actually focus on business.

Brendon tells me to focus on school.

Ryan...

He's not so prickly now that he's madly in love with Leighton, but he's still somewhat... unapproachable.

I swallow hard.

I need to under sell how much I want this. "That's what I'm studying. Business."

"So why Art History?"

"And Fashion Design."

"You thought it would be an easy A."

"Easier than some of my options. Nothing is an easy A for me."

He nods. "I get that."

"You do?"

"Most people who are good in school don't end up tattoo artists."

Probably true.

"Brought home straight Cs all through high school."

"I managed Bs." Just barely. And only because of Kaylee's help. But I did. "Mostly."

"That's good."

"Maybe."

"It is. Especially if you worked for it." His blue eyes get intense. It means something to him, me believing this. Taking his compliment.

"Will you show me more? About running the business?" I press my palms together. Pretend as if I'm utterly apathetic to the thought of learning more.

"If you get at least a B on this test."

Fuck. "You're offering me more learning as a reward for learning?"

"Yeah."

"Fine. But you should know something, Hunter."

"Oh?"

"If you're going to keep making my life difficult, I'm going to do the same."

"Difficult, huh?"

I nod.

"All right. Noted."

"Good."

"Now, tell me the defining features of the impressionist movement."

I do.

He quizzes me for an hour. Then another.

It feels like we go all night.

We don't stop until I'm about to fall asleep at the table.

Hunter practically carries me up the stairs. He makes sure I brush my teeth and change into my pajamas.

He practically tucks me into bed.

For the first time in forever, I fall asleep easily. Go without a nightmare.

He's annoying as hell.

But I like having him here.

I like him, period.

Three months without feeling a thing for any guy, anywhere, and I like the one guy I can't have.

Figures.

EMMA

I wake to the smell of coffee.

There are twelve ounces of a single-origin blend inside Hunter's fancy hourglass carafe.

It's good.

Sweet.

Caring.

If things were different...

No. They aren't different.

Hunter is my temporary roommate.

We can be friendly, but that's all we can be.

I push thoughts of him aside as I fix my breakfast, get ready, drive to school.

I focus for long enough to ace my test.

But the second I turn the thing in, my head goes back to him.

Those deep blue eyes.

That soft smile.

The hard muscles.

I spend my business class fantasizing about him.

About pressing my lips to his.

Tearing off his jeans.

Wrapping my legs around him.

And him driving into me again and again.

IT'S A NICE DAY. IT ALWAYS IS THIS EARLY IN FALL. BIG YELLOW SUN. Bright blue sky. Warm breeze.

The streets are buzzing with a mix of tourists and locals. A family gawking at the tall palm trees. Two surfer boys carting their boards home. A couple on beach cruisers laughing as they stop at a red light.

It's picture perfect.

The same as the shop.

Leighton is behind the counter, twirling a lavender strand around her index finger, pretending to work on her laptop as she watches her boyfriend.

And there's Ryan, in his usual all black outfit, working on some guy's backpiece, staring at his girlfriend with gaga eyes.

It's still weird, seeing him happy. He was never a jolly guy, but it wasn't until his ex cheated that he really turned into Mr. I Hate The World. He came in every day like he had forgotten what the sun looked like.

Leighton was always into it. Into him, I guess.

It's hard to blame her. He's super-hot. Tall and lean with lush curly hair and intense blue eyes. Like Hunter's.

Not that I'm thinking about Hunter's eyes.

He's just right there.

In Brendon's usual suite.

Tattooing something onto a pretty brunette's wrist. She looks up at him like he's the only person who can comfort her.

Which is normal.

Women are usually looking for comfort when they get tattoos. Guys are usually trying to act like it doesn't hurt.

I'm used to watching the guys flirt.

It shouldn't bother me.

I shouldn't care that Hunter is flirting back.

"Hey, Em." Leighton's wave is big. Friendly. She moves out from behind the counter to hug me. "I'll get out of your way."

"There's plenty of room." I set my backpack on the counter. Move straight to the shop's Keurig. Fix a cup of medium roast.

Too much coffee is a bad idea. Kaylee is always reminding me, reminding herself really, that excess caffeine leads to anxiety.

But I'm running on four hours of sleep.

I need the energy.

Especially if I want to stay on top of Hunter.

I try to keep my attention on the *drip, drip, drip* of the coffee machine, but it keeps drifting back to Hunter.

To his sandy brown hair.

His broad shoulders.

His strong back.

He's just so...

His arms look so safe. Do they feel like that too?

What the hell does that feel like?

I don't remember.

It's been too long.

Finally, my coffee finishes. I add a packet of cream. Half a packet of sugar in the raw.

Mmm. It's not as good as the stuff Hunter made this morning, but it's still sweet, creamy, rich caffeine.

I take my seat behind the counter. Make small talk with Leighton as I settle in for the afternoon.

There isn't a ton to do. I keep the shop clean and stocked. I schedule appointments, send reminder emails and phone calls, update the shop's social media.

Ignore the texts from Kaylee.

She's checking in.

She's worried.

It's sweet that she cares, but I can't get into that now.

She doesn't know. But she suspects. And if she asks—

I don't want to lie about this.

I don't want to talk about it, period.

"Done." Hunter sets his tattoo gun down. He looks up at his client like she's the stars in the sky.

She lets out a heavy sigh. Stares back at him like he's everything she wants.

They laugh over some joke as he cleans her up and brings her to the counter.

She shows off her new ink. *Carpe Diem* surrounded by poppies.

It's nice.

Obvious, but nice.

I force my lips into a smile. "How cool." I'm not jealous of the attention he's giving her.

I'm not.

"I know." Her light eyes go wide as she stares at the ink. She turns back to Hunter with a smile. "Thank you." She throws her arms around him and squeezes tightly. "I'm in love."

My stomach twists.

Which is ridiculous.

Because I'm not remotely jealous.

I print her receipt and set it on the counter. "You're lucky. Hunter does great work."

"Yeah." She turns back to me. Picks up the pen. Writes a fat tip. Sighs. "It's everything I imagined." She looks back to him, her smile ear to ear. "Can you please stay here permanently?"

"I'm working on it."

She fishes something from her pocket. A business card. "Call me if you move somewhere else." Her cheeks flush. "Or… if you just want to call me."

He watches her leave then he turns to the counter. His eyes find mine. They bore into mine.

Demand an explanation for my expression.

I'm frowning.

Not because I'm jealous.

Because...

I...

Uh...

Well, I'm not letting him realize it.

"You should ask her out." I bite my tongue so I won't add *if you want to date someone with absolutely no standards.* I mean, really *carpe diem?* Could she be more cliché?

"I'll keep that in mind."

"Really. She's pretty."

"Yeah." His eyes flit to the door for a quick second. Then they're back on me. "You don't fool me."

"Oh?" I force a smile. It's awkward and stilted, but it's there.

"You won't get me out of your hair that easily."

My laugh is impossibly fake.

Hunter stares at me. He sees through me like I'm made of glass. "How late are you here?"

"Until six."

"Me too."

"Great." My head fills with images of the two of us walking home together. Fixing dinner in the kitchen. Sliding our empty plates off the table then climbing on top of it. "You making dinner tonight?"

"You don't want the dinner I make."

"Oh."

"I'll pick something up on my way home from the gym."

"Great."

He heads back to his suite. Devotes all his attention to his sketchbook.

Maybe...

Maybe this will work.

I pull out my cell. Text my brother.

Emma: How's Jersey?

Brendon: Humid. What are you up to?

Emma: I can't ask my brother how he's doing?

Brendon: Question stands.

Emma: How long is Hunter staying at our place?

Brendon: We haven't discussed a timeline.

Emma: Oh.

Brendon: He giving you trouble?

Emma: He's around a lot.

Brendon: Is it really that bad?

Yes.

But then…

It's not too.

He teases me about my music.

Fixes me coffee.

Compliments my cooking.

He even watches movies with me.

It's nice, having someone there.

Having him there.

Emma: Bad is relative.

Brendon: Worse than me?

Emma: I'm just wondering if you meant what you said about me babysitting him.

Brendon: Keep an eye on him, yeah.

Emma: Why?

Brendon: Because he needs it.

Emma: That's not an answer.

Brendon: It's not mine to tell.

Brendon is a freaking safe. He's not going to crack.

There's no sense in pushing it.

Brendon: Are you okay, Em? Kay hasn't been texting.

This is the trouble with your best friend dating your brother.

Even when she has every intention of keeping my secrets, he figures it out.

Kaylee only texts me and my brother.

So if she's with him and not texting, he knows I'm staying quiet.

There's a lot I want to say.

But not yet.

Not until I figure it out.

I'm not admitting I want Hunter around.

I'm not giving him—or my brother—the satisfaction.

Emma: Hmm, what could be bothering me? It's not like my adult brother assigned me a babysitter even though he's sleeping with a woman two months younger than me.

Brendon: If I thought it was that, I wouldn't be concerned.

Emma: Enjoy your vacation.

Brendon: I love you.

Emma: Love you too.

I set my phone face down on the counter. Lose myself in replying to the shop's emails. Try to avoid watching Hunter work.

Fail.

Eventually, I finish work. Switch to studying. Then to watching his final client.

This time, it's a cute guy getting something on his bicep.

They finish.

I flirt through check out.

Hunter stares without comment.

Then he stretches his arms over his head with a sigh. "You heading home?"

"No." All right. This is it. Time to start fighting fire with fire. "We're going to the gym."

"*We're* going to the gym?"

"Yeah."

He stares back at me *what the hell?*

71

"You were right. You're just looking out for me. I shouldn't fight you."

He arches a brow.

"I'm going to do the same. Like Brendon asked." I slide my textbook into my backpack and pull the zipper shut. "You're babysitting me."

"Yeah."

"Well, I'm babysitting you too."

HUNTER

E mma steps into the gym and flashes the guy at the counter a megawatt smile.

His eyes go straight to her. "Ms. Kane, right?"

"Yeah." She presses her palm against the counter. "Alan, right?"

He nods. "Been awhile."

She nods. "Yeah. I'm not the gym type. Getting back in shape though." She pats her stomach over her hoodie.

It's a ridiculous claim.

Maybe Emma isn't a body builder.

But she's hot, any way you cut it.

Those leggings are tight on her long limbs.

And, fuck, the way that sheer black mesh skims her skin—

I want to tear those things off.

To dive between her legs.

Lick her until she's screaming.

My heart thuds.

My blood races.

It's a normal reaction at the gym.

Almost.

She unzips her hoodie and hangs it over her arm.

Her tits strain against her tight black sports bra.

That's all she's wearing.

Fuck me leggings and a tiny sports bra.

She's trying to kill me.

I suck a breath through my teeth.

Shrug my shoulders.

Fail to direct my blood back to my brain.

There's something wrong with me.

I'm magnetically drawn to shit that's bad for me.

"So..." She motions to the weights on the left. Then to the cardio machines against the wall to the right. "What are we doing today?"

"We?" I ask.

"Yeah."

"You're gonna workout with me?"

She turns back to me. Stares into my eyes like she's best assessing how to fuck with me. "Sure."

"Really?"

"You don't think I can?"

"I'm sure you can."

"Good." She folds her arms over her chest. Sits on a bench. "Well..."

"Well?"

"What's the workout of the day?"

"Push."

She nods *let's go then.*

"You really think I'm gonna get into trouble here?"

"Yep." She motions to the rack of weights behind us. "Better stay busy."

My thoughts straighten.

She's right.

I can get into plenty of trouble here.

Every gym with serious lifters has at least one guy with a steroid hookup.

And he knows a guy who can get his hands on oxy fast.

Fuck, I barely did that shit. Alcohol was more than enough to get me trashed.

But I wasn't picky either.

Anything to eviscerate my thoughts.

Right now...

This is supposed to be my coping mechanism.

Where I work my shit out.

With her here—

I like Emma.

Too much.

I can't concentrate when she's around.

I can't let her know that.

"Help." I motion to the weight racks. "Bring me a forty-five-pound plate."

She stares like I'm crazy.

"You can lift it."

She shakes her head.

"Your backpack is heavier."

Her lips curl into a smile. "What do I get if I can?"

"What do you want?"

She shoots me a *really* look.

"Be reasonable." I'm keeping an eye on her. Even if it kills me.

"Okay. How about you tell me why you're staying with Brendon?"

I should tell her. Eventually.

But not now.

Not yet.

I need someone else thinking I'm worthwhile.

The way she looks at me—

Fuck, I need her to keep looking at me like that.

And to stop.

She's doing something to me.

Something I should be able to resist.

"That bad, huh?" She unfolds her legs. "I guess you really do need a babysitter."

"What do I get if I win?"

"How do you win?"

"You can carry the weight."

"That's how I win."

"How great that we both win."

She rolls her eyes. "That isn't how competitions work."

"All right." I know her well enough to bait her. "I'll bet you can't get through my entire workout."

"Well, duh. Not at whatever you're lifting. I spend time outside the gym."

"You have an issue with something?"

"No." Her gaze shifts to my shoulders. My chest. My arms. "You look pretty good."

"Pretty good?"

"You're hot, yeah, but at what cost?"

"I like working out."

"But you could be watching TV."

I can't help but chuckle. "At whatever weight challenges you."

"So you think I'm going to give up."

I shrug *maybe*.

Her eyes narrow. "Fine. But I want a prize."

She presses her red lips together.

Fuck, she has pretty lips.

Lush. Soft. Perfect around my—

No.

I can't let my head go there.

It doesn't matter how much I want those perky tits in my hands. Or how much I want that smart mouth—

"If I win—" I steer my thoughts back to the conversation. "I'll buy you coffee."

"You'll do that anyway."

"Ask for something else."

"You do the dishes. For a week."

"All right. And if I win."

"Doesn't matter. You won't." She offers her hand.

I shake.

Her smile widens.

Determination spreads over her expression.

It calls every ounce of my attention.

I want to keep pushing her.

To bring out that fire.

To be around this fierce girl.

She skips to the weight rack.

She struggles with the plate, but she manages to bring it back to the seat.

We take turns loading the bar.

I claim a free bench for her.

She slides the last weight onto the right side. "That good?"

"Yeah." I secure the weights. Take a seat. "You're warmed up now."

"Uh-huh."

"Lie down." I motion to the bench next to mine. "You're gonna use the bar."

She stares at me like I'm crazy.

"It's lighter than the plate." All right, the same weight as the plate. But close enough. "You've got it. Trust me."

"Okay, but if I can't, bet's off."

"Fair."

She sits on the bench. "I want to state, for the record, that this is a waste of time."

"Is it?"

"Yeah. Why spend all your time at the gym?"

"It feels good, getting stronger," I say.

"Getting bigger?"

"Well, yeah."

Her gaze flits to my crotch. It's a quick second. But it's as clear as day.

Her eyes meet mine.

Her cheeks flush. "Does that ever happen?"

"Do I ever get hard at the gym?"

"Yeah." She motions to the women on the treadmill. "There are attractive women here." She arches her back, thrusting her chest in the air. "I mean, look at me."

Fuck, I'm looking too closely.

She's so tall.

Long and lean with slight curves and soft skin.

I shake my head. "You ever hear guys talking about a pump?"

"No…"

"Blood's flowing to your muscles during a workout."

"Exactly."

"This place is kind of a sausage fest."

"Yeah." She makes a show of checking out the guy at the lat pull down. "There are some hotties here."

"Now you'll have an excuse to hang out."

"I've seen better."

I can't help but smile. She's ridiculous.

I shake it off. Slide onto my bench. Lift the barbell. This is supposed to be a warm-up set. It should feel light.

But with Emma watching me…

Fuck, it's weird.

I close my eyes. Focus on my form. My breath. The strain in my chest.

"It doesn't look too hard." Her voice is soft. Curious. "Heavy. But simple."

"It is." I push out another three reps. "You need me to show you how to do it?" Two more.

"Okay."

There.

78

"But you have to promise it won't turn me into a dumb bro."

I can't help but laugh.

"I mean, look at you, Hunter. All that blood pumping your muscles. Fleeing your brain."

"How do you figure?"

"You're here when you could be having sex."

"Shit, that escalated."

"Well TV only gets so far."

"You ever figure this helps me do that?"

"Well, yeah. I mean, it's not like women are flocking to you for your charming personality."

My lips curl into a smile. "So if you think about it, this is the smartest thing I could be doing."

"No. I don't think so."

My chest warms. It feels good, teasing her. Too fucking good. "On your back."

"We're doing it like that?"

"Yeah." If I start ordering Emma around... Fuck. "On your back."

She slides onto her back.

"Wrap your hands around the bar."

"Like it's a dick?"

"Why would that be my example?"

"You're lifting a giant rod. Why would I think there's something phallic about that?"

"You're making me think about how I hold my dick."

A wicked smile spreads over her lips. "Am I?"

"Just grab it."

"Well, if you want it *that* badly." She wraps her hands around the barbell. "Too hard?"

"No. You're good."

"Noted." Her brown eyes light up as she laughs. "What's the point of this?"

"If you want to lose to me..."

79

Fire fills her eyes.

It's out of the question.

She nods a *let's do this.*

I get into position, ready to catch the weight if it's too heavy for her. "Lift the bar above the guardrail."

She grimaces as she pushes the bar up.

"You've got it." I keep my hand over the bar. "Now lower it to your chest."

Slowly, she lowers her arms.

"This is a push motion. This is where it really starts."

"Now you tell me."

"It's been easy, hasn't it?"

"No. It's fucking heavy."

I can't help but chuckle.

"What's funny about that?"

"It is fucking heavy."

"Well, yeah." Her eyes narrow. Her lips press together. With a grunt, she pushes the weight up.

"Don't lock your elbows."

"What?"

My fingers brush her arm. "Keep a soft bend here."

"Oh." She finishes the movement. Takes a deep breath. Lowers slowly.

"You have good form."

"Thanks, I guess."

"Let's go for five."

She groans. "Fine."

But she's faking that discontent.

It's like with her studying.

Maybe she's not into the idea of chest presses.

But now that she's here, she's ready to destroy them.

She destroys everything she takes on.

And, fuck, I want to be around to watch that.

I want to see her spread her wings.

I…

I need to find a better way to resist her.

There is something.

I hate it.

But it's the only idea I've got.

EMMA

For the first time in a long time, the shower feels the way it should.

Clean and fresh and hot as hell.

I close my eyes. Imagine Hunter here with me.

His hands in my hair.

His lips on my neck.

His body pressed against mine.

I don't touch myself.

But, for the first time in a long time, I want to.

I want to lose myself in fantasies.

To come thinking of him.

Groaning his name.

It's so not happening.

But that doesn't make it any less appealing.

After, I dress, head to the kitchen, decide what to make for dinner.

There isn't much—I need to pick up groceries tomorrow—but there's enough for chicken piccata.

I turn on the stove, heat a pan, melt butter, pick up the chef's knife.

Stop at the sound of Hunter's voice.

"Hey." He moves down the stairs. Across the living room.

"Hey." I try to make my voice even. Like I haven't been thinking about him naked.

Like I'm used to thinking about guys naked without fraying at the edges.

Seeing Vinnie…

I can't think about that or I'll fall into that memory.

And that isn't happening.

"I just started." I turn the heat down so the butter won't burn. The last thing I need is the irritating beep of the smoke detector. "It will be a little while. Chicken breasts take forever."

"You want help?" His voice is steady. Honest.

I remember a lot about Hunter. He was always honest. And he was always starting shit.

This calm, duty bound, responsible guy—that's not the Hunter I used to know.

But then it's been awhile.

We change. Grow up. Get smarter.

Go through shit that scars us.

"I thought you were useless," I say.

"Terrible."

"So you're really asking for a lesson?"

His chuckle is soft, but it still feels good.

I want him close.

Not in a sexual way.

Not even in a platonic way.

I mean, I do want that.

But I also want him here.

I want someone who will scare off all the Vinnies in the world.

I hate needing that.

But I do.

"Em, are you sure you're okay?" he asks.

No. I'm falling back into those thoughts. They're always around the corner, waiting to pounce. I need to push them aside. To focus on this. "If you're here for a lesson, I'm putting you to work."

"I'm good with my hands."

I try to laugh at the joke, but I don't get quite there. "Here." I set the knife on the cutting board. Press my palms together to steady them. "Butterfly the chicken."

He stares at me like I'm crazy.

"Cut it in half lengthwise." I demonstrate the gesture. "When you unfold it, it has the shape of a butterfly."

"All right." His chuckle gets a little louder.

"Try it." I move to the sink, run the water until it's warm, wash my hands.

Hunter presses two fingers against the chicken breast then slides the knife through it.

He unfolds the chicken on the cutting board.

"Huh." He tilts his head to one side like he's trying to find the right angle. "I guess, if you use your imagination."

"Which you should have. As an artist."

"Don't really think of myself as an artist."

"It's in the job title."

"Still." He turns back to me.

I turn back to the sink. Pretend I'm still washing my hands. "How do you think of yourself?"

"Fuck, that's a loaded question."

Yeah, it is. And there's something about him. This quiet contemplation. Like there's an ocean of torment beneath those blue eyes.

He wasn't like that before.

Or maybe I didn't realize it.

I'm not sure I noticed those kinds of subtleties. More his abs.

I move to the stove. Turn the burner to medium. "Your job."

"Artist sounds so temperamental. Like a guy who's going to throw his latte if someone questions his vision."

"You met my old boss?"

His chuckle is louder. Heartier. "No. But I had my own."

"Yeah?"

He nods. "The shop where I apprenticed. Guy who taught me was great. A hard-ass, yeah, but he gave a shit. He challenged me. He wanted the world for me."

"Then?"

"Then?" His voice drops.

There's a story about what happened at his old shop.

A story he doesn't want me to know.

I want it.

I want to know him.

And not just because he's here or because he's hot or because he's good at scaring off creeps.

Because he's Hunter.

I press my lips together. "The pan's warm. Let's fry this breast. Put it on the pan with the flat side down."

He picks up the chicken breast, turns, steps to the stove, sets it down.

He's right there.

He's so close.

I want to reach out and touch him. To tear off his t-shirt. Unzip his jeans. Run my fingers through his hair.

I want to know that Vinnie didn't change anything.

That sex can still feel good.

That I can still want someone.

I haven't. Not since that… bad date.

It's been three months and I haven't wanted anyone.

Don't get me wrong. It's not like I was expecting to fill the months with hookups.

But I see guys all day. At school. At the department store where I still work once a week. At Inked Hearts.

Hell, the clientele at Inked Hearts is flush with hotties. Every day a surfer boy or celebrity or bodybuilder walks into the shop and takes his shirt off.

Sometimes, twice a day.

Sometimes, twice an hour.

But for three months, I've been staring and nothing...

No ache between my legs.

No desire racing through my veins.

No flutter in my stomach.

Sure, I flirt well enough. It's easier, actually, when I'm not attracted to the guy. There's nothing at stake.

Sometimes, I get numbers.

Then I throw them away.

Go home and tell myself that everything is the same.

That I'm busy with school and work.

It was okay as long as I avoided Vinnie.

But now...

No.

I'm here.

He's there.

I never have to see him again.

It can continue not being a big deal.

"Em?" Hunter asks.

"Yeah?" I press my palms into the tile counter. Hunter is a good guy, but that doesn't mean I can trust him.

He's trying, yeah.

But he's still Brendon's spy.

"What's next?" he asks.

"Oh." Right. We're cooking dinner. Not losing ourselves in our thoughts. It's weird, being stuck in my head. I've never been a daydreamer. I'm not used to it. "This." I flip the chicken breast with a pair of tongs.

"Then?" He moves closer.

His bare arm is pressed against mine.

My breath catches in my throat.

Desire buzzes through my veins.

I need more of it.

I let my eyelids flutter closed.

I try to conjure images of me and Hunter. Of his hands on my thighs, his lips on my neck, his cock driving inside me.

But they're wrong now.

Vinnie is always lurking around the corner.

Whispering something about how I want it with that awful vodka-soaked breath.

"Em?" Hunter asks. "What's next?"

"I thought I told you to cut the other chicken breast."

He motions to it, butterflied on the cutting board.

"Oh." I clear my throat. Motion to the meat thermometer sitting on the counter. "We need to get to one sixty-five. Why don't you check it?"

He picks up the meat thermometer. "How do I do that?"

"Slide it inside the thickest part."

"Oh?" He raises a brow.

"Are you allowed to make sex jokes?"

"According to who?"

"I don't know. Are you using your judgment or Brendon's?"

"You want to remind me that your brother wouldn't appreciate it?" he asks.

No. I don't actually. I just… I don't want to need a babysitter. "I'm just looking out for you."

"Oh?"

I take the meat thermometer and demonstrate. "Wouldn't want him kicking you out." It's supposed to be teasing, but it's not. I want him here. I really do.

"I know I'm annoying—"

"Very annoying."

"But I'm just trying to look out for you. Promise."

"What if we have different ideas of what that means?"

"Tell me."

Uh-huh.

"Really."

"I'll think about it."

He flips the chicken and sets the tongs down on a paper towel. "If you'd prefer I skip the dirty jokes—"

"No. Keep the jokes. Just, watch the quality."

"Oh?" He copies my *really* expression.

My lips curl into a smile.

It pushes away everything circling through my head.

I want to be here. Focusing on dinner. And the hot guy inches from me.

This should be easy.

Simple.

"So…" I push those thoughts further away. Focus on the way Hunter's deep blue eyes fill with concentration as he checks the temperature. "How are you going to pay me back?"

He arches a brow. "For?"

"Teaching you to cook."

"Thought I was helping."

I motion *eh, a little*.

He chuckles. "Harsh."

"Truth hurts sometimes."

"What do you want?"

A kiss. A touch. A fuck. Something to make me feel normal again. Please, please, please, make me feel normal. "All I'm doing tonight is studying."

"Studying what?"

"Biology."

"Perfect."

My groan fills the room. "You know biology?"

"No. But I know how to quiz."

"Generous."

"Thanks." His lips curl into a smile.

My knees knock together.

God, he's so handsome.

And, right now, he isn't looking at me like a kid who needs protection.

Right now, I actually believe there's a chance we'll be more.

EMMA

My phone buzzes against the wood table. I suck another sip of iced Americano from my straw. Wipe my wet hands on my dress.

It's a simple white sundress. The perfect canvas to pair with my red wedges and my leather satchel.

Cute. Comfortable. Stylish.

I should feel like a badass.

But I don't.

I'm off.

And not the way I've been off for the last three months.

No. This is a new kind of off.

A Hunter Keating off.

My phone is buzzing with a text.

It's from him.

I can feel it.

I'm developing a Hunter sense.

I turn my cell over, and sure enough, it's there.

Hunter: You got out of school at one.

Emma: I'm off today.

He should know that. We discussed my schedule last night.

We discussed everything last night.

After work, we went to the gym again.

Then we made dinner together.

Watched *Mulan* together.

I even sat on the couch while he booted up *Daredevil.*

So obvious why he likes it.

The brooding superhero must be Hunter's role model. They're both serious and duty bound and smolderingly hot.

Ugh.

I roll my shoulders, but it does nothing to soothe me.

It's not that it annoys me that he's looking out for me.

It's that it doesn't.

My chest is warm.

My stomach is fluttering.

My limbs are airy.

Hell, my fingers are already sliding over the keyboard, tapping out detailed directions to my location.

I want him here.

I hate that I want him here.

But I really fucking want him here.

Hunter: You're supposed to volunteer what you're doing.

Emma: Your subtlety is lacking.

Hunter: Not my strong suit.

Emma: Clearly.

Hunter: Where are you?

Emma: None of your business.

My fingers itch to tell him. All of me itches to tell him. To have his tall, strong, safe body nearby.

It's only getting worse the more we text.

I like him more than I did yesterday.

And, yesterday, I liked him more than I did the day before.

I just…

I really like him.

Hunter: All right.

Emma: All right?

It can't be all right. I need him engaging me. I need him capturing my attention.

Hunter: Then I won't tell you about my date.

My stomach twists.

He...

I...

No.

He's not going on a date.

He can't go on a date.

Not when we're...

When we could be something.

Emma: Your what?

Hunter: Date.

Emma: With who?

Hunter: A woman I know.

Emma: From where?

"Hey Emma!" My classmate Collin calls my name.

I force myself to look up.

This is nothing. It doesn't matter that Hunter is going on a date.

I don't care.

I'm not jealous.

It...

I...

Fuck.

"Hey. Those are nice jeans." I force a smile. Collin does look good—with the fitted jeans and the messy blond hair, he's pure surfer boy—but it only appeals in an abstract way.

Compared to Hunter, he's so...

Not Hunter.

"I'm gonna order something." He motions to the counter.

"What's good here?"

"You suggested this place."

He nods *oh yeah*. Motions to my drink. "What's that?"

"Americano."

"Is it good?"

I take a long sip. Let out a sigh of bliss. "Is it that obvious?"

His laugh is nervous.

Because he likes me?

Or because my moaning is too much?

Hard to say.

He nods *right on* in that California surfer boy way then steps into line and turns to the menu.

He likes me.

I should follow in Hunter's footsteps.

Invite Collin.

Make this into a double date.

Watching him suck face on his date is as bad as staying home, imagining him sucking face.

No.

They're equally bad.

My fingers glide over my cell case. It's the perfect shade of electric purple. Bright. Bold. Eye-catching.

Buzz.

I turn my cell over.

Hunter: As you'd say, "none of your business."

Emma: You don't know any women. All you do is work and go to the gym.

Hunter: In the three days you've lived with me?

Emma: Three days is enough.

Hunter: Believe it or not, I knew people before I started crashing at your brother's place.

"It's kinda cold in here, huh?" Collin slides into the table, into the seat next to mine. "They have a housemade hazelnut milk here. How cool."

I nod. Whatever he said, it's totally cool.

Emma: Was it a client?

Hunter: Maybe.

Emma: Pink hair?

"I was actually thinking we'd do a coffee shop. For our business proposal," Collin says.

I force myself to look into Collin's eyes. This is our second week of school. I barely know him. I certainly don't know if I can trust him. "I was thinking something with more inventory. A shoe store. Or a boutique."

"But so much of a boutique is trends and style."

"And coffee isn't?"

Emma: Carpe diem girl?

He laughs. "Not for me. I always whisper my vanilla latte order so no one will make fun of me."

"I won't tell."

His laugh gets louder.

I'm charming him.

He's flirting back.

He's interested.

And he's cute.

I should go for it. Ask him out. Get back in the game.

Sure, I'm not going to fall in love with him. But we might have a nice time together.

We might even hook up.

I might be capable of normal.

I won't know until I try.

"Coffee shop could be good. A hipster place like this." It's cute. White walls. Brown tables and chairs. Framed photos of coffee beans and roasters.

Collin turns as the barista calls his drink order.

He motions *one minute.*

I pick up my phone immediately.

Hunter: You would have a problem with carpe diem.

Emma: Why not write "I'm a cliché" on her wrist?

Hunter: Maybe she wants to seize the day.

Emma: Maybe she wants to prove she's tough enough for a tattoo.

Hunter: Are you jealous?

Emma: No.

That's ridiculous. I don't even. I… Ugh.

Hunter: You're ink free.

Oh.

Emma: I'm just saying. You can do better.

Hunter: What about my atrocious personality?

Emma: You have abs. That's more important than personality.

Hunter: To you?

Emma: To girls who tattoo carpe diem on their wrists.

Hunter: And you're too cool to seize the day?

Emma: If you need a tattoo to remind you to seize the day, you're not doing it.

Hunter: Probably true.

Emma: When's your date?

Hunter: Where are you?

Emma: Coffee shop on Main. Working on a group project for my business class.

I send the address.

Hunter: Thank you.

Emma: Where's your date?

Hunter: A restaurant.

Emma: Which one?

He sends the name of a casual Italian restaurant by the promenade.

Hunter: We're doing dinner and a movie.

Emma: Whose idea was that?

Hunter: Why? Is it too obvious for you?

Emma: Kinda, yeah.

Hunter: You shouldn't speak so ill of Alice.

Emma: I shouldn't?

96

Hunter: She has great tits.

My cheeks flush with some mix of nerves and anger. He's trying to get a rise out of me.

He's trying to make me jealous.

I think.

Emma: And when are you and Carpe Diem seizing the night?

Hunter: That's carpe noctem.

Emma: An answer?

Hunter: Tomorrow. After work.

Emma: Good to know.

Hunter: When will you be home?

Emma: Late.

Hunter: Approximately?

Emma: Nine or ten.

Hunter: You have dinner plans?

Emma: I'll work it out.

Hunter: Em.

Emma: Yeah?

Hunter: That place closes at six.

Emma: And?

Hunter: Get back to your project.

Emma: Or?

Hunter: I'll see you tonight.

Emma: Until then.

WE COMPROMISE ON THE CONCEPT. USE A COFFEE SHOP THAT SELLS a lot of beans online, so we have a mix of long-term and short-term inventory.

Over two hours and two more shots of espresso, we get there. Outline everything we need. Divide the work evenly. Joke about our stuffy professor.

Flirt.

It's easy.

Like with guys at the shop.

I don't care what happens with Collin. I don't care if he likes me. If he asks me out. If he goes home and fucks himself thinking about me.

It's a sick joke of human nature. The less invested we are, the easier things feel.

And it is easy.

Until the door swings open and Hunter steps inside.

He's fresh from work. Backpack on his shoulders. T-shirt hugging his chest. Jeans slung low around his hips.

His eyes meet mine. He nods a *hello*. Like he just happens to be here at ten minutes to closing.

This cafe is close to the shop.

A ten minute walk.

Five if you're fast.

But there are closer places. Better places.

I'm not buying this as coincidence.

He moves into the line casually.

Collin follows my gaze.

Stares at Hunter the way guys stare at other guys. Sizing Hunter up. Trying to see how he compares.

He doesn't.

But he's a decent guy.

A good time.

In theory.

"What are you doing tomorrow night?" I press my palms into the table.

"Studying." Collin turns to me. "You?"

"You want to get dinner?"

"With you?"

"Yeah." My gaze refuses to budge from Hunter. He leans in to order his drink. Flashes the barista a wide smile. Laughs at her joke. "As a date."

"Really?" Surprise fills his voice.

"Yeah."

"Yeah. Of course." He smiles like a kid who just won a trip to space camp.

It should be flattering.

But it's flat instead.

Six month ago, I'd have been humming with ideas about how I'd rock Collin's innocent world.

Now...

My thoughts scatter as Hunter's eyes find mine.

I should hate that he's here.

But I don't.

I really, really don't.

Collin follows my gaze. Frowns.

Okay, I have to make this normal.

No. I have to make this happen. To make tomorrow happen.

"Hunter, hey." My lips curl into a smile. It's good to see him. It shouldn't be this good, but it is. "Funny seeing you here."

He chuckles. "Yeah."

Confusion spreads over Collin's face.

I introduce them and motion for Hunter to sit.

He does.

"Hunter and I work together. At Inked Hearts," I say.

"The tattoo shop in Venice?" Collin's voice gets bouncy. Well, more bouncy.

I nod.

"You work there?" he asks.

"I know." I rub my upper arms with my palms. "I'm kind of... square."

"Nobody would call you square." Collin's laugh is nervous.

"There's a running bet on what her first tattoo will be." Hunter shoots me a curious look. Like he's trying to figure out where we stand.

"Oh?" Collin gives me a slow once over. "A butterfly on your lower back?"

Hunter and I share a look.

A tramp stamp?

Really?

Either he thinks nothing of me or he's completely out of touch.

"No." Hunter chuckles. "Carpe diem. In a big, bold font. Right here." His fingers brush my forearm.

It's a quick second, but it still fills me with nervous energy.

God, that feels good.

Like nothing has ever felt bad.

I sit up straight. Force a smile. Regain my composure.

"Hunter is an artist. If that wasn't obvious." I motion to the tattoo on his chest, the one peeking out from under his v-neck. *Quod Me Nutrit Me Destruit.*

What nourishes me also destroys me.

So angsty.

And dramatic.

And broody.

And completely Hunter like.

"Shop's only five blocks away," Hunter says.

More like ten, but who's counting?

"We're just finishing up." I slurp melted ice from my drink. "I guess we can walk together."

Collin's brow scrunches in confusion.

Not explaining this whole thing. "I need something at the shop." I motion for him to play cool.

He does.

"I guess I'll see you tomorrow night." I slide my laptop into my backpack. "I was thinking seven. At that Italian place by the promenade."

"Funny coincidence," Hunter says.

"Oh?" I play dumb.

"I'm meeting a friend for dinner there tomorrow," he says.

Collin looks between us with confusion.

"Maybe we should join," I say. "Make it a double date."

"Yeah, I guess we should." Hunter's chuckle is low. Deep. "We can head over together. After work."

"Perfect." I stand and blow Collin a kiss. "Until then."

"Yeah. Sure." He nods. "Until then."

Hunter stands with me. Motions to the door.

I follow him outside.

It's a beautiful evening. Warm air. Cool breeze. Orange light of sunset casting a soft glow over the sidewalk.

Hunter turns back to the coffee shop and shakes his head. "You're using that poor kid."

"My date isn't about you."

"Uh-huh."

"And you and Carpe Diem?"

"I hate to break it to you, Em, but you're not my type."

It's bullshit.

It's there, in those intense blue eyes.

He's trying to convince me he isn't interested.

But he is.

And...

Fuck, that only makes this more confusing.

HUNTER

"**F**uck, Hunter. You're gonna make me look bad with all these mock-ups." Dean steps into my suite. He leans against the wall, the picture of cool, and motions to my sketchbook.

"That's the goal," I tease.

It's funny.

Dean is the same as he always was. Nobody can make him look bad. He's built like a water polo player, he aces the laid back surfer boy vibe, and, well…

He makes himself look plenty bad.

He wants everyone to know he's obnoxious.

"You gonna show me this cool shit, or what?" Again, he motions to my sketchbook. Adds a *give it.*

My shoulders tense reflexively.

When I was wasted all the time, it was easy for me to share my work. Because that's all it was. Work.

I didn't pour my soul onto the page.

My drawings were plenty good. I captured what clients wanted.

I was a competent craftsman.

But that was it.

I'm not used to baring my soul.

Or sharing it.

I try to make my voice casual. Get halfway there. "You don't get enough of giving feedback with your shadow?"

"She's not here."

"I'm sloppy seconds?"

"Of course."

I hand over the notebook. Suck a breath through my nose. Exhale slowly.

This is a good sign. He's trying to help me out. Showing camaraderie.

He wants me here.

Yeah, my drawings show what a mess my head is, but—

I study his expression as he takes in the work.

He nods, digging it.

"Fuck, this is some moody shit." He flips backward, working his way past the last few days of drawings. "Exactly what I'd expect from you." He stops on an In Memoriam. Shaded roses surround a nameless tombstone. "This for anyone in particular?"

"It was," I lie. "A client who got cold feet."

"Shit. Send it to her."

"No."

He looks back to me. "Is it for a woman?"

"Yeah. Why do you ask?"

"Has that look."

"You wouldn't get roses?"

He pulls his t-shirt up his stomach to show off a side tattoo. Roses outlined by the state of California. "Most guys aren't secure enough in their masculinity for that shit."

"You know there isn't anyone here to gawk at your bod," Emma calls from the counter.

"What about you, Em?" He turns to her and pats his stomach. "Look me in the eyes and tell me you don't enjoy the view."

She shakes her head, but she can't hide the smile spreading over her lips.

He's fucking with her.

He's obviously into Chloe.

With Chloe even—nobody tells me shit about what's going on.

But my stomach still twists.

Fuck, I need to get over this.

Emma is gorgeous, sharp, and charming.

She's also off limits.

We're friends, at best.

I need to prove that to her. And myself.

Our double date is a necessary evil.

She needs to believe I'm not interested.

"She's always playing coy. That's our thing. Right, Em?" He winks as he lifts his t-shirt a little higher.

She makes a show of rolling her eyes.

Dean turns back to me. "You can try the same thing."

"Subject Emma to my stripping?" I ask.

"Yeah. She'll be into it." He winks again. "I see you checking Hunter out. It's only when I'm not there to soothe your lust for eye candy."

She laughs. "How do you know if you aren't there?"

"I'm always here." He draws a circle around the room. "I'm everywhere, all the time."

"Uh-huh." She shakes her head *you're ridiculous*. "Hunter is like Brendon. Doesn't want to do anything to disgrace himself."

"Disgrace himself?" Dean pats his stomach. "With that bod? I don't think so."

"True." She presses her palm into the counter to fight her blush.

Her nails are pink today.

A pale pink that nearly blends into her skin.

It's subtle, quiet, completely unlike her.

Or maybe I don't know shit about her.

A few dinners and an entire season of *Daredevil* don't make us best friends.

Only…

Fuck, at this point, this is the closest relationship I have.

"Girl needs a show." Dean shakes his head. "And you're gonna leave her high and dry. That's disgraceful."

Emma laughs.

"Unless. You got some sort of embarrassing tattoo I should know about?" Dean holds his hand over his mouth to stage whisper. "It can be our secret?"

I shake my head. Stripping for attention has never been my thing, but modesty isn't what's keeping my clothes on.

It's my inability to handle Emma's stare.

Whenever I catch her looking—

Fuck.

My balls tighten at the thought of her attention.

"You're a party girl." Dean turns to Emma.

"I am?" She raises a brow. "Since when?"

"Not 'cause you're—" He brings his hands to his hips to mime thrusting into someone.

I have to hand it to Dean.

He doesn't half-ass shit.

He's all in, all the time.

Emma bursts into laughter. "Glad to know I'm not too slutty for you."

"Em, please. You're nowhere near my record," he says.

"Which is?" she asks.

"You think I can count that high?"

"I think you're over-compensating because you don't want me to realize how much you love your girlfriend," she says.

"Why would I hide that?" he asks.

"You should ask a shrink that," she says.

He chuckles. Brushes it off. "Not sex and drugs party. An actual party. You threw one for Kaylee's birthday."

"So?" she asks.

"Hunter's birthday is coming up," he says.

"Oh yeah." Her eyes light up. "It is."

"So. Party time." He motions *let's go*.

"Okay, sure. Any other demands you want me to follow? You know I live and die to satisfy your whims." She rolls her eyes.

"What was that? I hear *satisfy you*." He winks at her. "If you're in for an exciting—"

"Thirty seconds," Ryan calls from his suite.

"That's a compliment, you know." He blows Emma a kiss. "That's how badly I want you."

She makes a show of dodging it. "Only if you finish the job after."

"After?" He shakes his head. "First."

"Always?" she asks.

"Of course." He nudges me. "Am I right, Keating?"

"Yeah." My jaw cricks. He's not actually offering to fuck Emma, but the thought still finds its way into my head.

"Fuck. Nobody wants to hear about your dick," Ryan says.

"He hasn't even started with the piercing talk yet." Emma laughs.

I turn to her and raise a brow.

She nods.

"Why?" I ask.

"Why not?" he asks.

"Fuck. Ow." And I thought getting sober was painful.

"Yeah, but now he has an extra excuse to bring up his dick thirty times a day. It really worked out for him," Emma says.

"Went six weeks without fucking anyone," Dean says.

"That's not that long," Emma says.

"Even myself."

"Still..." She folds her arms. "I could do that blindfolded with my hands tied behind my back."

"Oh shit, you're into that too?" he teases.

She sticks her tongue out. "Hell no."

"Never?" I ask.

"Never what?" Her eyes find mine.

"You've never wanted a guy to tie you up?" I ask.

The teasing drops from her voice. "I'd rather be in control."

"What is it with you Kanes?" Her brother's reputation for tying women up is legendary. As is his girlfriend's interest in being tied up. "Always with the kinky shit."

Ryan steps into my suite and motions for Dean to shut up. "How much is my brother fucking with you?"

Dean blows Ryan a kiss. "I love you too."

"He's fine." Truth be told, I like Dean's obnoxious jokes.

He gives me shit.

But most of his attention is on his apprentice. And most of mine—

Emma is right there. Behind the counter. Studying. Or pretending to study. Wearing a tight white blouse that hugs her tits just so.

"Poor Chloe." Emma looks up from her text book. "She takes all of Dean's shit now."

Dean steps into the main room and shoots Emma a megawatt smile. "Don't tell me you're jealous."

"Of you and Chloe?" Emma laughs. "In some parallel universe where I want you?"

"I see the way you look at me, Em. You don't have to admit it to these idiots." He places his finger over his mouth *our secret*. "I know what you're after."

"Uh-huh."

He winks.

"God, I can't believe I actually bought Kaylee's story about hooking up with you." She shakes her head, sending strands of chestnut hair in every direction.

"Em, baby, you have no idea how good my fake sex with Kay was." He fans himself. "You know I've got a cock piercing."

Emma laughs knowingly. "We were only talking about it thirty seconds ago."

Dean looks back to me. "You believe this shit? Striking out."

"Yeah. 'Cause it's not obvious you and Chloe are—"

Dean motions to Ryan.

Emma laughs. "You realize we all know you're together?"

Dean motions to me. "Not Keating."

"Welcome to the club, Hunter," Emma says. "How does it feel, being in the know?"

"Good." My eyes find hers.

Her cheeks flush.

Ryan chuckles as he surveys the empty room. "What the fuck are all three of us doing here when it's this dead?"

"Hunter works for a percentage and you two own the shop. I'm the only one here who gets a salary," Emma says. "Why aren't you off with Chloe?"

"What makes you think she wants anything to do with me?" Dean asks.

"Good body." Emma laughs. "What else?"

Ryan pulls out his cell. Smiles at the notification—no doubt a text from his girlfriend. "I got an hour to my next appointment. Can I trust you two not to burn the place down?"

"No." Emma points to us. "Look at them. Miscreants."

Dean nods *it's true.*

Ryan's chuckle is hearty. He pretends like he hates his brother, but his affection is clear as day. "You're doing good shit, Hunter. Really. Think about if you'd want to say."

"Sure." I slide my hand into my front pocket.

It's a great offer. Exactly what I need.

Yeah, I'd rather work at Blacklist, but I can't afford to wait until Chase lets go of this grudge.

I need a job now.

I need a job here.

Which means I'm staying on Brendon's good side.

I'm keeping my hands off Emma.

Whatever it takes.

HUNTER

Emma presses her red lips together as she descends the stairs. "What does that look mean?"

She's a vision. Black cocktail dress. Fuck me heels. Long hair pinned to her head.

Elegant neck on display.

It's like she's offering her flesh to me.

Begging me to wrap my arms around her and scrape my teeth over her skin. Not enough to hurt. Only enough she feels it everywhere.

I want to make her shudder. And shake. And groan my name.

I stay put.

If rehab taught me anything, it's wanting something without taking it.

I still fall asleep every night craving bourbon.

But I've stayed away for months now. I go to meetings. I distract myself. I avoid temptation.

If I can give up booze, I can keep my hands off her.

"Hunter?" Her dark eyes fill with curiosity. And a hint of insecurity.

She cares what I think.

Not in some shallow *I want you to find me hot* way.

She actually gives a shit about my opinion of her.

I don't have anything eloquent to say. But I have to get this out. "You look gorgeous."

"Oh." Her cheeks flush.

"Grown up."

"I'm nineteen."

"I'm twenty-seven."

"Really?" She moves into the living room. Stares at me like she's assessing the claim.

"Yeah."

She nods. "I guess you're the same age as Brendon."

"You guess?"

"You just seem so… Immature."

"Right back at you."

Her laugh lights up her eyes. "See. Look at you, lashing out after an insult."

"You'd never do that."

"Never ever." Her lips curl into a tiny smile. Her eyes meet mine.

Something passes between us.

This understanding.

I'm not sure what it means.

Only that I want more of it.

I want to know the Emma behind the sharp comebacks and the fierce fashion.

I want to understand all of her.

To peel back the walls around my heart so she can understand all of me.

But I don't understand myself half the time.

I'm still sorting my shit out.

I'm a mess. And she shouldn't have to clean me up.

Fuck. I'm getting distracted again.

There are a million reasons why this can't happen.

I need to stop getting lost in what ifs.

I'm going on this date.

Convincing Emma I'm not interested.

The end.

Emma turns as she assesses me. She shakes her head. Something about how I'm ridiculous.

But in a way she likes.

She's smiling.

Blushing even.

It's too fucking obvious that she wants me too.

That we should cancel this pointless attempting at stemming our feelings. Go to her bedroom. Get horizontal.

Fuck, I want to make her come.

I never feel like that.

I want women, yeah.

I'm plenty generous when we do get down to it.

But it's not because I'm craving their satisfaction.

With Em—

I want to make her feel good.

However I can.

"Could you?" Her voice pulls me back to the room.

Her brother's place.

My temporary place.

Because he's the only person willing to help me piece my life back together.

Fuck, I need to get my head in gear here.

I shrug my shoulders. Shake my head. Channel thoughts of baseball.

It helps.

Emma motions to the black coat hanging on a rack by the door.

It's elegant. Modern. Perfect for her. "You want to wear it?"

"No. Just hold it for me."

That's the ultimate boyfriend task, but there's no sense in bringing that up.

"You ready?" I grab my keys from the table. Slide them into my pocket.

She checks her reflection in the window.

"You look perfect, Em."

Her blush deepens. "I know."

"You staring 'cause you're vain?"

"Making sure my boobs look good."

Fuck.

My body ignores my apprehension.

My cock stirs at the thought of her perky tits.

Damn, I want to strip her out of that dress.

Tear off her panties.

Carry her to the couch, spread her legs, dive between them.

I arrange the coat in front of my crotch.

Breathe deeply.

Try to name the Dodger's lineup in my head.

Fuck, I hate baseball.

I hate everything that isn't making her come.

I move outside. Open the passenger side door for her.

She shoots me a curious look, but she still slides inside.

I do the same. Turn the key. Pull out of the driveway.

Her chest spills into her dress as she leans forward.

She doesn't ask permission.

Goes straight to blasting some band that was popular when I was in high school.

They're good.

But they're too nostalgic. They bring me back to a time when shit was okay.

I drank like a fish, yeah, but only at parties. Only on weekends. Only when everyone else was getting wasted.

My brothers cared about me.

My friends didn't look at me like I was broken.

No, that's bullshit.

High school sucked.

Mom was always wasted.

I hated half my friends.

Struggled to pass most of my classes.

Failed to gain my older brother's approval.

I was already drinking myself numb.

I was already fucked.

"Are you always this spacey?" Emma asks.

"They played this song at my prom."

"You went to prom?" Her nose scrunches. "Really?"

"Fuck yeah." I snuck in a flask. Spent the entire dance getting drunk with my date. "You know what happens after?"

"No offense, Hunter, but I don't believe you waited until prom to lose your virginity."

I chuckle. "That hurts."

"Mhmm."

"And you?"

"I went to prom with Kaylee."

"She was your date?"

"What's funny about that?" Her eyes bore into mine. They're intense. Defensive. She cares about her best friend. Cares about their friendship.

"It's sweet."

"Well, it's not like I had a virginity to lose at that point."

"Oh?" I turn onto the main drag.

"Oh?" Her hearty laugh fills the car. "Is that supposed to convince me you're all cool and collected when it comes to my sex life."

"We're two people talking."

"I'm still waiting for the lecture."

"On Vanilla Latte?"

Her lips curl into a smile. "Vanilla Latte?"

"That's what he ordered, isn't it?"

"How do you know?"

"Lucky guess."

"You're a snob."

I shrug. "So are you."

Her smile spreads a little wider.

I nod *you are*.

She motions *a little*.

Fuck, the look on her face. Her expression is easy. Joyful.

I want that.

All of it.

I like her, yeah.

But it doesn't have to be sexual.

I can make her feel good without making her come.

I can be her friend.

I can get close without touching her.

I tease her. "Does he have any idea what he's getting into?"

"You're supposed to be worried about me, not him."

I am. But I can't let her know that or she'll get into trouble just to annoy me.

I was the same way when I was her age.

"You seem like you can handle yourself," I say.

Her gaze flits to the mirror. "Mostly."

"If you can't, call me."

"You're going to be there."

"In the future. If you need help. If you're scared. If you're too drunk to drive. Whatever it is, call me."

"Forever?"

"Yeah."

"What about when you move out of Brendon's place?"

"Shit, that happens after forever. I forgot."

She tries to hide her smile but doesn't quite get there. "So you'd be cool if I wanted to go back to his place?"

Fuck no. But I have to convince her I am. I have to convince her I'm not interested.

I turn onto Ocean. This place is close, but it's not quite close enough to walk. Not in Emma's shoes.

"On the first date?" I ask.

"Oh my God. Slut-shaming much."

"Seems a little fast."

"Oh yeah, I bet you've never had sex on the first date."

"Never." My poker face cracks immediately. "I'm practically a virgin."

"Uh-huh." She turns to me with a wicked smile. "Plausible."

"You shouldn't stereotype like this."

"Oh?"

"Just 'cause a guy has tattoos…"

"You and Brendon weren't exactly quiet during your conversations."

"He was always quiet."

A laugh falls from her lips. "Okay, sure, he was quiet. But you? Not so much. You were bragging about a new conquest every other day."

Before I discovered just how much I enjoyed alcohol, sex was my preferred method of distraction. When I realized I could combine them—

I was a slut by anyone's definition.

"I'm just surprised you're off this whole 'why don't you commit to celibacy' thing." Emma sets her purse in her lap. Plays with the zipper. "Brendon and I don't really talk about sex. God knows I don't want to hear what he does to my best friend. But he does realize that I have sex."

"Do you?"

"How is that any of your business?"

It's not. But I still want to know. And not just because I'm responsible for her. "We're friends, aren't we?"

"Hmmm. Maybe. That's kinda stretching it."

"That hurts." It's supposed to be a joke, but it doesn't feel like one. I burned almost all the bridges I had. I'm lacking friends. And Emma—we have a connection. One that means a lot to me.

"Don't do that whole Dean feigned melodrama thing. I can only handle one person like that."

"Don't meet my younger brother."

"Chase?"

"No. Wes."

"Oh yeah. Lighter hair and a lot more sass?"

"Exactly." I stop at a red light. We're right in downtown Santa Monica. Surrounded by quaint shops, trees lined with blinking lights, the orange glow of sunset. "You actually planning on banging Vanilla Latte?"

"His name is Collin."

"Question stands."

"Should I reiterate that it's none of your business?"

Probably. "Let's make a deal."

"Is this another quid pro quo thing?"

"Yeah."

"Why not just offer information voluntarily?"

"All right. I'm gonna tell you the last time I had sex."

"And I want to know because…" She fails to pull off her shrug. Her pupils dilate. Her tongue slides over her lips. Her fingers dig into her bare thighs.

She wants to know.

She's desperate to know.

I wish I had a better story.

Something deserving of that kind of interest.

"Two months ago." Right when I got into rehab. When I was desperate for any kind of distraction. "Guess you'd call it a fuck buddies thing." More like *fuck our way into ignoring our problems thing*, but close enough.

"Commitment. Not what I expected from you." She shifts in her seat. Uncrosses then recrosses her legs.

"No. Just… convenience."

"Convenience how?"

"She was my neighbor."

"And you rocked her world?"

"Yeah."

"Did she rock yours?"

"No."

"Damn." Her laugh breaks up the tension in her brow. "You could sugar coat it."

"Would you?"

"No, but… that's me."

"And you?"

"We talked about this whole quid pro quo thing."

The light turns green. I press the gas. Focus on the road.

"Have you always slept around?" she asks.

"Yeah."

"Why?"

"Huh?" I turn to face her, but it doesn't help me figure out her intentions.

"Well, you know my brother. He was screwing around because it made him feel in control of his life when he wasn't."

That's awfully perceptive.

"Or Walker. He enjoyed sex. But he was also afraid of getting hurt. Because he's got issues with his sister. She's an addict. Or Ryan. He went the other way. Totally avoided intimacy after his ex cheated. He's only been with his ex and Leighton."

"That's sweet."

"Yeah. Hard to believe too. Guy that looks like him." She makes a show of fanning herself. "He could clean up." Her voice is easy. Casual.

But there's something about her expression.

She's trying to make me jealous.

It's petty.

Stupid.

Effective.

I know it's a ruse. That she's pushing me.

But I hate the idea of her wanting someone else.

I can see her and Ryan in some tiny room. Her tugging at his black t-shirt. Him pinning her to the wall. The two of them groaning in ecstasy.

He's madly in love with his girlfriend.

Emma isn't interested.

But I'm still seething.

I push it aside. Reach for something else. Something I can handle. "And Vanilla Latte?"

"What about him?"

"Is he as hot as Ryan?"

"That's a stupid question."

"Why?"

"You have eyes."

"Not attracted to men."

She shoots me a *really* look. "You can still tell when a guy is hot. And Collin… he's cute. But he's not on Ryan's tier." She leans back in her seat. Smooths her dress over her legs. "What was your sex life like?"

"What?"

"What were you getting out of it?"

"Do I need to explain the mechanics?"

"Yeah, you came, sure. You can come by your hand."

"It's better—"

"Is that really all it is? You were treating women like your own personal fleshlights. Because if so, you're a fucking asshole."

I am an asshole. But that's not it. "Sex was a distraction."

"From…"

"Dealing with my shit."

She unzips her purse. Pulls out her red lipstick. Applies another coat. "That suits you."

"Does it?"

"Yeah. You're like... You're trying to be more miserable than Matt." She references the *Daredevil* protagonist who...

He is a miserable motherfucker. But he's got a sense of humor. And he sure as hell enjoys beating people up.

"But, like, instead of getting your rocks off with violence, you do it with sex. Which is probably healthier," she says.

"Score one for me."

"He has magic powers, so..."

"So we'll give him one for those."

She laughs. "Are you two competing?"

"You're the one comparing us."

"I guess so."

"How do I stack up?"

Her eyes find mine. "Really?"

"You won't hurt my feelings if you like him better."

"Well, you're both incredibly annoying."

"That means a lot."

"Hypocrites. He's always telling his friends to stay out of things even though he's out there kicking ass."

"True."

"Whereas you're all 'never touch a man,' even as you're making plans to fuck Carpe Diem." Jealousy seeps into her voice. She clears her throat. Smooths her dress. "And, um, well, I guess you're taller."

"Another one for me."

She laughs. "Better hair."

"Body?"

"Hmm. He is super-hot. But you... You're pretty good too."

"Fuck, I'm so flattered. How do you do it?"

She laughs. "Your ego is big enough."

"I thought I was pathetically begging you to compare me to a TV character?"

"Yeah, but because you think you're better than he is."

Better? No.

As much of a fucked-up mess? Maybe.
But at least I'm off my drug of choice.
I've gotten pretty good at resisting booze.
If I can figure out how to resist Emma...
Then I'm golden.

HUNTER

The host leads us to a table in the corner. Pulls out Emma's chair. Offers me the wine list.

I shake my head. "My friend is only nineteen."

Emma shoots me a *really* look. It's pure *don't be such a drag.*

She believes I'm doing this for her.

Because I don't want her drinking.

That I'm not fun.

That's perfect.

"So..." She picks up her napkin and folds it in her lap. "You worked at Blacklist Tattoo for a long time."

I turn to her and arch a brow.

Her checks just barely flush. "It's all on your Instagram."

"You're stalking me?"

"It's public. And I was looking for the shop. We're always pushing for more followers."

"Probably easiest with Dean."

She chuckles. "Yeah. He tends to show off his abs."

"And your brother?"

"He used to be like you. All pics of tattoos. Nothing else. But once he started dating Kaylee, it was all cute pics all the time. It's disgusting." Her nose scrunches in distaste. "I'm not sure which of them is more popular."

"That must be hard."

"It's not a big deal." She presses her lips together. "I'm happy for them."

"Still."

Her voice drops to something more earnest. "I miss her. She's still my best friend. But I... I know he comes first."

"I'm sure she comes first."

"Oh my God." Her entire face scrunches. "Gross."

Fuck, she's adorable. "Don't you think?"

"I think I'd rather jam breadsticks in my eyes than discuss this." She motions to the empty table. "Where are the breadsticks?"

I hail the server. Request bread, and water.

She shoots me that same *you're such a drag* look.

She's playing it up.

She's not the type to bust out a fake ID for eight dollar a glass wine.

I keep pushing her. "Your brother seems like a generous guy."

"Oh my God, Hunter!"

I can't help but chuckle. "Just need a yes."

"Yes, I'm sure my brother insists on his girlfriend coming first. Did you really need my opinion on that?"

"Yeah."

"Why?"

"Your reaction is priceless."

She shakes her head. "I can do the same thing to you."

"Try me."

She presses her lips together, racking her brain. "Are you generous?"

"Yeah."

124

"Why?"

"What do you mean why?"

"Is it a love of watching women come? Is it obligation? Is it your affection for your one-night stands?"

I stare into her eyes, trying to figure out her intentions.

Instead, my thoughts shift to her.

To us.

To her slipping that black dress off her hips. Tossing aside her lacy bra. Sliding to her knees. Running her red lips over my cock.

Her on her back, her legs spread, her cunt pulsing against my lips.

Fuck, I bet she tastes good.

I want to know.

I want to watch her writhe under me.

To hear her groan through her orgasm.

"Hunter? Hello?" she asks.

"Yeah?"

"Are you there?"

"No. Thinking about making women come."

Her blush goes all the way to her chest. "Oh."

"What was the fucking question?"

"Why do you do it?"

If it was her, it would be obvious. How much I need her satisfaction. How badly I want her groan. How beautiful she looks when she comes.

Fuck, what do those dark eyes look like when they're filled with bliss?

"Hunter?" she asks.

"Still thinking about making women come."

"Oh my God. You're ridiculous."

"Yeah. But you brought it up."

"You did, actually. With that question about Brendon."

I guess I did.

Concentration continues to elude me.

125

Everything but the perfect fantasy of my name falling off her lips—

"I think you're torturing me on purpose."

A great idea.

"Should I give up on an answer to the question?"

"The what?"

"You're doing this on purpose."

"Doing what on what?" I ask.

"You are."

I shake my head.

"Yeah. But I guess this is an answer too. If you're just that fixated on watching women come."

Not women. Her. But she doesn't need to know that.

"Okay, since this isn't going anywhere. New subject."

"That was a tactful transition."

"Thank you. I appreciate that." She flips me off.

I laugh.

She does too.

Fuck, the way her eyes light up.

She has such gorgeous eyes. A deep brown with flecks of honey.

And, fuck, the way she lines them in black.

She looks like a goddess in that makeup.

Don't get me wrong. Emma is just as beautiful fresh faced as she is in makeup.

She's beautiful in everything.

"Let's talk about work," she says.

That might be a more loaded topic. "What about it?"

"Ryan really likes you. And he doesn't like anyone. Him inviting you to join the shop... that's practically rolling out the red carpet."

Maybe. He's not a guy for pleasantries. Or bullshit.

He said he wants me there.

He must mean it.

It's hard to accept that.

To see myself as someone people want around.

I want to deserve that.

To believe I deserve that.

"Are you going to take the job?" she asks.

"Probably." I want to make things work with Chase. I'm not giving up on him. But I'm not giving up on paying my own rent either. I can't wait until he's over hating me to take a paying gig.

Emma's gaze shifts from me to the corner of the room.

To Collin.

He's heading over here in jeans and a t-shirt.

He's not even trying to impress her.

Fuck, I hate the smarmy little asshole and he hasn't done anything.

I hate him for existing.

For wanting to touch Emma.

He goes around the table to hug Emma.

She hugs him back with awkward posture.

She's usually better at faking interest. She charms clients' pants off, even when they're obnoxious.

"You look beautiful." He takes the seat across from hers. "You too, Hunter."

"He kinda over-did it." Emma laughs as she gives me a long once-over. Her eyes linger on my slacks. My black belt. My button-up shirt.

"Now you tell me?" I try to make my voice teasing, but it's not quite there.

"You look good. Handsome." Her blush spreads to her chest. "But Carpe Diem—"

Collin's brow furrows with confusion.

"Alice," I say.

"She asked you out, right?" Emma asks.

"Yeah," I say.

"She wants to go home with the hot tattoo artist. Not"—She

gives my outfit another long once-over—"the guy who works at a bank."

Collin chuckles. "That is a bank look."

"You could have said that before we left," I say.

"I know." Her lips curl into a smile. "But then I wouldn't be able to make you all awkward and uncomfortable."

"How long have you guys known each other?" Collin's voice is shaky. Threatened.

"Too long," Emma says. "He was my brother's best friend when they were kids."

"Oh." Collin studies my expression. "So he's like an older brother to you?"

"Yeah." Emma's gaze flits from Collin to me. "A stuffy, no fun, over-protective older brother."

Collin's expression relaxes.

"And she's a total brat," I say.

"Oh, a brat, huh?" Emma raises a brow. "I've heard about that one."

Oh fuck no. My head is not going there. I'm not thinking of Emma throwing back sassy responses to my dirty demands.

No fucking way.

"Is that part of your daddy thing?" Emma asks.

No.

That's bullshit.

But if Emma is into it—

I want her however I can have her.

In my car. At the shop. On the fucking moon.

It doesn't matter as long as she's groaning my name.

Emma turns to the entrance and clears her throat.

She's watching Alice walk inside.

Alice looks gorgeous in her flowing floral print dress.

But staring at her only makes me think of all the ways she compares to Emma.

She's shorter. Softer. Less sassy.

Less interesting.

Completely uninteresting.

That's not fair. She's nice. Pretty. Smart. Honest.

But she's not Emma.

She hugs me. "You look good. Too bad you're stuck babysitting."

I nod. Bite my tongue so I won't blurt out all the shit in my brain. Right now, it's fucking obvious. I don't feel anything hugging Alice. I don't crave her presence. I don't even want to flirt with her.

Yeah, she's hot.

I could take her home.

Distract myself by fucking her.

Either I'll enjoy it.

Or I'll be more of a mess.

I still haven't untangled sex and booze.

I don't trust her to help me do it.

I don't crave the satisfaction.

Or even the release.

Better to go home. Think of Emma. Fuck myself.

I will.

Later.

I lead Alice to the table. Pull out her chair for her.

Emma offers her hand. "It's nice to see you again."

"Thanks." Alice shows off the ink on her wrist.

It's technically perfect—sharp lines, soft shading, bright colors, rich blacks—but it's lacking vision.

This could be anyone's design.

Sometimes, that's necessary. Sometimes, the client wants something boring or cliché. Part of the job is keeping my ego in check.

But when it's every fucking piece…

"I love it." Emma smiles knowingly. "There's something so comforting about the idea of seizing the day. Don't you think?"

Collin nods *hell yeah*.

I fight my chuckle. "I prefer seize the night, but yeah."

Alice blushes. Her light eyes spark with desire.

I try to return the gesture.

Fail.

She turns to Emma. "Hunter tells me you're his cousin."

I said she's like a sister, but close enough.

Emma laughs. "You could say that. We grew up together. He's basically my older brother. So when my brother went out of town, he asked Hunter to babysit me."

"You're a little old for that," she says.

"Thank you." Emma smiles. "But men don't always see reason."

Alice laughs. "No, they don't."

I shoot Collin a look. "This is at our expense."

He shrugs, sheepish. Completely enamored with Emma. "My dad is the same way with my sister."

"It's sweet that you care." Alice smiles at me. "I have a little sister too. I worry. Even when I shouldn't."

"God, I have like… a million older brothers. All the guys at Inked Hearts treat me like a little sister," Emma says.

Alice smiles. "It's good, having all that love in your life."

Emma smiles too. "Yeah, it is." Then she turns to me and smiles wider. "Even if they're obnoxious."

"You looking at me?" I ask.

"Not looking at anyone else." She turns to Alice. "You know Hunter is going to join full time?"

"Really?" Alice's eyes go wide. "That's great." Her voice is genuine She's happy for me.

She's happy for me.

I wish it meant more.

That I wanted her instead of Emma.

That would be so much easier.

But pretending I don't feel shit is how I got into this mess.

I'm not pursuing Emma.

But I'm not lying to myself either.

I want her.

I'm resisting her.

It's as simple as that.

"You never told me how you got into doing tattoos," Alice says.

Emma looks to me. "Yeah. How did you?"

"My older brother Chase was an artist." It's weird, thinking about him. About when he was still speaking to me. "I always wanted to impress him, so I started taking all the same art classes he did. When he started working as an apprentice, he brought home a tattoo gun. Showed me how to tattoo bananas."

Alice hangs on every word.

Emma too.

"First time I tried it, I fell in love. It was a rush, marking something forever." Once upon a time, it was the best feeling in the entire world.

"And you?" Emma clears her throat. "Alice, what do you do?"

"I'm an office manager," she says.

"I guess that makes two of us," Emma says.

"Emma runs the front desk at Inked Hearts," I say.

"Must be a lot," Alice says.

"Less than you'd think." Emma turns to Collin. "We're in school together. At SMC." She calls Santa Monica College by its initials. "I'm studying business and fashion. I'm going to own my own boutique one day."

"Ambitious." Alice studies her carefully. "I bet you have an eye for it."

Emma beams. "Thanks." She motions to me. "Probably should have told Hunter to dress down."

"No. He looks good. Like the guy you bring home to Mom." Alice smiles. "There's something sexy about seeing a guy with tattoos in a suit. About being the only one who knows about his inner freak."

"Inner freak?" I raise a brow.

"Oh yeah." Emma laughs.

I can't help but laugh. "I'm more vanilla than you'd think."

"Somehow I doubt that," she says.

"It's true." I shrug. "Vanilla as hell."

Emma turns to her date. "Do you believe that?"

He swallows his discomfort. "No. I don't think so."

"What about you?" she asks.

He stares with confusion.

She laughs. "Don't worry. It will come in time."

We fall into getting to know you small talk and teasing.

I try my best to focus on my date, but my gaze keeps shifting back to Emma.

And hers keeps shifting back to me.

Even with that, it's good. Easy.

Until the server stops by to take our order.

And Alice whispers something about splitting a bottle of wine.

I make up a lie about not wanting to drink in front of Emma.

Alice buys it, but my palms still get sweaty.

My heart still pounds like a drum.

I don't drink.

That's all I have to say.

It should be easy.

But it's not.

It's really not.

HUNTER

A ll through dinner, then a superhero movie at a theater on the Third Street Promenade, I watch Emma and Collin.

He's a good kid. Polite. Friendly. Respectful.

He holds her hand during the movie.

But that's it.

Alice and I get closer. She cuddles up to me like she wants to soak in all the comfort I can offer her.

But I don't know how to offer her comfort.

I wish I did.

I wish I was good at this.

But I'm not.

I absorb most of the movie—the plot isn't all that complicated —but it doesn't hit me the way it usually does.

It's not comic fatigue either.

I still love this stuff.

Still read graphic novels in my spare time.

Hell, watching *Daredevil* with Emma is the most fun I've had in ages.

Though… that's not exactly about the show.

It's watching it with *her*.

After the movie ends, Emma and Alice head to the bathroom.

They reappear with their makeup fresh and their smiles wide.

Alice's is real.

Emma's isn't.

She joins her date on one of the green iron benches on the promenade. This late, this far into fall, it's quiet. The street isn't teeming with tourists. The shops are all closed.

"Hey, Hunter." Emma's eyes bore into mine.

I stare back, trying to figure out what she's saying. "Yeah?"

"Collin invited me to a party at UCLA." She presses her red lips together. Digs her soft pink nails into her bare thighs. "I'm going to go for a few hours."

She's asking my permission.

Or looking for me to say no.

I try to figure it out, but I don't.

"Is that a good idea?" I check the time on my cell. "It's late."

"Thanks for the concern, Dad." She makes a show of rolling her eyes. "I'll be fine."

She watches Alice close the distance between us. Fights a frown.

I'm not closer to convincing Emma I'm not interested.

This is my chance.

And Collin… he's a teddy bear. If I can trust her with anyone, it's him.

Still—"If you're home by one."

"Oh my God." She tries to feign irritation, but it doesn't land. "I can't wait until I find my own place."

"I was the same way when I was your age." Alice slides her arm around my waist. "Do you kids have the address to your party?"

"Yeah." Emma nods. "I'll text it to you."

"Call if you need anything," I say.

"What could I need?" she asks.

"A ride," I say.

"Okay. Sure." She nods.

"Don't get in a car with someone who's been drinking," I say.

"And you're going to be sober?" she asks.

Fuck, that's it. "Guess so."

Alice frowns.

"All right. But don't wait up." She motions *lets go* to Collin.

"One a.m."

"You don't have any authority, Hunter." She waves goodbye. "But I'll think about it."

She nods another goodbye and follows Collin around the corner, back toward the restaurant.

Alice slides her arms around my waist. She looks up at me with a smile. "He seems like a good kid."

"Yeah." He seems safe. But you never know with guys. They're good at hiding what pieces of shit they are.

"What do you think?" Alice motions to the bar across the street. "One can't hurt."

I bite my tongue.

"A guy your size. Do you even feel a drink?"

Fuck, I used to hang out at that place. It's a wine bar. Trendy. Loud.

Tempting.

"I was thinking coffee," I say.

"Maybe at my place." She presses her palm to my chest. "Unless—"

"I can't stay late."

"I won't keep you."

EMMA

My purse vibrates against my lap.

It's almost enjoyable.

Hell, if I were alone on the couch, my eyelids pressed together, my thoughts on stripping Hunter out of that suit—

I can work with that.

I mean, I don't exactly need my cell's buzz. I have a vibrator.

Brendon made this huge, awkward thing about letting me pick out one when I was fifteen.

God, it was weird.

It completely killed the thrill of masturbation for a while.

And, well, killing a fifteen-year-old girl's desire to masturbate is quite an accomplishment.

A nineteen year old's…

I haven't.

Since that night.

It's school. Work. Stress.

All those extra shifts I picked up at the department store over the summer.

It's not like I was working myself to the bone so I wouldn't have free space in my brain.

It's not about him.

And it's not like the tension in my chest is about him either.

It's just…

It's been a while since I've been alone with a guy.

My purse buzzes again.

Collin looks to me curiously. "You gonna check that?"

"It's just Hunter."

"Oh." His eyes narrow. His brows furrow. His fingers curl into the steering wheel.

"He's so annoying. As bad as my brother."

"You two seemed pretty friendly."

"That's the only way to keep him off my back."

"Yeah."

"Trust me. It is." I guess, this time, I'm the one responsible for Collin's insecurity. It's obvious I'm into Hunter. That I want to drag him back to my room, unbutton his slacks, and wrap my hand around him.

Fuck, I want to touch him.

To taste him.

To lose myself in fucking him.

I want to be able to do that.

To feel normal.

Maybe it's not possible.

But actually wanting him without Vinnie creeping into the picture—

That's progress.

Even if I'm soothed rather than annoyed by his check-in texts.

Even if I'm comforted by knowing he's waiting to swoop in.

I'm a fucking damsel in distress.

How the hell do women deal with this all the time?

I spent the vast majority of my life sure I could take care of myself. Desperate to prove I could take care of myself.

And I could.

Until I couldn't.

Hunter: I can play bad cop if you need an out.

Emma: Why would I need that?

Hunter: Why did you stare at me like you wanted me to say no?

Because I'm not sure I can handle this.

Because I haven't been alone with a guy in three months.

Because I don't remember how to enjoy parties.

There are too many reasons.

Emma: You really think I need your permission to go to a party?

Hunter: You asked for it.

Emma: So your date would buy your 'Emma is like a sister story.'

Hunter: What story?

Emma: You get hard thinking about your sister?

Hunter: Don't have a sister.

Emma: You aren't denying it.

Hunter: A pretty girl was staring at my cock. It was involuntary.

Emma: And earlier tonight?

Hunter: What about it?

I mean. I'm not sure he was hard. But the way he was holding my coat, blushing, staring—

God, I want that.

I want to make him hard.

To *feel* how much he wants me.

I haven't wanted that in a long fucking time.

Emma: You were staring at my tits.

Hunter: Isn't that the point of your dress?

Yeah. It's for me. Because it makes me feel good. Because it makes me feel sexy. Because I need to believe I'm in control of that.

But…

139

Well, I'd be lying if I said I didn't want Hunter staring at my chest.

Emma: Not for your sake.

Hunter: I'm a man. I like tits. It's not personal.

Emma: You weren't looking at Alice's.

Hunter: I was. You just didn't notice.

"Em?" Collin mutters a curse as he slams on the brakes. "Everything okay?"

"Yeah. He just wants to make sure there won't be any drugs at the party. You know what parents are like."

"Parents?"

"My brother is my legal guardian. My parents died when I was a kid."

"Oh, fuck."

"They were in a car accident."

"Shit." He turns to me with an apologetic frown. The stoplight casts a red glow over his light skin.

It should be beautiful.

But it's not.

"I'm so sorry, Em." He reaches out to place his palm on the back of my hand. "That sucks."

"Yeah." I pull my hand to my lap. I appreciate the thought, but I don't need empty platitudes."

Are you okay?" he asks.

"It was a long time ago."

"Still. You must miss them."

"Yeah." My fingers glide over my cell. I bite back the defensive responses that will get him to back off. I've done enough to this poor guy. "But I don't really want to talk about it."

"Sure."

"Where is the address? Hunter wants it."

Despite the mention of Hunter, Collin's expression stays soft. "On my cell." He motions to his phone, currently plugged into the speaker.

I pick it up. Find the address in the maps app, send it to Hunter.

Emma: Don't wait up.

Hunter: That isn't funny.

Emma: You should enjoy your date. Find out what cliché Alice has tattooed on her ribs.

Hunter: Now, I know you're jealous.

Emma: In your dreams.

Hunter: Rib tattoos hurt like a bitch.

Emma: I'm aware.

Hunter: You're too scared for the needle.

Emma: Or maybe I have no desire to mark my skin forever.

Hunter: One day, you're going to care enough about something to need it on your skin.

Emma: And your Latin quote?

Hunter: What about it?

Emma: What nourishes me also destroys me? Really?

I set my cell in my lap to fiddle with Collin's. It's really trusting of him, keeping his attention on the road while I have every opportunity to check for nudes or texts with other girls.

I don't.

I do care about respecting people's privacy.

I go straight to the streaming app. Switch the music from a hip-hop playlist to The Smiths.

Collin makes that *really, this* face, but he keeps his lips zipped.

This is what always happens when I tell people about my parents.

They get all quiet and awkward and apologetic.

Hunter: It does.

Emma: What specifically?

Hunter: Aren't you at a party?

Emma: Aren't you getting a drink?

Hunter: Staying sober in case you need a ride.

Emma: I can Uber.

Hunter: Over my dead body.
Emma: Really? You'd die over me taking a ride share?
Hunter: Yeah.
Emma: That's a little melodramatic.
Hunter: So am I.
Emma: You really are.

SOMEONE'S PARENTS ARE OUT OF TOWN.

A big Brentwood house (in a perfect shade of Bruins blue) is booming with the *wub wub wub* of club music.

Its yellow fluorescent lights glow against the dark sky.

College students stand on the deck, sipping from red Solo cups. A few sit at a trendy green patio table, puffing cigarette smoke into the cool night air.

It's a normal party.

But it feels like I'm stepping into another dimension.

I haven't been to a proper college party since... Since Vinnie.

Fuck, that asshole doesn't get to be some sort of dividing line in my life.

There's no pre-Vinnie and after-Vinnie.

There's college.

I'm here at a college party like a normal sophomore.

Maybe my date isn't the most shining guy in the universe. Maybe he doesn't make my sex ache or my stomach flutter or my chest fill with warmth.

But it's like that saying goes.

I'm going to dance with the one who brought me.

I link arms with Collin as I step into the party. We pass friends playing a card game on the coffee table. Plates of snacks against the dining table. A row of bottles in the kitchen.

"Let's get a drink." I go straight to the makeshift bar. Fill a plastic cup with plenty of ice and rum and enough coke to make the whole thing palatable.

Collin fixes something with a lot of orange juice. "Damn, Em. You can put it away."

"Uh-huh." I swallow another gulp. Let the cheap booze warm my throat and cheeks. "This is your friend's party?"

He nods.

"Introduce me," I say.

"Yeah, sure." Collin leads me through the crowded living room. To a den around the corner.

Big leather couches. Clean white carpet. High ceilings. Skylights looking out at the stars. And those massive sliding doors that open to a lush backyard.

Collin motions to a muscular Asian guy sitting on the couch between two women in fuck me heels. "Hey Steve."

Steve nods.

"This is Emma."

"The hottie." He nods a hello. "I can see why he's always talking about you."

The compliment should make me blush, but it doesn't. Still, I play my part. "You're just saying that."

"Maybe." He laughs. "I say a lot of shit." He and Collin exchange a look, then he turns back to me. "Glad you joined us, Emma. We were just getting ready to play seven minutes in heaven."

Seriously? We're not fourteen. No self-respecting college student needs an excuse to head upstairs with a partner.

Collin laughs. "Not sure she's impressed."

"We're a little old for that," I say.

"How about seven inches in heaven?" Steve teases.

It's a funny enough joke.

If it was Dean making it—Dean would never dare suggest he's only seven inches—I'd laugh.

This…

It doesn't feel right.

"All right." Steve nods to the couch across from his. Motions for us to sit. "How about we play a different game?"

"Let me guess. Ten fingers," I make my voice as teasing as I can.

"I was thinking truth or dare." He smiles.

Collin nods.

I just barely stop myself from rolling my eyes.

This is not a college party.

This is just... sad.

But that's not ruining my night. I'm having fun. I have fun. That's who I am. Who I've always been. "All right. But I want to go first."

He nods.

I take a seat on the white leather couch.

Collin sits next to me. His knee taps mine. His fingers brush my thigh.

I wrap my arms around my chest. "It's cold in here, huh?"

Collin nods, grabs the blanket that's draped over the couch, sets it on my lap.

"What a gentleman," the blond girl coos.

"Steve, right?" I tuck the blanket around my thighs. So he won't get any ideas about us fooling around under it. That could be fun. If it was me and Hunter and we were desperate to touch—

Fuck.

I need to get my head in the game.

Sure, I want Hunter.

But Hunter is off with Carpe Diem.

Hunter isn't happening.

This party, me having fun tonight—that is happening.

Steve nods. "Shoot."

"Truth or dare," I ask.

"Truth." He grins.

Okay, let's get this started. "How many people at this party have you fucked."

His expression gets sheepish. "One."

"Who?" I ask.

"Not your turn anymore," he says.

Collin leans in to whisper. "You remember the redhead in the kitchen?"

Not at all.

He moves closer. So his breath is warming my ear. "It was her."

My shoulders tense, but I shake it off.

Steve asks one of the girls something about when she lost her virginity.

She dares her friend to kiss Steve.

Then the friend turns to Collin and he picks dare.

"I dare you to kiss Emma." She smiles like she just aced a test in her hardest subject.

It's a standard dare.

It's totally normal.

It's totally fine.

He looks to me. "What do you think?"

This is where I say yes. "Not here."

"Ooooh." Steve claps. "Fucking escalating. Nice."

I bite my tongue. "I better refill first."

"Yeah." Collin stands and offers his hand.

I take it. Let him slide his arm around my waist as he leads me to the kitchen.

I swallow my last drop of rum and coke.

Pour another glass and swallow a mouthful.

It warms my throat.

Calms the nerves spinning around my head.

This is a party.

A dare.

It doesn't mean anything.

Only... if I can't kiss him.

Fuck, that means everything.

Collin presses his palm into my lower back. He leads me through the living room, up the stairs, all the way to a dark bedroom.

I step inside and swallow another sip of rum and coke.

He flips the switch.

Yellow light floods the room.

It's a teenage girl's bedroom. The posters of hot musicians are a dead giveaway.

My room is the same.

Well, it was.

Until I tore down everything.

Collin closes the door, shutting out the noise of the party.

It's just us.

And the bed.

And the silence.

"This is nice." He takes a seat on the hot pink comforter.

I press my back into the wall. Take another sip.

"Don't worry about that dare, Em. It's a dumb game."

"Yeah."

"I just want to talk to you."

I've heard that before.

"I really like you."

"Thanks."

"You're funny. Smart. Hot." His cheeks flush. "Not sure what you want to do with me."

I'm trying to figure that out.

"Did you like the movie?"

I barely watched it. I was too busy keeping my guard up. "It wasn't my favorite."

"What is?" He motions to the bed. "If you want."

I do. I want to be able to sit there. And I want to rest my feet. These shoes are murder.

But I can't bring myself to move closer.

"What?" I pull my jacket a little tighter.

"What movie is your favorite?" he asks.

"Oh, that's easy. *Hercules*."

"Really?" He lets out a soft chuckle. "It's so… cute."

"And?"

"You just seem…"

"Not cute?"

"No. You're really pretty."

God, I'm way too defensive.

It's not his fault.

It's really not.

"Thank you." I force myself to push off the wall. I can sit on a bed next to a guy. That isn't a big deal. "I love Disney movies. My best friend and I are always watching them."

"Kaylee, right?"

"Yeah. She's my roommate too. But… well… we have to look for a new place."

"Oh?"

"Trouble with our landlord. Not interesting stuff." Deep breath. Slow exhale. Focus. I'm having fun on this date. Not thinking about Vinnie.

Collin isn't like that.

He's a nice guy.

He's safe.

This is it. I'm getting back on the horse.

I'm capable of this.

Collin looks up at me. "I'm still in my parents' place."

"That sucks."

"They're annoying. But their house is huge. And close to school."

I nod, even though I'm not absorbing his words. I'm too focused on moving toward the bed.

There.

I take a seat a few feet away from him.

I fold one leg over the other. Smooth my coat. Press my lips together. "You're a sophomore too, right?"

He nods.

"Where are you going to transfer?"

"Here, hopefully."

"UCLA?"

He nods.

I nod back. Everyone wants to transfer to UCLA. It's easier transferring as a junior than getting in straight out of high school, but it's still competitive. "Me too."

"You're smart enough."

"Smart isn't really my thing."

"But you are. You did most of the work on our project."

"I did okay."

He shakes his head. "All that stuff about managing inventory and marketing. I don't know any of it."

"I guess I picked up a lot at Inked Hearts."

Collin scoots a little closer.

I suck a breath through my teeth.

This is normal.

We're talking.

That's all.

"Does your friend normally play truth or dare?" I ask.

"No." He laughs and scoots a little closer. "He's trying to be a wingman."

"He's not good at it."

"I know. But then… I'm not very good at this either." His hand goes to my waist.

He pulls my body into his.

Then, all of a sudden, his hands are on my arms.

And his lips are on my lips.

And everything tastes like orange juice and vodka.

And my heart is beating so, so loudly.

I freeze.

This is too familiar.

The vodka.

The music.

The pressure of his hands.

He's not Vinnie. This isn't like that.

But, it's all there.

My head pounding the couch.

His belt scrapping my thigh.

The tug of rubber as he forced himself inside me.

At least he used a condom.

At least I didn't have to worry about that.

At least...

Collin pulls back. "Em? Are you okay?"

No. "Excuse me." I stand. Hug my purse to my chest. "I... bathroom." Somehow, my feet move toward the door. My hand wraps around the handle.

I get all the way to the bathroom down the hall and click the door locked.

The room is dark. Calm. Empty.

But it's spinning.

Everything is spinning. From rum or memories or my heart pounding so fucking fast.

I don't know.

But I know what I need.

I need to not be here.

I need Hunter.

I pull out my cell and call him.

HUNTER

My cell buzzes against my jeans.

I reach for it. Stop myself.

I'm too expressive when it comes to Em. If she's telling me she's about to fuck this guy but she's out of condoms, I'll lose it.

I scan the room for a private spot.

Alice's place is cute. White walls. Poppies on the windowsill. Seashells lining the mantle.

It's straight out of a home and garden magazine.

Beach casual. An easy, breezy decor that will make guests dream of salty air and crashing waves.

She crosses her legs as she brings her mug to her lips.

We're only halfway into our coffee.

I'm trying to find that thrill.

But staring at her tits isn't doing anything to motivate me.

They're nice tits, yeah.

She's hot.

She's eager.

Interested.

But it's not enough.

I don't need another empty fuck.

The hole in my gut is big enough.

I'm not doing anything to tear it wider.

Alice finishes her last sip. "You mind if I switch to wine?"

"No." Yeah. I was never a wine drinker, but it's not like I was picky. Whatever it took to get trashed. "But I have to admit something."

"Yeah?"

"I can't stand wine." My cell buzzes again.

"No." She presses her hand to her chest. "Really?"

"Tastes like vinegar."

"Take that back."

"I have to speak the truth."

She laughs. "God, you're lucky you're already here."

Once upon a time, I would have thought that too. I would have been over the moon fucking an eager babe who wanted to ply me with wine. But now—

All I can think about is Emma.

"Not liking wine is a deal-breaker." A laugh spills from her lips. "Wine is life."

"I know what you mean." Maybe that's the cliché Latin phrase tattooed to her ribs. *In Vita Vinum.*

That's another reason why I shouldn't be here.

It's hard enough avoiding booze when it's far away.

When there's a gorgeous woman begging me to drink?

Fuck, I need to get out of here.

"Where's your bathroom?" I ask.

She motions to a room down the hall.

My heart thuds against my chest as I lock myself inside.

I'm not sure if it's the calls or the wine or the combination.

I make a mental note to go to a meeting first thing in the morning.

Wipe my palms on a towel.

Splash cool water on my face.

Then I pull out my cell to check her text.

Emma: Are you still free?

Emma: I could use a ride.

Emma: But if you're busy fucking Carpe Diem, I'll summon a ride share.

There are two missed calls.

She's acting calm, but if there are calls, she must be freaked.

I hit the button to call her back.

She answers with a shaky voice. "Hunter."

"You okay?"

"Yeah. I just… I overreacted to something." Her words run together. She's nervous. And a little drunk.

"You called twice."

"Did I fuck up your date?" There's no fire in her voice. None of the usual sharpness. Just fear.

"What happened?"

"I need a ride."

"Are you drunk?"

"No." She lets out a heavy exhale. "Maybe."

"Em—"

"Forget it. I'll call an Uber."

"No. Stay there. I'll be there soon."

"If you're mad—"

"Stay there." I hang up the call before she can argue.

In the living room, Alice is sipping a glass of red wine.

She has this easy smile, like she really believes everything will always be okay. "Everything okay?"

No. I slide my cell into my pocket. "I gotta go."

"Oh." Her fingers curl into my forearm. "I guess you're—"

"Have a good night."

She yells some goodbye as I run out the door.

153

I park on the street. Pull out my cell to text Emma.

Hunter: I'm here.

Emma: I'm coming.

Hunter: I can come in.

Emma: This will be faster. Just stay there.

What the hell has her so scared?

I hate it.

I want to do whatever it takes to fix it.

The song switches to the next. I pick up my cell. Switch the album to one of those pop-punk bands Emma likes. I need to offer her some kind of comfort.

This is a nice neighborhood. But so was mine.

My heart thuds against my chest.

My stomach twists.

My limbs get heavy.

Finally, she steps onto the deck.

She wraps her arms around her chest as she descends the stairs.

I open the door for her.

She slides inside and clicks her seatbelt. "Thanks."

"You okay?" I put the car in drive.

"Yeah." Her voice is shaky. "Just ready to be home."

"You sure?"

She nods.

It's not true. She's not okay. But staying here isn't helping matters. I pull onto the street, do a U-turn in a driveway, head back toward San Vincente.

She settles into her seat. "I thought you only listened to guys who mumble about their pain."

"And this—" I nod to the stereo as the vocalist's words run together.

For a split second, she smiles. "He's a bit of a mumbler."

"Hot?"

"Eh... The voice is hot. The face and body not as much."

"Harsh."

"Truth hurts sometimes." This time, her smile lasts a few seconds. Then it's gone and she has that same nervous expression.

Her dark eyes are full of fear.

"What happened, Em?"

"Nothing. I just needed to be home."

"Where's Collin?"

"Hanging with his friends. He was having a good time. I didn't want to ruin that."

"He try something?"

"Oh my God, Hunter, can we not?"

"No."

Her gaze shifts to the window. She watches storefronts run together. A frozen yogurt place. An expensive gym. A strip mall full of local chains. "Where's Carpe Diem?"

"At her place."

"Oh." She presses her lips together. They're not red anymore. Her lipstick is worn off.

It's not like her.

She's religious about reapplying her makeup.

"Did you already fuck her?" Her voice doesn't quite hit teasing. "Doesn't really speak well to your performance."

"What happened?"

She ignores me. "Did you go back to her place?"

"Yeah."

"So I cock blocked you?"

"That doesn't matter."

"It does to me."

"Why?"

"Because... I... I'm not a cock blocker." Her fingers curl into her seatbelt.

"I wasn't gonna fuck her."

"Why not?"

"She's too nice."

"Isn't that a good thing?"

"No. That's all she is to me. Nice."

"And you only want premium pussy?"

"That's a douchey way to put it," I say.

"Guess I spend too much time with Dean."

I stop at a red light. We're less than a dozen miles from Emma's place in Venice, but it feels like we're in another dimension. Brentwood is clean, rich, empty, soulless.

I study her expression, but it doesn't help. She's defensive. I get that. But not why. "What happened with Vanilla Latte?"

"Nothing."

"Em, you're shaking."

"No." She forces herself to sit upright. "I'm fine."

"How much did you have to drink?"

"I don't know. Enough."

"Enough?"

"I wanted to relax." She makes eye contact through the mirror. "Is that not allowed?"

Green light falls over her as the stoplight changes. I have to break eye contact to look to the street. It's empty, but better safe than sorry. "Approximate it."

"I wasn't pouring shots. I don't know." She wraps her hand around her seatbelt. "Why does that matter?"

"Drinking fucks with your judgment."

"Don't." She leans in to turn the radio up. "Nothing happened. I just wanted to be home."

That's bullshit.

But pushing her isn't working.

The street curves to the left. It's a long stretch of empty road. Then more lights.

They're all green.

It's like the city wants us home as quickly as possible.

My sedan glides over the streets until I hit Eleventh. I get into the left lane. To head back to her place.

"You went back to Carpe Diem's place?" she asks.

"Yeah."

"But you weren't planning on fucking her?"

"I wasn't sure yet."

"So…"

"I didn't feel that spark."

She clears her throat. "Do you really need that?"

"Yeah." Now.

"But you always… you weren't discriminating."

"Things change."

"Oh." She rests her head on the window. "Well, what happened? Where did it go wrong? Spell it out for me."

If that's really what she wants.

I need to soothe her.

Whatever it takes.

"She invited me to her place," I say. "We had a drink."

"So it's okay for you to drink—"

"Coffee."

"Oh."

"She made her intentions clear."

"How?"

"I know when a woman wants to fuck me."

"But what did she do? Specifically?"

"It was the way she looked at me. The way her hand would linger on my arm or my leg. She'd lean in. Lower her voice to a whisper so I had to get closer."

"Good moves."

"Yeah." I swallow hard. I don't like her knowing moves. I don't like the implication. "And Vanilla Latte?"

"His friends wanted to play truth or dare."

"Really?"

"Yeah. It's so stupid and high school. But I'm not going to be a wet blanket."

"Why not?"

She shakes her head. "I'm not going to be that girl."

"Which girl?"

"The one who can't handle shit."

The light flashes green. I turn left. Keep most of my attention on the road. "What shit is that?"

"You know what I mean."

I shake my head. I don't, but I sure as hell don't like any of my ideas about it.

"You go to parties."

"I did."

"Why'd you stop?" Her voice is vulnerable, not accusatory.

But I still don't know how to answer. "It stopped being fun."

Her brow furrows with confusion. "Do you not want a birthday party?"

"Do I have a choice?"

"No." Her lips curl into a smile.

It's only a second, but I still feel it everywhere.

"It's on your actual birthday. After the shop closes. I need people to invite."

"Em, I appreciate that—"

"But?"

"I know you're trying to distract me," I say.

"Why do you care? I didn't fuck anyone. I didn't get arrested. I'm not physically hurt. You can report back to Brendon. Tell him everything is fine."

"It's not about your brother."

She turns to the window. "Whatever."

"We are friends."

She says nothing.

"I care about you."

Still nothing.

"If you're not ready to talk, that's fine. But I need to know you're okay."

She stays silent.

I turn my attention to the road.

Emma turns up the stereo.

A peppy melody fills the car. It should make the silence easier, but it doesn't. It underlines it.

We stay like that for the rest of the road. As I park. As she storms into the house and up the stairs.

Maybe I should give her space.

But I don't.

"Seriously, Hunter, I'm tired. I need to sleep." She steps out of her shoes. Bends to scoop them into her hands.

I stare back at her.

She sighs *fine*. "I overreacted to something."

"Did he try something?"

"Try something?"

"Touch you?"

"He kissed me, yeah."

The words drop like a thud. They bounce off the white walls and the modern furniture. Echo around the dark, empty house.

Bile rises in my throat.

"Are you jealous or worried?" she asks.

Both. "Did you want him to kiss you?"

"Yeah."

That doesn't make sense.

She's terrified.

Shaking.

"You're right. I drank too much. Got mixed up. That's it." She turns and reaches for her door handle. "Thanks for the ride."

"Em—"

"I'm going to bed."

"If there is something, anything… You can tell me."

"Right."

"We are friends."

"You've only said that three million times now."

"Anything you tell me stays between us."

"How can I trust that?"

"You have my word."

"That's it?"

"It's all I have."

She stops for a second. Considers it. Shakes her head "Good night, Hunter."

Emma steps into her room and slams the door closed.

I stare at the fucking door, trying to figure out what the hell I'm supposed to do here.

She's screaming *go away*.

But I'm not leaving her terrified.

I'm not leaving her.

I wait in the hallway until her room quiets, then I head to my room.

I try to sleep, but it's no good.

She's the only thing in my brain.

She wants nothing to do with me.

But I'm going to protect her.

Not because Brendon asked.

Or because I owe him.

Or because I owe the fucking universe a karmic debt.

Because I need to know someone's protecting her.

19

EMMA

Why is it so bright in here?

My eyelids flutter open then squeeze shut.

That isn't the soft white light of a beach morning.

Which means it's not early.

Which means I'm already late.

Fuck.

I force myself to roll out of bed. My feet hit the ground. My hands go to my hips. My eyes stay closed.

My head throbs as I stumble to the bathroom.

I push the door closed. Click the lock. Flip the light off.

There. That's better.

That's a reasonable level of illumination.

My reflection stares back, ragged and tired. My hair is a limp tragedy. My makeup is smeared. My under-eye circles are dark.

I might as well have a sign on my head reading *I drank too much last night. Please, Hunter give me a lecture. Then start poking my bruises. Ask all those questions I can't answer.*

If he wants to know to tell Brendon, he can go fuck himself.

But if he really does care…

If I really can trust him…

God, I want that.

I want him.

I want to be able to sit on a bed next to him, climb into his lap, kiss him like the God damn ship is going down.

I go through my morning routine. Shower. Wrap a towel around my chest.

Step into the hallway prepared to pretend his stares annoy me.

But the house is quiet. Empty.

He's not here.

He doesn't work today, but he isn't here.

I guess it's possible his claims about having a life were true. It's possible he's somewhere besides the gym. That he's not making a point of avoiding me.

I find my cell. Pray it's not as late as it seems.

It is. It's a quarter to eleven and I'm due at Inked Hearts thirty minutes ago.

Thank God I'm the only one who checks the schedule.

I ignore my texts from Kay, dress in the first clean thing I find, grab the cup of coffee that's sitting on the counter, curse Hunter's considerateness, and run the five blocks to work.

All right, I don't run—I don't do running—but I hustle.

The shop is clean, bright, quiet. Ryan's tattoo gun buzzes.

Dean and Chloe are actually working. As in, he's concentrating on a piece and she's staring with awe, and their client is mumbling something about classic rock.

I fix a cup of medium roast in the Keurig, turn the music on, find ways to stay busy.

For an hour, I restock drinks, check schedules, scour social media for tattoo posts to like and share.

My headache fades to a dull throb.

My nausea subsides.

My stomach stays twisted.

It's Hunter.

I want to believe it's just Hunter.

I want to keep telling myself this story about how nothing has changed.

But I'm not really buying it anymore.

I switch the music to something that fits my mood, then I pull out my cell and face my best friend.

Kaylee: OMG Em. How could you not tell me about Hunter?

Emma: It's not a big deal.

Kaylee: Brendon showed me his Instagram.

Emma: And?

Kaylee: And? Like you didn't see that smoking hot pic of his new rib tattoo?

I may have seen it.

I may have stared.

I may have actually considered fucking myself to the incredibly hot picture of Hunter's torso.

Kaylee: Brendon says he's staying at the house.

Emma: He is.

Kaylee: Am I supposed to buy this blasé attitude?

Emma: Yes.

Kaylee: I'm not.

Emma: You're on vacation. Go have fun.

Kaylee: I'm worn out.

Emma: Gross.

Kaylee: From our day in New York. It's so much more amazing than I remember.

Emma: Slightly less gross.

Kaylee: I won't tell Brendon.

She's usually good about keeping my secrets. No, she's always good about keeping my secrets.

I press my lips together.

Look around the room for some kind of sign.

There's nothing. Just the hum of the tattoo gun and Chloe and Dean exchanging barbs. I swear, it looks like she's flirting with his client. But why would she be flirting with his client? She's not the flirty type. And she's super into him.

Like crazy in love with him.

Maybe it's some foreplay thing they do.

Leighton and Ryan are like that. He gets off on watching her thrust her tits into customer's faces.

It's weird. But kinda hot too.

Emma: What about when he's picking up your phone to look at your nudes?

Kaylee: OMG, Em!

Emma: You're right. You send those straight to him.

Kaylee: No comment.

Emma: OMG, you do not.

Kaylee: No comment.

Emma: Kaylee Hart!

Kaylee: Do you really want to know?

Emma: God no.

Kaylee: Would you even care if I had nudes?

Emma: I don't want to think about my brother's spank bank.

Kaylee: Well...

Emma: I will... What's the text equivalent of hang up?

Kaylee: You won't.

Emma: I miss you.

Kaylee: I miss you too. But I'm back soon.

Emma: Then you have school.

Kaylee: We've made busy work before.

Emma: True.

Kaylee: All summer, you were working nonstop.

Emma: Also true.

Kaylee: Was there a reason for that?

Emma: I told you. I'm saving.

Kaylee: Your parents had a million dollar life insurance policy.

Emma: And?

Kaylee: And Brendon never spent any of your half.

Emma: Do you two really talk about that?

Kaylee: When we talk about the future.

Emma: And marriage and babies?

Kaylee: Yeah. Of course.

Emma: Gross.

Kaylee: You asked.

Emma: Do you want to have a baby?

Kaylee: Not now. But one day, yeah. At first, I was scared of the idea of taking care of anyone but myself. But now... I don't know. I feel more like I'm capable. He'd be such a good dad.

He would, but, seriously, this is too much mushy stuff.

My cell flashes with an empty picture message. It's still loading.

Emma: If those are your boobs, I will burn this place down.

Kaylee: The house or Inked Hearts?

Emma: Inked Hearts.

Kaylee: Does their insurance cover arson?

Emma: Not by an employee.

Kaylee: The shop is safe. I promise.

It's a picture of her and Brendon at the Empire State Building. They're hugging. They're beaming.

She's joyful a lot of the time.

But he—

It's rare seeing him this happy.

They're madly in love.

Sometimes, it's hard to accept. I was so used to her being *my* best friend. I knew she had a crush on him. But I thought it was that he was hot. I didn't realize how deep it went.

Now...

I'm happy for them.

But I miss when I was Kaylee's favorite person in the world.

When she went to me before she went to Brendon.

It's hard, losing that.

Emma: Cute. Disgustingly cute. You're both disgusting.

Kaylee: Thank you.

Emma: You're welcome.

Kaylee: I do remember Hunter.

Emma: You do not.

Kaylee: I do too. He always smelled like booze.

He did.

Emma: He doesn't.

He smells good. Like salt and that earthy shampoo.

Emma: And he got all weird about me getting drunk last night.

Kaylee: Emma Kane!

Emma: It was a party. I was on a date.

Kaylee: With someone you trust?

Emma: I have two dads right now. I can't take a mom.

Kaylee: Seriously, Em. You know I worry.

I know. And, somehow, it's not obnoxious when she does it.

Kaylee: How'd he know you were drunk?

Emma: I asked him for a ride.

Kaylee: Was everything okay?

Emma: Seriously, Kay. I have a babysitter.

Kaylee: Say yes and I'll drop it.

Emma: I can lie.

Kaylee: Yeah, but you won't.

She's right.

I hate lying to her.

It's even worse than lying to myself.

Kaylee: Listen, Em.

Emma: Whatever that is, let's not.

Kaylee: No deal.

Emma: I'll beg.

Kaylee: That only works on Doms.

Emma: Ew.

Kaylee: And it doesn't actually work.

Emma: EVEN MORE EW.

Kaylee: If you don't talk, I'm going to keep discussing my sex life.

Emma: Talk about what?

Kaylee: How about the super-hot tattoo artist currently staying across the hall?

Emma: It's no big deal.

Kaylee: You do realize I've also lived across the hall from the object of my affection?

Emma: Hunter is a babysitter, not an object of affection.

Kaylee: I remember your crush.

Emma: It was a long time ago.

Kaylee: He's only gotten hotter.

Emma: Irrelevant.

Kaylee: Very relevant.

Emma: It's nothing.

Kaylee: Fess up.

Emma: Mostly, he's annoying. He's always around. And now he's talking about how we're friends and how I can trust him.

Kaylee: Can you?

Emma: I don't know. Maybe it's a double agent move.

Kaylee: Is he the type?

Emma: I don't think so. But I'm not sure.

I don't add *I no longer trust my judgment in guys. Not after Vinnie.* But it's there.

Kaylee: Do you like him?

Emma: I don't want to.

Kaylee: But you do?

Emma: He's annoying.

Kaylee: YOU DO!

Emma: Maybe.

Kaylee: So? What's the game plan?

Emma: He's way into this whole 'you're just a kid, I can't see you as a sexual being' thing.

Kaylee: I doubt it.

Emma: He's not going to go for it.

Kaylee: I thought the same thing.

Emma: But Brendon was so obviously into you.

Kaylee: Really? Because I remember you being surprised and pissed.

Okay, that might be true.

But in hindsight, it was super obvious.

Kaylee: Do you want to make it happen?

Emma: I don't know. I want to find him irritating, but I like when he's around. God, last night, I was so freaked, but the second I heard his voice it was okay. Even though he was totally judging me for drinking.

Kaylee: What happened last night?

Emma: I overreacted.

Kaylee: To?

Emma: I was on a date. He kissed me. I wasn't feeling it.

Kaylee: Oh.

The two letters speak volumes.

It's like with my new lack of judgment.

We both know it's there.

I never told Kaylee what happened with Vinnie. But she came home to me sobbing in the shower after my date.

She saw the way everything changed.

How I went from flirting with him, wearing cute stuff around the building, generally being my take charge self to...

Whatever this is.

Maybe she doesn't know for sure.

But she's got a pretty good idea.

Kaylee: Listen, Em. Whatever reason you have for moving out, it's okay. I'll tell Brendon there was a noise complaint. I'll drop it if that's what you need. But you should talk to someone. Even if it's a professional.

Emma: Am I that crazy?

Kaylee: You haven't gone on a date since.

I swallow hard.

Kaylee: Something is up. Whatever it is, I'll support you. But you can't keep pretending nothing happened.

Emma: It's just awkward with Vinnie.

Kaylee: It's never been awkward before.

Emma: This is different.

Kaylee: I know.

Emma: Can we not do this now?

Kaylee: No, Em. We have to do this.

Emma: Or?

Kaylee: Or nothing. I'm still coming home. We're going to find a place together. Then we're going to marathon Disney movies and stuff ourselves stupid with chocolate chip pancakes.

Emma: Good.

Kaylee: I'm prodding because I love you and I don't like seeing you hurting.

Emma: I'm not.

Kaylee: You are.

Emma: I miss when we were talking about Hunter.

Kaylee: Promise you'll get help and I'll drop it.

Emma: Can you just drop it?

Kaylee: Not until you promise.

Emma: Okay. I will.

Eventually.

She's quiet for a minute.

Deciding if she believes me.

Or thinking about telling Brendon.

Or planning an intervention.

Something.

My shoulders relax as my phone buzzes with her reply.

This is okay. Normal. Good.

Kaylee: He is really hot.

Emma: Stupid hot.

Kaylee: What's he like?

I can talk about this. I can talk with her. Maybe I can't talk about *that* yet, but I can talk about this.

Emma: He's bossy.

Kaylee: Hot.

Emma: Not like that.

Kaylee: I bet like that.

Emma: What if I'm not into it?

Kaylee: Have you tried it?

Emma: Not really.

Kaylee: You should.

Emma: This is getting gross again.

Kaylee: What do you think Hunter is into?

Emma: I don't know. He's all broody and serious. But he's funny too.

Kaylee: Lots of pent-up feelings.

Emma: Exactly.

Kaylee: I bet he's intense.

Emma: I think so. I saw him naked.

Kaylee: Really?

Emma: Yeah. When I dropped by. He was getting out of the shower.

Kaylee: And?

Emma: And?

Kaylee: You know what I'm asking.

Emma: He does have a lot of ink, yes.

Kaylee: And?

Emma: Whatever could you mean?

Kaylee: His cock?

God, it's weird, seeing her use the word cock. But it's not like I'm suffering any illusions about how much my brother has corrupted her.

Emma: I saw that.
Kaylee: And?
Emma: Huge.
Kaylee: Was he hard?
Emma: Getting there.
Kaylee: You gonna get him there?
Emma: I'm working on it.

20

HUNTER

My cell sits on the passenger seat, reflecting the sun, daring me to text Emma.

There's some way to fix this.

To soothe her.

Convince her I deserve her trust.

I need to figure that out before I push her.

The song switches to the next. Another radio hit. Damn, I have to hand it to Emma. She knows how to pick music that cuts all the way to my bones.

My thoughts swirl as I park on the street and feed the meter.

When I close my eyes, I can feel her fear. The way it furrowed her brow. Shook her voice. Curled her shoulders.

Then I open my eyes and the only thing I can feel is my thudding heart.

It's right there.

Blacklist Tattoo.

Same bright sign.

Same big windows.

Same art lining the walls.

This place was home for years.

For most of my adult life.

Now...

I know I'm not welcome here.

But the degree is up for debate.

I swallow hard as I cross the street.

A red sports car stops just in time. The driver yells a curse, but the words don't flow through my ears.

The last time I was here, Chase pushed me out the door.

I deserved it.

He has every right to hate me.

To make good on his promise and never speak to me again.

I still remember the day that switch turned. He'd scheduled an intervention a few months earlier. Issued an ultimatum—stop drinking or get out of his life forever.

I promised I'd stop.

Picked up a bottle that same night.

When he caught me drinking at work, that was it.

He was done with me.

I wish I could say that was what inspired me to get clean. But it took another few months of drinking my money and an ultimatum from my parents—no rehab, no rent—to even consider putting down the bottle.

Even then... I didn't plan on getting sober.

I was going to do my time, get out, get drunk as soon as possible.

It wasn't until I was clearheaded enough to give a fuck that I actually wanted to change.

Now...

I'm still not sure where I'm going.

Only that I want to be better.

To stay sober.

To fix the shit I broke.

A short dude steps onto the sidewalk. Shoots me a *what the fuck's your problem* look.

He's a new customer. Or one I forgot in a blur of bourbon.

Either way, he's not impressed by the way I'm staring.

It's not helping.

I've got issues with the twelve step program, but that whole *only make amends if it's not making shit worse* thing?

That's a good policy.

I've done enough damage.

If my friends and family aren't read to forgive me—

I have to be okay with that.

Somehow.

I suck a breath through my nose, then I step into the shop.

My feet barely touch the ground.

Same flash tattoos in black frames. Same clean white walls. Same heavy guitar riff flowing through the speakers.

Chase has the same favorite band as Emma.

That can't be a win.

I laugh. For a second, I believe my brother and I are close enough I can tease him about his music.

Then I see him standing behind the desk, stern look on his face, posture screaming *go away*—

All that joy fades.

He doesn't want me here.

But Wes—my younger brother is standing next to Chase—is smiling.

Chase looks the same as he did the day he tossed me on my ass. Tall. Broad. Imposing.

He's an inch taller than me now, two maybe, but I never managed to outgrow seeing him as my tough older brother.

Wes has always looked small to me. Like he needed protecting. But he doesn't. He's not. He's the same height as I am. And he's utterly unaffected by everything.

He's wearing his usual aloof grin. Like he's ready to start shit right away.

Like he doesn't care that I'm here.

Usually, Chase is all steel and ice.

Usually, I don't have a clue what he's thinking.

Right now, his deep blue eyes are filled with pure disdain.

It's as clear as day.

My older brother hates me.

The buzz of a tattoo gun ceases.

That's Griffin, in the corner. Not a blood relative, but close enough to be a brother.

He's a good guy. Loyal. Idealistic. Straightforward.

Which makes his *what the fuck is this* look all the more concerning.

"Hunter…" Griffin whispers something to his client. Sets his gun down. "You look—"

"Like shit." Wes shrugs. "Sobriety hasn't been kind to you."

"Thanks." A chuckle falls off my lips. It's more nerves than anything. But it's good to see Wes. It's good he's the same. "I've been working on it."

"Yeah, I can tell. You wearing red eyeliner or something?" Wes motions to my eyes. "Maybe some light foundation. Like during your goth phase."

"That was to impress a girl," I say.

"So he says." Wes motions to Griffin.

But Griffin doesn't take the bait. He stares at Chase. His brow furrows. His lip corners turn down.

"Fuck, it's like a funeral in here." Wes moves out from behind the counter. "And Hunter isn't even rocking the My Chemical Romance look." He offers his hand.

I take it.

He pulls me into a hug.

Pats my back. Stage whispers. "Fuck, maybe I'm the only one glad you're here, but I am."

"Thanks." I step backward.

Chase's eyes stay fixed on mine. He's practically screaming *what the fuck do you think you're doing here?*

He's still my larger than life big brother.

But I can see the signs of strain. The frown on his lips. The tension in his shoulders. The tiredness in his blue eyes.

He looks so much like Mom.

Same deep eyes. Same dark locks. Same vicious stare.

Wes turns to our older brother. "Hate to break it to you, Chase, but you haven't mastered telepathy yet."

Chase's stare deepens.

"You know this tension is bad for your heart." Wes taps his chest. "Why don't you take him outside, hit him, get over it?"

"No." I take a step backward. "I get it."

"Fuck that. You're looking buff as hell, Hunter. Don't tell me you're still afraid of your big brother," Wes says.

Of him? No. Of disappointing him—I could write an essay about that.

"You do look good," Griffin says. "Even without the eyeliner."

"You got any I can borrow?" I try to tease, but it doesn't land.

Wes is the only one laughing.

And it's hollow.

Fuck, if Wes can't pretend everything is okay—

This really is dire.

"Are you here for a reason?" Chase's deep voice echoes through the room. It drowns out the thrashing guitars. The hum of the air-conditioning. The pounding of my heart.

"I want to apologize." It's not what he wants to hear. He wants something he can fix, something that will get me out of here. A last paycheck. A sketchbook I forgot. A client who needs a referral.

He's willing to deal with Hunter Keating, tattoo artist.

Not Hunter Keating, brother.

Fuck, I shouldn't be here. Even if it's my only option. "I

177

am sorry."

"That's great, right, Chase?" Wes shoots Chase a look.

Chase stays firm.

Wes's shoulders rise with frustration.

I'm going to fix this.

That means giving my brother room. "I should go."

"Fuck that. Stay. Help me with this mock-up." Wes motions to his sketchbook. "The perspective is off."

"Not my strong suit," I say.

Wes struggles to fight a frown. "Then tell me what you want for your birthday. It's next week. And I can't exactly buy you a bottle of Jim Beam this year."

Griffin shakes his head *fuck, did you really say that?* He turns back to his client and picks up his gun. "I'll see you around."

"I'm good," I say. "Really."

"Fuck that. I'm getting you something," Wes says. "If you want it to be appropriate—"

"Just come to my party," I say.

Wes and Griffin share a look.

Griffin shrugs.

Wes turns to me. "Fuck yeah. Is it gonna be dry or—"

That's a good question. "It's at Inked Hearts. On Friday. Starts around eight or nine." My eyes flit to Chase. He's still staring with disdain. "Hope I'll see you there."

Wes nods.

Griffin too.

Chase…

Well, I get the message.

I nod a goodbye to my brother, then I turn and leave.

He wants nothing to do with me.

It's fair.

I can give him space.

I can wait forever.

Whatever it takes, I'm fixing this.

HUNTER

Emma looks up from her spot on the couch.

Her dark eyes cut through me.

It's not like my brother's stare.

There's no hate in it.

There's frustration, yeah, but there's relief too.

"Hey." I press the door closed. Leave my keys on the dining table. I want to be here. I want to help her. To earn her trust.

There's something easy about being with her.

I don't feel like a useless fuckup.

I feel like I'm worth something.

Like I'm capable of helping her.

I don't know how to do it.

But the way her eyes are lighting up—

If she wants me around, I'm going to be around.

"Hey." She takes a long sip from her oversized mug. "I tried using the pour over."

"Yeah?" The room does smell like coffee.

"But I couldn't figure it out." Her lips press together—they aren't red today. She isn't wearing a hint of makeup. "So I made drip instead."

I shake my head. "Not with the single-origin?"

She bites her lip. "Yes with the single-origin."

"Em, you didn't." Using coffee that good to make something as shitty as drip is wrong.

"I figured it would be easy." Her lips curl into a half-smile. "I mean, if you can do it, how hard can it be?"

"You want me to show you?"

Her smile widens as she nods.

"What about that?" I motion to her mug.

"There's always room for more coffee."

"It's getting late."

"It's still light out." She stands and crosses the room. "Besides, it's Saturday."

"Is this how you party?"

"Coffee, chocolate chip pancakes, and Disney movies. Best party in the world."

Fuck, I can't think of anything that sounds better.

Maybe I'm stupid or reckless or self-destructive.

I don't care.

I need this connection.

I need her.

"Hunter, hello?" Her ass brushes my hip as she moves past me. "Are you going to show me or do I need to walk to the place down the street?"

I motion to the kitchen. "After you."

She steps into the small space.

I follow.

She's right there. Her crotch pressed against the counter, her tank top hiking up her lower back.

She reaches for the top shelf. Picks the single-origin Kenyan beans. Sets the bag on the tile counter. Sinks into her heels.

Fuck, this is a bad idea.

She's soft.

Touchable.

My hands are begging for her long legs.

I slide them into my pockets. Clear my throat.

I'm not touching her.

My cock is going to have to get over that.

I'm going to have to get used to mental images of pinning her to the counter.

I place the scale in front of her. "This is an exact science."

"Isn't that boring?"

"It's meditative." I grind the beans then scoop exactly sixty grams into the pour over.

"You don't seem like the type." Her eyes flit to the counter. She clears her throat. Presses her fingers into the tile.

"I'm working on it."

"Yeah, you're kinda… off."

"That obvious?"

She nods. "Where were you today?"

"I went to the old shop. To see my brother."

"Oh." She swallows hard. "I'm guessing it didn't go well."

"It went as well as it could."

"But—"

"Chase hates me. For some shit I did. He… I betrayed him."

"How?"

"Broke a promise."

She studies me carefully. "You do realize you're being incredibly vague."

I chuckle. "Yeah."

She fills the kettle, sets it on the stove, turns the burner on. "Unlike you. I'm not going to try to manipulate you into sharing by offering some quid pro quo bullshit. But, well, trading gossip during the Disney movies is an important part of the party. If you want to join."

"I'm invited?"

"Yeah. You're an integral part."

I arch a brow.

She motions to the carafe. "We need coffee."

"Damn, Em. You know how to bruise a guy's ego."

"Your company isn't too bad either."

"Shit, don't sweet talk me now."

Her smile spreads over her cheeks. "The gossip is normally about the shop. Or school. Or boys. Mostly boys. But I can make an exception for you."

"My brother is a guy."

She laughs. "Yeah, but guys as in guys we want to bang. Your brother—"

"You'd like him."

"Would I?"

I nod. "He's a little taller than me. Darker hair. Darker eyes."

"Brown?"

"Deep blue."

"He does sound hot."

I chuckle. "He is."

"It's good, you can admit that."

"Is it?"

"So many guys are uptight about that."

"I touch guys all day."

"And women."

"But mostly guys."

Her smile spreads over her lips. "Shit, I should become a tattoo artist."

"You could."

She shakes her head. "I couldn't take the pressure."

"I was like that at first."

"Really?"

"Yeah."

"How'd you get over it."

"Booze, at first."

Her eyes go wide. "Oh."

"Then time." I check the temperature gauge on the kettle. It's getting close. "It's not for everyone."

"Glad you realize that."

"What does speak to you?"

"Besides fashion?"

"Yeah."

"I do love fashion. Being able to turn into someone else in an hour. It's funny, how differently people treat me if I'm in something like I wore last night. Or if I'm in this." She motions to her pajama shorts and tank top. "Or if I put on some trashy leopard print dress."

"You don't own leopard print."

"I do. I swear."

"Really?"

"Yeah. It's not my favorite. But it has a certain aesthetic."

I'm sure she looks fantastic in any print.

"I love movies too. Letting them wash over me. And music. I have no talent. I can't play an instrument. I can barely carry a tune. I have enough rhythm to dance. But God, when I close my eyes, and I feel the bass, and I let the melody wash over me—there's nothing like that."

"Be honest: you listen to Bayside when you fuck."

Her cheeks flush. "I haven't."

She might as well scream *I want to.*

God, she's adorable blushing.

My balls tighten.

My pulse races.

That was the wrong thing to ask.

My body is going haywire.

It's tuned to her.

The desire in her eyes. The heave of her chest. The nervous scrape of her fingernails.

She wants me.

She's holding back.

But, fuck, seeing how she wants me too—

Not good for keeping it in my pants.

"I'll, um… I'll have to keep that in mind." She clears her throat. "I don't usually listen to music. I don't want to pollute it."

"You've never wanted to share it with someone?"

"Only Kaylee. But I'm not into girls." Her eyes find mine.

"What?"

"Guys used to get all *oh my God, you're so close, you must experiment* with us."

"Really?"

She nods.

"Did you?"

"Oh my God." She pushes me. Softly. Then harder.

Hard enough my ass hits the counter.

Fuck, it gives me ideas.

"I never got that," I say. "Why watch two girls go at it?"

"I think guys believe the women are going to invite them to join because they just desperately need a dick."

"Do they?"

"They? I don't know."

"Do you?"

"Are you allowed to ask that?" Her eyes light up.

"I won't tell if you don't."

"I could stand to get laid, yeah. You?"

"Don't need a dick no."

"Oh my God. That was so lame."

I laugh. "It was." Behind me, the kettle steams. I turn the stove off. Check the temperature. 205. A little hot. "Like I said, it's been awhile."

"For me too." She presses her lips together. "Why did you stop sleeping around?"

"I was never into it. It was more… something to do."

"A hobby?"

"You could say that." If I hadn't been so desperate to impress Chase, it would have been my only hobby. I check the temperature. Perfect. "Here."

I show her how to pour the water over the beans. It's a simple spiral pattern, but it takes a lot of practice to get the nuances.

"So that's it. Chicks, tattoos, and coffee?"

"The coffee is recent."

"You want me to believe you weren't sucking down Americanos to keep you *up* all night?"

"Never experienced that benefit of caffeine."

She chuckles. "You know what I mean."

"It was energy drinks back then."

She sticks her tongue out. "Vile."

"Yeah." I feel the same way now. Hell, I'm disgusted by vanilla lattes now. But back then—"I just wanted the high."

"They make caffeine pills."

"Had them."

She nods *reasonable.* Presses her ass into the counter. Stares into my eyes.

We're farther away. There's two feet between us. But now we're eye to eye.

It feels closer.

But not close enough.

"What else?" she asks.

"Comics."

"Of course."

"More graphic novels now. But still comics sometimes. I've been into them since the first time Chase loaned me his *The Amazing Spider-Man*. Fuck, what was the issue?"

"How did you get from there to art?"

"It's not interesting."

"Well…" Her cheeks blush. "It's not uninteresting."

We stare for a long moment.

Until the timer beeps.

185

I instruct her on how to pull the filter.

Her voice gets soft. Uncertain. "This is way too many steps."

"You want good coffee or you want minimum effort coffee?"

"I prefer blackmailing you into making the coffee."

"Sure."

"Sure?"

I nod. "You cook most nights. It's the least I could do." I want to take care of her. To make sure she's eating every meal and sleeping every night and finding comfort in—

In my arms.

With me.

"Okay." She tries to avoid blushing as she looks me in the eyes.

She's never shy.

It warms me everywhere.

I stare back at her. "Come here."

"And?"

"With the carafe."

She picks it up. Moves closer. Closer.

There.

She's inches away.

I step aside to give her room.

She slides into the space between me and the counter. Her ass brushes my crotch as she turns.

I should move.

But I don't.

I keep my body behind hers, my crotch against her ass, my chest against her back, my arms around hers.

Slowly, I bring one hand to her wrist. "I'll pour."

"Oh." Her chest heaves with her inhale. "Do you... um... are you still into comics?"

I take the carafe. Grab cups. Pour. "I lost interest for a while."

"Because?"

"High school bullshit."

"They weren't cool?"

"Yeah."

"And the art?"

"What about it?"

"When did you start drawing?"

"Chase talked me into this summer class at the community center when I was fifteen."

"And?"

"Once I realized about the naked women, I was sold."

She chuckles. "I thought you were kidding about that."

"I was." Water pours over the beans, flows through them, drips into the container. "And I wasn't."

"You're disgusting."

"Thanks."

She breaks our touch. Slides out from my grip. Pulls open the fridge door and grabs the half and half. "Hunter?"

"Yeah?"

"You know how you're all annoying about wanting to know things?"

I nod.

"It's been less annoying." She presses her palms into the counter. "I… I'm glad we're friends."

"Me too."

I'm pretty sure she's the closest friend I have.

22

HUNTER

Watching Disney movies while downing copious amounts of coffee and chocolate chip pancakes is a hell of a party.

The most fun I've had in a long time.

The most fun I've had sober... ever.

We talk about nothing and everything through *Mulan*, *The Lion King*, and *Inside Out*.

Apparently, the Disney marathon has relaxed enough to include Pixar.

I lobby for the addition of *Star Wars* and *Marvel*.

Emma sticks her tongue out and mutters something about being done with Matt Murdoch's brooding bullshit.

But when I get home from work on Sunday and start season two of *Daredevil*, she joins me on the couch.

She mocks the show at every turn.

Rolls her eyes at every one-liner.

Complains endlessly about the mismatched plot lines.

But, the next night, she joins me for another few episodes.

She scoots closer.

Until we're close enough to touch, kiss, fuck.

We're too close.

But we're still not close enough.

WES BREAKS THE SILENCE.

It's Tuesday afternoon. I'm two appointments down and dreading the third. It's not just that this client is a known pain in the ass.

Or my itch to move.

Or the way Emma is sitting at the counter, pretending she's not staring.

It's how completely out of my depths I am.

This is supposed to be an epic piece.

It's supposed to be fucking art.

For once, I actually poured myself into it.

This old-school lighthouse is my client's vision.

But it's mine too.

The tiny beacon of hope in the darkness.

A metaphor for the world.

Rocky shores most of the time.

Barely anything to guide the way.

But something.

And, fuck, when you find that, you need to hold on tightly.

I swallow hard.

It's everything, hearing from Wes, but that isn't the beacon of hope that's guiding me.

My beacon of hope is sending me to even more treacherous waters.

Wes: Do you realize there's a babe doing your bidding?

Hunter: A babe?

Wes: She sounded hot. This Emma who called the shop to invite everyone to your birthday party.

Hunter: Even if she did, is she really "a babe?"

Wes: Yeah. She is. Should have seen Chase's face when he picked up.

Fuck, I can see it now.

Hunter: He was delighted?

Wes: Yeah, like a polar bear in Arizona.

Hunter: That's specific.

Wes: Our AC is busted.

Hunter: And you're running?

Wes: We're closed for the day.

Hunter: Only for the day?

Wes: For a few days. Cash flow issues. We'll work it out.

If Wes is mentioning any issue, it's already huge.

Blacklist Tattoo is in trouble.

Wes, Chase, and Griffin are talented artists. They'll find new gigs easily. But not together.

This means the end of our surrogate family.

If I can still claim my place in *our* family.

Wes: You aren't telling me about this Emma babe.

Hunter: How do you know she's a babe?

Wes: Get with the times, Hunter. I checked her social media.

She posts a lot. Mostly her outfits. Or her makeup.

And, fuck, those outfits—

It's always something clingy or low-cut or short.

Like now.

She's wearing a white blouse. It's low enough on her chest to show off the lace of her black bra. It's not an all lace thing. Just a trim.

I saw it when I was packing her shit.

When I close my eyes, I can see her in it.

In nothing but that black bra and a matching thong.

She's here, teasing Chloe about work, studying between social media updates.

We're friends.

I'm not going to set her on that counter, roll her jeans to her ankles, and dive between her legs.

I need to go home.

Fuck myself until I can't come anymore.

That's the only way to keep my cool around her.

But there's no way I'm missing a minute of our time together.

We have plans tonight.

The gym. Dinner. The rest of season two.

I need that.

Her proximity. Her laugh. Her touch.

I need more.

But I'm taking what I can get.

My cell sings with a text alert.

Wes: You fuck her?

Hunter: That's Brendon's kid sister.

Wes: Shit, she's that Emma?

Hunter: Yeah.

Wes: She looks different.

Hunter: Her hair is a different color every month or two.

Wes: Damn. He could snap your neck like that.

I could hold my own against Brendon if it came to that.

But I'm not letting it come to that.

Hunter: I've been crashing at his place.

Wes: "Keeping her entertained" while he's away.

Hunter: Don't.

Wes: You think I was born yesterday? I know how you go through women.

Hunter: Not anymore.

Wes: Oh yeah, now that you're so busy not drinking?

Hunter: Did you have a point?

Wes: "Hey, Wes, nice chatting with you. You are the only brother who will talk to me, but I'm going to be an asshole to you anyway. I just love burning bridges."

Hunter: Don't talk about her like that.

Wes: You like her or something?

Hunter: Doesn't matter.

Wes: Fuck, it doesn't. Girl is throwing you birthday parties. You should hear the way she says your name. Like it's her favorite chocolate or some shit.

Hunter: You coming to the party?

Wes: Fuck yeah. Gotta see you fuck shit up with this girl.

Hunter: Your support means a lot.

Wes: You're welcome.

My shoulders relax.

He's fucking with me, yeah, but that's Wes.

This is the most normal conversation I've had in ages.

Wes: Chase isn't working tomorrow. If you want to come by.

Hunter: I thought you were closed?

Wes: We'll be open in the morning.

Hunter: I'll think about it.

Wes: Griffin is lukewarm toward you, and everybody else here thinks you're a piece of shit. But none of them will actively kick you out.

Fuck, he really hasn't changed.

Hunter: That's a warm welcome.

Wes: I was just thinking that.

Hunter: Great minds.

Wes: You gonna tell me what you want for your birthday or do I need to buy you a fleshlight?

Hunter: Live your dreams.

Wes: Not sure you'll like that.

Hunter: Honestly, Wes, I just want you there.

Wes: Don't get all sappy and shit.

Hunter: It comes with the territory.

Wes: Well stop. I get enough of that with Griffin. If you're gonna have feelings, at least hide them behind your steely blue eyes the way our big brother does.

Hunter: I'll keep that in mind.

"Hunter, hello!" Emma calls from the front desk. "Are you there?"

I shake my head. "Checked out."

"No. Check this out." She motions for me to come here.

I do.

She turns her laptop around to show off the results to her last art history test.

A big, fat 92 percent.

"I'm a genius." She motions to the Keurig. "You should worship me with a coffee tribute."

"Sure." I chuckle. "I'll drink coffee in your honor."

She shakes her head and pats the spot next to her. "No, you'll bring me coffee."

"How about I buy you an Americano?"

"Really?" Her dark eyes fill with doubt. "What's the catch?"

"Really." The catch is I need to get my eyes off her tits or I'm going to do something I can't take back. Fuck, she looks good in that white blouse. Professional. Like she really is training to own a business.

"You're being nice."

"I'm always nice."

"No." She looks to Chloe, who's back in Dean's suite, working on a mock-up with him. "Hunter's usually a jerk, right?"

Chloe makes that *kinda* motion.

"Hot though." Dean winks at her.

Emma makes a show of rolling her eyes. "Not everything is about that."

He scratches his head. "It's not?"

She looks to me. "You know what this means, right?"

"No."

"You promised you'd take me through running the shop."

"Now?"

"No." She presses her palms into the counter. Her nails are

purple today. A deep shade that's almost black. "Tonight. After dinner."

"And *Daredevil?*"

"Well... yeah." Her cheeks flush. "But not because I like it."

"Of course not."

"I watch it for your sake."

"Uh-huh."

"Otherwise, you might get confused and think it's good."

"That would be awful."

"Yeah, I wouldn't want your taste to degrade that fast."

I can't help but chuckle. "I appreciate your concern."

"It's because I care about you."

"You're sweet."

"I do what I can."

MY CLIENT DIGS THE WORK. LOVES IT EVEN. I FINISH THE PIECE ON a high. Float to the gym. Take all of Emma's teasing in stride.

All right, I enjoy her teasing.

Especially the way she eggs me on about lifting more and lifting harder because "I'm not going to impress any babes at this rate."

We walk home together.

She issues orders as we cook dinner. Assigns me the chopping, measuring, stirring.

Sighs over her perfect carbonara.

After her shower, she's clean and wet and dressed in a tiny tank top and shorter shorts.

She settles on the couch and pats the spot next to her.

With each episode, she moves a little closer.

Until she's right there, her thigh against mine, her head on my shoulder, her fingers brushing my forearm.

Fuck, I want her there.

I want her there too badly.

I make an excuse about how we need to get to the shop now. Before it's too late.

But it's already too late.

I'm falling for her.

23

EMMA

Starlight falls over the concrete. It mixes with the soft yellow glow of the streetlights. Then the neon signs of the shops across the street.

It's a beautiful night. Crisp. Clear. Cool.

I pull my arms over my chest. Rub my palms against my triceps. We're getting into fall now. It's still warm all day—it's warm all day, all year—but the nights demand sweaters.

Or maybe tall, broad men with safe arms and long embraces.

The stoplight turns green. The walk sign flashes.

My wedges click against the concrete as I follow Hunter into the street.

With the two inches of lift, I'm eye to eye with him.

Or more like eye to back of head. With him in front of me.

God, he walks fast.

I hustle to catch up with him. Exhale slowly to hide my straining breath.

It's not just moving quickly.

It's him.

He makes me fluttery.

Nervous.

Happy.

Even when I want to slap him for his bullshit, I want to stick around.

The back of my hand brushes his.

It's nothing. Barely a touch. But it still sends warmth straight to my stomach.

"You cold?" He steps onto the sidewalk.

I swallow hard. "A little." Not so much with him this close. Those flutters take over. Make it impossible to notice the goose bumps spreading over my arms.

He's just…

He's annoying and bossy and over-protective.

He likes action shows with inexplicable plots, can't chop vegetables to save his life, and steals my chocolate at an alarming rate.

But I still want him around.

I like him.

More even.

I don't love him yet—I've never even considered loving someone—but this is more than like.

There must be something in between.

Some *he drives me out of my mind, his lips are so kissable, his trust is so tantalizing.*

His smile makes me think of cheesy pop songs.

His hurt cuts right to my heart.

I stop breathing when I think about him.

"Here." He slides his leather jacket off his shoulders. Drapes it over mine. "Better?"

"Yeah. Thanks." I bring my hands to the lapel to hold the jacket to my chest. It's too much for the weather, but I still want it closer.

It smells like him.

And it's…

It's so sweet and normal and boyfriend, Hunter offering me his leather jacket.

"What is it you want to know?" He turns right. Toward the shop.

"Everything."

"You have me for an hour." His footsteps are strong. Steady. "Get specific."

"I watched three episodes of *Daredevil.*"

"By choice."

I shake my head.

He turns to me and raises a brow.

His blue eyes meet mine.

They fill with that spark he gets when he's teasing me.

When he smiles.

His smile is too rare.

I want more of it.

I want it every minute of every day.

"No." I try to make my voice even, but it's not. I'm too light. Too airy. Too intoxicated. "I had to be there. To help you understand all the adult themes."

"Did you?"

I nod. "All those guys who died? That's traumatizing."

"Hate to break it to you, Em, but I've read comics since I was a kid. Henchmen are always dying." He fishes his keys from his pocket, unlocks the door to Inked Hearts, pulls it open, motions *after you.*

I nod a thanks and step inside. It's weird, being here alone. Sometimes, I open the store, but I never manage to arrive first. One of the guys is always here prepping for an appointment.

They're dedicated.

Even Walker and Dean. They act like they're easy, breezy surfer boys—well, with Dean it's more obnoxious, trouble-making surfer boy—but they're devoted to their craft.

Moving closer to that, learning the skills I need to bring my boutique to life—fuck, it makes me dizzy.

I shrug the jacket off my shoulders and lay it on the counter.

Hunter clicks the door locked behind us. His footsteps fill the room as he moves forward. "Em?"

"Yeah?" I press my palms into the black plastic. My nails are too chipped. It's time to change the purple polish to something else. Something that feels right. I pick a color that suits my mood.

Right now... this is red. A deep, crimson red, like the rose tattooed to Hunter's hip.

Ahem.

Not that he...

I'm not...

God, I so am.

"You decide where you want to focus?" he asks.

"You're the teacher."

He nods.

I force myself to look him in the eyes. "Give me some options."

"Fair." His soft lips curl into a half-smile. "You manage the schedule?"

I nod.

"And the social media?"

"Yeah."

"You ever see the books?"

"Sometimes. Ryan is secretive about it."

Hunter chuckles. "He's secretive about everything."

"Those are strong words for you."

"Oh?"

I nod. "I still don't know why you're crashing at my brother's place."

"Ran out of cash."

"Because..."

"Because I spent it."

"Really? Is that how money works?"

He moves around the counter. Turns on the computer. Types his login.

"You don't seem like the type of guy who can't balance his checkbook."

"Shit. Do I really seem like I use a checkbook?"

My lips curl into a smile. It's the perfect response. And it's so Hunter. Defensive. But funny too. "Honestly, Hunter, if you ran out of cash because of stupidity, I'd like to cancel this lesson."

"Is that a threat?"

"Yeah."

"Not your best work."

It's not. He's doing this as a favor to me, not the other way around. "Still. If you're showing me the books."

"Not these books." He motions to the spot next to him. "I don't have access."

"Really?"

"You thought I would?"

"I guess you're still a guest." I move around the counter. Until I'm three feet from him. Then two. "Did you think about Ryan's offer?"

"Yeah."

"If you're broke, seems like a good deal."

He rolls his shoulders back. "I'm gonna take it. Just have to figure out some other shit first."

Like whatever it is that used up all his money.

And got him to leave his last job.

Or maybe he got fired.

I couldn't really tell from the reaction I got when I called Blacklist Tattoo.

But then if someone called here for dirt, I'd purposely lead them astray.

I can gossip about my friends all I want. But if someone else starts shit, they're going down.

"I did some stupid shit," Hunter says. "Made some bad decisions. That's how I ended up broke."

"Now?"

"Not exactly rolling in it."

"But…"

"I'll get there." His fingers brush my wrist. "You know how much I make?"

"Not exactly."

"Explain how my salary works." His eyes meet mine. They bore into mine. They demand something. Something that isn't educational.

But I do need to learn this. "You don't get a salary."

He nods.

"You basically rent the chair here. Like at a hair salon. You charge clients something within the shop's rates and pay the shop a percentage. Then you get tips. Well, minus the percent I get."

"What did I make this week?" He turns the screen to me.

It's his records.

I guess he has access to those.

I scan them carefully. Add the numbers in my head. Get a rough approximate. "Shit, really?"

"Really…?"

It's more than I expected. A lot more. I pull out my cell, check my math with the calculator, relay the number to Hunter.

He nods. "So the shop?"

I do the math. Show him the results.

He nods.

"How many hours did I work last week?"

I check the time sheet. Reach for something to write with. "This is too much to keep in my head."

"Fair." He grabs the sharpie we keep on the counter. His fingers brush mine as he hands it over.

It's barely a touch, but it still makes my stomach flutter.

He's so close.

And he smells so good.

I barely manage to hold my poker face. "Paper."

He bends, grabs a spare sketchbook from beneath the counter.

I scribble a note about Hunter's hours.

"Let's figure out how much the shop made." He points to the computer. "Assume all the other guys made the same for every hour they worked."

I nod.

"You know the schedule. Do the math."

Okay, that's simple. How much they made per hour, times the shop's commission percentage, times hours worked. But that info is on my account, not his. I motion to the computer. "I need that."

He nods.

His body brushes mine as he steps aside.

Then mine brushes his as I take my place.

There's barely any space here.

But he's still too far away.

My fingers fumble over the keyboard. It's impossible to focus. To do this math.

He's so close.

So there.

So attentive.

Deep breath. Slow exhale.

I run through the calculations twice. "There." I show Hunter the number.

He nods. "How much is that a month?"

"There are four weeks and two days in most months."

He motions *go ahead*.

I do the math. "Are you sure you're not an algebra tutor?"

"Is that your kink?"

My cheeks flush. "What?"

"I've got my daddy thing—"

"You don't really."

"You're all about teacher/student."

"No, I..." I swallow hard. Fuck, it's weird feeling awkward with a guy. I'm usually good at flirting. I'm usually smooth. But between the last three months and all the fluttering in my stomach... "Yeah. I want my professor to bend me over and spank me with a ruler."

"Fuck." He doesn't sell it as teasing. His pupils dilate. His tongue slides over his lip.

"I... Uh..."

He stares back at me.

I stare back at him.

What the hell are we doing here again?

We shouldn't be talking. Or working. Or thinking.

We should be getting naked.

Touching.

Making each other come.

I want to see him, feel him, touch him, taste him.

Not just because he's hot.

Or because I want to prove I can do this.

Because he's Hunter.

Because he loves bad action TV. Because he can't chop to save his life. Because he's bossy and overbearing and incredibly sweet.

"I... Uh..."

"You finish the math?" His fingers brush my wrist.

"Yeah. Umm..." I force myself to concentrate. Do the calculation. "This right?"

He moves closer as he checks.

He nods.

I shudder.

He stays there—right there—as he takes me through an expense report.

His fingers brush my hip.

My neck.

The small of my back.

Then his body is behind mine.

And his breath is warning my ear. "How are we doing?"

Please touch me. Forget about the shop. Forget about my brother. Forget how badly you need this job.

Erase everything else.

"Good." My heart thuds against my chest.

I'm not used to wanting someone.

For three months I haven't.

Hell, since I jumped up to five foot seven (at fourteen; I'm five eleven now) and developed breasts (also at fourteen, and, well, they aren't much bigger now), I've been the one making boys nervous.

But Hunter isn't a boy.

He's a man.

And he's practically untouchable.

"At the end of the year, everyone is taking home a nice profit. Even after the salary they pay themselves." I force myself to look him in the eyes. "But, if you think about it, we could do a lot better."

"Yeah?"

"We have three suites, plus the one in back. With the shop hours, we could have artists here from ten to seven, all day, every day. We could stay open later even. You won't have a client every hour. But we could add shifts. Fill the chairs more. Hire a few artists. More if we moved stuff around."

"Ryan won't like that."

"He might. He… he does want to hire you."

"You should pitch it to him."

"Maybe." I bite my lip. I want to feel like an important part of the team. But no one sees me that way. "He won't listen."

"Make him."

"Easier said than done."

"Maybe. But you're tough."

I turn toward Hunter. "He's like you. No one can make him do anything."

"How do you know?"

"About you?"

He nods.

"We've been arguing nonstop."

"I've done your bidding."

"Only when you want to. And how you want to. You… you basically tricked me into acing my test."

"Offered you a deal."

"If anything, I've done your bidding."

He shakes his head.

"Okay, I haven't. I… no one makes me do anything either." Not even myself.

I bite my lip. Press my palms into my thighs.

I want to touch him. He's right there. And he's staring at me with all this pride.

God, it's intoxicating.

His fingers brush the back of my hand. My forearm. My shoulder. "Like what?"

"Hunter." I swallow hard.

His hand cups my cheek.

My eyelids flutter together. "Why are you so over-protective? You barely know me."

"I know you."

"A little."

"Because you don't let me in."

"You don't either."

He moves closer. "I want to know you, Em. I want in your head."

"I want that too." I lean into his touch. Soak up the softness of it. The hardness of his calloused fingertips.

He brushes a stray hair behind my ear.

He stares down at me.

My eyelids flutter closed.

I rise to my tiptoes.

Press my lips to his.

It's soft. A hint of a kiss.

Then it's more.

His lips close around my bottom lip.

His fingers skim my jawline.

His need pours into me.

There's so much neither one of us has said.

So much we want to say.

My hands go to his hips.

His go to my back.

He pulls my body into his.

But it's only for a moment.

Then his hands are gone.

And he's pulling away.

Staring dumbstruck.

Fuck. That's bad. "I…" What the hell can I say when he's staring like that?

For a moment, we're in limbo.

Then he blinks, and everything clicks into place.

"Em…"

It's everything he has to say.

"You're amazing, but—"

"Don't."

"It's not you."

"Seriously, Hunter. Don't." I take a step backward, but there's nowhere to go. I'm pressed against the counter.

I try to slide out of the space.

His fingers curl around my wrist.

For a moment, he holds me tightly.

What the hell does he think he's doing?

He doesn't get to say *you're amazing, but*.

Fuck him for that.

I don't care what his reason is.

"Em…" He releases me. "It's not you."

"Whatever." My cheeks flame. Fuck him.

He doesn't get to flirt and help me and touch me and then turn around and say *we can't*.

"I'm going home." I push past him. Move around the counter. Grab my purse. Leave his jacket.

"I'm not a good guy."

"How many times do I have to say 'don't'?"

He opens his mouth to speak.

But I don't stay to listen.

I move to the door.

Outside.

The air is cold. It nips at my cheeks, chest, chin.

Without his jacket, it's freezing.

Or maybe that's reality dawning on me.

I'm amazing, but I'm not as important as his bullshit reasons.

24

EMMA

I avoid Hunter. Sleep late. Study at the library. Eat dinner in my room. Blast music so I won't hear his footsteps or the low roar of the TV.

It's supposed to feel good, ignoring him.

But it doesn't.

It only makes me emptier.

Lonelier.

I text Kaylee nonstop. Discuss anything but Hunter or, God forbid, Vinnie.

It's a relief, talking to her, but I'm still holding my cards too close to my vest.

I'm still crumbling under the weight of this.

MY PERFECT *I'M NOT SEEING OR HEARING HUNTER; I BARELY KNOW HE exists* record falters when I arrive at Inked Hearts Thursday afternoon.

It's a nice day. Warm. Sunny. Peaceful.

Except for Chloe and Dean bantering, the shop is quiet. The music drowns out the buzz of tattoo guns and the low hum of conversation.

I alternate between work and studying—Ryan is obliging about letting me study during down time—but none of it distracts me.

I'm acutely aware of Hunter's presence.

He's right there. Hunched over a pretty girl, one hand on her side, the other adorning her lower back in ink. It's a yoga thing.

She's a yoga teacher and she's all bendy and smiley and blond.

Not that I stalked her social media.

She publicly tagged the shop. And Hunter.

It's not like I was looking.

Or like I'm jealous.

If she wants some guy who pulls this bullshit *it's not you, it's me, I'm a bad person, I can't own my decisions*—

Fuck him for touching her.

Fuck her for laughing at his joke.

Fuck everything.

I dive into art history, but it makes me even more aware of his presence. This was so much easier when he was drilling me. I mean, uh...

I can still taste his lips.

Feel the pressure of them.

The warmth in my chest.

The ache between my legs.

He kissed me back.

He does want me.

But...

Why are relationships so confusing?

"Oh my God, isn't it awesome?" Yoga Girl bounces to the front desk. She smiles at me. This big, genuine, loving smile.

She's so sweet and nice and cute.

And I want to punch her in the face.

She tilts her head to the right as she lifts up her t-shirt. She can't quite see her new ink, but I can.

It's good. A Buddha meditating, surrounded by lush petals.

It's not exactly what I expect from Hunter, but it's him all the same. He has this way of drawing with the bare minimum of detail and extra shading. Like something out of a comic book.

This is softer and brighter than his usual thing—the boy is dark, whether he wants to believe it or not—but it's still him.

I can feel him in it.

Which only makes me hate Yoga Girl more.

It's not her fault.

It's his.

He's an asshole with bullshit excuses.

Fuck him for staring at me with those piercing blue eyes.

For making my knees weak.

For making my heart ache.

Fuck him for hurting.

He did this to himself.

He did this to me.

He doesn't get sympathy now.

"It's great." I force a smile as I tally Yoga Girl's total and print a receipt.

She smiles, fishes a wad of cash from her wallet, presses it into Hunter's palm. "Thank you so much."

He nods. "Of course."

"Really." She doesn't give him time to slide the money into his pocket. Goes right into throwing her arms around him and squeezing tightly. "It's so awesome."

He hugs back awkwardly. "My pleasure."

She releases him. Looks around the shop like she's looking for more people to hug.

So not into that.

I make a show of taking a seat.

She gives Hunter one last hug then she bounces out of the shop.

He slides the cash into his pocket.

I bury my nose in my text book.

"Art history test?" he asks.

I say nothing.

He stands there, waiting.

I pretend to ignore him.

We stay like that for a solid two minutes.

Finally, he gives up.

"All right." His fingers brush the counter. "If that's the way you want it."

Fuck him for that.

Fuck him for everything.

I mean, if I could fuck him I wouldn't want to throw up every time I saw a smile.

But fuck him for that too.

Hunter doesn't have time to leave. Ryan interrupts.

He leaves his suite to move to the counter. Stretches his arms over his head, accidentally showing off his taut abs.

I try to convince my body to want him, but it doesn't happen.

Only Hunter will do.

He turns to Ryan. Nods a hello.

Ryan nods back.

Hunter's eyes flit to me. "Emma wants to tell you something."

No. I want sleep. And Disney movies. And an alternate universe free of Hunter's excuses.

"About the shop," he says.

"No. I want coffee." This is my idea. I get to decide when I share it.

I slide out of my chair. Move around the counter. Brush past Hunter with as much cold shoulder as I can manage.

But that does nothing to help my case.

Now, he's whispering something to Ryan.

And Ryan is nodding.

I focus on fixing a medium roast. On its *drip drip drip* and the comforting scent of coffee. On pouring exactly the right amount of half and half and adding just a touch of sugar.

Fucking Hunter.

He's ruined this too.

Now that I'm used to his fancy pour overs, this K-cup screams of mediocrity.

I slide my shoulders back, suck a deep breath through my teeth, march to the counter as casually as possible.

Ryan's eyes meet mine. They get big. Intense. "You think we should hire more artists?"

I fight my desire to glare. "It's what the math suggests."

Ryan brushes a wavy strand behind his ear. "How many?"

"Well…" I step behind the counter. Pull up the Google Doc I made. "We're limited by space, but we could fit another suite in here. And we could get more strict about kicking people who aren't working to the lobby."

He nods.

"We could hire three or four artists. Easily." I turn the screen so it's facing Ryan.

He's so quiet and intense.

He's always like that.

But I'm not usually seeking his approval.

My eyes flit to Hunter.

He nods some *way to go* nod.

I try my best to ignore it.

To not feel the warmth in my chest or the flutter in my stomach.

It's worse that he's being all supportive and encouraging. It would be easier if he was a dick. Then I could convince myself I was wrong about him.

But right now, with those blue eyes trained on me…

He kissed me.

And it was…

It was everything.

Why is he…

Why are we…

UGH.

"This is thorough." Ryan's eyes meet mine. "You're good at this."

"Maybe." It's weird, accepting a compliment about my intellect. But Ryan is always straightforward. If he's saying this, he means it.

"These are projections, Em. Good ones. You forget I went to college?"

Yeah, actually.

"Studied business," he says.

That's vaguely familiar. He did it to make his parents happy. Started working as an artist soon after.

I guess he learned something, because the shop is doing well. And he's the guy who runs it.

"What are you taking now?" he asks.

"It's a two-oh-one class." I sell the confidence. Math doesn't come easily to me, but I pay attention and I work hard.

"You're a natural." He studies the numbers carefully. "You ever think about focusing on business?"

"Like an MBA or something?" I fight my desire to cringe.

He chuckles. "I was the same way when I was your age."

"What was it like, living before the invention of television?" I tease.

"Tough." He looks to me. "It doesn't have to mean working at some giant company. Could be this." He motions to the shop.

"Hate to break it to you, but I already have this," I say.

He just laughs again. "You could be me."

"Please God no."

Hunter laughs.

Ryan shoots him a look, but it's only for a second. His poker face breaks and he shrugs. "Fuck, no one would want that."

I nod. "No one." Ryan's funny. He's always been a good sport about mocking his misery. Even now that he's no longer miserable. He and Leighton are like... disgustingly happy.

"You could run a shop," he says.

"That's already what I want to do." Does no one listen? "I want to own my own boutique."

"You could run this shop."

"Isn't that your job?"

"Yeah. But it could be yours instead."

I stare back at him. "Like an actual, official Inked Hearts manager?"

He nods.

"The guys would kill you," I say.

He smiles. "All the better."

"You'd be good at it," Hunter says.

Ryan shoots me a look. "After college."

"That's almost three years," I say.

"We could make it official, you being assistant manager," he says. "But you'd have to commit more hours to the shop. Drop that other job."

I like my other job.

I like having a life outside my brother.

But actually having more responsibility—

That's fucking amazing.

"I'll think about it," I say.

"Never worked so hard to give someone a promotion." Ryan chuckles.

"You should," Hunter says.

I ignore him.

He doesn't get to offer me life advice now.

I'm so...

UGH.

He's standing there all happy and sure of himself. Like he did this. Fuck him.

If he's spilling my feelings, I'm spilling his. "Hunter wants to stay."

"Oh?" Ryan turns to Hunter.

"Yeah. So that's one artist down," I say.

"Only took us a year." Ryan chuckles.

I motion to Dean and Chloe.

"She's got another eighteen months before she's doing her own shit," he says.

"Really?" Learning to tattoo takes a long fucking time.

He nods *really*.

God, eighteen months learning under Dean.

At least she's actually getting *under* Dean.

That will do a lot for their sanity.

"Hunter?" Ryan asks. "You want to work here?"

"Yeah," he says.

"Fuck, don't sound so excited," Ryan says.

"If Ryan is mocking your enthusiasm, you know it's bad," I say.

Ryan flips me off.

I return the gesture.

"What's this about excitement?" Dean calls.

Chloe shoots him a *really* look.

He nods. "Yeah, sunshine. You gotta listen for your cues."

"Who here would even want to have sex with you?" she asks.

"Not everything is about sex," he says.

She looks to me. "You believe this?"

"I believe he believes it," I say.

"Hmm." Her dark eyes fill with fire. "I'm not sure I do."

"You want to gossip or you want to work, sunshine?" He taps the sketchbook they're hovering over.

"You sound like Ryan," she stage whispers.

He cringes in feigned disgust. "Fuck. I better shower right away." He stands. Shoots her a wink. "You can watch."

"Can I?"

"Of course." He moves to the sink. Makes a big show of washing his hands.

She rolls her eyes.

But she smiles too.

She's totally into it.

Ryan shakes his head at their shenanigans. Turns to Hunter. "I'll get you a contract next week."

"Sure." He nods.

Ryan actually smiles. He offers his hand. "You're a good guy, Hunter. Glad to have you here."

"Thanks." Hunter shakes. Manages to hide the awkwardness in his frown.

"Talk to Emma about working you into the schedule." Ryan nods a goodbye and heads back to his suite.

Hunter stays put.

I stare at my hands.

We're quiet for a long moment.

He breaks the silence. "Listen, Em—"

No way in hell. "Do you have any days you can't work?"

He stares back at me *are we doing this?*

I nod. Hell yeah, we're doing this.

He frowns, but he concedes.

And then he leaves.

That's how little he cares about fixing whatever it is that's broken between us.

EMMA

I t should be easier working my second job schilling lingerie, but it's not.

It's slow.

My thoughts keep flitting back to Hunter.

I want to hate him.

I'm trying, so hard, to hate him.

But my heart isn't in it.

I focus on fixing the displays in the front of the store. The newest one is particularly beautiful. A black chemise with lace cups and sides and a matching thong.

Classy. Elegant. Upscale.

It's interesting, seeing what different women pick out.

Sheer white chiffon for a honeymoon.

Slick red satin for a girl's night out.

Soft pink lace for a date with a smart, worldly guy.

It's there, in the sale rack—the lingerie set I bought for Vinnie.

Really, it was for me. Lingerie is always for women, so we can feel better about ourselves. Men appreciate it, sure, but they can't tell the difference between La Perla and H&M.

This bra and panty seemed elegant. Mature. Subtle.

Like the kind of women he'd want.

When we flirted, it was never compliments about my tits. It was teasing about art or music or wine.

I was in over my head, pretending I knew what he was talking about, but I didn't care.

I was so into him.

I loved that he was older. That he was wiser. That he was a consultant with a schedule that had him traveling constantly.

I felt important the first time he invited me over.

I dressed up in my fancy new lingerie and a classic black sheath.

He cooked this fancy Halibut dinner and poured glass after glass of wine.

Then it was dessert and cocktails.

Amaretto and vodka and vanilla cake.

I drank too much.

Got fuzzy.

It all blurs together now.

His smile.

The ever so slightly condescending tone to his voice as he explained Plato's *Allegory of the Cave* to me.

The sigh as he leaned in to kiss me.

His hands under my dress.

My palms against his chest as I tried to push him away.

The way he pretended he was okay to stop.

The change in his posture when he stopped pretending.

I still remember that look in his eyes.

The one that said *I'll take whatever I want, so you might as well give it to me.*

I did.

I froze.

It was easier to close my eyes and tell myself it was okay.

To convince myself I wanted it.

That he was sloppy.

That it was a bad date.

Not a sexual assault.

But...

My fingers curl around the pale pink bra. This one isn't my size, sure, but it's the same garment.

It's been so long that it's on sale.

It was trendy then.

Now it's out of season.

The nylon lace is rough against my fingertips.

It's a familiar feeling—most of my bras are made out of nylon —but this exact fabric, this exact pressure...

For three months, I've been telling myself this doesn't matter.

But it does.

Only...

What the hell do I do with that?

I can't wallow in it. I'll fall apart.

I can't share it with anyone. Brendon will kill Vinnie and I can't ask Kaylee to keep this from him. I can't put that on her shoulders.

Hunter...

I thought I could trust him.

But I can't.

Not if he's going to run away when I need him most.

I set the bra on the rack. Scan for something that actually suits me. Something that will make me feel like I'm attached to my body.

The black chemise in the front of the store is perfect.

Practical but still sexy.

Still Emma Kane.

I slip into the dressing room to try it on.

I stare back at my reflection until it's a blur of black fabric and pale skin.

It's beautiful.

But it's still so fucking weird.

I buy the lingerie. I tell myself it's an important first step. That I'm reclaiming my body.

But I'm not sure I believe it.

AT HOME, I LAY THE CHEMISE ON MY BED. NEXT TO MY DRESS FOR Hunter's party. I'm not in the mood to celebrate him, but I'm a woman of my word.

I text Dean to make sure everything is prepped. Despite the tattoo artist's aloof act, he's an excellent party host. And he's really insistent about celebrating birthdays in style.

I move to the bathroom, lock the door, strip out of my work clothes.

I never spend a lot of time staring at myself naked.

I have my insecurities, sure, but I'm usually happy with my body.

Right now...

I feel so naked.

I mean, I know I'm naked.

But I've never felt that way. I was never awkward or shy. I'd walk about the house in nothing. Leave my underwear everywhere. Skip panties if I'd gone too long without doing laundry.

Now, I can't even look at myself in the mirror.

I step into the shower. Turn the water on. Try to scrub away the day.

My hair needs a gentle touch—I'm taking a break from dying it every color in the rainbow to let it grow out, which means it's a classic but plain shade of brown—but I'm rough. Impatient.

I scrub until I'm raw.

I still remember showering that night. Wanting the water to erase everything, but feeling just as violated.

I'd watched enough *Law and Order SVU* to know I was doing all the wrong things.

I should have gone to the hospital, done a rape kit, filed a report.

But that would have meant admitting what had happened.

And I couldn't.

I can barely think it now.

I linger in the shower, water pounding the tension from my back, until someone is knocking on the door.

Hunter is saying something.

I turn the water off and wrap myself in a towel.

He knocks again. "You okay?" His voice is soft. Caring.

He's only asking about the shower. About why I'm spending an hour locking myself into the bathroom.

He's not asking about his bullshit rejection.

But I still want to pour my heart out.

His proximity brings safety.

When I close my eyes, I can see myself in that chemise. In front of him. Inviting him to touch me.

Fuck, I want that so badly.

I want that to be okay.

"I have to get ready." I cinch the towel tightly.

"That isn't an answer."

He isn't getting one.

I suck a breath through my teeth. Muster all the *I don't give a fuck* I can manage. Step into the hallway.

He's standing in jeans.

Only jeans.

He slides one hand into his front pocket. Runs the other though his hair.

His pupils dilate as his eyes trace my body.

It's different than with other guys.

I want him staring.

I want him tearing off my towel, wrapping his arms around me, pinning me to the wall.

Erasing that awful memory.

That can't be that last time someone touched me.

It can't.

His eyes fix on mine. They're so blue and piercing and full of hurt.

I want to wipe it away.

Fuck him for that.

"We need to talk," he says.

No. I know what he wants to talk about. And I'm done. "I have to get dressed."

"Too bad."

I push past him.

His skin feels so good against mine.

He's warm and hard and inviting.

But fuck him for that too.

"Emma." His voice drops to something demanding. "Stop."

My knees go weak. Fuck, maybe it is hot when he gets bossy. Or maybe it's the hurt dripping into his voice.

He is worried about me.

He does care.

Just not enough to pull his head out of his ass.

"Are you going to apologize for your hypocrisy?" I ask.

He says nothing.

"Or tell me you realized I'm more important than whatever it is that's keeping you away?"

Still nothing.

"Then what the fuck could we possibly have to talk about?" I don't give him a chance to respond.

I move into my room.

Slam the door.

Drop my towel.

He stays in the hallway for a moment. Waiting for me. Giving me time to get over my anger, I guess.

Not happening.

I ignore him as much as I can. Don my chemise and my little black dress. Towel dry my hair and apply texturizer.

I hate going out with wet hair, but heat styling is out of the question. My hair is way too fried for that.

Eventually, he moves into the office. His room. Whatever.

He shuts his door.

I focus on my makeup. My heels. My purse.

But, still, when I look in the mirror, I don't see Emma Kane, confident, sexy, badass.

I see a vulnerable girl who can't protect herself.

Hunter is standing in the hallway, both hands in his jeans, black sneakers pressed together.

"You look older." I push my door shut. Hug my purse to my shoulder. "You're turning forty-five, right?"

"Feels like it."

I press my lips together, even though that will mess up my lipstick.

I already feel safer. Less vulnerable.

All it takes is his proximity.

I trust him to keep me safe.

I guess that's what Brendon wanted.

I should hate it.

But I don't.

I really, really don't.

EMMA

"**I** know what you're thinking." Dean jumps—actually jumps —up to the counter. He motions to an empty spot of ceiling. "It's not enough."

It's a lot. The shop is decked—*Happy Birthday* banner over the entrance, black balloons bouncing against the roof, giant mocha chocolate cake stacked with candles.

Hunter chuckles.

Then blushes.

Oh my God.

It's so…

He's so…

It's wrong how hot he is.

How impossible it is to hate him.

"Yeah, that's exactly it." Walker chuckles as he nods hello. "Happy birthday."

He offers Hunter a hug.

Hunter accepts it. Barely even looks awkward.

Walker turns back to his girlfriend. Wraps his arms around her.

Iris looks as stylish as always in dark wash jeans and fuck me pumps. But *fuck me, I'm a dirty secretary* pumps. Not *fuck me, I'm in the clubs for a one-night stand* heels.

They started as a fuck buddies thing earlier this year. He fell hard. She resisted.

She had a secret, one that caused a mountain of drama, but they got through that.

And now they're…

They're more dirty than cute.

But they are cute too.

Iris turns to me. "You really do throw a party, Emma."

I shrug like it's nothing.

Her expression gets sheepish. "I wish I hadn't ruined the one you threw for Walker's birthday."

"Don't worry about it." It was memorable. "Besides, that was more Dean."

Dean chuckles. "It was all him." He nods to Walker, who shrugs *I guess it was*. He and Dean are best friends. They fight sometimes and constantly give each other shit, but they're clearly close.

"The main thing I remember happened right over there." He nods to the office, where they once had very loud sex.

It was his birthday.

But still…

I don't need to hear that.

"What do you think, sweetness?" His lips brush her ear. "Want a repeat?"

Her blush deepens. "Later."

"Can you veto this?" I turn to Hunter. Try my best to pretend as if I'm totally relaxed discussing sex with him. "Make it your birthday wish."

"Fuck that. I want my free audio porn." Dean's voice booms.

"The amateur stuff is the best."

Leighton makes a show of rolling her eyes. "He mentions that five times a day." She greets me with a hug. "You okay?"

I nod. "Long day at work."

Leighton worked here for a long time, but we were never really friends. Friendly, sure. But she's like everyone else here. Her loyalty is to Brendon first.

"If you want to talk…" She pulls back with a smile. "Well… I'll probably be gushing over my boyfriend. But you can always pull me away." She turns back to Ryan and blows him a kiss.

He catches it and presses it to his chest.

She giggles like a schoolgirl.

It's cute.

But disgusting.

That's enough love for one night.

I'm glad my friends are happy. Really.

But I can't stomach their romance right now.

Not with Hunter standing right there, pretending like he isn't wanting me, refusing to explain why we can't be together.

I go through my hellos. Everyone from the shop is here except for Chloe.

"Where's your shadow?" I ask Dean.

"I like to imagine her in her bedroom," he says.

"That's gross."

"Is it?" He raises a brow. "Or is it so hot your panties are drenched?"

I shake my head.

"You want me to go into detail?" He motions to Walker. "Or call my boy over? Get him narrating his last tryst?"

"Is it a tryst with your girlfriend?" I ask.

Dean shrugs. "You think I know shit?"

"You're smarter than you let on," I say.

He chuckles. "Am I?"

I nod.

"Hate to break it to you, but it doesn't take a lot of brainpower to connect these dots." He motions to my chest. Then to Hunter.

Who's still pretending he's not watching.

"You look hot as fuck," Dean says. "Pretty sure your mission is working. Assuming your target is turning twenty-eight today."

I try to copy his coy shrug, but I don't pull it off.

Okay. New subject.

Anything but Hunter.

Even if he is staring.

Even if his attention sets me on fire.

Even if I desperately want him to tear my clothes off.

I turn back to Dean. "You have to be careful with Chloe. Ryan will kill you if you scare her off."

"Ryan's been waiting for a reason to kill me since I was born."

"Oh?"

He nods. "It's some fucked-up Greek tragedy shit."

"Haven't heard that one."

"Then Disney shit. Like *The Lion King*."

"Like *Hamlet*?"

"Yeah. Kill me. Take my place."

"Yeah, Ryan really wants to be the court jester."

He presses his hand to his heart. "Oh, Em, you don't mean that." Dean's gaze shifts to something behind me.

I don't have to look to know.

My Hunter sense is tingling. He's moving closer. And, fuck, am I really making comic book references in my head?

I'm already in too deep.

"Damn, Em, without your brother here, we can get into some real shit." Dean flashes me an effortless smile. He nods hello to Hunter. "What are you thinking?"

Hunter surveys the scene carefully. "What kind of shit do you normally get into, Em?"

"The usual. Drugs, sex, mayhem." I try to make my shrug

casual, but it's really not happening. My body is magnetically drawn to his. "I better start. Get a drink."

Dean motions *after you* then turns to Hunter. "You want something."

Hunter shakes his head. "Not right now."

Dean shrugs *suit yourself*.

It's funny.

Hunter used to drink a lot.

Now, on his birthday, he's refusing booze.

I tell myself it doesn't matter.

That I don't care what he does or why.

But the thought still bounces around my brain.

What the hell is his deal?

I let Dean pour me a rum and coke. Shift into bantering with my friends.

Dean teases about playing Never Have I Ever.

Leighton rolls her eyes and settles into Ryan's lap.

Walker makes dirty jokes until his girlfriend is blushing.

Everything is okay. I'm with my friends. I'm laughing. I'm buzzed.

Then the door swings open.

A guy with gorgeous blue eyes—the same as Hunter's—steps inside. He runs a hand through his sandy hair. Flashes me a panty-melting smile. "You must be Emma."

"Wes?" God, he's exactly as Hunter described him.

He nods. "The one and only."

I offer my hand to shake.

He takes it, bows—really bows—and places a kiss on the back of my hand.

I giggle. "Not sure this is the occasion."

He straightens himself. "It's always the occasion for theatrics." He holds up an enormous wrapped package. "Where can I put this?"

I lead him to the counter.

It's not flush with presents, but there is something from everyone.

We want Hunter to belong.

To believe he should be here.

He…

I…

Ahem.

Wes's gaze shifts to Hunter (he's still pretending he's not watching). "Can I tell you a secret, Emma?"

"Sure."

"Thought you sounded hot as fuck when you called Blacklist."

"Oh. Thanks." My gaze flits to Hunter for a second, then it's back on Wes. "I mean, that's kind of weird, since I don't know you—"

"You were at our place once. For a party," he says. "You were little. Ten, maybe."

"Oh. With the basketball hoop in the pool?" I ask

He nods. "Exactly."

"What is it about this place? Why all the rich parents?"

"Nepotism."

I can't help but laugh. "True." There are a lot of friends and blood relatives working here, myself included.

"Looked at your Instagram," he says. "You've got nice tits."

My cheeks flush. My body is devoted to Hunter, but Wes is charming. For a second, I forget that everything is fucked. "Thanks."

His gaze shifts to my chest for a moment, then it's back on my eyes. "Is that working?"

"I wore this dress because I like it."

"Right." He leans in to whisper in my ear. "You need help making him jealous?"

"I don't know what you—"

"Yeah, you do."

Okay, I do.

It's stupid.

It's petty.

It's completely necessary.

"Okay," I whisper.

Wes brushes my hair behind my ear.

His fingers linger on my neck, my shoulder, my arm.

It's not like with Vinnie.

But it's not like with Hunter either.

The pretense is obvious.

"Look at him," Wes whispers.

I do.

He brushes my hair behind my ear. "He wants to deck me."

"Something tells me that's a typical thing for you."

Wes's laugh bounces around the room. "Yeah. But Hunter stole my thunder for a while."

"Did he?" I bite my tongue. I have to play this cool. To pretend like I know what Hunter did. That's my only chance of getting info.

"Yeah. You must know what he's like by now."

"Brooding and difficult?"

Wes chuckles. "That what you like about him?"

"More his abs."

"Lots of guys with abs in the world."

"Like you?" I offer.

"Yeah, but you're not my type."

"I don't believe you."

He laughs. "That obvious?"

I nod. "Why… why are you the only one from Blacklist here?"

"I'm the only one who wants to see his face."

My gaze flits to said face.

He's not hiding his stare anymore.

He's not hiding his jealousy.

His brow is furrowed. His eyes are wide. His hands are fists.

It shouldn't feel good.

But it does.

This is all I can get from him.

"That good?" Wes asks.

"Yeah."

"We need to escalate?"

Probably, but I can't handle that. "No. I think this is enough."

He raises his voice. "Fuck, Emma. You gotta give a guy a warning before making a proposition like that."

"Do I?" I raise mine too.

"Yeah. But if you insist..." He steps back enough to offer me his hand.

I go to take it.

Hunter marches over.

Stops me.

His fingers brush my wrist. "Can we talk?"

I stare at Wes like I'm madly in love with him.

I'm not. But he's hot, tattooed, and devil may care. It's easy enough pretending.

"About what?" I try to keep my gaze off Hunter, but my eyes betray me.

"Now," he says.

Hunter and his brother share a look. I'm not sure what they're saying, but it must be meaningful, because Wes turns to me and nods a goodbye.

"Call me, Emma." He winks. "I've got no problem being sloppy seconds."

Hunter shoots his brother a *get real* look.

Wes shrugs and joins the conversation on the other side of the room.

Which leaves me and Hunter alone.

He motions to the now clear back office. "There."

He's not saying *let's go someplace where I can fuck you*.

But that's exactly what my body hears.

HUNTER

I suck a breath through my teeth.
Close my eyes.
Exhale slowly.
It does nothing.
I'm still seeing red.
My veins are still buzzing.
What the fuck does Wes think he's doing touching Emma?
The office door slams shut behind me.
Emma sits on the desk. Folds her arms over her chest. Stares.
Her dark eyes fill with the hurt she's been wearing for days. "Well?" Her voice is low. Impatient.
Not that I'm any better.
My thoughts are a jumbled mess.
I need to get my shit together.
To make this up to her.
Justify dragging her from the fray.
I reach for something sensible to say. Find only platitudes. "We need to talk."

She scoffs. "That's rich."

"Em—"

"No. My friends call me *Em*. You do not call me Em."

Fuck, I need to cool it. I need a clear head for this conversation.

Slow inhale.

Steady exhale.

Oxygen flows through my veins. Competes with the anger.

Loses.

Her brow knits in frustration. "Let's talk, Hunter. Let's talk about how you're a fucking hypocrite."

Maybe.

I'm too far past logic to say.

None of that matters.

Protecting her is the only thing that matters.

"You can go fuck some blonde dolt, but I can't even flirt—"

"I didn't touch her."

"'Cause I cock blocked you."

"I told you. I didn't want to."

"Fuck you."

"You know what I was thinking the entire time I was there?"

"How you're an asshole."

"How much I'd rather be with you."

Her cheeks flame red. Her throat quivers. Her fingers slam the desk. "Fuck you."

"Em—"

"YOU DON'T GET TO CALL ME THAT."

"I'm not—"

"Yeah, you are. You chose to end this. You don't get to turn around and say you'd rather be with me."

She slides off the desk.

I move in front of the door to block her.

She tries to push past me.

I grab her wrist.

She pulls her hand back. Holds it to her chest. Stares like I'm the devil. "Happy birthday, Hunter. Save your talk for someone who gives a fuck."

She pushes past me.

Slams the door on her way out.

My heart begs me to follow her.

But I manage to find the one scrap of logic left in my brain.

I've hurt her too much.

Whatever happens, I'm not pouring salt in the wound.

THE MAIN ROOM IS BUZZING WITH LAUGHTER AND CONVERSATION, but the second I step out of the office, the mood changes.

Emma's angry exit is in the air.

Ryan shakes his head.

Leighton shoots me a worried glance.

Dean shrugs like he has no idea what's going on.

He and Wes are locked into some sort of *who gives less of a fuck* competition.

Fuck, the two of them together is either the best or worst thing that could happen.

They aren't the same—Dean tries so much harder to get a reaction, Wes tries so much harder to convince people he doesn't care about their reaction—but they're both devil may care attention whores.

Wes always made Blacklist Tattoo interesting.

Difficult.

But interesting.

And now he's here.

Fuck, that means a lot.

Even if he's flirting with Emma to piss me off.

Even if he's here to taunt me.

He's still here.

I nod a *hey* to my brother. Cross the room to him. Spot Griffin.

He's sitting on one of the benches in the lobby, his arm around a pretty redhead, his lips pressed into a *baby, I can't wait to fuck you senseless* smile.

His dark eyes flit around the room.

Catch mine.

He nods a hello.

There's so much in it.

In him being here.

That's all Griffin has to do. Show up and nod and I instantly get exactly what he's saying.

He whispers something to his date then plants a kiss on her lips.

It's not soft and sweet. It's a dirty, carnal *I'm going to fuck you six ways from Sunday* thing.

But there's still a connection between them.

He's always fucked around because he enjoys it.

He's always savored his *experiences*.

We've all been the benefactors of his generosity. Guy has a hell of a mouth. His replays are more evocative than any porn I've ever seen.

His date slips away with an *I'll miss you* smile.

He nods to the bench opposite his.

It shouldn't feel like such a big deal, him inviting me over, but it does. For a long time, I thought that was it. That none of my friends or family would ever choose to see me again.

Now, two of them are here.

This is good.

Shit with Emma is fucked.

But this is really fucking good.

I suck a breath through my teeth. Exhale slowly. There's no more anger coursing through my veins.

Only a lightness.

It's just as overwhelming.

No one told me that when I was getting sober.

No one explained that good would be as hard to handle as bad.

Griffin nods to Wes, who seamlessly extricates himself from his conversation with Dean and heads over.

We're right under the speaker.

It's blasting one of Emma's CDs.

That same one Chase loves.

It's bizarre.

But perfect too.

Griffin stands and offers me a hug.

I accept it.

Wes does that handshake hug thing.

"Thanks for coming." I don't know how to handle these interactions. Not sober. I suck a breath through my teeth. Exhale slowly. I need to stay present. To be honest. That's all I can offer.

It's one moment at a time.

I can handle one fucking moment.

Griffin nods. "You look good."

"I miss the eyeliner," Wes says.

"Sober," Griffin says.

Wes chuckles. "Fuck, dude, you aren't supposed to come out and say it."

"Are you?" Griffin's eyes flit to the half a dozen bottles lined up on the bar.

There's a lot, and some of my favorites too.

The comfortable numb is still appealing.

But I don't want to drink.

It's too obvious that will fuck shit up.

Maybe that isn't the world's best reason for staying sober.

But I'm getting there. "Three months now."

"Good." His dark eyes fill with relief. "You fucked shit up real bad, Hunter."

Wes nudges him. "You gotta say it like that?"

He nods.

Wes shakes his head. "Say *fuck, Hunter...* shit. How do you say that?" He shakes his head. "You did fuck shit up."

"Well aware," I say.

"Chase is too busy fapping over his righteous indignation to be here," Wes says.

I shoot him a look. Yeah, it hurts that my big brother wants nothing to do with me. But I get it. I'm the one who failed him, not the other way around.

"He's still pissed," Griffin says. "I am too."

"Jesus, Griff—"

"You think your unfazed bullshit is gonna help him?"

"What bullshit?"

"You're twenty-three, dude. We know you have feelings."

Wes scrunches his nose in distaste.

"Look at your brother. Tell him you love him."

Wes shakes his head *never*.

"I love you, Hunter." Griffin pats his chest. "I'm not afraid to say it."

"Why don't you two get married?" Wes mimes brushing these disgusting feelings from his shoulders.

"Love you too." Griffin blows him a kiss.

He ducks to dodge it. Stands. Wipes his brow with relief.

"Is marriage too much, too fast? Should you start with going to AA together?" Wes teases.

"If you want me there." Griffin nods.

"Ugh." Wes throws his hands in the air. "It wasn't an actual suggestion."

"It's a good idea." Griffin chuckles. "You're perceptive some-times, Wes."

Wes cringes.

I try to keep my expression casual. It's a thing, Al-anon, meet-ings where people bring friends and family. Meetings where friends and family go alone. To figure out *their* shit. Or how they can help the people they love.

The fact he's offering...

Fuck, I'm not nearly as afraid of feelings as Wes is, but this is too mushy for me.

I nod. "Thanks."

"You gotta stop." Wes shakes his head. "I'm not here for this shit."

"Why are you afraid of intimacy?" Griffin teases.

"'Cause you're not a hot chick with fantastic tits." Wes chuckles. "That would be something—"

"You'd fuck me if I was a chick?" Griffin teases.

"Fuck no. You're too earnest and shit."

"See." Griffin turns to me. "You gotta keep an eye on him. Or he's gonna be numbing himself too."

"I know," I say.

Wes feigns offense. "I'm right here."

"Fucking shit up. As usual." Griffin laughs. He reaches over and musses Wes's hair.

Wes slaps his hands away. Actually frowns as he's fixing it. "Don't fuck with the hair."

"'Cause all the babes here are checking you out?" Griffin asks.

"Fuck yeah." Wes nods to Leighton then to Iris. "I see them looking."

"They're taken," Griffin says.

"Doesn't mean they're dead. You never look when you have someone?" Wes asks.

Griffin nods *true*.

This is fun. Silly.

I hate to ruin the mood.

But I gotta ask. "How is Blacklist?"

Griffin frowns.

Wes shrugs. "Got some troubles, but we'll figure it out."

"It's not your problem, Hunter," Griffin says.

"You guys closing?" I ask.

"Could go that way." Frustration fills Griffin's dark eyes. It spreads over his face. "But, seriously, Hunter. You've got enough shit on your plate. Don't worry—"

"We could hire you," I say.

Surprise spreads over Wes's expression.

And Griffin's.

They share a look.

It's not good.

Fuck, if Wes is readable, it must be bad.

"Hunt…" Griffin's eyes turn down. "I wish I could."

"Yeah." I know where he's going with this, but I let him finish anyway.

"Inked Hearts is a fucking institution. But I promised Chase I'd stick with him. And—"

"He just has to stop fucking himself over this." Wes rolls his eyes. "Fucking guy has his head so far up his ass."

"He made his feelings clear," I say.

"Asshole needs to get over himself." Wes shakes his head. "I didn't make any fucking promise. If you're offering me a gig, I'm here. That Emma chick was hot. All the other women who work here the same?"

Is he fucking with me?

I can't tell.

But then it's Wes.

Of course he's fucking with me.

"Yeah. Dean's girl is too," I say. "At least, I think she's Dean's girl. I'm not in the loop."

"Dean has a girl?" Wes shakes his head. "Fuck. Times change."

"Yeah." Griffin chuckles, but that frustration is still there, in his eyes. "They really fucking do."

HUNTER

Griffin and Wes insist on walking me home.

We say goodbye with a handshake and a high-five, then I slip into the house.

It feels more like home than it did a week ago.

Even with Emma sitting on the couch, glaring like I'm the scum of the Earth.

It's obvious right now.

There's no stomaching the distance between us.

She *is* my closest friend.

She's exactly what I need.

I have to fix this.

But only if it's what's best for her.

"You okay?" It's a stupid question, but it's all I've got.

She says nothing.

All right, I need to aim a little lower. "You eat dinner?"

"Yeah. Leftovers." Her eyes flit to me for a split second, then they're back on the screen. "If you don't mind." She motions to the TV.

It's playing *Hercules.*

Her favorite movie.

Easy to see why. The tough yet vulnerable heroine is pure Emma. Style and sass and a heart she doesn't want to admit to having.

I nod. "Good night."

Her voice softens. "Good night." She watches me move up the stairs and into the hallway.

Even as I slip into the bathroom and turn the shower on, I can feel her attention.

There's a lot of frustration there, yeah.

But it's not because she hates me.

It's because she wants me.

And, fuck, do I want her.

I'm not acting on it.

Or running from it.

I have to face it.

Whatever that means.

At the moment…

I close my eyes. Wrap my hands around my cock. Let my thoughts flit to Emma.

Her perfect tits.

Her soft thighs.

Her low groan.

I come harder than I have in a long fucking time.

AFTER MY SHOWER, I LOCK MYSELF IN MY ROOM AND SPILL MY thoughts onto the paper until my hands are numb.

Sketching helps.

But not enough.

It's too late for clarity.

I rise, piss, wash my hands, brush my teeth, turn off the light in the hall.

The room glows from the light of the TV downstairs.

Emma is on the couch. Silent. Still.

She's asleep.

Peaceful.

I'm tempted to leave her there—I've done enough to disturb her today—but I need to bring her this little bit of comfort.

I move downstairs quietly. Wrap my arms around her. Lift her to my chest.

She stirs as I ascend the stairs.

Her eyelids flutter open.

Her dark eyes fix on mine.

For a split second, she stares at me like I'm everything she wants.

Then she blinks and her eyes are closed again.

She rests her head against my chest.

Digs her fingers into my back.

She's quiet as I carry her into her bedroom and lay her on the bed.

It's the first time I've *really* seen her bedroom.

It's different than the room at her apartment.

That was sparse. Empty. Soulless.

This room is brimming with life.

Posters of musicians line the walls. The desk in the corner is covered with lyrics and doodles. The closet is packed with clothes in every shade of the rainbow.

Same crimson comforter and plain white sheets.

I lay her on the wide bed.

She rolls onto her side. Reaches for a pillow.

Her guard is down.

She's inviting me into her heart. Her life. Her space.

My throat tightens. My heart thuds against my chest.

I want that.

I want to be in her life.

To deserve a place in her life.

But there has to be a line somewhere.

I need to draw it in extra thick sharpie. Black against stark white. Something obvious. That we'll both see.

I need her closer.

But I can't be hers.

I don't know how the fuck to reconcile the two.

Only that I'm lacking the self-control to keep my hands off her.

I stand. Wipe my palms on my jeans. Flick the light switch.

The silver glow of the moon flows through the window.

The intimacy of this is terrifying.

And exhilarating.

Fuck, I want to be here. I want to lie next to her, wrap my arms around her, hold her all night.

That's over the line.

But there must be something I can do.

Some way I can comfort her.

"Good night, Em." I reach for the door.

"Wait." She slides to the right. Pats the spot next to her. "There's room." She brushes her long hair behind her ear. "Kaylee sleeps here all the time."

I try to find that line.

To figure out what's best for her.

It's no good.

Clarity is a million miles away.

Emma saves me from figuring out my shit. "I'm sorry I stormed off. I just… I don't know. I guess I don't really have a leg to stand on. I was trying to make you jealous."

"You were?"

She nods.

"Why?"

"You know why."

Yeah, but I want to hear those words again.

I want them on her lips.

It fills me someplace that's been empty for too fucking long.

"It felt good, getting a reaction. I know I'm not supposed to say that. But it did." She sinks her fingers into her crimson comforter. "Sometimes... it seems like you don't care. I hate you for that."

"I do care."

"No, Hunter, you don't get it. I never trust someone like this. It means a lot."

"I know."

She shakes her head. "You don't know. You don't know me."

"I want to."

"No." Her fingers dig into the crimson comforter. "You don't get to say that. You don't get to say shit like *I want to know you* then turn around and say this can't happen."

There's the line.

I need to be all in or all out.

Her everything or her nothing.

Fuck, that isn't good for me.

But it's fair.

If that's what she wants, it's what she wants.

Her eyes turn down. "I hate that you won't choose me."

Right now, she looks tiny and vulnerable.

She's not.

She's thin, yeah, but she's nearly as tall as I am.

She's at least as tough as I am.

Tougher.

She's strong enough to let her guard down.

Whereas I...

Fuck.

There's only one thing I can say to help her understand this.

I force the words from my lips. "I'm an alcoholic."

"What?" Her dark eyes fill with surprise.

"I got out of rehab a few weeks ago. That's why I'm here."

"But you… you were always sneaking bottles over."

I nod.

"You always smelled like bourbon."

"Yeah."

"And all the liquor in the house is missing."

"Yeah."

"I thought… that you just liked to party."

"So did I."

"Oh." She sits up and presses her back against the wall. "So you… um… what do I say here?"

"Whatever you're thinking."

She stares at me for a long moment. "Brendon knows?"

"Yeah."

"Anyone else?"

"Everyone at Blacklist. Some old friends."

"But no one… fuck, there was so much booze at your party." Her face goes white. "Did you…" Fear fills with eyes.

Did you have a drink?

Did you fuck everything up?

Are you lost forever?

"No." I keep my voice steady. I'm not good at much, emotionally speaking, but I'm pretty good at not drinking at this point. "I'm still sober."

"Oh. Good. I…" She looks to me. "Why didn't you tell me?"

"You looked at me like I was worthwhile."

"You are."

"Maybe." I press my palms into my quads. Fuck, I want to touch her. I'm dying to touch her.

And not just sexually.

Yeah, I want to make her come.

But I also want to hold her all night.

I want to be her everything.

To live in a universe where that's a possibility.

I don't.

It's not.

I need to get over it.

I try to shake it off. Fail. "Everyone who knows stares like I'm a fuckup or a train wreck."

"Oh." Understanding fills her eyes.

"My brother put the pieces together six months ago." I press my palm into her soft white sheets.

"Chase?"

"He planned this huge intervention. Got everyone there. Even the shop owner. And my fucking parents. Which is rich."

"They're—"

"Not sure I've ever seen my mom sober."

"I'm sorry."

I shake my head. I want her sympathy. But I want to deserve it. I'm the one who fucked-up this. I made bad decisions. Chose alcohol over everything else. I need to own that. "He gave me an ultimatum. I could keep drinking or I could keep working at the shop."

"That's fucked-up."

Maybe. But not to Chase. "He was trying to help."

"Yeah, but everyone knows you don't take an addict's word." Her dark eyes fill with sympathy. "No offense."

A laugh falls from my lips. It's funny, her swerving around my feelings. My whole fucking life is swerving around feelings. Either, I'm walking on eggshells or I'm the eggshells someone's avoiding. "No. It was stupid. Naïve even. He's usually not like that."

"I know the type." She pushes herself up. Onto her back. Hugs her knees and pulls them toward her chest.

She's wearing these tiny black shorts.

They show off every inch of those long legs.

I want those legs wrapped around me.

Pressed against my cheeks.

Fighting my hands.

I want to make her come.

It's impossible to push the thought aside.

"You are the type," she says.

"Now. Then... I was... you met my brother."

"Wes?"

I nod. "You like him?"

She half-smiles. "Yeah. He showed up."

He did. And it means the world. "I was like him. Obsessed with being the life of the party."

"I remember."

It's easy to forget I've known her for ten years. That she knows exactly who I used to be. Well, the more presentable version of that guy. "I managed work okay. I was buzzed constantly, but I did my best work like that. I was looser. Freer. Less worried about fucking up someone's skin."

She turns her body toward mine.

"Since I was your age, I did whatever it took to stay buzzed. Or wasted. I was running from something. From everything, I guess. There was always this hole in my gut. I don't know if it was my parents' apathy or my inability to connect with my friends or something else entirely. I didn't feel it long enough to understand it."

"Now?"

"I'm still running from it."

"Is it working?"

"No."

Her laugh is soft. Giving. "Maybe you should try casual sex again."

"Em..."

"I don't mean me. I don't... I don't know..." Her smile is more sad than anything. "What happened with your brother?"

"I promised I'd get sober. Didn't. When he figured it out, he kicked me out."

"Oh."

"We lived together back then. He changed the locks. Sent all my stuff to our parents. I convinced them he was overreacting. Used the money I had to get my own place. Drank the rest."

She nods.

"When I ran out of cash, I tried to beg my parents for rent money, but they weren't hearing it. Not unless I went to rehab."

"And you did?"

"Yeah. I thought I'd make it through the thirty days—I thought it was thirty days." I can't help but chuckle. "I thought I'd dry out then go right back to my life."

"But?"

"It's awful, being out of it, needing a drink like you need oxygen. Just better than the alternative."

"You were self-medicating?"

"Yeah." I press my lips together. "I got put on meds. For depression. It's a common thing. I thought it was bullshit, but it helped."

"You're…"

"I don't know. Could be that all the alcohol fucked-up my brain. Could be that I was always drinking my way out of that. I… I'm still not good with feelings."

"I can tell."

My laugh breaks up the tension in my chest.

"So, um… the meds. Is that why you didn't fuck Carpe Diem?"

I arch a brow.

"They can have that side effect."

I chuckle. "No. The first prescription they gave me did—"

"You couldn't get it up?"

I can't help but laugh. "You don't sugar coat shit."

"Why should I?"

"I could. But it took more effort. And I didn't have the drive."

"Now?"

"This one is better."

"So you do want to?"

Fuck, how I want to. "Yeah."

"Oh. Good." Her cheeks flush. "I mean... I... you know I want to fuck you."

"I know." I bite my tongue so I won't add something about how I want to fuck her. This is it. My chance to draw the line. I try to figure out how to articulate it. To explain that I want to be her friend more than anything. That I can only be her friend.

She interrupts me. "Wes still came to your party."

"Yeah. And Griffin."

Her eyes brighten. "Really?"

I nod.

"They forgive you."

"Going that way."

"You..." She looks up at me. "I'm glad you're telling me this. Really, Hunter. I can see it's a big deal. And I know what it's like shouldering a secret."

I nod.

"But if this is supposed to be the reason why we can't—"

"I can't."

"But..."

"I'm sorry, Em. There are so many fucking reasons why I can't."

"Oh."

"I hate hurting you. I do." All right, this is it. I can explain where I stand. "I want to be your friend. I want that more than anything. But it's all I can offer."

"Oh."

"If that isn't enough, fine." I swallow hard. "Tell me to fuck off. I will. But I'd rather stick around."

"Okay. I... Uh... I'll think about it." She pulls her comforter to her chest. "I... uh... I should probably get to bed."

"Yeah."

She scoots closer.

Close enough to kiss me.
Her lips brush my cheek.
A goodbye kiss between friends.
It should satisfy.
Clarify where we stand.
But it doesn't.
It screams of possibilities.
Of everything we could have.
Of how badly I want to kiss her.

EMMA

Ugh.

It's too early.

Only bright light is streaming through my window. Afternoon light.

I roll over. Grab my cell from the bedside table. Check the time.

Super ugh.

Why do I work Saturdays?

I mean, I work pretty much every day. But still. Saturdays are the worst. I can feel how much everyone else is off, enjoying their weekend.

I rise, go through my morning routine, move downstairs, toward the smell of coffee.

Hunter is leaning against the counter, fingers curled around a mug, muscle tank dripping with sweat.

All of him is dripping with sweat.

Fuck, he looks good. Like he's in the middle of a particularly athletic fuck.

My eyes close. For a quick second, I see it. Him stripping out of his gym shorts. Throwing me on the bed. Tearing off my panties. Prying my legs apart.

Promising to split me in half.

It's messy and dirty and hot as hell.

Then his arms are on my wrists and I just…

Half of me is there. In it. Craving Hunter's touch.

The other half…

"Em?" His voice is soft. Curious, not concerned.

I guess it doesn't matter if I'm ready for sex.

Hunter made his feelings clear last night.

He trusts me.

He wants me.

He cares about me.

But we're never going to be more than friends.

"Em?" he asks again, a little louder.

It brings my attention to the room.

The hair sticking to his forehead.

The flush reddening his cheeks.

The ink trailing over his shoulder.

"Where's my coffee?" I try to keep my voice light. Teasing.

Last night was too much.

It means the world to me, him sharing his past.

There's no question.

I'm going to be his friend.

I hate that I only get his friendship.

But it's a hell of a lot better than losing whatever it is that's between us.

"Here." He offers me his mug.

I shake my head. "You make it too sweet."

He chuckles. "Do I?"

"Yeah. Way too sweet."

"The one teaspoon of honey?"

"Disgusting."

"Snob."

"It's your fault, you know."

He moves into the kitchen. Sets his mug on the counter and starts fixing another cup of pour over.

"I can no longer stand the taste of the K-cups."

"They're shit."

"See. You caused this snobbery," I say.

"Yeah, you never bought five-dollar Americanos before I started crashing here."

"Never."

His eyes flit to me. His lips curl into a smile.

It makes my knees weak.

He's so pretty.

And handsome.

How can one man be both?

Those blue eyes are beautiful.

That chiseled jaw is positively Disney prince.

He's just so fucking hot.

"I occasionally order vanilla lattes," I say.

He shoots me a look of feigned horror. "No."

"Only when I have a sugar craving."

His chuckle fills the room.

"What?"

"Your life is a sugar craving."

"Just because a girl likes to eat chocolate chip pancakes for dinner on occasion—"

"On occasion?"

"During parties."

"Watching Disney movies?"

"If you don't want to eat my chocolate chip pancakes…"

His smile spreads over his cheeks. Lights up his eyes. "Anything but that."

The electric kettle steams. He grabs it. Carefully finishes the pour over. Sets a timer for exactly four minutes.

"You just get home from the gym?" *How about we hop in the shower together? Get clean before we get dirty?*

He nods.

"Without me?"

"Didn't realize you were in for leg day."

Mmm. Leg day. That's when he does all the shit that gives me a view of his ass. "I am."

"Yeah?"

"I'm gonna… what's it called. That thing." I hinge at my hips to demonstrate the movement.

"Deadlift?"

"Yeah."

His gaze goes straight to my chest.

My boobs are about to pop out of my tank top.

There's victory in getting his attention.

But it's more bitter than sweet.

I can't have that.

Why remind myself?

I clear my throat. "Yeah. I'm gonna deadlift two hundred pounds."

"Now?"

"Don't be ridiculous." I could barely lift the bar last time. "I have to work up to that."

"Uh-huh."

"Yeah." I move into the kitchen. Get close to him. Close enough my hand brushes his. "I can't let you have fun without me."

He turns to me. Stares into my eyes.

He's such a perfect height.

Just a little bit taller than I am.

My head fits into the crook of his neck.

His hands are at my hips.

This is so…

"You think about what I said?" He presses his ass into the counter. Moves away from me.

"Yeah." I force myself to take a step backward. I was dead tired last night, but it still took forever to find sleep. I kept thinking about the hurt in his eyes and the regret in his voice.

He was practically begging me to be his friend.

I want to give him that.

But then…

I still want to slap him for rejecting me. For rejecting us.

I can't blame him. Not really.

But that doesn't make it easier.

"It's a good idea." I play with the hem of my tank top. There's nowhere to put my hands. Every place screams *I want you to touch me.*

The timer beeps. He pours the coffee into my oversized white mug. Slides it across the counter.

I find the half and half in the fridge. Fix my java.

Mmm. Perfect. "Thanks."

He nods *sure thing.*

"So… um… Believe it or not, I don't really have guy friends," I say. "Besides the guys at the shop."

"I'm not a guy at the shop?"

"You didn't sign the paperwork yet."

"Still."

"What um… what do we do?"

"You think I know?" Vulnerability streaks his eyes.

This matters to him.

A lot.

He's fresh out of rehab.

His friends are still partying or unwilling to talk to him.

He doesn't have anyone.

"With my friends—" all right, I spend ninety-five percent of my time with Kaylee, but still—"we mostly eat chocolate and talk about hot guys."

"Chocolate, huh?"

"Dark chocolate. Eight-five percent or bust."

"And the pancakes?"

"There's no sugar in pancakes."

He chuckles.

"What?"

"Didn't say anything."

"Is it too many carbs?"

His laugh bounces around the room. "I prefer eating food for dinner."

"Aren't you fancy?"

"Yeah." He picks up his mug. Takes a long sip of his coffee. Let's out a moan of pure satisfaction.

It's so…

Mmm.

My cheeks flush.

My sex clenches.

It's the first time I've heard a guy moan without going *there*.

It's the first time I've wanted it.

Fuck, I want it so badly.

"I like chocolate," he says.

"And hot guys?"

"Can you do better than Matt Murdoch?"

"Hot guys does not mean comic book stuff."

"Is he hot or not?"

"Not the point."

"But is he?"

"Well, I mean…"

"You love his brooding ass."

I say nothing.

"Admit it."

I feign indifference.

"You complain about the lack of nudity every episode."

"That's just being sensible."

"Admit it, Em."

"I admit nothing."

"He's a certified hottie."

"He is..."

Hunter's eyes find mine. He raises a brow.

I fight my blush. "He is... attractive."

"We're making progress here."

"It doesn't mean comic books."

"It's Disney."

Technically true.

"If you'd rather not watch three more episodes tonight..."

"I'll think about it."

His smile is smug. It's *I know you'll be there.*

He's right.

I hate that he's right.

But he really, really is.

AFTER HE SHOWERS AND I DRESS, WE WALK TO WORK TOGETHER.

It's a busy day—Saturdays always are—but I'm still flush with free time. I alternate between watching him work and studying.

I'm about to crash from lack of coffee when Dean slides up to the counter.

His eyes flit between me and Hunter. "He make that shit up to you yet?"

I play dumb. "What shit?"

"Whatever got you storming out of the office." Dean leans in to whisper. "Don't tell me he came early and failed to finish the job."

"If that happened, do you really think I'd tell you?"

His smile is wide. Knowing. "I could help you out."

"By cheating on your girlfriend?"

"Em, you think so little of me."

261

No, actually. Dean would do a lot of shit, but he'd never do that. He's smitten. Still, I make a point of rolling my eyes.

"Just gonna give you some tips."

"Just the tip? Hmm, when have I heard that before?"

"Guys are still using that line?"

"No. But you trod it out every other week."

"This about the amateur porn?" His expression gets dead serious. "Or the Prince Albert?"

A laugh spills from my lips. Then another.

I press my arm against my stomach to hold back my giggle fit, but it doesn't happen. Dean is just…

He's so fucking ridiculous.

"If I have to hear another word about your cock, I'm gonna riot," Walker calls from his suite.

Chloe looks to Dean—she's sitting in his suite, on his teal chair, perfecting a sketch.

Her smile is smaller, but it's as wicked as his.

It's incredibly *yes, let's talk about your cock somewhere more private. And by talk, I mean fuck hard and fast.*

My stomach pangs with jealousy.

I don't want Dean.

But I do want that.

It's hard having a couple working here. They're just so… adorable and dirty in equal measures.

Despite her short black hair, heavy eyeliner (which looks so amazing with her almond eyes. She's half-Korean, half-Italian, all badass), tattoos, and combat boots, she projects innocence.

But Dean is dirty as all hell.

I'm sure he's corrupted her.

Fucked her every way a person can be fucked.

Hunter is just as dirty.

But he's unwilling to share it with me.

He's adamant about this whole *we're only friends* thing.

"Shit, Em, what were we talking about?" he asks.

"How quickly guys come." I make my voice loud. So everyone can hear. Okay, so Hunter can hear.

It works.

Hunter looks up from his client—a burly guy getting something on his calf—and raises a brow.

His client whispers something.

Hunter whispers back. Laughs. "Even Jed knows you're a two pump, chump, Dean."

Dean jumps—actually jumps—onto the counter.

I push my books aside. "Step on my textbook and you die."

"You gonna sic your boy on me?" Dean asks.

"Maybe." I look to Hunter. "Would you kill Dean if I asked?"

"Think I'd have to get in line." His lips curl into a half-smile. "But yeah."

My chest warms. Dean called Hunter my boy. Hunter didn't correct him.

It doesn't mean anything, but it feels good all the same.

"We're gonna have to wrestle for that one," Walker says.

Chloe jumps in. "He's dying by my hand or not at all."

Dean blows her a kiss. "Sunshine, I can't think of a better way to die."

She blushes.

"And fuck knows none of you can take Chloe," Dean says.

Walker nods.

Hunter too.

She is a total badass. She reconnected with Ryan at their Aikido dojo. There are a lot of rumors about whether or not she kicked Ryan's ass (Ryan plays along, says she did, but she admits she's never come close. Either way, she's masterful. I've seen her throw Dean over her shoulder. Multiple times. He's way into it. Or maybe just into her touching him).

Dean leans in to whisper. "Is he treating you well?"

"We're just friends," I say.

Dean nods *uh-huh.* "That hurts, Em, that you think I'd narc to Brendon."

"Or maybe that you can't keep your voice down?"

"Maybe." He laughs. "But mostly the thing I said."

"Really." I press my lips together. "I'm not as enlightened as you. Can't work with someone I'm fucking."

He gives me that same *uh-huh* nod. "It's 'cause he's not packing enough heat, isn't it?"

"Why are you so obsessed with dicks?"

"Like you aren't thinking about it right now."

Uh… No comment.

He smirks. "That's what I thought."

"You think he'll be happy here?"

"I think he'll be happy in your bed."

"Seriously."

"I'm dead serious."

He is.

And he's right.

I want to honor Hunter's promise.

I want to respect his wishes.

But sometimes being a friend means showing someone they're wrong.

Hunter and I both need more.

We need to be together.

I just have to make him see that.

EMMA

After work, Hunter takes me through another business lesson. This time it's projections. We look at years of historical data. Models based on a few months or a year. Compare our estimates to reality.

There are formulas, sure, but there's an art to it too.

By the time we get home, my brain is fried.

I zone out while we cook.

Hunter helps. He even sets the table.

We savor eggplant Parmesan together.

We barely even joke about the phallic implications of the vegetable.

Then we retire to the couch.

Watch more *Daredevil*, drink too much coffee, eat too much chocolate.

I try to keep my distance, but with every episode, I move a little closer.

I rest my head on his chest.

Soak up the smell of his soap.

The warmth of his skin.

The *thump-thump* of his strong, steady heartbeat.

ANOTHER MORNING, ANOTHER LIVING ROOM FILLED WITH THE scent of coffee.

And the even more delicious sight of Hunter in my raspberry towel.

He's no longer dripping, but he's wet.

Light bounces off his slick skin. Calls attention to the deep lines of his muscles.

How can one man be this endlessly yummy?

It's wrong.

I barely manage to walk across the room. I'm knock-kneed and nervous. It's not like me, but that's the Hunter Keating effect.

He nods to a mug of coffee sitting on the counter. "Sumatra."

Mmm, that's a good one. I brush against him as I wrap my hands around the mug.

He's right there and he's wet and warm. His skin is soft, but his muscles are so hard.

He's just so...

Mmm.

I swallow a sip of coffee. Let my moan fill the room.

Fuck, this is good. But it's nothing compared to him.

"You're wet." I bite my tongue. I need something more subtle. More articulate.

"Just got home from the gym."

"You're supposed to invite me."

He raises a brow *really*.

"Yeah. I'm gonna get swoll. Like you." I flex my barely there bicep.

He chuckles. "Doesn't seem like your hobby."

If it wasn't for the whole teasing Hunter thing (okay, and the staring at his bod thing), I wouldn't get anywhere near a weight.

It's bad enough when Kaylee decides she wants to take up jogging and "invites" me to go with her.

"I thought about inviting you," he says.

"But you realized I'd embarrass you in front of your gym bros?"

He laughs. "You would. But that wasn't it."

"It's my epic skills, isn't it?"

He shrugs *true*. "You looked peaceful. I didn't want to wake you."

"You watched me sleep?"

"Checked if you were up."

Still. He watched me sleep.

It's sweet.

It's pure *I want you as more than a friend*.

But I can't remind him of that.

I have to keep him relaxed. So he doesn't go on the defensive.

"Creepy," I tease.

He nods *that's me*. Takes a long sip of his coffee. Sighs with pleasure.

Mmm, that sound.

It's music.

Better than everything on my emo playlist.

And that's a hell of a playlist.

"Your brother texted." He pushes off the counter. Does nothing to secure the towel clinging to his hips.

I watch the berry fabric with rapt attention.

I need that towel gone.

I need him naked.

I need the intimacy. The honesty.

Like the night he told me everything.

I've never felt like that before.

I've never wanted it this badly.

God, I need to touch him.

I need to connect with him.

I need to get ahold of myself.

Ahem. "Brendon offer some bondage tips?"

"How'd you know?"

Fuck, I didn't think this over. I can't joke about my brother's sex life. It's just… ick. "You offer anything in exchange?"

"Not sure my masturbation stories are worthy."

I hide my blush behind my cup of coffee. He's teasing, but it's there in his eyes—he wants me hot and bothered over the thought of his hand around his cock.

Fuck, what a thought. "How could those possibly fail?"

"Figured Dean can pull it off."

My laugh does nothing to ease the ache in my sex. "Is that what you call it?"

He chuckles. "Nobody calls it that."

"There are a lot of euphemisms."

"You're not the euphemism type."

"Still."

He moves into the kitchen. "You want eggs?"

"You're cooking them?"

He nods.

I exaggerate my concern. "Is that really a good idea?"

"You've taught me so well."

"Even so…"

"Trust me."

God, those words do things to me. I nod an okay. I do trust him. I doubt his ability to cook anything, but I trust him. "And bacon?"

"Is there another way?"

"I'm more… you're gonna laugh."

"Probably."

"More into chocolate oatmeal for breakfast."

He does laugh. "Of course."

"It's perfect. The fruit is sweet. The cocoa powder is bitter. It's chocolate nirvana."

"That's a lot to live up to."

"Should probably just give up."

He nods.

"So… was there anything notable about your self-love?"

"Self-love." He half-smiles. "That's a sweet way of putting it."

I nod.

"More like self-abuse sometimes."

"Go on."

He shakes his head. "Pretty sure friends don't discuss this."

"Pretty sure they do. At least our mutual friends."

He laughs *true enough*. "Hate to break it to you, Em, but I'm a gentleman. Not gonna discuss how often or hard I come."

My blush spreads to my chest. "Then you won't hear about my—"

"For the best."

Okay. I need to pull back. He has to come to this conclusion himself. "What else did Brendon say?"

"Something about how much he loves tying up his girlfriend."

Ugh. I stick my tongue out.

Hunter's laugh gets lower. Heartier. "Fuck, your face."

Yes, please, do. "He didn't."

"No. He didn't. But for someone so—"

"Watch it."

"Open." He laughs over his euphemism. "You really hate hearing about your brother's sex life."

"And I suppose you're just begging for details?"

"Never have to beg." He grabs a pan, sets it on the stove, turns the burner on. "Wes is always offering."

"Of course he is."

"Chase is more quiet. Now Griffin—he's got a gift."

"Oh yeah?" I motion *go on*. I want to hear one of Griffin's dirty stories. I want those words on Hunter's lips. If he connects us with sex—that has to help.

And, well, I always like dirt.

Hunter shakes his head. "I wouldn't do him justice."

"Paraphrase."

He studies my expression. Decides this is a good enough idea. "He was flirting with this sweet blond chick in a long dress. She was modest. Innocent. Kept talking about church and volunteering. Then he gets to her bedroom and it's a fucking dungeon."

"Really?"

"Yeah. She changes into this black corset and boots that go up to her cunt and she orders him onto his back and sits on his face."

"Was he into it?"

"Way into it."

"So he…" I clear my throat. "He's submissive?"

"No." Hunter chuckles. "He's open-minded."

"Slutty?"

Hunter nods *yeah*. "He's not like me."

"Not wounded and broody?"

He shoots me a teasing *watch it*. "He likes sex for the connection."

"No fear of intimacy."

"Yeah." He pulls the eggs from the fridge. Cracks them in a bowl. Whisks them. "But no real desire to commit either."

"One-night stands left and right?"

"More flings."

"Get in, get out, avoid getting hurt?"

"Something like that."

"I get that." I wrap my fingers around my cup. Bring it to my lips. Sip. Sigh.

His eyes flit toward me. They light up with desire, but his posture stays cool calm.

God, that towel is so right around his hips.

He's just…

I just…

MMMMM.

"I guess that's how I've always operated." I press my palms into the mug. Soak up its warmth. "It's never been a conscious thing. I've just never found a guy who interested me enough."

"You're a lot to handle."

"Hey."

"It's a compliment."

"Is it?"

"Yeah." He pours olive oil on the pan. Grabs the handle and tilts the pan so oil slides over the surface. "You're a strong woman. You know what you want. You don't take shit. Guys your age are dumb boys. They aren't gonna be able to handle you."

"Maybe."

"Probably can't even handle their own laundry."

That's true. But it's not encouraging. It only digs that *we can't happen* knife into my chest.

Maybe I've got it wrong.

Maybe this is his subconscious taking over.

He wants me to know how desirable I am.

He wants me.

He just—he has to connect the dots.

"Guys can be idiots."

He pours the eggs over the pan. "That guy who was at your old place. Was he like that?"

What?

How the—

Fuck.

His voice is even.

There's no sign he knows.

But then…

Why else would he mention it?

"Vinnie?" I ask.

He nods.

"No. He was older. Wiser. Worldly."

"Did you like that?"

"Yeah." My chest tightens. "He made me feel smart. Special. But I… he wasn't really the best guy."

"What happened?"

"He just didn't…" I can't tell him. I want to. But I can't. I can't say it out loud. And I definitely can't have him looking at me like a victim. "You know when you really like someone, you see their flaws through rose-tinted glasses."

He nods.

"Eventually, they broke. I realized he was condescending and pretentious. That he didn't respect me. That he saw me as a silly plaything."

As someone who wouldn't fight back.

I guess he was right.

That happened and I did nothing.

I let him get away with it.

I haven't even told anyone.

Something changes in Hunter's expression.

Like he knows.

But how the hell could he know?

"What, um…" My fingers curl around the handle of my mug. "What did Brendon actually say?"

"Asked if you were looking at apartments."

"He wants me out that badly?"

Hunter turns the eggs over. "I think he does."

My laugh breaks up the tension in my chest. This can be okay. Vinnie can stay a distant memory. At the very least, I can have one fucking day without his presence ruining the mood. "You're not supposed to say that."

"I get it. I would too."

"Hey."

He motions to my backpack, currently sitting on the couch. "You leave your shit everywhere."

"You walk around the house in nothing."

"You never do the dishes."

"I cook, you clean."

"You demand coffee."

"I say thank you."

He shakes his head *you do not*.

"Well, thank you."

"Your sweet talk won't save you."

"It's 'cause he wants to bang his girlfriend."

"Won't she live with you?"

"Yeah, but she'll come here to that giant bed and its—" My nose scrunches. "Under the bed restraints."

"And you're into it?"

"God no."

"Maybe the way Griffin's fling was?"

"Maybe you sound like Dean right now."

He laughs. "I was thinking Wes, but yeah, I do."

"Am I that awful of a roommate?"

"No. But then my last roommate was a manic depressive who spent most of his time talking about cocaine."

"He set the bar high."

"Exactly." He scoops the eggs from the pan and places them on two plates. "I pulled a few listings."

"Oh."

"We can go before work. You're on at two, right?"

"Yeah." Same as him.

He brings the eggs to the table. Takes the seat opposite mine.

"Thanks. For breakfast."

"You can sweet talk me all you want, Em. It won't help your case."

He's right.

I need something stronger.

I need to convince him we belong together.

EMMA

Tragically, Hunter changes into jeans and a plain white t-shirt. I suits him more than it should.

I stare more than I should.

Even as we get into the car, argue over the music, discuss the list of places to visit, I stare.

He's so pretty.

Touchable.

Fuckable.

I have to keep my wits about me.

To guide him to this realization with a light touch.

I have an idea about how to do that.

It's not my finest work.

But it's something.

I shoot Kaylee a text about our apartment hunt.

She texts back a request for pictures. And a gushing *I miss you*.

I miss her too.

It's hard, being away from my best friend.

But then—

I'm not ready to say goodbye to my little universe with Hunter.

As soon as Kaylee and Brendon get back, this is over.

We're no longer roomies.

It's easy for him to stick with *just friends* when we're living at separate places.

When he's reporting to my brother at work every day.

Fuck, I'm short on time here.

Still.

I have to be patient.

To do this right.

I straighten my thoughts as we park in Santa Monica.

It's a beautiful day—warm, sunny, bright—and this neighborhood is suburban paradise. Rows and rows of cozy houses with green lawns or succulent gardens. Teslas everywhere.

Hunter leads me into an old apartment building. It fits into the beachy aesthetic. Cozy and worn and charming.

He even opens the door for me.

I shudder as I step inside.

It's hot.

Way too fucking hot.

Seriously, it's a breezy seventy outside, but the hallway is a sauna.

I tug at my tank. Try to let some air cool me off.

Then Hunter steps into the tiny space and pushes the door closed and I give up on cooling off.

He's so close.

So tall and hard and safe.

We're so alone.

This isn't my brother's house. It isn't a place marked with reminders of why we shouldn't.

It's fresh.

Clean.

New.

Tiny.

Seriously, what the hell?

This place is half the size of the pictures.

"What a gorgeous view." I motion to the window looking out on the apartment building next door. "My favorite shade of cream."

"I was thinking the parking lot." He motions to the right side of the window. The spaces in front of that apartment building.

"Does this place have parking?"

"One spot."

That's workable. Kaylee bikes everywhere. And we can get a permit to park on the street.

But it will make entertaining a pain in the ass.

Not that it was easier at our old place.

Or Brendon's place.

Thank God for ride shares, I guess.

"You love it?" he asks.

I shouldn't—it's small and cramped and too fucking hot—but his proximity is enough to convince me. "It's a start."

"Yeah?" His fingers brush my hip as he moves past me. He goes to the window. Looks out at the view. Shakes his head. "You can do better."

"What about you?"

He arches a brow.

"Are you going to live with Brendon forever?"

"Yeah, we're going to start our own buddy show—"

"Brooding and Brooding-er."

He chuckles. "Exactly."

"Which is which?"

"You tell me."

"Hmm." I make *L*s with my hands. Hold them up to frame Hunter. "As hard as you try, he's still Brooding-er."

"Fuck, Em." He mimes being stabbed in the gut. "You're as brutal as always."

"Okay, how about The Dom and The Celibate?"

"Oh? You want to talk about his sex life?"

No. I want him to say he's not fucking anyone.

Or to admit he wants to fuck me.

At least to himself.

"Was thinking it would be more about your challenge avoiding temptation," I say. "We could always have some pretty girl stumbling over herself. Somehow falling out of her dress. That's good for ratings."

"Probably is."

"Do you watch any comedies?"

He chuckles. "Fuck off."

"So brooding."

"Do you?"

"What?"

"Watch comedies?"

Uh… "Sometimes."

"Like what?"

"Like *Seinfeld*. *Friends*. All that stuff from the 90s. It was the golden age."

"*Seinfeld*?"

I nod.

"Isn't it all about them being unable to communicate directly?"

"Yeah."

"Don't need extra lessons."

"You're good with me."

"Maybe." He turns back to me. Stares into my eyes. "Should we get out of here?"

"After we check out the bedrooms."

He nods and moves to the other end of the room. To the hallway.

But it doesn't go to bedrooms.

Only to a single bathroom.

Hunter chuckles. "Fuck, who put these listings together?"

"An idiot," I tease.

"He's probably used to getting by on his looks."

"Aren't they always?"

I move around the room, trying to imagine our stuff filling the space.

It's not quite as small as my bedroom, but it would still be a struggle.

There's no way we'd have any privacy.

I motion to one corner. "I could sleep there." Then to the other. "Kay could sleep there. I could watch her fuck my brother when he stays the night."

"Does he?"

"Usually, they go to his place. Our place, I guess."

"To spare you?"

"It's a bigger place."

"With the under-the-bed restraints."

My nose scrunches in distaste.

He chuckles. "You ever try those?"

"No. Have you?"

"A few times."

"Which way?"

"Both."

"Oh." That's not what I expected. For all his talk about how empty his fucks were and how little he gave, I wouldn't expect him to allow someone to tie him up.

Not that I want to.

I mean, I don't not want to.

Fuck, it's hot in here.

"What else?" I ask.

"What else?"

"Did you try?"

"Everything."

"Why?" I move closer. Until I can feel the heat of his body. God, I'm on fire.

He turns toward me.

His eyes fix on mine.

There's no wall between us.

Between *Emma* and *Sex*.

He's discussing this.

Opening up to me.

It's perfect.

"Sometimes, because I was drunk. Or because I didn't care what we did as long as I got off." He runs his hand through his hair. "But mostly 'cause, deep down, I wanted to feel it more."

"More intensely?"

"Not physically."

"You wanted a connection."

He nods. "At the time, I thought it was nothing. A distraction."

"That's what you told me."

"Yeah. It was. But I think there was a part of me that always wanted more."

"It must have been lonely."

"Yeah. Nobody knew the real me. Not even me."

"Now?"

"Now..." He chuckles. "Hate to break it to you, Em, but you're my best friend."

My lips curl into a smile. "That sucks for you."

"It's not so bad."

It's a quick drive to the second apartment.

It's a beautiful place. Big. Clean. Miraculously air-conditioned.

But even with all eight hundred square feet, there isn't enough space for the desire racing through my veins.

I want him.

I want him too much to stay friends.

If I can't make him see the light—

God, I don't want to think about that possibility.

I really, really don't.

I move through the wide, open main room into a short hallway. Then the bedroom on the right. It overlooks the cozy neighborhood. A big blue house. A white and grey one-story. An apartment complex with a modern design.

Hunter steps into the room.

The air changes. Gets sharp. Electric.

His breath fills the space.

My heart pounds.

My sex clenches.

My knees wobble.

We're alone in a bedroom. What might become my bedroom.

This is everything it's supposed to be.

Only it's not.

"You like it?" he asks.

I take a deep breath. Force my thoughts to straighten. Yeah, I need to show him the light. I also need to find a new place for me and Kay.

I can't let Vinnie fuck that up too.

Our new apartment needs to be as awesome as our old one.

This place is nice. Two bedrooms. Close to the beach. Big windows.

It's a little more expensive, but we can still make it work.

"Yeah." I turn back to Hunter. Stare into his gorgeous blue eyes. "What do you think?"

"This neighborhood isn't you."

Maybe. This is the part of Santa Monica filled with families and quaint cafés. "Walker lives over here."

"Does he?" Hunter closes the space between us.

I swallow hard. "A little closer to the promenade. But yeah. He, uh…" I lose track of my words. Who cares where Walker lives when Hunter is this close?

His hip brushes mine.

Then his arm.

The back of his hand.

He brings his palms to the window. Stares at the picturesque blue sky. "The neighbors probably call the cops if the music is too loud."

I laugh. "Probably."

"How will you live if you can't blast Bayside?"

"I have headphones."

"You're gonna blow out your eardrums."

"I'll keep it reasonable."

"Good." His fingers brush my ear. "Would hate if I couldn't talk to you anymore."

"You could. You'd just have to shout."

"What if your hearing goes completely?"

"We'd learn sign language together."

"That's a commitment."

"Yeah, but you already told me I'm your best friend."

He smiles. "Using that to manipulate me already?"

"Stating facts."

He turns. Rests his ass against the wall. Stares back at the hallway. "I'm not sure I see it."

I do. Kinda.

My bed could go against the wall.

My dresser next to it.

The closet has plenty of space for my stuff.

Then my vanity in the corner.

No, there's only room for my vanity or my desk.

And there's no way I'm giving up on my desk. I poured my heart into that thing over the last year. Every time I felt something strong, I channeled it into that desk. Found the right lyric to express it. Scribbled in the right color.

Hell, I even drew on it.

And I can't draw for shit.

If I can see that, then maybe this can work.

"You're thinking something," he says.

"About my desk."

"It's cute."

"You mean with the writing?"

He nods.

"Kaylee did that first. I stole her idea."

"Great artists steal."

"Who said that?" I ask.

"I did."

"Did not."

"Did too."

He shoots me a look.

Oh. "You trying to trick me." I push him playfully. "Asshole."

He nods *yeah*. "Is there rhyme or reason to it?"

"I guess it's whatever I felt at the moment. The lyrics that captured my mood. Or a drawing. It's a collage of the last year."

"Huh."

"What?"

"Nothing."

"Something." It's in his eyes. He's thinking something.

"The desk at your apartment?"

I nod. "Yeah, I decorated the one at home back in high school. What's the difference?" They're both white desks covered in various shades of marker.

"There's a vibe to that desk," he says. "Maybe 'cause it was the only decoration in your room."

"Oh."

"It seemed hurt. Angry."

"No. I just…"

"You've been hurt."

"By you."

"Yeah." He stares into my eyes. "I'm sorry."

"I…" Uh… "Thank you."

"If there's anything you want to talk about—"

"Not right now." Eventually, yeah. But not with this wall between us. Not with him trying so hard to resist me. "But thanks."

He nods *sure*.

I move into the hallway. The main room. The kitchen.

Hunter follows a few paces behind.

It stays in the air.

The possibility of telling him.

Of easing the burden on my shoulders.

Of finding some understanding.

God, I want that.

I want that as much as I want to tear off his clothes.

And I really want to tear off his clothes.

I try to focus on the modern kitchen.

It's all stainless steel and high-end appliances.

Gas stove.

Enormous fridge.

High pressured sink.

Dishwasher.

Actual dishwasher.

God, I can see this. Making pancakes with Kaylee. Making dinner while she sits on the couch.

Or with Hunter helping chop and dice.

And sliding his arms around my waist. Setting his head into the crook of my neck. Pulling me close and kissing me like he'll never get enough.

I slide onto the counter. Press my knees together. Suck a breath through my teeth.

It does nothing to clear my head of delicious mental images.

It only makes them more vivid.

Be patient, Em. Wait for him to come to you.

But, God, he looks so good in that white t-shirt.

Those jeans slung low around his waist.

Those blue eyes fixed on me.

I can afford to push him a little.

I have to push him a little.

"Can you help me with something?" I press my lips together.

He moves closer. "Here?"

"Yeah." I spread my knees about six inches. My skirt is tight around my thighs. It's not exactly a *fuck me on the counter* skirt.

Unless he slides it to my waist.

And peels my panties to my ankles.

And…

"With?" He moves closer. Closer. Until he's standing in front of me.

"I have to see if this place is the right height."

"Really?"

"Yeah. So help me demonstrate."

"You do realize it will depend on the guy."

"You're a guy."

"Not the guy you're—"

"We could have figured it out already."

He shakes his head *you're ridiculous*, but it's there in his eyes.

He wants to play this game.

He wants me.

Hunter moves closer.

Until he's just barely between my legs.

I spread them as wide as I can.

So my thighs brush his hips.

Fuck, that feels good.

He's so close.

Closer than anyone's been since before.

But I'm not thinking about that.

I'm thinking about how I want to wrap my legs around him.

How I want to dig my hands into his hair.

How I want to unzip those jeans and stroke him until he comes.

He slides his fingers under my thighs. Lifts my legs just enough to pull us into position. Stares down at me like he's daring me back.

He's challenging me to something.

But I don't know what it is.

Only that I want it.

Just as quickly, he sets me down. Steps backward. "Well?"

"Perfect." My heart thuds against my chest.

"You're gonna share this apartment."

"I'll clean up after."

He cocks his head to one side, assessing my words. "You realize I'm taller than most guys."

"I like tall guys."

"All women say that."

"Yeah, but I'm five eleven. I should get first dibs."

He moves into the main room. "Is that how relationships work?"

"Yeah. Of course. Hot people stick together. Smart people stick together. Tall people stick together."

"Fucked-up people?"

"Exactly."

HUNTER

Emma's eyes go wide as she steps inside the third apartment.

Hard to blame her.

This place is perfect.

Wide, open living room. Huge windows. Shiny kitchen.

Real estate agent in a fashionable striped dress.

She adopts a perfect customer service smile as she extends her hand. "Sandy Lovejoy."

Emma shakes and introduces herself.

I do the same.

"I love when couples tour together." She presses her hands together. "It's so sweet."

Emma raises a brow *play along?*

I shouldn't.

I should draw a line in the sand now.

Tell her it isn't ever happening.

That I'm not thinking about her lush thighs.

Or her soft lips.

Or her flushed cheeks.

It's in the air.

She wants me.

I want her.

The only thing in the way of our bodies connecting is me.

With every minute, it seems less and less sensible.

I need to protect her, yeah.

But maybe I'm all wrong about the how.

She lights up around me.

Opens up to me.

Maybe this is what's best for her.

Maybe I'm punishing myself, telling her to stay away.

Or maybe my self-destructive steak has taken over my brain.

Hard to say.

"Hunter, sweetie." Emma wraps her arms around me. Shoots me a look. *I gave you a chance to say no.* "Is it that obvious?"

Sandy laughs. "I can always tell."

Emma beams with victory. "Hunter and I said we wouldn't be one of those couples." She turns to me with wide eyes. "But, sometimes, I just can't contain myself." Emma stares into my eyes like she's madly in love with me. "You feel like that too, baby?"

My heart pounds against my chest.

My limbs get light.

My balls tighten.

Her affection feels real.

I want to believe that.

I want to believe I deserve her.

"He's shy," she stage whispers to Sandy. "I love the shy ones, don't you?"

"There's something about them." Sandy nods. "Let me show you to the bedroom."

"Oh." Emma winks. "Yes, please."

We follow Sandy down the hall.

The bedroom is as nice as the rest of the apartment. Plenty of space. Beige carpet. White walls. Huge windows looking out on the picture-perfect street.

Fuck, that's a lot of natural light.

And Emma...

She looks like an angel, surrounded in the soft glow.

It's wrong for her.

But right all the same.

I'm so fixed on her I barely notice the thick slice of ocean in the view.

It's beautiful. Deep. Peaceful.

I've never appreciated living in Southern California. It was a fact of life, not a slice of paradise. But when I'm with Emma...

I see the beauty in the bright sky, the blooming flowers, the crashing waves.

Her dark eyes.

Her lush lips.

Her long legs.

That skirt is short.

And her shoes are tall.

She has two inches on me in those wedges.

Maybe it should bother me, but it doesn't.

"Tell me—" the real estate agent moves into the hallway and motions for us to follow. "How did you two meet?"

We follow her into the other bedroom.

It's a little bigger, with a mirrored closet door and a view of the pool.

Emma goes straight to the window.

Stares at the aqua water like it's everything she wants. "There's a pool?"

"Yes." The agent launches into a discussion of the pool's hours and awesomeness.

Emma's gaze stays on the water as she nods along.

My head fills with thoughts of her in a tiny black bikini. Lying on a pool chair. Beckoning me to come closer.

My heart thuds.

My cock stirs.

I need to strip her out of that skirt.

I need to dive between her legs.

I need to bury myself in her.

No pretenses. No bullshit. No excuses.

Just the two of us connecting.

I've never had that.

I want that so fucking badly.

Not some abstract concept of intimacy.

A connection with Emma.

"Hello." Someone knocks on the apartment's front door. "Is this the open house?"

"Yes, one moment!" Sandy calls to the door. She turns to us with a serene smile and hands an application to Emma. "You'd be a lovely addition to the building."

"Thank you." Emma beams.

"Hello?" The prospective tenant calls.

"Sorry, I better go." Sandy moves into the main room and launches into a speech about the apartment.

"Think she uses that line on everyone?" I ask.

Emma shakes her head. "I'm adorable."

She is, but—"I'm surprised you can admit that."

"Should I deny it?" She pulls a pen from her purse. "Come here."

I arch a brow.

"I'm going to use your back."

"Use the floor."

She presses her foot into the carpet. "Your back is harder."

Probably true, but hearing the word *hard* on her lips…

Not good for mission *don't touch Emma*.

Not that it's going well.

That voice in my head, the one that's supposed to tell me that this is a bad idea, is silent.

But I can't tell if that's because my cock has it gagged and bound in the closet.

Or if it's because I'm finally capable of seeing myself as more than a piece of shit.

"What do I get in return?" I tease her back. Keep it light. Keep my head away from thoughts of her groaning *fuck, you're hard*.

All right, I don't manage the latter.

But I do try.

"You get a reason to complain." She laughs. "Exactly what you always wanted."

"You sure about this place?"

"Yeah." Emma nods to the vent above her. "Feel that." She leans her head back, thrusting her chest into the air. "Sweet, sweet air-conditioning."

It is a rarity around here.

But, fuck, that's not where my head is going.

Her outfit is normal. Casual. Something stretchy and comfortable.

And tight as hell.

She looks so fucking good in the soft fabric.

Like the tough as nails woman who can handle anything.

Even a guy who can barely articulate what's in his head.

"What about your roommate?" I ask.

Her lips press together. "Good point." She fishes for her cell. "We need to send photos."

"The listing—"

"Isn't enough. We need amateur stuff."

I raise a brow.

She chuckles. "It is the best."

"Feel like I've heard that somewhere."

"Yeah, who is it that mentions it ten times a day?"

"You, probably," I say.

Her laugh gets louder. "You know me. Can't stop talking about porn." She hands her phone to me.

I open her camera app.

Frame the image the best I can.

I don't know a lot about photography, but I do know composition.

Click, click.

Emma shakes her head. "I didn't look cute."

"Yeah, you did."

"No. I need a pose. Count me down."

I arch a brow.

"You know, three, two, one."

"Okay…"

She turns. Places her hand on her hip. Blows the camera a kiss.

Fuck, it's adorable.

Sassy. Sweet. Emma.

"Three, two, one." *Click.*

"Take a few. So I have options."

"You think your best friend cares if you look cute?"

"I asked for pictures, not sass."

"You didn't specify that."

She laughs. "You're usually good at following instructions."

I raise a brow.

"Oh my God, stop with that."

"I didn't say anything."

"You said everything." She moves to the other side of the room and poses.

Click, click. "No idea what you're talking about."

"Uh-huh."

We move into the hallway.

Click, click.

"Why are you so obsessed with that anyway?" she asks. "Do you have a secret desire to be tied up?"

No.

I miss the freedom that came with letting go of control.

But I don't miss the act itself.

Whenever I sobered up, I hated that feeling of blankness. Of not knowing what I'd done. Or why I'd done it.

"I just think you'd look good in leather boots," I say.

"Well, obviously." She hikes her skirt up her thigh. "I have the legs for it."

Fuck, does she.

"The thing is"—she leads us into the main room—"I look good in everything."

"And modest too."

"Thank you." She stretches her arms wide. Smiles.

Click, click. "How do you do it?"

"It's hard. I have to practice humility every day. But I'm so good at it."

"Amazing."

"I know, right?"

I double over with a full-blown belly laugh.

She does that to me.

Gets me like no one else does.

Hits me somewhere no one else reaches.

I need more of her.

If that really is what she wants—

If it really is what's best for her—

"Okay. I'll get the bathroom." Her fingers brush mine as she takes my phone. She skips to the room. Snaps a few photos. Skips back. "You think it will help our odds if we make a show of kissing goodbye?"

"Why would we kiss goodbye if we're leaving together?"

"Yeah, true." Disappointment flares in her eyes. It's a quick thing. A second. Then she's all smiles. "We could make out. Let the happiness of finding a new place overtake us."

"We could?" I raise a brow.

She moves closer enough to whisper. "Sandy is really into us."

"You think she wants to watch?"

293

"She's dying to watch." Her fingers brush my hair. My ear. My neck. "But I'm only willing to give her a hint of a show."

"No penetration?"

Her fingers curl into my hip. "Definitely not."

"Not sure I can agree."

"Don't be such a guy."

"Oh?"

She nods. "There are plenty of other ways to have sex."

"Go on."

"I'm just saying. It's not all about penetration."

"Yeah?"

She pulls back enough to look me in the eyes.

Only she can't.

She's blushing.

Staring at her shoes.

"I... Uh... it's getting late, yeah?" She slides her cell into her purse. "Maybe we should grab lunch before work."

"Sure."

"Good."

"But, Em—"

"Yeah?"

"You're gonna have to explain this whole 'it's not all about penetration' thing to me."

Her smile gets wicked. "Use your imagination."

Already there.

WE DRIVE TO THE SHOP. GRAB TACOS. THEN COFFEE.

Emma's hand brushes mine as we walk back.

We're already late.

But I can't bring myself to rush.

It feels too good doing nothing with her.

Doing everything with her.

This is something off a postcard.

Blue sky. Palm trees. Gorgeous brunette staring at me like I'm her favorite thing in the universe.

She's already my favorite thing in the universe.

Maybe I'm still a mess.

But if she's looking at me like this, I can't be all that bad.

This can't be *that* terrible of an idea.

We walk the last block.

Stop in front of the sandwich shop next door.

Out of view of Inked Heart's windows.

"Oh." Her cheeks flush. "I still haven't sent those pictures." She pulls out her cell. Opens the camera app. Shows me the screen. "Which do you think?"

"There nudes I should know about?"

"You already had my camera."

"Wasn't looking."

"No, you perv."

"I asked to respect your privacy."

"Or so you could know to look."

I shake my head.

She nods.

I force my eyes to the cell. Select a few photos. They aren't the ones that capture the apartment best.

They're the ones that capture her the best.

She's beautiful, bright, vibrant.

I love seeing this side of her.

Don't get me wrong. I like pissed, difficult Emma too.

But seeing her joy—

Fuck, this is better than any bourbon.

Than anything.

My fingers brush hers as I hand the phone back.

She taps the screen a few times.

Hits send.

Swallows hard. "Hunter, I…"

"We're late."

"I know." She slides her cell into her back pocket.

I move closer.

Her fingers brush my hip. My side. My shoulder.

I bring my hand to her cheek.

Maybe I'm out of my fucking mind.

Maybe I'm the most self-destructive idiot on the planet.

Right now, I don't care.

My eyelids flutter closed.

I lean in.

Bring my lips to hers.

She kisses back hard.

Like she needs this as badly as I do.

I'm ready to kiss her forever.

But this familiar voice interrupts.

She jumps back.

Turns to Dean—he's standing outside the door, shaking his head in some mix of *you're ridiculous* and *about time*.

"I was just." She clears her throat. "Mind your own business."

He holds up his hands *I'd never.*

Her eyes flit to me. "I, um, we really are late."

"Yeah."

"I…" She grabs my wrist. Kisses me again. Quickly. Then she turns and rushes into the shop.

Dean and I watch her get behind the counter.

He turns to me, apprehension filling his blue eyes. "You know what you're doing?"

No.

But I'm starting to figure it out.

HUNTER

The air-conditioning hums as I step into Inked Hearts.

The door swings shut behind me.

Wes's laugh fills the room.

He's at the counter with Ryan. Making some joke.

Wes leans into the counter. "Em, sweetheart. You give any thought to that whole sloppy seconds thing?"

"I don't want to break your heart, Wes, but I like quiet guys." Her eyes flit to me. Her cheeks flush. Her chest heaves with her inhale.

Fuck, it's obvious there's something between us.

It's practically written on our foreheads.

Somehow, Ryan doesn't notice.

"You're here till seven, right?" he asks me.

I nod.

"Meet me in the office after your last appointment. We'll sign your paperwork." He extends his hand.

I take it. Shake.

A lightness spreads through my limbs.

This is happening.

I'm working at Inked Hearts.

I'm kissing Emma.

I'm figuring out my shit.

Fuck, it's hard to believe.

I want to prove I deserve this gig.

To prove I'm worth her trust and affection.

I can't do that overnight.

But I can commit to making it happen every fucking day.

Ryan shoots Wes a cutting look. "If she reports you for sexual harassment…" He shrugs *there will be nothing I can do.*

"Would you do that, Em?" Wes asks.

"Haven't done it to Dean yet," she says.

"So there's a record for me to break?" Wes's blue eyes light up.

She laughs. "Yeah, if you want to get fired."

"Or killed," I add. "You've seen her brother."

"Yeah." Wes meets my gaze. "Brendon is bulging—"

"Oh my God, we're so not doing that." Her nose scrunches in distaste.

"But he's a softie, deep down. Besides, what's he gonna say? 'You can't date my badass little sister even though I'm two years older than you, dating a chick two months younger?'" Wes asks.

"Since when do you date?" Ryan asks.

"Since Em." Wes winks at her.

Ryan shakes his head *I've had enough of your nonsense—and that means all of you*—then heads to his suite.

"Gotta use polite language in front of the lady," Wes says.

"I'm not a lady," Emma says. "If you want any chance, you should realize that."

He presses both hands to his heart. "Baby, I love the way you hurt me."

"We've spoken twice in the last ten years," she says.

"It's more like three or four times," he says.

She laughs, charmed.

He has that effect on people.

Maybe I should be jealous—he is flirting with her.

But it's obviously a put on.

Besides, she's not kissing him.

She's kissing me.

I turn to my brother. "What are you doing here?"

He pulls out his cell. Shows off a screenshot of a drawing. "This look familiar?"

It's the piece I've been working on all week. For the guy with the empty Instagram who desperately wanted something on his bicep.

Fuck—"You're—"

"Could it really be anyone else?" he asks.

Of course it's him.

He's supporting me in the most obnoxious way possible.

That's pure Wes.

And this…

Well, if he's gonna fuck with me, I'm gonna fuck with him.

"Sit down." I motion to the teal chair in my suite. "Gotta make sure I find the most painful needle possible."

"Good." He winks at Emma. "Want you to know how much punishment I can take."

"Is someone spreading a rumor about me being a Domme?" Her eyes flit to me.

I shrug. I wouldn't be surprised if Dean was spreading a rumor like that, though I don't really see it.

If anything, Emma needs to let go. To let someone else take control.

But if she insisted on tying me to her bed—

I certainly wouldn't turn her down.

My cock stirs at the thought.

I need to fuck her.

To taste her.

To make her come.

Tonight.

Right now, I need to keep my blood in my brain.

Wes's tattoo is going to take all my concentration.

Wes takes a seat. Blows Emma a kiss.

I get everything I need from the office. Pull a stool over. Prep him for the temporary tattoo.

"She's into me." He motions to Emma, who's not doing anything to hide how much she's staring.

"You think you're cute, huh?" I ask.

He grins *I'm adorable.*

"You can act as asinine as you want—"

"Slow down with the vocab quiz, Hunter. I didn't get sixty days to read and talk about my feelings."

"You wouldn't last two minutes in rehab."

"You're talking about that?"

I should.

I should be able to tell people *hey, I don't drink 'cause I used to have a problem* like it's not a big deal.

"If you can use your inside voice." I press the transfer paper to his skin. Wet it with a cotton ball. Hold it in place.

"What was that, Mom?" He makes a point of raising his voice.

All right, that is the kind of thing Mom used to say. Back when she gave a shit. "Shut up or I'll write *I love Dawson Leery* on your arm."

Wes cringes. "At least give me Pacey."

"In your dreams."

He shudders.

"Still can't believe you dressed up for Halloween."

"Did you see how hot that chick was?"

"And how she went straight to the guy dressed as Pacey?"

"Fuck, how am I supposed to know Joey ends up with Pacey? I mean, if I'd seen the show, it would be obvious. Because who would want to be with a sentimental fucker with a Peter Pan syndrome, but—"

"Not that you ever watched."

"She liked playing it while we were making out."

"Uh-huh."

He makes a point of holding up his crossed fingers. "Cross my heart and hope to die."

"Stop moving." I peel the paper from his arm.

Fuck, it looks awesome. Lyrics on a scroll that's curving around a thorny rose.

I grab the mirror and angle it so he can see.

For a second, his poker face falls.

His blue eyes fill with wonder.

And nerves.

He blinks, and he's back to the poker face. "Fuck, when did you get so good at this shit?"

"Had sixty days of—"

"Lifting from the looks of it."

I chuckle. "Helps clear my head."

"Fuck, dude, I thought we discussed the feelings."

"You know Dean works here?"

"You're right. And he's got that smoking hot apprentice too." He makes a show of standing and looking around the shop. "Where'd she go?"

"They're at lunch."

"Damn. She's got a nice ass."

"She'll kick yours."

"So I hear."

I push him into the chair.

He shoots me a look. "Didn't realize you were into that shit." His gaze shifts to Emma. "How's she like it?"

"Thought you were angling to get in her pants?"

"Can't be sloppy seconds unless someone has gone first."

I wet a cotton swab with rubbing alcohol. Clean off the temp tattoo. Pick up the stencil. "Never realized my self-destructive streak rubbed off—"

"Do not need to hear about you rubbing off."

"You're nervous."

"No." He shrugs his shoulders.

"Stop moving." This time, I pin him to the chair.

Wes clears his throat. "Nervous you're gonna fuck it up."

That's fair. It's not true, but it's fair.

"You afraid it's gonna hurt or that it's forever?"

"Just told you."

"Some bullshit."

Again, he shrugs.

"You keep doing that, I am gonna fuck it up."

His eyes flit to Emma then to me.

I have my back to her.

But there's a mirrored wall in front of me.

I can see her standing in front of the computer. Her chipped nails on the keyboard. Her teeth sinking into her lips.

Her makeup is all worn off.

That's the pink of her lips.

She looks up from the computer.

Through the mirror, her eyes catch mine.

Her blush is positively coquettish.

Like she's a school girl and I'm the teacher she's dreaming about.

And, fuck, now *that* idea is in my head.

A tiny plaid skirt hanging off her hips. That long hair in pigtails. Those soft lips—

"Fuck, dude, get your rocks off later." For a split second, all the playfulness drops from Wes's voice. Then he shrugs and it's back. "I'm paying by the hour."

"This one is on me."

"Fuck that. I'm not gonna owe you shit. I'm paying and I'm leaving a fat tip."

"You shouldn't announce that. Then Emma won't be incentivized to flirt."

"Girl doesn't need an incentive. Look at me."

I chuckle. "You ready or not?"

"I was born ready. You?"

That's a tough question. A long time ago, Chase did Wes's first tattoo. I did the second.

The crooked crescent moon is still there, on his wrist.

He's still proud of the battle scar.

I get it. I feel the same about my first few tattoos. They're shitty as hell, but I wouldn't trade them for anything.

I guess…

Well, it's actually really fucking sweet that Wes loves something I gave him.

Not that he'd ever admit it.

"All right." I press one hand to his shoulder to hold him in place. "On three."

He nods.

"One." I turn the needle on. "Two." I press it to his skin.

He mutters a curse. "Asshole."

"Always works."

"You're still an asshole."

"No arguments here." I trace the first letter. It's a thick, blocky font. A lot of ink.

But Wes takes it like a champ.

"You realize your girl is watching?" he says.

I keep my eyes on my work. "She's not my girl." Whatever this is, it's none of his business.

"Looks like she wants to be."

"Yeah."

"And you're turning that down?"

"What are you doing here, Wes?"

"Fuck, this the thanks I get for supporting my brother in his new place of employment?"

"You're right. It means the world to me that you're supporting me. In fact, I think I gotta turn off this gun so I can give you a hug."

His groan is pure agony.

My laugh hits me everywhere.

Wes is so… Wes.

I still can't believe that he's here.

That shit is okay.

"Listen, Wes—" I finish the first word. Move onto the second.

He groans. "Fuck, this spot isn't supposed to hurt."

"It's a needle on your skin."

"I know it's a fucking needle. This is my job too. Jesus." He uses his free hand to brush the dust from his jeans. "Why am I surrounded by know it alls? God, it's only gonna get worse working here."

"Been thinking—"

"Never a good idea."

"Can't help it."

"This about rehab again?"

"It's basically two months to turn over your mistakes."

"Fuck, you know how bad I want to shudder right now?"

I laugh. "Yeah." I move onto the third word.

Wes mutters a curse.

"Take a deep breath."

"I hate to break it to you, Hunter, but you're not a lithe chick with a yoga ass."

"Fuck. Really?" I make a show of reaching for my ass. "Feels pretty firm."

His nose scrunches in distaste. "Not gonna listen to your advice on how to breathe."

"But you go to yoga classes?"

"Well…"

I laugh. Has my little brother always been this girl crazy? "What was her name?"

"Claire and she was hot. And, fuck, that sweet voice. I could listen to her say anything."

"How about 'Wes Keating is a pig'?"

"I heard that." He laughs. "Around—"

"Date three?"

"I tried to tell her I don't do commitment."

"Uh-huh."

"All right, maybe it slipped my mind. But I thought she—"

"You're an asshole."

"Yeah, but I'm here." He sighs as I pick up the gun. Curses as I move onto the next word.

"Halfway done."

"Really?"

"With the words."

He nods like he doesn't mind the pain. "Been thinking about being here."

Me too.

I want my brother here.

I want someone in my corner.

But—"That will fuck shit up with Chase."

"I can handle Chase."

"I can rescind the job offer."

He shakes his head. "Already sweet talked Ryan."

I arch a brow.

"What do you think I was doing here early?" His voice is honest. "Signed my paperwork this afternoon."

"Chase is gonna kill you."

"Yeah, but he's gonna kill you first."

Maybe.

Or maybe there's forgiveness somewhere in his heart.

Stranger things have happened.

"Now, you gonna tell me about the hottie in the short skirt or not?" he asks.

"How many times I tell you not to talk about her like that?"

"More times than you offered details."

"You know, I admire your optimism." I move onto the next word. "No matter how many times I say no, you keep asking."

"I'm tenacious."

"Annoying is another way to say it."

"Still not hearing details."

"We're friends."

"Uh-huh."

"Cross my heart and hope to die." I finish the first line and move onto the next.

"It's sweet, that you'd swear on that."

"I try."

"There's only one thing?"

"Yeah?"

"You're still wearing her lipstick."

HUNTER

The piece comes together, bit by bit. The thick black words. The deep red petals. The sharp green thorns.

Wes sighs as I turn off the gun.

It's weird, seeing him this vulnerable.

Treating him like any other client.

He's a hell of a lot more bossy and difficult than any of my clients.

I clean him up, give him the standard after care speech, take him to the mirror.

The pretenses fall from his expression. "Fuck, Hunter." He traces the design in the air. "This is good."

"Thanks."

"Seriously. All that time in rehab was good for you."

"You figure?"

He looks up at me and shakes his head. "Fuck, dude, you're so serious now."

"Now?"

"Hell yeah, now. You even remember how you used to act?"

It's farther away every day.

I can't wait until that phase is a distant memory.

At the moment—"I see your point."

He nods *hell yeah you do*. "I get the whole brooding tattoo artist thing. I'm sure the chicks dig it. But you gotta tone it down."

"I'll keep that in mind."

He shrugs. "Trying to help you, dude."

In his way, he is. "You really working here or you fucking with me?"

"I start next week."

"We're doomed."

He flashes me that classic Wes Keating smile. "Would you expect anything less?"

I walk him to the register.

He flirts with Emma enough to make her blush.

Insists on paying. And leaving a generous tip.

Tries to high-five me goodbye.

I pull him into a hug instead.

He's right.

I'm not the guy who was blackmailed into rehab.

I'm a better version of myself.

Maybe I'm not at a hundred percent yet.

But I'm getting there.

Bit by bit, I'm getting there.

***

WITH MY THOUGHTS ON EMMA, THE DAY IS A CRAWL.

I want to be done.

To be alone with her.

To figure out what the fuck we're doing.

She leaves a little after five.

I finish touching up a short dude's back piece. Walk him to

308

the counter. Print his receipt.

Except for the moan of some miserable musician, the shop is quiet.

It's just me and Ryan.

I guess this is his music.

How am I surrounded by people who like this whiny shit?

Don't get me wrong.

It's not all bad.

And I certainly understand torment in the soul.

Hell, this is actually a pretty fucking great band. Catchy melodies. Awesome riffs. Epic solos.

But hearing music Emma loves to play isn't doing shit to speed time.

When I close my eyes, I see her singing along. Blushing. Smiling to deflect the attention. Digging her nails into her skirt.

Fuck, I need to be there.

This is it. Our last day alone.

I need to make the most of it.

"Fuck, man. This is nice." My client finishes checking out his freshly blackened back piece. He holds up his hand.

I high-five him. "Thanks."

"I barely groaned too."

I can't help but chuckle. He grunted though every stroke. Classic tough guy. Insisting it doesn't hurt despite his frequent grunts. "Gotta save that for your girl."

He laughs. "Gotta save it, but not for a girl."

"Oh."

"Get that a lot."

"Wouldn't guess."

"Boyfriend tells me the same thing."

I let him gush about his boyfriend.

It's sweet.

But it only makes me want Emma more.

After I walk him out, Ryan heads to the counter.

His blue eyes fix on me. Fill with Ryan like intensity.

He's wearing all black, same as always.

Only he's smiling.

Which is…

Well, that's pretty fucking normal at this point.

He's crazy about his girlfriend.

I finally get that.

How one person can change your outlook on the entire world.

It happened to him.

It's happening to me.

It's better than any drink I've ever had.

And I've tried them all.

He raises a brow *you ready for this?*

I'm not.

But I want to be.

I move to the counter.

"You sure you know what you're getting into?" he teases.

"Yeah." My fingers curl around the pen. It's a normal plastic thing. One of the gel rollers Emma loves.

It's not a thick fountain thing reserved for special occasions.

But that's perfect in its own way.

"You sick of us yet?" he teases.

"Getting there."

"Give it six months. You'll be clawing at the walls," he teases.

"Yeah, you look ready to get out of here," I tease back.

His low chuckle bounces around the room. "I love this place."

I do too. "Have any advice?"

"You know that shit they say about honesty being the best policy?"

"Yeah."

"Not everything is everyone's business."

Fuck, it's like he knows.

I study his expression. Try to find a clue. But the man is a brick wall.

I shake it off.

Pick up the pen.

Sign on the dotted line.

He does the same.

Then he offers his hand.

We shake.

"Congrats, Hunter. You're officially a part of Inked Hearts."

I nod.

"You're fucked."

I can't help but laugh.

Not yet.

But with what I'm going to do after this…

This is the best decision of my life.

Or the worst.

EMMA

The door swings open then slams shut.

Hunter tosses his keys on the dining table.

He kicks off his shoes and socks.

Moves directly to me.

His steps are bouncy.

Packed with enthusiasm.

It's all over his gorgeous blue eyes.

He moves into the kitchen. Brings his hands to my hips.

"It's official." His fingers curl into the fabric of my dress.

"You're at Inked Hearts?"

He nods.

My chest warms. It's perfect. It's everything.

But this…

What the hell is this?

I stare into his baby blues. Find nothing but affection.

I'm not sure what it means.

But it has to be good.

I need it to be good. "Should we celebrate?"

"Yeah." His eyes flutter closer.

Mine follow.

He leans in. Brushes his lips to mine.

It's soft.

Then it's harder.

I suck on his bottom lip.

Scrape my teeth against it.

His fingers dig into my skin.

He groans against my mouth.

It's heaven.

It really is.

When I pull back, I'm breathless. Dizzy. Unable to articulate anything running through my head. "Hunter, I…"

"Yeah?"

"Are we… what are we?"

"I want to be with you, Em."

"Like boyfriend girlfriend?"

He nods.

My shoulders relax. "Really?"

"Fuck yeah." He wraps his arms around my waist. "You're the best thing that's ever happened to me."

"But… Brendon… and—"

"We'll figure it out."

"You sure?"

"Yeah."

I stare back into his eyes. So I can feel that certainty.

There isn't a single hint of doubt in his deep blue eyes.

This…

We…

Holy shit…

I dig my fingers into his hair. "Say it again."

"I want to be with you."

I rise to my tiptoes.

Press my lips to his.

Any reservations in my brain fall away.

I part my lips to make way for his tongue.

Arch my body into his.

Tug at his hair to pull him closer.

God, he tastes good.

And this—

This is everything.

I need to be with him. To tear his clothes off. Touch him.

Fuck him.

But that—

Can I really handle that?

He pulls back. Presses his forehead to mine.

His voice gets low. Growly. "I need to make you come."

My sex clenches.

"If you need to talk first—"

I shake my head. No talking. No thinking. No inhibitions.

I need him erasing the past.

Okay, maybe that's too much to ask for.

As long as that's not the last time someone touched me.

As long as he replaces that—

I can do this.

I have to do this.

I take a step backward. Hook my fingers into his belt loop. "Bed."

He wraps his arms around me and lifts me to his chest.

My fingers dig into his cotton t-shirt as I hold on tightly.

This is a hell of a ride.

But it's only beginning.

The rest…

Fuck, I really hope I can handle this.

He sets me down outside my room.

I turn the handle, press the door open. "After you."

He steps inside.

I follow. Close the door. Press my back against it.

This is already a lot.

The last time I had a guy in my room…

I can't even remember.

He brings his hand to my hips. "You're nervous."

"A little."

"I'll go slow."

I shake my head. "No. I… I want to." My eyes go to the bedside table. "Do you have condoms?"

He shakes his head. "I got tested before I left rehab."

"Me too. I mean, I did, last month. I'm safe. But I'm not on birth control."

He nods, taking in the information. "Sit on the bed."

"What?"

"I need you coming on my face, Em."

"But—"

"We can stop there."

"I can't."

His lips curl into a half-smile. It's equal parts affection and desire. "I'll pick something up tomorrow."

"But tomorrow—"

"Then after this." He tugs at my t-shirt. "We can negotiate all you want after you come on my face."

My sex clenches.

The demanding tone to his voice sets me on fire.

He wants this so badly.

Wants my bliss so badly.

It's hot as hell.

My knees knock together.

I fall onto the bed.

I'm not sure I can handle penetration.

But this—

I can do this.

He sits next to me. Pulls me into his lap.

I kiss him hard.

Slip my hand under his t-shirt.

Soft skin. Hard muscles.

And that's Hunter.

It's different than touching other guys. Better.

I want everything all at once.

But I want to go slow too.

I want to take my time exploring every inch of him.

Maybe…

Maybe enough time has passed. Maybe I'm ready. Maybe I really can forget my inhibitions.

I dig my fingers into his skin as I kiss him back.

His tongue slides around mine.

His hands go to my hips.

He pulls my body against his, so I'm grinding against him.

His cock brushes my sex.

There's all this fabric in the way, but it still feels so fucking good.

I want that.

I want him.

I push his t-shirt up his stomach.

He breaks our kiss to pull it over his head.

Fuck, he looks good in nothing but his jeans.

All tall and broad and inked.

But I don't have time to gawk.

He's already tugging at my dress.

I help him do away with the garment.

Then the beige bra.

The black panties.

It doesn't hit me until I'm naked.

This is really happening.

I'm *really* naked.

But, God, the way he's staring makes my sex ache.

I need him.

I'm scared, yeah, but I really, really need him.

He slips off the bed. His hands go to my hips. In one swift gesture, he pulls me to the edge of the bed.

Hunter lowers himself onto his knees.

He's right between my legs.

He's so, so close.

God, I want that.

I lean back. Press my eyelids together. Take a deep breath.

Slow inhale.

Steady exhale.

It's been a long, long time.

There are ugly memories in the back of my head.

But I can do this.

Fuck, I want to do this.

I gasp as his lips close around my nipple.

He sucks on my tender skin softly. Then harder. Then hard enough it hurts in the best possible way.

I dig my hands into his hair.

Wrap my legs around his waist.

It's more his chest, with him kneeling between my legs, but I don't care.

As long as I feel more of him.

Get him closer.

I stare into his eyes.

Watch those baby blues fill with the perfect mix of bliss and need.

He's there.

He's lost in this.

I can be there too.

I'm capable of feeling good.

My thoughts scatter as he drags his lips to my other nipple.

He tortures me with soft flicks of his tongue, circles, zigzags.

He fills me with this perfect mix of bliss and need.

I'm aching, desperate, empty.

Finally, he brings his hand to my sex.

It starts as the brush of the back of his hand.

Then his palm.

His first two fingers.

His thumb.

My fingers curl into the crimson bedspread.

I lie back.

Close my eyes.

This is a lot.

There's too much going through my head.

I need it gone.

I need to be here, in this moment, with him.

"Please." *Erase the past. Fix this broken part of me. Make this better.* I can't ask for any of that. So I go for the next best thing. "Make me come."

He presses his lips to my hip bone as he rubs me with his thumb.

Softly.

Then harder.

Then—

Fuck.

A groan spills from my lips.

He's good at this.

He's really fucking good at this.

"Hunter." I reach for him. Get his shoulder.

I can't add everything I want to say.

But this is a start.

It's a really great fucking start.

He sucks on my skin as he rubs me with his thumb.

He tortures me with soft, slow circles.

My thoughts flit away.

My breath gets heavy.

My groans fill the room.

Those ugly memories drift to the corner of my mind. They're not gone, exactly, but they're not here either.

CRYSTAL KASWELL

I'm *here*.
In this moment.
Feeling his thumb against my clit.
Well, most of me is.
There's just that one part—
"Please." I can't ask for everything I need. I can't add anything.
So I say it again. "Make me come."
"Yeah, baby?"
The pet name sets me on fire. My nod is heavy. Needy.
Not just for release.
For everything.
I reach for him again.
Get his chin. His cheek. His head.
I knot my hand in his hair.
He looks up at me, those deep blue eyes filled with pure lust.
Then he brings his mouth to me.
He licks me up and down.
Slowly.
Softly.
Again and again.
Pleasure floods my pelvis.
I wind tighter and tighter.
I'm already so close.
It's already so intense.
I…
We…
Fuck.
I sling one leg over his shoulder.
Then the other.
He tortures me with long, slow flicks of his tongue.
He winds me tighter and tighter.
Bit by bit, my thoughts fade away.
I melt into the bed.
He brings his mouth to my clit.

Plays with different strokes and speeds until he—

"Fuck." I tug at his hair. Hold him closer. "Hunter—"

"Say my name again, baby."

My nipples pang. God, I love this pet name.

I love this.

It's everything it's supposed to be.

I'm almost completely *here*.

I'm so fucking close.

"Hunter." His name rolls off my lips. It sounds good there. Right. Like my favorite lyrics.

His fingers dig into my thighs.

He holds me in place as he works me.

Every flick of his tongue winds me tighter.

Brings me closer.

He keeps that same, steady pace.

He's impossibly patient.

It's sweet, sweet torture.

I savor it until I can't take it anymore.

Until my body takes over.

My hips buck of their own accord.

He holds me in place.

To steady me.

To remind me he's in control.

It's hot as hell.

But it brings me back to that night.

I...

Too many things mix in my head.

I open my eyes. Stare down at him. Focus on everything present in the room.

The crimson bedspread.

The silver sharpie scribbles on my desk.

The light pouring through the window.

His sandy hair.

His strong hands.

His soft tongue.

Fuck, he's so good at this.

His grip on my thighs softens.

I relax into the bed.

Bring my hand to his hair.

Guide him into place.

He moves with me.

He's listening to me.

I'm safe.

I trust him.

I…

Fuck.

"Hunter."

He groans into my skin.

It pushes those thoughts back to the corner of my mind.

I try to push them further.

But it doesn't work.

Deep breath.

Slow exhale.

I just… we just…

I'm almost there.

I focus on the feeling of his soft, wet tongue.

The tension in my sex.

The pang in my nipples.

He winds me tighter and tighter.

Almost.

Almost.

There.

With the next flick of his tongue, I come.

I unravel.

Pleasure spills through my pelvis. My torso. My limbs and toes.

My sex pulses.

My breath hitches.

My groans run together.

Hunter pulls back. Presses his lips to my thigh.

Then my stomach.

He climbs up the bed, lies next to me, pulls me into his arms.

And, for the first time in forever, I really do believe everything is going to be okay.

EMMA

Hunter steps into the living room, wet hair sticking to his forehead, raspberry towel wrapped around his hips.

I try to pull my jaw from the floor.

Fail.

He stares back with *fuck me* eyes.

My knees knock together.

My sex clenches.

I forget my satisfaction in favor of the hunger growing below my belly.

I need him again.

I need him like this.

I need him naked.

But I need logic too.

We're still lacking condoms.

And I'm still... uncertain of my limits.

I reach for some hint of sense. Find little.

"Showing off?" It's more awkward than teasing. I'm too flushed and fluttery to tease him properly.

"No." He crosses the room toward me. "This is showing off." He drops his towel.

God, he's hot.

And he's so—

"My eyes are up here, Em."

"Your cock is down there though."

His chuckle fills the space. "Shit, is that where it is?"

I think I nod, but, honestly, I'm not sure.

"I don't want to break your heart, Em, but I brought these too." He waves something in his hand.

A fabric.

It's black.

Or maybe navy.

Really, who cares?

He bends.

Pulls on a pair of black boxers.

It makes him ten percent less distracting.

He's still so fucking yummy.

I want that.

I really, really want that.

But I'm not remotely sure if I can handle it.

He stands and crosses the room to me.

His hands brush my hips.

One inch at a time, he presses his body against mine.

Then it's his lips.

I kiss back hard.

He feels so good. So safe. So mine.

I've never wanted that before.

But, right now, I do.

I really, really do.

I pull back with a heavy sigh.

I want to tear off those boxers and drag him to my bedroom.

But first things first.

"So…" I motion to the door.

He raises a brow.

"We need something."

"Something?"

I clear my throat again.

"Oh." His chuckle is soft. "Now?"

"We could eat first. I mean, I did. But did you?"

He shakes his head.

"I made lasagna."

"Yeah?"

My cheeks flush. "What?"

"Just you."

"What about me?"

"You're Em."

"Obviously."

"Lasagna is perfect." He brings his hand to the back of my head and pulls me into a kiss.

I have no idea what he's saying, but I can't complain about the way he's saying it.

I kiss him harder.

His tongue slides around mine.

His fingers curl into my scalp.

Right now, I believe it.

That I'd drop to my knees immediately if he asked.

Fuck, I want that.

It's the only thing in my head.

I need to make him come too.

I need it in this deep, visceral way.

When our kiss breaks, I'm dizzy.

I don't know what to say.

Only that I need to stay here. In this perfect world of ours. "It's in the fridge."

"Thanks." He pulls back to grab the lasagna.

"I… uh…" Oh. That's it. "We need to celebrate your job."

He motions to my bedroom upstairs. "Didn't we?"

My cheeks flush. "I, um, I was thinking cupcakes."

His lips curl into that same knowing smile.

Something between *I love making fun of you* and *I love everything about you*.

It's as intense as anything we did upstairs.

And as scary.

I've never loved anyone.

Never trusted anyone that much.

But the way he's looking at me—

God, I could get used to that.

I really, really could.

"You have a problem with cupcakes?" Again, I fail to sound teasing. I'm in a permanent state or fluttery awkwardness.

"It's not that big a deal."

"Fuck that. It's huge."

His cheeks flush.

I swear to God, I die.

That's so…

He's so…

Ahem. "Your life is a train wreck, right."

He laughs. "Damn. Where's the sugar coating?"

"In the cupcakes."

His laugh gets lower. Heartier. "Fair." He grabs a spatula. Scoops a slice of lasagna onto a plate. Puts it in the microwave. "Yeah, my life is a train wreck."

"This is your first step to fixing that."

"Rehab was the first step." He hits the timer. Turns back to me. "But, you're right. It's big."

"Exactly. You have a job."

"And the best girlfriend in the world." He wraps his arms around my waist.

I giggle. "Say that again."

"You're the best girlfriend in the world."

"You're my boyfriend." It's surreal.

"Yeah." He brushes a stray hair behind my ear. "Am I not the best?"

"That's still to be seen."

"Brutal."

"As always."

"Yeah." His lips curl into that same smile. The *I love everything about you* one.

It makes my cheeks flush.

It makes my knees weak.

I have to hold onto the counter to stay upright. "You, um... can you help with the cupcakes or what?"

He nods.

I motion to the cabinet. Take him through grabbing all the ingredients as I find a bowl and a mixing spoon.

He places his body behind mine.

Helps me measure all the dry ingredients. Up to the chocolate chips.

The microwave beeps. Even though I motion for him to grab his dinner, he ignores it.

"You think this is too much chocolate?" I ask.

He presses his lips to my neck. "You have that category?"

"True." I pour another handful of chips into the batter. "And fuck you."

"Still don't have condoms."

God, I'm tempted to do something stupid.

Ask him to pull out.

Come on my back or my chest.

Or in my mouth.

Fuck, that's...

It's still tempting as all hell.

But first things first.

"I hear excuses." This time, I finally make my voice teasing.

He plants another kiss on my neck.

Mmm.

"I hear groaning," he murmurs into my skin.

"That was terrible."

"Still hear it."

"Hunter..."

"Yeah?"

"Um..." I reach for something to say. Find nothing. I'm too lost in this. In my head. "Your dinner."

"Aren't we making cupcakes."

"You should eat."

This time, he listens. He steps backward, grabs his lasagna and a fork, shifts onto the counter. "Fuck." He chews. Swallows. "This is amazing."

"What did you expect?"

"I don't know."

I flip him off.

He chuckles.

"I ever cook anything less than amazing?"

"No."

"So why the surprise."

"You're not the cooking type."

I motion to the bowl full of cupcake batter. Then to the oven. "Put it to three seventy-five."

He reaches for the knob. Turns it.

"How am I not the cooking type?"

"You're not going to like it."

"Tell me anyway." I grab the muffin tray. Fill it with foil liners.

"You're not exactly nurturing."

"Fuck you."

He laughs. "Told you."

I laugh too.

He's right.

Mostly.

"It's not that, exactly." I fill a pan with batter. "More that I have limited love to go around. I save it for the people who really deserve it."

His eyes find mine. "Like who?"

"Kaylee. And Brendon. He's annoying... but he's a good brother."

"You're sweet."

"Sometimes." I fill another row of cupcakes. "But only to people I like."

"Fuck, not good news for me."

I flip him off again.

He slides off the counter. Sets his plate down. Wraps his fingers around my wrist. Nips at my index finger.

I laugh.

"It's rough. My best friend doesn't like me," he says.

"Maybe you should have picked someone kinder."

"No." He rests his palm on my cheek. "She's perfect. We're perfect."

My entire body warms. "I... Uh..."

He's right. This is perfect.

But it could be more perfect.

If we...

If I...

Fuck, I'm not used to feeling shy and awkward.

I have to do it.

Go for it.

"I was thinking." I step back. Fill the last liner with batter. Lick the spoon.

"Yeah?"

"Maybe... maybe we don't have the condoms yet."

He arches a brow.

"But that doesn't mean we can't..."

He stares back at me, hanging on every word.

Fuck, I have to say it.

I can say it.

I'm capable of fun and dirty and uninhibited.

I was once.

I will get back there.

My heart thuds against my chest.

My fingers dig into the plastic.

My gaze stays on the floor.

"I was thinking… that I want to suck you off."

EMMA

My heart thuds so loudly, I hear it between my ears.

It's the only thing I can hear.

It overpowers the air-conditioning, the oven, the exhale falling from Hunter's lips.

For a second, he stares back at me.

His lips part.

His pupils dilate.

His hands go to my hips.

"Fuck, Em—" He kisses me hard.

I close my eyes.

Part my lips to make room for his tongue.

This is what I want.

Him claiming me.

Him out of his fucking mind.

I slide my hand into his hair to hold him close.

My hips rock against his.

His hands slip under my tank top. Up my stomach. Over my chest.

He toys with my nipples as he swirls his tongue around mine.

It's aggressive.

Impatient.

It's perfect.

But it's so much.

Too much.

I pull back with a sigh.

Stare up into his gorgeous blue eyes.

I really do trust him.

And if I trust him…

I should be able to do this.

I think I can do this.

Maybe.

I bring my hand to his wrist. Walk backward to lead him to the couch.

My calves hit the leather cushions.

His hands curl around my ass.

In one swift motion, he lifts me and sets me on the couch.

I push myself onto my knees. Press my palm against his chest. Drag the other over his torso.

Fuck, he feels good.

Wet.

Warm.

Hard.

I savor the feel of his soft skin against my fingertips.

Then I bring my hand lower.

To the rough waistband of his boxers.

Slowly, I push the garment off his hips.

My eyes go wide.

He really is huge.

It's more obvious this close.

And, God, he really is close.

I want to wrap my hand around him.

And run a million miles away.

This is everything I want.

And everything that terrifies me.

I swallow hard. Look up at him as I brush my palm against his tip.

His eyelids press together.

A sigh falls off his lips.

"Fuck."

God, that feels good.

This is Hunter.

My...

He's really my boyfriend.

This is really...

Deep breath.

Slow exhale.

I'm in control here.

As long as I'm in control, I can do this.

I press my lips to his chest.

He groans as I pump him. "Em."

My name rolls off his lips like poetry.

It makes my sex clench.

Makes my nipples ache.

God, I already want to come again.

But I want this more.

I want this so fucking badly.

I run my thumb over his tip.

Revel in the groan that falls off his lips.

I try a little to the left, the right, the top, the bottom.

Harder.

Faster.

Slower.

Softer.

I study him like he's a work of art.

He is.

And this...

Fuck, it feels so good watching pleasure spread over his expression.

Deep breath.

Steady exhale.

I can do this.

I really, really want to do this.

Slowly, I shift off the couch.

Onto my knees.

He looks down at me with reverence.

Hunter shudders as my lips brush his stomach.

I drag them lower.

Lower.

There.

My lips brush his tip.

He tastes good. Like soap and like Hunter.

I stare up at him as I take him into my mouth.

Fuck, it's been a long time since I've done this.

I'm rusty.

Awkward.

But technique isn't what I need.

I need to study his reactions.

To figure *him* out.

And figure me out too.

I take my time tasting every inch of him.

Then testing different speeds.

Different strokes.

Swirls of my tongue.

The top of his tip.

The bottom.

"Fuck, Em."

God, the way he says my name is perfect.

That's what I need.

Us connecting.

Nothing in the way.

I wrap my hand around his cock.

Then I bring my mouth to his tip.

Toy with him until his groan is bouncing around the room.

Then I take him deeper.

Deeper.

As deep as I can manage.

He's big. Even with my hand, I can't cover him completely.

So I use my hand like an extension of my mouth.

Stroke him as I drag my mouth over him again and again.

One of his hands curls into my hair. It settles onto the back of my head.

Guiding.

I swallow to relax my throat.

He groans as I take him deeper.

Move faster.

Then he's tugging at my hair.

Pushing the back of my head.

Not guiding.

Pushing.

I…

I can't.

I pull back.

Force my lips together.

Force my voice to steady. "Softer."

He nods with hazy eyes.

But there's something in his gaze.

The magic disappears.

He's not lost in this. In me.

He's aware something is wrong.

That I'm…

Fuck.

I swallow hard.

I am doing this.

We're doing this.

"I don't like it rough." It's a reasonable enough explanation. And it's true. I was never into that. Even before… ahem.

I close my eyes.

Bring all my attention to this.

To Hunter's heavy breath.

And his soft touch.

His fingers curl into my shoulder.

It's gentle. Impossibly gentle.

He's reassuring me.

I hate that he has to.

But right now…

I need to do this.

I open my eyes.

Stare up at him.

I brush my lips against his tip.

Then I take him into my mouth. Wrap my hand around him.

He watches me carefully for a moment.

Then he relaxes. Lets go of the doubt creeping into his head.

His eyes close.

His lips part.

His fingers curl into my skin.

I take him as deep as I can.

Then I pull back and do it again.

He loses himself in me.

It's fucking beautiful.

It's fucking everything.

His groans fill the room as I work him.

They get louder. Lower. Deeper.

Then they run together.

And his fingers dig into my skin.

It's hard.

But not in an *I'm pushing you* way.

More in *I can't control my hands because you're driving me out of my mind* way.

"Fuck, Em."

His cock pulses.

I wait until he spills every drop, then I swallow hard.

He blinks his eyes open and stares down at me with that same hazy expression.

Like I'm some angel sent to save him.

I'm not.

I can barely save myself.

But it still feels good believing it.

Believing that there aren't any ugly complications on the horizon.

HUNTER

After too many cupcakes and lots of TV, Emma and I climb into her bed.

I wrap my arms around her.

Hold her all fucking night.

Fall asleep next to her.

It's nearly perfect.

Even if I wake up with fear in my gut.

I want to believe I'm a worthwhile guy.

That I deserve her.

That there isn't any legitimate reason for Brendon—or anyone else—to object to this relationship.

But I'm not there yet.

And this is it.

The day her family returns.

The day our world dissolves.

I don't want it to change anything—this is paradise—but it might.

That's how life works.

It's hard, tearing myself away from her.

I want to lie here all day.

I want to die in her fucking bed.

But that's an actual possibility.

If Brendon walks in on us like this—

That can't happen.

I brush my teeth, dress, fix coffee for both of us.

The gym is more quiet than usual.

Or maybe my thoughts are louder.

My head is tuned to Emma. To the way she blushes when I tease her, the way her eyes light up when she tastes a perfect cupcake, the way she groans when she comes.

There's a lot I love about Emma.

But now that I've seen her come—

Fuck, it's impossible to think about anything else.

She owns my thoughts through my entire workout. On my walk home. As I enter the Kane place.

The house is buzzing with laughter and conversation.

She and Kaylee are sitting on the couch, sharing a cupcake, oversized mugs of coffee in front of them.

Thank fuck Brendon isn't here.

I'm not sure I can handle his stare.

I want to scream this from the mountaintops.

I want the entire world to know how much I adore her.

Her cheeks flush as her eyes meet mine.

It makes my heart warm.

Fills me someplace that's usually empty.

Her joy is mine.

And, God, seeing her with her best friend, downing coffee and chocolate, tapping her fingers along with her favorite emo album—

It's so fucking Em.

It's everything.

"Hey." Her eyes find mine.

"Hey." It's all I can say. I'm not articulate. I'm too fixed on her.

She turns to her best friend. "You've met Hunter before, right Kay?"

Kaylee looks the same as always. Long champagne-blond hair, green eyes, and powder blue glasses.

She's wearing a dress straight out of a *Mad Men* episode, this grey and purple thing with a Peter Pan collar.

Fuck, how do I know what a Peter Pan collar is?

"Yeah." Kaylee stands. Smooths her dress. Glides across the room.

I almost expect her to curtsy.

She radiates regal energy.

"Nice to see you again, Kaylee." I shake her hand.

She shakes with a firm grip. "You too." She turns back to Emma. "Emma talks about you a lot."

"Brendon talks about you a lot," I say.

She blushes. "Anything bad?"

"Dirty, maybe. But not bad," I say.

Emma holds out her hand *stop*. "Don't with that. I've had enough of it… uh, for the last year."

"He brought it up." Kaylee shrugs.

Emma shakes her head *I know better*.

Kaylee laughs and returns to the couch.

They trade whispers.

It's sweet.

Cute.

Right.

I'm glad Emma has all this love in her life.

She deserves it.

She deserves the fucking world.

I don't know Kaylee all that well, but I can tell she's good to Emma.

That's what matters.

"Em was just telling me about the apartment you found." Kaylee crosses her legs and smooths her dress.

They exchange a look that gets both of them giggling.

"It's really nice," Emma says. "There's another open house today. We should go. Sign the papers."

"You need me to play your boyfriend again?" I ask.

Emma and Kaylee exchange another look.

"Long story," Emma says.

Kaylee shakes her head knowingly.

Fuck, they're cute.

So teenage girl.

'Cause they are teenage girls.

Emma is nineteen. A kid just starting her life.

And she...

Fuck, I'm not doing this right now.

She wants me.

I care about her.

I'd do anything for her.

Even convince myself this relationship makes sense every day, forever. As long as I have logic on my side, it's happening.

One day, I'll be there. Believe I'm a guy with value. Believe I'm good enough for her.

Not yet.

But one day.

Upstairs, a door swings open. Steady footsteps move into the hallway.

Brendon steps onto the stairs, his hair wet, his black t-shirt sticking to his skin.

He shoots his girlfriend a panty-melting look.

Emma makes a show of feigning gagging.

Kaylee's expression gets apologetic. "Sorry. I forget."

"Uh huh." Emma makes air quotes. "Forget."

"He's just so..." Kaylee's cheeks flush as she gawks at her boyfriend.

"Please stop." Emma hides behind her hands. "Didn't you two spend your trip having sex?"

"We were staying with my parents!" Kaylee says.

"So now I'm going to have to spend the next few weeks listening to you have sex?" Emma scrunches her nose in distaste.

"Imagine if you had your own place." Brendon raises a brow.

"Yeah. Imagine if I had a brother who respected boundaries," Emma says.

"Well, actually," Kaylee starts.

"Please don't," Emma stops her.

Brendon descends the stairs and greets me with a hug. "You survive my sister?"

"Barely," Emma says from the couch. "I think I drove him crazy."

"But you made lasagna. So I forgive you," I say.

Her smile gets goofy.

Kaylee whispers something in her ear.

Emma nods.

"She doing okay?" he asks.

"I'm right here." Emma folds her arms over her chest. Makes a show of pouting.

He turns to her. "You doing okay, Em?"

"Thank you for asking, Brendon. I'm a little overworked and under caffeinated, but I'm good." She smiles.

He and Kaylee share a look.

"You sound like a cyborg," Kaylee says.

"But I meant the thing about caffeine." She stands and offers her friend her hand. "The place on Abbot Kinney?"

"Mmm." Kaylee takes her hand. Lets Emma help her up. "Genius. Then the apartment?"

Emma nods.

Kaylee waves goodbye to her boyfriend.

He takes her hand, pulls her into a hug.

Then she's rising to her tiptoes and he's leaning in and they're kissing like they'll never get enough.

Emma shoots me a *can you believe this shit?* look.

Brendon releases Kaylee.

Emma grabs her. "Leaving now." She takes a step toward the door. "Love you."

It's meant for her brother, but fuck, it still feels good hearing those words on her lips.

"Love you too." He nods a goodbye then turns back to me. The softness in his expression fades to an intense concern.

"Is Emma okay?" he asks.

My pulse races.

It's one thing convincing myself I deserve Emma when it's the two of us.

When she's staring at me like I'm the sun in her sky—

When she's unfurling for me—

Then, I can see all the evidence.

It makes sense.

With Brendon staring at me like I'm supposed to be her knowing babysitter—

Fuck, I don't know what to say.

I don't even know what to think.

"She's a good kid." That's true. Sure, there's something wrong. Something she won't tell me. But it's not like I can say *she's cagey about sex sometimes. I think something happened. There was this asshole at her old apartment. I have a bad feeling about him.*

Even if I could share that without the part about her sucking me off—

It's not mine to tell.

"She give you a hard time?"

"A little," I say. "But it was good. Nice to hang with a normal person."

He nods with understanding. "And you?" *Are you staying sober?*

"Yeah." It's been hard. But less so the more time I spend with

346

her. It's not that she's my new drug. More that she makes it easier to see why I need to stay sober. She makes me see all the good in the world. "It's hard sometimes, but yeah." I run my fingers through my hair. Fuck, I need a shower. And a confession box.

"Did you tell anyone?"

"Yeah. Emma figured it out."

"Oh." Surprise drips into his voice. "Did I make it obvious?"

"No. It just came up."

"Is that okay?"

"Yeah."

His brow relaxes. "Good." He pats me on the shoulder. "Thanks for taking care of her."

"Sure."

"Really. I know she's a brat, but she's all the family I've got."

I nod.

"You're a good guy, Hunter."

He might as well say *you betrayed me, you piece of shit.*

But I smile back anyway.

EMMA

Kaylee presses her hands into the railing and looks toward the beach. "You can see the ocean."

"I know."

"I can smell the salt."

"Our house is on the beach."

"Yeah, but this will be ours." She puts an emphasis on the last word. So we both know that she and I are still our own *our*.

That it's still us against the world.

Even if the world sometimes involves my brother.

"I can see it." She turns back to the living room. Draws an outline of our couch. Then our TV.

"A big overflowing bookshelf." I point to the corner.

"Yeah." She pulls the door wider and motions *after you*.

I step inside.

She follows. Closes the balcony door. "Some cacti maybe."

"Since when do you want plants?"

"Since we got a balcony."

I nod *fair enough*. Point to the shiny counters in the kitchen. "That fancy tea kettle there."

"Next to—what was it Hunter made you this morning?"

"A pour over."

She laughs.

"What?" I know I love coffee, but she rarely mocks me for that. She's equally obsessed with tea.

"You're so into him."

I motion *a little*.

She shakes her head and motions *a lot*.

"He's really—"

"Hot."

"Yeah. But sweet too. Caring."

"It was written over both your faces."

"Oh."

She looks me in the eyes. Shakes her head.

She doesn't have to say it.

We both get it.

Brendon doesn't know.

Yet.

He can be oblivious.

But he can be smart too.

He'll realize soon.

"You okay keeping it a secret?" I ask.

"Yeah, but it won't stay a secret that long." She presses her lips together. They're a soft shade of pink. It's girly and sweet and perfect for her. "It's obvious."

"Still."

"Of course, Em. Anything you say is ours."

"Okay."

She moves through the hallway. Into the first bedroom. "I can really see us here."

"There's a pool."

"Shut up."

I take her hand and lead her into the other room.

She trots to the mirror. Presses her nose to the glass. "Oh my God."

"Right?"

"It's… it's really nice."

"Yeah."

"But, um… our last place was nice too." She clears her throat. "I'm fine moving. I just… Are you?"

"Yeah."

"We're only half a mile from the old place."

"I know."

"Is that enough distance?"

The entire planet isn't enough distance. But—"I'm not letting my life revolve around it."

She makes that *hmmm* noise that means she doesn't believe me. "Emma…"

Fuck, it's bad.

She's calling me Emma.

"Does Hunter know?" she asks.

"Know what?" I play dumb.

She opens the window. Inhales like she's trying to smell the chlorine from up here. "You don't have to admit it out loud."

"Okay."

"I don't want to push you. Really."

"I know. I just—"

"Did you have sex?" She turns back to me, her green eyes wide. Earnest.

Fuck, she looks so innocent.

In some ways she is.

I'm glad she's never been through it.

But it means she doesn't get it.

No matter how hard she tries.

"Hunter and I?" I ask.

"No, you and Dean." She shoots me a *seriously* look.

"He and Chloe are official."

"They could be into threesomes."

"Over her dead body."

She nods *true*. "Did you?"

"He ate me out."

"Yeah?" Her eyes light up.

It's like when we were in high school, gossiping about guys without a care in the world.

I nod a yeah.

"And?" She play swats me. "Emma Kane, you better not be withholding details!"

"He was… skilled."

"That's it?"

"I sucked him off too."

"Yeah?" Her voice gets bouncy. Excited. "And?"

"He's huge."

"So you didn't—"

"We didn't have condoms."

"You know you can still get an STD from oral."

"Thank you, Mom." I clear my throat. She's right, of course. But—"We discussed that."

"And?"

"He got tested while he—" I can't say he was in rehab. That's his business. "He got tested a few months ago. And he hadn't been with anyone for a while."

"Really?"

"Yeah." I press my lips together. "And you know, I haven't… since Vinnie. And we used a condom. So…"

"Emma."

"Can we not?"

She shakes her head.

"It's… it's not a big deal."

She says nothing, but it's written all over her face.

It is a big deal. A huge deal.

And I'm not selling my apathy.

Not even a little.

I move into the hallway. Find some sort of response. Something to say besides *I know it's pathetic that I can't admit I was raped. But I can't.* "This um. It has a really nice bathroom."

"I remember." She follows me into said bathroom.

Which doesn't help me run away from this.

The shower makes me think of that night.

Of trying so hard to scrub it all away.

Of her finding me pruned and crying.

Her voice is soft. "You don't have to admit it, Em. But please stop pretending like it's not a big deal."

"Okay."

"I don't want to scold you. I... I hate this." She brings her hands to my shoulders. "I hate this so much. I hate that he hurt you. I want to kill him."

"Me too."

"It's still hurting you. I hate that the most."

"It's..."

"If you say it's not, I'm going to slam you into that wall."

"Are you into that now?"

"No." She laughs. "Maybe if we switch positions—"

"Gross."

"Brendon could—"

"Ew."

"We'll probably have sex in here."

"Don't need to hear that."

"Against the wall," she adds.

"Nuh nuh nuh nuh nuh. I can't hear you."

She laughs.

I do too.

It helps.

It pushes this further away.

Reminds me there's good in the world.

"Are you going to tell Hunter?" she asks.

I sit on the edge of the tub. Press my knees together. "I don't know. He… he shared stuff with me."

"Yeah?"

"He was scared about it. That I'd think of him differently."

"Did you?"

"Yeah. But in a good way. I understood him more."

She sits next to me. Places her hand next to mine. "It feels good, letting someone in."

"Yeah. When you told me about all that stuff last year… I was hurt at first. That you didn't think I'd accept that."

"I know."

"But that was my fault. Not yours."

"I did keep my relationship with your brother a secret."

"Yeah. But even so… It was never about me. I needed to see that. I just…"

"You're not sure he will?"

"Maybe." That's part of it. Guys can get really defensive. And I love that. I love the idea that Hunter would punch the asshole who hurt me. That he'd do anything to protect me. But—"I don't want him to see me differently."

"Why would he?"

"He's going to think I'm a victim."

"Do you?"

"No… I don't know…" Sometimes. But I hate that word. I hate the sympathy and vulnerability that come with it. I hate everything about it.

"You get to define who you are, Em."

"Yeah, but I can't control what he thinks."

She nods. "You trust him?"

I nod. "I want to tell him… I think I have to." My fingers dig into the ceramic. "Sex isn't the same."

"Not good?"

"No. It's good. But I… it's around the edges. When we were…"
I clear my throat. "He got aggressive."

"Yeah?" Her voice is soft. Caring.

It's like her.

But I hate it.

"Can you say something dirty about it?" I tap my toes against
the tile floor. "Please?"

"Aggressive how? Like grabbing you? Or spankings? Or
fucking your mouth?"

"Oh my God. Mental images!"

"Because that can be really hot."

"Ew."

"If he's holding you in place and—"

"Oh my God, stop." I make a point of covering my ears.

But she doesn't. "And he's going so deep you can barely take it.
Staring at you with this intense look that screams *you're mine*."

Disgusting.

So disgusting.

But exactly what I need to hear to make this better.

"He was pushing the back of my head," I say.

She tries to keep it light. "Hot."

But my head won't go there. "Yeah. It was. But then, it was
like… I could just feel *his* hands and I… I had to stop it."

"Did he—"

"He did. He was cool about it. Like it was just a preference.
But then… I don't know. He must know something is up."

"It's yours to tell."

"Yeah. But… I… I want to fuck him so badly."

"I get that."

My gaze shifts to my wedges. "I'm not sure I can."

"You don't have to do it now."

"I do."

She laughs. "You *can* wait."

"Yeah…"

"Or tell him what to expect."

I shake my head.

"Seems like it's waiting then."

My nose scrunches.

She laughs.

"Can we be done talking about this?"

She nods.

"Tell me about your trip."

"I'm going to mention how much my parents cunt-blocked us."

"Oh my God, Kay, I swear… Since when do you say cunt?"

"Since your brother."

"When… you know, I don't want to know."

"I wasn't going to tell you."

"I don't believe you."

"Well, I mean… if you want to know that badly." Her smile is sweet.

It feels good, having her in my corner.

But thinking about telling Hunter.

About not knowing how he'll take it—

That's fucking terrifying.

EMMA

For the better part of a week, Hunter and I make do with stolen moments.

Touching hands while we're making dinner.

Getting a little too close while we're watching TV.

Staying at work late so we can make out in the back room.

As soon as Kaylee and I are approved for our apartment, Hunter lobbies for us to tell Brendon.

It's a reasonable idea.

Except for the fact I have no idea how my brother will react.

What if he kicks Hunter out? Or lobbies for his dismissal from Inked Hearts? Or hurts him enough to send him straight to a bottle?

There's no reason to risk that.

To risk us.

Not when our world is about to open up.

It's only two days until Kaylee and I move into the new place.

A place where there's all the room in the world for me and Hunter.

For us to *celebrate* my independence properly.

If I can handle it.

God, I hope I can handle it.

"Em, babe, tell me this is yours?" Wes steps into the living room with two enormous cardboard boxes in his arms.

They go all the way to his mouth, but I can still tell he's smiling.

He's ridiculous.

"Why would that matter?" I slice through the packing tape with a pair of scissors.

"'Cause I'll see your room."

"It's empty."

"Can still imagine you there."

"Doing what?"

"What girls do in their rooms." He takes two steps toward me. "This shit's heavy."

"Did the big black words reading Bathroom not give it away?" I tease.

He shakes his head. "Never know what kind of games you're playing with me."

"It belongs in the bathroom."

"Damn. What a loss."

"You can imagine me showering."

"With a detachable showerhead." He raises a brow.

I... Oh. My blush deepens.

Wes winks, turns, moves to the bathroom.

Those boxes are heavy—I couldn't pick up one of them—but he moves with ease. Sets them down softly. Jumps back into the hallway.

It's just in time for Griffin to step inside.

I guess today is my first time meeting Hunter's friend. He's

BREAKING THE RULES

different than anyone else I know. Mostly quiet. Exceedingly honest. Good at giving Wes shit.

He's hot. Tall and broad with dark tattoos and darker features. There's intensity in his eyes, but there's joy too. He's not quite on the Brendon or Hunter tier of brooding.

He nods a hello. Sets my bright red suitcase on the carpet. "Which room is yours?"

"How'd you know?"

He motions to my bright red nails. "Brendon told me."

"Fuck Brendon." Dean steps inside, his arms wrapped around an enormous box. "I'm the one directing this shit."

"Lord help us." Chloe follows him inside. She nods a hello and holds up a takeout iced coffee.

"Is that what I think it is?" I ask.

She nods. "Courtesy of Hunter." Her dark eyes light up. She sets the drink on the counter. Raises her eyebrows.

She's trying to be subtle, but it's not really her strong suit.

"Thanks." My fingers curl around the plastic. Mmm. Iced Americano. Is there anything better?

"He was insistent on bringing it right away." She takes a sip from her takeout cup. Lets out a sigh of pleasure.

"Sunshine, you keep doing that, I'm gonna take you right here." He nods to the kitchen counter then moves into the living room and sets the box in the corner.

"Right here?" Her eyes lock with his.

"You prefer another spot?" He motions to the balcony. "So everyone on the street can see us?"

Her cheeks flush.

"Personally, I think it's wrong you're depriving the world of the beauty of our lovemaking."

"Personally, I think you're an idiot," she says.

"We all do," Griffin adds.

Dean ignores him. "Em's room has a mirrored closet."

Chloe blushes.

359

Griffin rolls his eyes *this again* then moves down the hallway.

I guess I should be more helpful. And less lost in daydreams of coffee and perfect boyfriends. "No sex in my apartment."

"Em, how could you?" Dean teases.

"You gonna invite her?" Wes asks.

Dean shoots Chloe a *you into that* look.

She shakes her head. "No offense, Em."

"None taken. I know you're more into blondes."

She laughs. "That's exactly it." She and Dean share a look.

He crosses the room to her. Wraps his arms around her. Spins her. Actually spins her.

She giggles as she wraps her arms around his neck. Then whispers an *I love you* in his ear.

He whispers it back.

It's sweet.

Which is weird.

Since when is Dean sweet?

Wes shakes his head. "All that affection is disgusting, huh?"

"Jealousy isn't attractive." Griffin steps into the living room. Crosses to Wes. Musses his hair.

Wes slaps his hand away and shoots him a death glare.

Griffin lets out a low, hearty chuckle. "Can you tell he's trying to get in your pants?"

"You wouldn't fit." I tug at the belt loop of my skinny jeans.

"Had that problem before." Wes laughs.

Oh, God. I set him up for that perfectly.

Am I really that out of it?

"Just need time and tenderness and a little lube. Anything for you." He winks as he moves out the door.

Griffin follows with a *you're ridiculous* head shake. Though he seems entertained by Wes's antics.

"You've got competition." I turn to Dean. "He might be more obnoxious than you are."

Dean motions being stabbed in the gut.

Chloe giggles.

Then he plays it up. Stumbles backward. Falls onto his ass. Splays out like he's dead.

It's Dean.

Entertaining.

But—"You here to help or to make a fool of yourself?"

"Dean's always here to make a fool of himself." She crouches next to him. Reaches for his pocket. "Should we raid his stuff?"

I nod.

She slips her hand into his front pocket.

He looks up at her. "Fuck, I feel like Sleeping Beauty in a porno. Skipping the foreplay?"

She laughs. "Yeah, I'm going to give you a hand job right here."

"I'd rather fuck you. But if that's what you want…" He turns to me with a shrug. "Sorry, Em. But I can't deny my girl—"

"Girl?"

He nods.

"I'm not a girl."

"You prefer woman?"

"Yeah."

"Can't deny my woman."

"You will deny her." I point to the door. "Carry more things."

He jumps—actually jumps—to his feet.

Chloe stands with him. Kisses him goodbye.

Then he moves out the door.

She turns to me with an apologetic shrug.

"I know, I know. You're madly in love and he has that Prince Albert." I try to sound annoyed, but I'm not. They're cute. And their affection is palpable. I want that for them. I want the world happy and in love.

I'm one of those sappy idiots I used to mock.

"He didn't bring it up," she says.

"That's growth."

Her eyes get dreamy. She shakes off her mental images of her boyfriend's dick and turns to me. "You want me unpacking or bringing in boxes?"

"Do I have to separate you and Dean to get you to behave?"

"Not sure anything can get him to behave."

Probably true. "You really like him, huh?"

Her smile gets as dreamy as her eyes. "He's a good guy. And—"

"The massive cock."

"It doesn't hurt."

"Does it ever?"

She laughs. "If I try to move too fast."

"He doesn't make sure you're—"

"Sometimes I'm impatient."

"I know the feeling."

Right on cue, Hunter steps inside. He's holding a coffee tray with four drinks—two light iced things, two hot beverages.

He nods a hello.

Chloe shoots me a knowing look.

My cheeks flush. She's known about my crush on Hunter for a long time. But not so much about our relationship.

"Why don't you deliver these?" I suggest.

She nods a sure and takes the tray from Hunter.

He grabs the iced drink on the right.

"That a vanilla latte?" I tease.

"You tell me." He offers me a sip.

It's not a vanilla latte, but it is awfully sweet and creamy. "Are you feeling okay?"

"No." He looks behind us. Checks the coast is clear. Then he sets his drink on the counter, wraps his arms around my waist, leans in to kiss me.

Fuck, he tastes good, like sugar and coffee.

But this is such a bad idea.

Brendon is supposed to stay with the moving truck. He and Kaylee are in charge of that half of operations.

Hunter and I are in charge of this half.

But what if he needs a break? Or water? Or the bathroom?

Concern flits through my brain.

Then Hunter's tongue slips into my mouth, and all that concern fades.

This is what matters.

Nothing else matters.

I still jump at the sound of footsteps.

Wes steps into the apartment with a heavy box in his arms. He looks at us and shakes his head *so obvious*.

Griffin follows him inside. He and Wes share a look, then he turns to Hunter. "You might want to skip the lipstick if you're gonna try to hide this thing you're doing."

My cheeks flush. "Oh. I…"

"Fuck, Grif, do you listen to yourself?" Wes shakes his head. "You're not supposed to articulate these thoughts."

He shakes his head *what good will that do* and sets the box down in the corner.

Wes's expression gets apologetic. "You do look good in red, Hunter."

Hunter blushes. His fingers go to his lips. "That bad?"

"No. You're definitely a spring," Wes says. "You could even handle a lighter red. Coral maybe."

Hunter shoots Griffin a *what is he talking about* look.

Griffin shrugs.

"It's a fashion thing," I say. "Your features map to a season. I… it doesn't matter." Hunter is wearing a little of my lipstick. And he totally could pull it off if he wanted to go that way. "I can wear the stuff that won't kiss off."

"Don't." He leans in and brushes his lips to mine. "I like tasting you on my lips."

"Fuck, I hope he's not talking about lipstick." Wes sets his box next to Griffin's.

Griffin just shakes his head. *What's wrong with you two?*

He's right.

363

We're going to tell my brother about this eventually.

Until then…

"We should probably cool it while he's downstairs," I say.

Hunter's eyes turn down. But he still nods. "Yeah." He goes to kiss me again. Stops himself. "Good thing you're the smart one."

"Too much blood in your muscles," I say.

"One in particular," he says.

Wes chuckles.

Griffin too.

I just blush.

And, well, check for confirmation of his claims.

The bulge in his jeans is inviting.

But now is so not the time.

Wes and Griffin shake their heads as they walk out the door.

Which leaves us alone.

I look up at Hunter. Press my palms into my sides so I won't touch him. "Can I trust you to stay here and help unpack?"

"Yeah." He wipes the lipstick from his mouth with his thumb. "But you can't give me that look."

"Which one."

"That one."

"I'm not."

"You are."

I shake my head. "I'm just looking."

"Maybe that's enough." He drops his voice to a whisper. "I need more of you."

"Me too."

He brushes a stray hair behind my ear. "Tonight?"

"It will be late."

He nods.

"I'll be exhausted."

"You won't have to move."

"Just lie there and starfish?"

"I was thinking more that I'd hold you. But yeah. If that's what you're into."

I shake my head.

"Guess I'll have to come bearing coffee."

"You're prefect."

"I do what I can."

41

HUNTER

Usually, moving is a nightmare. But this is different. More like a party.

Yeah, it's torture keeping my hands off Em. Watching her bend to unpack boxes or suck coffee from her straw or reach for something on a high shelf.

But it's everything having my friends here. Wes and Griffin showing up to help someone they barely know just because I asked.

It's a long day. The guys from Inked Hearts work in shifts—someone has to be at the shop.

Everyone stops by to lend a hand or drop off a housewarming present.

The place swells with love and support.

It warms me everywhere, knowing Emma has that.

I don't even care that we're keeping this a secret. That it could explode at any moment.

Only that she's mine.

A LITTLE PAST TEN, I KNOCK ON EMMA'S DOOR.

There's whispering inside. Then giggling. Footsteps.

Emma pulls the door open.

Her dark eyes fix on mine. Fill with love and affection.

She wraps her arms around me, rises to her tiptoes, presses her lips to mine.

My fingers curl into her hips as I kiss her back.

It's been too long.

Way too fucking long.

Her sigh is heavy. Needy. "Come in."

I do.

Kaylee is sitting on the couch, watching TV.

"I interrupt?" I ask.

"No." Kaylee stands. "I was just about to head out."

"You don't have to." Emma shoots her best friend a look.

"No, I do. I have a ton of work to catch up on and the library is open until midnight." She motions to the hallway. "I'll be two minutes."

Emma nods. Turns back to me with wide eyes and a wider smile. "I was promised coffee."

I motion to the gift bag in my left hand.

She claps. "Let me see."

"You're supposed to accept gifts with grace."

"Fuck that." She claps again. "I love presents."

"Your place is packed with them."

She laughs. "Can you even tell which boxes are new?" She motions to a row of half unpacked boxes lining the living room wall. Then to another on the kitchen counter.

No one would accuse the apartment of Martha Stewart perfection.

It's barely unpacked.

And a mess.

And completely Emma.

Of course, the TV, couch, and mugs are all in their proper place.

I set the purple gift bag on the counter.

"Can I?"

I nod.

She pulls out the cream paper with glee. Her brow furrows with concentration as she reaches in. Runs her fingers over the gift.

She looks to me *what is it?*

I shrug *open it and find out.*

A laugh falls from her lips as she pulls out the box. "Perfect."

She sets the pour over on the counter.

"There's more," I say.

"I'd hope so." She peers inside the bag. Pulls out the scale. The electric grinder. The bag of single-origin beans. "It's an involved process."

"Some things are worth extra effort."

Her eyes meet mine. They say something, but I'm not sure what it is. Only that I want it.

Fuck, it's weird how much I want every thought in her head.

How much I want to pry her open.

She slides her arm around my waist. Rises to her tiptoes to press her lips to mine. "Thank you, Hunter."

"My pleasure." I rest my palm on her cheek. Rub her temple with my thumb. She's so fucking beautiful. I'm not sure I'll ever get tired of staring at her.

"Is it safe to come out?" Kaylee calls from the hallway.

"No. I'm completely naked," Emma teases.

Kaylee shakes her head as she steps into the main room. She hugs her best friend goodbye. "You're ridiculous."

"You love it," Emma says.

"I do." Kaylee waves a goodbye to me. "Take care of her."

"I will," I say.

Emma and her friend exchange a look.

Then Kaylee leaves.

And I get all of Emma's attention.

"I got you something too," she says.

"Yeah?"

She nods and grabs something from the drawer. Then she sets a box of condoms on the counter.

I can't help but laugh. "That's for me?"

"Yeah."

"Not us?"

"'I got you something' sounds so much better than 'I got us something.'"

I bring my hand to her hip. "Either way, I love it."

"Really?"

"Yeah, you shouldn't have."

"Hmm?"

"That one doesn't work here."

"It really doesn't."

My fingers curl into her skin as I kiss her. She tastes so fucking good and I can feel all this need pouring between us.

It's been too long.

I need to touch her.

To make her come.

To make love to her.

All that cheesy that only exists in pop songs.

She sighs as she breaks our kiss. "Give me a minute. I want to change."

"You look gorgeous." Too gorgeous. I'm ready to tear off her jeans.

"Even so." She grabs the box of condoms and takes a step backward. "Pour a... a drink, I guess."

"Water is a drink."

"Okay." She laughs. "Pour a water." She spins on her heels and disappears down the hallway.

It's sweet, her wanting to make this special.

But it's not necessary.

It's Em.

It's already perfect.

A sultry slow jam spills from Emma's room as I fill a glass with water. It gets louder.

Loud enough to set the mood without waking the neighbors.

The mood doesn't need setting.

But I appreciate the effort.

I've never been in a relationship where either one of us makes an effort.

There is something special about trying to make it special.

I really fucking like it.

Her door creeks open. "Come in."

I move down the hallway. Then into her room.

It's as messy as the rest of the apartment, and as Emma. The lyric covered desk, the posters of hot musicians, the crimson bedspread, the mirrored closet door.

And her.

Standing in front of the bed in black lingerie.

Sheer lace stretches over her sides and chest. Black satin skims her stomach and hips.

That thing barely covers her ass.

"You like it?" Her voice is shy.

Blood flees my brain at an alarming rate.

She swallows hard. "Is that a yes?"

"Fuck yes." I push the door closed.

She stares back at me.

Shy. Nervous.

It's flattering as hell.

But it won't do.

I need to set her at ease. "You buy that for me, baby?"

Her nod is heavy. "Made me think of you."

"You look fucking gorgeous."

"Yeah?" The skirt flies up as she spins on the balls of her feet.

She's wearing another scrap of lace under it.

Some tiny thing that shows off her perfect ass.

Fuck, I need my hands on her.

I'm impatient as all hell.

But if she needs slow, I'm giving her slow.

"You're torturing me, baby."

Her cheeks flush. She steps backward. Sits on the bed. Pats the spot next to her. "You think we should leave the lights on?"

"Yeah." I take the seat next to her. "I want to see every inch of you."

Her blush spreads down her chest. "I... I want this." Her eyelids flutter closed.

She digs her hand into my hair.

Presses her lips to mine.

Her kiss is hard. Hungry.

Her lips close around my top lip. Then it's the soft scrape of her teeth. Her tongue slipping into my mouth.

I rest my hand on her thigh.

She groans as I drag my fingertips up her leg.

Soft skin. Slick satin. Rough lace hem.

She pulls back with a sigh. "Hunter."

Fuck, my name sounds good on her lips.

I need more of that.

I need her lost in bliss.

I need her, period.

Her eyes blink open as I push her skirt up her legs. She stares up at me, begging for more.

I want to give her more.

Fuck, I want to give her everything.

But slowly.

We both need to savor it.

And, well—

I need to stay in control. To make sure she's okay every fucking step of the way.

I stare into her dark eyes as I drag my fingertips up her thigh. Over the slick fabric of her thong. Down her other thigh.

She spreads her legs a little wider.

I do it again. Up her thigh, over her panties, down her other thigh.

Her eyelids flutter together.

She arches her back. Tugs at my t-shirt to pull me into a deep, slow kiss.

I wrap one arm around her.

Slip the other between her legs.

She groans against my lips as I rub her over her panties.

I can feel her through the slick fabric.

She's wet.

Blood flees my brain.

I barely manage to hold onto control.

Her fingers dig into my chest, pressing the cotton of my t-shirt into my skin.

She tugs at my t-shirt. "Off."

I toss the thing over my head.

She lifts her hips to push her panties to her knees. "More." She presses her palm to my stomach. "Please."

My balls tighten.

I never thought I got off on women begging me.

But hearing *please* on Emma's lips—

Fuck.

I dig my fingers through her hair. Cup the back of her head with my palm.

She kisses me softly.

Slowly.

Then harder.

Faster.

Her tongue slides around mine.

She cups me over my jeans. Presses her palm against my cock, rubbing me through the fabric.

It's sweet torture.

I drag my fingertips up her thigh.

Slowly.

Until she's shaking with anticipation.

Until she's tugging at my hair like she's cursing my name.

She sighs as I bring my fingers to her clit. "Fuck."

Pleasure spills over her expression as I rub her.

A sigh falls from her lips.

Her fingers curl into the sheets.

Her lids get heavy.

I can't take my eyes off her.

She's too fucking beautiful.

I bring my fingers to the spot where she needs me. Move harder. Harder. There—

"Hunter," she breathes.

I keep that same speed and pressure.

Touch her just how she needs me.

Her groans get louder.

Lower.

Her breath hitches.

Everything runs together.

It's beautiful fucking music.

A hell of a lot better than the slow jam filling the room.

A hell of a lot better than anything.

A few more flicks of my fingers and she's there.

Her cunt pulses.

My name falls off her lips.

I rub her through her orgasm.

Give her a second to catch her breath.

Then I bring her to the edge again.

Her groans are agony as much as they're ecstasy.

Then they're all ecstasy.

They're beautiful fucking ecstasy.

She comes quickly.

Screams my name like it's a curse.

Then she's fumbling over my zipper. Rubbing me over my boxers. Driving me out of my fucking mind.

She pushes my jeans off my hips.

I shimmy out of them.

She grabs the condom laying on the bedside table. Presses it in my palm.

I rip it open and roll it over my cock.

She lies back. Pulls her skirt to her waist. Spreads her legs.

She stares up at me, her dark eyes filled with need. "Please."

My fingers curl into her thighs.

Slowly, I lower my body onto hers.

I pull her closer.

Closer.

There.

My cock strains against her.

She grunts as I fill her.

Her fingers curl into my back. A *fuck, give me more.*

Then something else.

She's digging hard enough to draw blood.

But it's not 'cause she's losing herself in ecstasy.

She's still.

I brush her hair behind her ear. Stare into her eyes.

She nods. "Please." The word falls off her lips again and again.

I pull back.

Untangle our bodies.

She shakes her head. "Please, Hunter." She blinks and a tear catches on her lashes. "I need this to be okay. Please."

"Em—"

She shakes her head. "We need to… This needs to… Please."

"You're crying."

"I just…"

"What's wrong, baby?"

"I... I..." She turns away from me. So I can't see her expression.

But I can still feel her fear.

She's terrified.

I think I know why.

But this is not the fucking time to push her.

I offer her my hand.

She ignores it. "If we're not going to... then maybe you should just..."

"No."

"But..."

"You don't have to say anything."

She doesn't.

"But I'm not leaving you like this."

Her eyes flit to me. Her cheeks flame red. A mix of embarrassment and shame.

Fuck, I hate that she's hurting.

I want to take every ounce of that.

But I can't.

I can only do this.

I wrap my arms around her.

Pull her closer.

Hold her as she cries into my chest.

42

EMMA

For a long time, Hunter holds me.

The room fills with baby making R&B jams.

With his steady breath.

And my shaky exhale.

I keep my back to him. Keep my arms around my chest. Keep my eyes on the wall.

I still remember staring at the *Breathless* poster on his wall.

At reading the credits again and again.

Trying to make time go faster.

To make it stop.

It didn't help.

Only scarred me from ever watching *Breathless*.

Not that it really appealed to me.

Thankfully, my brother prefers action movies to new wave. For all his pretension about music, the guy has low standards when it comes to film.

Even Kaylee rarely dabbles in foreign cinema.

I'm never in danger of entering our place and coming face-to-face with a reminder. Not on the TV, at least.

It's there every time I look at my wrists.

Or a pastel pink lingerie set.

Or a glass of vodka.

Hell, sometimes it's there for no reason.

My mind is playing tricks on me. Out to get me. Impossibly against me.

The playlist ends.

Hunter slips out of bed. Goes to my desk. Picks up my cell. "You mind?"

"No."

"You want silence or music?"

"Music."

"Something you love?"

"Okay."

A moment later, a familiar song fills the room. The first one on my emo playlist.

Fuck, I hope it's a good idea listening to this now.

I can't lose something else I love.

I can't have that asshole connected to anything else.

He's already ruined sex.

He doesn't get music.

He doesn't get Hunter.

"Kay will be here soon." I pull the comforter to my chest. "I made the playlist two hours, so we'd know when we had to stop."

"Ambitious."

"Thanks." I try to laugh, but it doesn't happen. "I still think I could have made it."

"You've been watching too many superhero shows."

"Oh yeah?"

"Yeah." His laugh is stilted. Awkward. "I'm not your boyfriend Matt. I can't go all night."

"You know, he's really wasting his powers beating people up."

Hunter pulls on his boxers.

"You don't have to do that."

"I know." He sits on the bed. Reaches over. Runs his fingers over my shoulder. "What should Matt do with his powers?"

"He could be the lover of the century."

Hunter laughs. "Yeah, he could."

"That's a waste." Matt (otherwise known as Daredevil) can sense minute changes in another person's body enough to know if they've been poisoned. If he turned those skills to sex—the man would be an unstoppable orgasm machine.

This time, his laugh is big. Hearty. Free of the reminder I ruined our perfect night. "Some people don't understand their gifts." He lies next to me.

Shifts onto his side.

Wraps his arm around my waist.

I nestle into his chest.

The comforter is between us, but he still feels good. Strong. Warm. Safe.

I really do trust him to protect me.

But I guess no one can protect me from my head.

The song shifts to the next. To something louder. With thrashing guitars and growling vocals.

It's the perfect fit for my mood.

But that doesn't really help.

Hunter's chest heaves with his inhale.

I can't quite feel his heartbeat, but there's still something soothing about feeling his breath.

He's still here.

He knows a lot and he's here.

It's not going to be a surprise. He saw how freaked I got around Vinnie. And after that party. And earlier tonight.

But the words still refuse to find my lips.

It's too much. Too heavy. Too ugly.

"You don't have to talk, Em." He runs his fingers through my

379

hair. "You can tell me anything. But you don't have to."

"Ever?"

"If that's what you need."

I nod, though I don't believe it. I can't keep this hidden forever. I can barely handle it now. But—"I don't want you to think I'm pathetic or broken."

"I couldn't."

"You don't know that."

"Yeah, I do." His fingers skim my ear. My jawline. My neck. "I can see why you'd believe otherwise. But you're wrong."

I shake my head.

He nods. "You're the strongest person I know."

"You don't know a lot of people."

"We had a dozen here today."

"Still."

"I'm not as strong as—"

"I'm never gonna think that about you, baby."

"Oh." I swallow hard. I don't know what else to say. I'm not arguing him out of his opinion. But he… he doesn't know this.

"I want everything in your heart."

"What about the ugly things?"

"Especially the ugly things." He pulls me closer. "But I have time."

"I don't. I want to fuck you."

He chuckles. "You're gonna have to be patient."

"I hate being patient."

"I know."

I close my eyes. Soak in the softness of his touch. The warmth of his breath. The bounce of the bassline.

This is a good song.

But that doesn't help either.

I try to practice the words in my head, but they won't come. I can barely say it to myself. How will I ever admit it to anyone else? "I guess it's obvious."

"How much you love emo music? Yeah. But I still love you."

"You—"

"Fuck. I… I do. But that's not what—"

"You love me?"

"Yeah." His voice is soft. Steady. "I love you."

"Oh." Warmth breaks up the tension in my chest. It's weird. So fucking weird. Part of me is stiff and awkward. Another part wants to float.

"I didn't mean to say that."

"You don't want—"

"This is about you, baby. This is your space. I don't want to push you."

"Okay."

"You don't have to say it back."

"Okay." I swallow hard. "I never have before."

"Me either."

"Really?"

"Yeah."

"Oh. Well… thanks."

"You're welcome."

My laugh is awkward. "This is weird."

"Yeah."

"I… Is it obvious what happened?"

He shakes his head.

"Really?"

"Yeah."

"I… do I have to say it?"

"You don't have to do shit. But I'm not gonna guess. I'm not gonna do that to you."

"Oh." I pull the blanket over my head. This is so big. Bigger than anything else in the room.

I want to tell him.

I really do.

Deep breath.

Steady exhale.

One word at a time.

"I guess what I told you was half true." My heart thuds against my chest.

Then Hunter wraps his arm around me.

And I feel a little steadier.

Steady enough to do this.

I think. "I did like Vinnie. And we did have this flirtation. I… I really wanted to impress him. Then one day, I was at his place, and we were drinking. Wine at first. Then cheap vodka."

"I know the type."

"Yeah." I thought I did too. But I was wrong. "We started making out. He was a little pushy but it was okay. Just sloppy. I thought maybe he was drunk. That it would be better another time." I can still remember that awful mix of vodka and amaretto. Thinking *oh fuck, he's a bad kisser. Is this over already? A bad kisser is always a bad fuck.* "I liked him. I wanted him to kiss me. But that was all I wanted."

He nods.

"Only he… he didn't stop." I suck a breath through my teeth. "At first, I thought maybe he wasn't getting the hint."

Hunter rubs my shoulder through the blanket.

"That he was kinda oblivious. But after the third time I moved his hand from my thigh, I pulled back. Said I wanted to take things slow."

His breath fills the room.

"He seemed apologetic. He said sure. We went back to making out. I got into this debate in my head. If I should leave. But he seemed like he was respecting me, and we were both kinda drunk, so I figured… I don't know. I've hooked up with guys before. I've never had an issue. It didn't occur to me that I would."

"You shouldn't have to."

"Yeah. Maybe. I… I think I knew, deep down. But I was scared to admit that possibility to myself. Because it was easier believing that he was drunk. That I had good judgment. That I could extricate myself from the situation at any point." I press my lips together. "It all happened so fast. We were kissing. Then he was holding me down, against the couch, and I was pushing him off. Then I was saying no. Asking him to stop. But he wasn't listening."

"Em..."

"It really fucking hurt. So I stopped fighting." My fingers go to my wrist. To the spot that was bruised for weeks. "I closed my eyes and I tried to leave my body."

"Did it work?"

"Not really." Even now, I can feel the pressure of Vinnie's hand. The strain of my muscles. The sense that my bones might snap.

He didn't seem that strong at a glance. But he was.

He had fifty pounds on me, easily. He could have snapped me in half.

Hunter could too.

But I don't know...

Even though I trust him not to...

My head keeps going there.

"It was like... I was getting bits and pieces of it. I'd block it out for a few seconds. Then I'd feel it again. My head banging into the couch. Or his hands on my wrists. Or the tug of rubber. It hurt. More than when I was new and inexperienced and I didn't know about foreplay and lube. It was... I don't know how to explain it. But it even felt violent."

"That must have been terrifying."

"It was."

"You lived next to him all this time?"

"He traveled a lot for work. And I... I told myself it was a bad date. Bad sex. It was easier believing that than believing I'd been raped."

"Did it help?"

"For a while. But one day... I was in the laundry room alone. And he came down. I froze. I couldn't move. Couldn't say anything. Couldn't even think to grab my cell and call for help. I thought it was going to happen again."

"Did he—"

"No. He... He doesn't care or maybe he doesn't realize what he did. I don't know. Or care. I just had to be away from him."

"I'm sorry you went through that."

I don't know what to say, so I nod.

"It is obnoxious that I want to kill him?"

"Only if you go out and do it."

"Fuck, I would. If I was there. If I saw that."

"I think that's legal. Right. Defense of a third-party?"

"You been watching *Law and Order*?"

"Yeah. Especially the *SVU* one. There's something soothing about it. Like pressing on a bruise."

"I can see that."

"Really?"

"Yeah. I watch stuff about addicts sometimes. Remind myself other people go through this shit too."

I nod.

"You are strong. Dealing with all that alone."

I shake my head.

"And telling me." He pulls me closer. "Your trust means the world to me."

"Me too. I means yours does. I mean... Will you say it again?"

"What?"

"All the good things."

"I don't think you're broken." He presses his lips to mine. "But even if you were, I'd still love you."

"Yeah?"

"Yeah."

"It would be so perfect if we had sex right now."

He chuckles. "Yeah. But I'm not that easy."

43

EMMA

I'm distracted at school.

And at work.

Hunter is there. Sitting on a stool. Tattooing a flower on a pretty girl's ankle. Laughing at something she's saying. Shooting me sweet glances.

I want to collapse in his arms.

And drag him to the back room.

And run away from the reminder that I still can't handle my shit.

We go to the gym together. He comes over. Helps with dinner. And with my art history.

We watch TV until Kaylee complains about the superhero shit. (She's super tactful about it).

Then we go to my room and make out like high schoolers who are saving it.

He tells me the ball is in my court.

That he isn't going to do so much as take off my top until I lead.

Which is ridiculous.
But sweet too.

44

EMMA

For weeks, we fall into a routine.

Texting while I'm at school.

Not quite flirting at work.

Going back to my place for dinner and TV and long make out sessions.

Sometimes, I get him off.

Sometimes, he gets me off.

I want, so, so badly to fuck him.

For that to be okay.

I'm almost there.

I'm so fucking close.

But the closer I get, the further away it feels.

EMMA

"**F**uck, why you gonna be like that?" Wes shakes his head as he walks his client to the counter.

The client—a long-haired hottie in a leather jacket and motorcycle boots—chuckles. "Only speak the truth."

"You believe this shit, Em?" Wes asks.

"You. Shit. Seems plausible," I say.

"Franklin doesn't believe we're in a torrid love affair," he says.

"Hmm... I wonder why. It's so believable. I mean, you have that great personality," I say.

"Fuck personality. I have this." He motions to his face. "Tell me I'm not beautiful."

Wes is a lot of things, beautiful included. "Too pretty for me."

"Em, baby. You don't realize my range," he says.

"This guy giving you trouble?" Franklin asks.

"No. He's kind of entertaining." I motion to Wes, who's still going on about his varying degrees of beauty. He could grow a beard. Or get a motorcycle. Or cover himself in grease. "Makes the time flow."

"Talks a lot," Franklin says.

"And thinks he knows best too." My gaze shifts to Hunter. He's tattooing a dolphin on a pretty girl's shoulder. It shouldn't bother me, him touching her.

It's his job.

But I hate it.

I hate that she's close enough to smell his shampoo.

I hate that she's not broken.

That she could drag him to the back room and fuck him without having to worry about freezing in panic.

I hate that she's incredibly sweet—a fucking conservationist, who literally spends her time saving marine life—and that I have no reason to hate her at all.

And that seeing him with her inspires this petty part of my mind. The part that desperately wants to make him jealous.

It's my job, yeah.

But I also want him jealous.

I bat my eyelashes. "Believe it or not, Wes isn't the most annoying guy who works here."

"No." Franklin leans in. Stage whispers, "Could anyone be worse?"

"You don't know the half of it," Wes says.

I nod. "There's Dean."

Franklin laughs. "With the hot apprentice?"

"Yeah. I think she gets more customers than him at this point," I say.

"She's got epic tits," Wes says. "Can't blame customers."

"She'll kill you for saying that." I mean, she won't. But she will shoot him a death glare. Chloe loves when Dean teases her. When anyone else makes lewd comments, she practically hops into aikido stance.

Okay, I'm pretty sure there isn't actually an aikido stance.

And Wes is the only one who does it.

But, you know...

The point stands.

"Have you had the misfortune of meeting my brother?" I motion to Brendon, who's currently in his suite, tattooing a guy who could give Franklin a run for his money in the long-haired, motorcycle riding hottie category.

"You're Brendon's sister?" he asks.

"God, you're friends, aren't you?" I ask.

He motions to the sleeve on his left arm. "Unfortunately for you."

"You didn't go back to him?" I ask.

"Wanted to try the new guy," Franklin says.

"Fuck, I feel like a piece of meat." Wes motions *go on*.

He doesn't.

I print Franklin's receipt. Press my chest together as I hand it over.

Hunter's gaze shifts to me.

He asks the ocean lover to take a break. Stands. Stretches his arms over his head.

It pulls his t-shirt up his torso.

Shows off his taut abs.

Which makes my stomach flutter.

I think I'm drooling.

And impossibly achy.

God, I'm always impossibly achy now.

I need to fuck him.

I…

I close my eyes. Picture it. The two of us in my bed. Him sliding his jeans to his ankles. Me tossing my dress over my head. Sliding a condom over his cock. Straddling him. Staring down at him as I take him.

It has to go like that.

I have to be in control.

After… practice, I can let go. Let him lead. Loose myself in him leading.

But not yet.

Not until I…

God, I wish I had a better term than practice.

Who says that?

I need to practice at sex so I can be really good at it. I've been warming the bench for a while because of an, erm, injury four months back. Almost five now, I guess. But I'm doing my rehabilitation and I'm ready to go back into the game. Just need practice.

How the hell did I pick up these sports metaphors?

This is worse than comic books.

Which are actually highly entertaining.

And full of super-hot guys in spandex.

Not that sports are lacking for hot guys in tiny clothes.

But…

Uh…

"Hey." Hunter presses his palms into the counter. Looks to Wes and Franklin with a *hey, maybe some privacy.*

They stay put.

"This guy bothering you?" Franklin asks.

"No." God, he has such pretty blue eyes. I never get tired of them. "He's here as eye candy."

"Oh?" Franklin chuckles.

"Yeah. Which means." I motion *take it off.*

"Call Dean if you want that," Hunter says.

"This is cruel and unusual punishment," I say.

Hunter shrugs *what are you going to do about it.*

"Torture you," I say,

"Already doing that," he says.

"How?"

"Sitting here staring."

"I don't stare," I say.

"You do too."

"Do not."

"And you wear these dresses that demand my attention."

"I like this dress."

"I do too." His voice drops as his gaze shifts to my chest.

Wes cuts in. "Fuck, dude, you gonna pull one of those 'it would look better on my floor' lines? 'Cause you should know that doesn't work." Wes looks to me. *Am I right?*

"Worst thing a guy could say about my dress," I agree.

"That's not how you hang clothes." Franklin nods.

Hunter chuckles. "What about I prefer your lipstick on my cock?"

"Fuck, that escalated." Wes shakes his head. "They think they're all coy and subtle about fucking."

"Oh." Franklin raises a brow.

Wes whispers something.

Franklin chuckles.

I mean, he's right.

We're so stupid flirting a dozen feet from my brother. Especially when I keep insisting we wait on telling him.

Brendon is in the zone, sure, but it only takes one loud comment to send him into caveman mode.

And that…

I so don't have the mental space for that.

"I don't remember anyone asking for your opinion," I say.

"What about me?" Franklin asks.

"Well, since you asked so nicely." I motion *go on.*

"You're a cute couple," he says.

Wes shakes his head. "That's betrayal."

"Speak the truth." Franklin holds out his hand.

Wes shakes. Walks him to the door.

Returns with company.

"Look who the cat dragged in?" Wes motions to Griffin, who's incredibly non-plussed.

"You asked me to meet you here," Griffin says.

"You're ruining the mystery, Grif," Wes says.

Griffin shakes his head in that *you're ridiculous* way of his.

He comes by a lot. To check on Hunter. Or meet Wes. Or just say hey.

He's a good guy.

He obviously wants to be here.

But he's just… not.

"You gonna take a gig here yet?" Wes asks.

"You think I'm gonna ditch Chase just because you asked for the five-hundredth time?" Griffin asks.

"He's a dick," Wes says.

"So are you."

"Less of a dick."

"See. He's even got a smaller dick!"

Griffin rolls his eyes.

Hunter laughs, but it doesn't hide the hurt in his expression. He's given his brother space for months now. But the space between them kills him.

Fucking Wes starts this conversation every time Griffin stops by.

Don't get me wrong. I like Wes.

But he's either oblivious to Hunter's pain or he's reveling in it.

Maybe his intentions are good. Maybe he thinks he's pushing Hunter. But…

Fuck anyone who hurts him.

"You all right, baby?" Hunter's fingers brush my palm.

I look to Brendon. Make sure he's focused on his client. "Brendon said you wanted to take me and Kay to dinner sometime."

"Yeah." Hunter nods.

"Like a double date?" I ask.

"Sorta." He reaches over. Brushes a hair behind my ear. Rests his palm on my cheek.

I lean into the touch.

Let my eyes close.

Let my body fill with warmth.

This is so stupid. So risky. So reckless.

And, right now, I'm so apathetic.

God, I need him touching me.

I need all of him.

All the time.

And I need—

Well, one thing at a time.

"Have an announcement to make," he says.

"You gonna fill us in on the dirt?" Wes asks. "Tell me you're finally getting that Evanescence tattoo."

Hunter shakes his head. "He can't let go of that."

"Can't blame him. Goth Hunter was a thing of beauty," Griffin says.

"You weren't there," Hunter says.

"I've seen pictures." Griffin chuckles. "You looked like a fool."

"Jesus, Griff! How many times do we need to have this conversation! Tact!" Wes shakes his head *what's wrong with you?*

They exchange that headshake pretty much... all the time.

I would tell them to leave.

But they're doing a great job blocking Brendon's view.

And, well, they're kinda entertaining.

Friends.

Family.

They're Hunter's family.

Maybe it's still fucked-up with his older brother. But it's something. It's a hell of a lot.

"No. Em gets to hear it first." Hunter rubs my temple with his thumb. "You free next Tuesday?"

I nod. "You free tonight?"

"Depends why you're asking." He plays coy, but we both know it's bullshit. We spend nearly every night together.

"I was thinking about that thing," I say.

"That thing?"

"Where the ball's in my court." I clear my throat. "I was thinking, um, that I want to, um…"

"She wants to bone you, dude. Even I can figure that out," Wes says.

"And I need tact?" Griffin shakes his head.

"Two things can be true," Wes says.

"Fuck, they're always ruining the moment," Hunter says.

"No. It's perfect," I say.

His eyes bore into mine. "You sure?"

"I think so."

He nods.

"My place?" I swallow hard. Adopt an impossibly easy smile. "Sevenish?"

The smile he returns is a hundred percent drunk in love. "You'll have to tear me away."

HUNTER

Emma twirls linguine around her fork. She brings it to her mouth. Sucks pasta from the silverware.

Chews.

Swallows.

Licks arrabiata from her lips.

Her cheeks flush as her eyes meet mine. "What?"

"Nothing."

The blush deepens.

It's a routine now. Staring at her, marveling in one of the things I love about her.

Her catching me staring.

Blushing.

Tripping over her words.

She hasn't said it back.

I thought it would bother me, but it doesn't.

I love her.

I love everything about her.

Her obsession with cooking Italian food.

The fact she plays the same dozen albums in rotation.

The way she blushes then stammers something about how I lack taste whenever I point that out.

Her smile.

Her dark eyes.

Her laugh.

There's no greed in my love.

No need for reciprocity.

I love her.

She isn't there yet.

Or she's scared.

Or unsure.

It doesn't matter.

I still love her.

It feels so fucking good.

Hell, even if this goes down in flames, if she decides she'll never love me, if she realizes that I am and always have been a piece of shit—

It will still feel good, loving her.

God damn, I'm so obnoxiously sappy now.

And I don't even care.

"You're still giving me a look." She licks arrabiata from her index finger. The tomato sauce matches the red of her nail. It's more orange. Her paint is more crimson. But it's Emma all the same.

"Thinking about how I'm going to rock your world."

"Rock your world? Really?" She stabs a piece of shrimp. "That's your dirty talk?"

"You want me to get started?"

Her pupils dilate. "Well..." She brings the shrimp to her mouth. Bites off half. Chews. Swallows. "You aren't eating."

I motion to my half empty bowl.

She motions back. "It's half-full."

"You're an optimist."

"Oh my God." Her laugh fills the room. "That's so bad."

"I'm gonna have to turn off the *Say Anything*."

"And put on what?"

"What kind of music is optimistic?"

"What do you listen to when you aren't being soothed by my amazing jams?"

"My taste isn't nearly so—"

"Good." She finishes her shrimp. "It's not as good as mine."

"I was going to say specific."

"Watch it." She swirls another forkful of pasta.

"Or you won't put out?"

"Oh my God, Hunter." Her cheeks flush. "You're so…"

"That a 'yes, Hunter, please turn on the dirty talk'?"

"If you want to win me over, you should start here." She motions to her speakers as they switch to a Bayside song. "Try 'Thank you for curating the perfect playlist, Emma.'"

"This is new?"

"You can't tell?"

I shake my head. I love that Emma loves this music. Hell, I like it well enough. But not enough to notice the subtle differences.

"You're really blowing this."

"Yeah?"

"Yeah." Her lips curl into a smile. "You're going to have to get up and sing if you want to win your way back into my good graces."

"Thought I was supposed to finish dinner."

"That too."

"And dirty talk you."

"You have a busy night."

"You don't want to hear me sing." I take another bite of arrabiata. It's great. Tender, rich, spicy.

"I do." She sets her fork down. Presses her hands together. "Please, Hunter, serenade me. I'll even put on something you like."

"What do I like?"

"That's what I'm trying to ask you."

It's a good question. I've never been into music. I like it, sure. But I've never been the type to curate playlists or surrender to a melody.

Honestly, the stuff Emma plays is my favorite.

It's her.

And that's better than anything.

Still.

I have a few ideas. "I want to surprise you."

She tilts her head to one side, assessing my claim. "I don't know. Access to the speakers… that's a big deal."

"Yeah?"

She nods. "Like giving you a key."

"Where's my key?"

"I'm always here." Her eyes meet mine. They flare with nerves for a second, then they're back to that fire.

She wants to fuck me, but she's scared.

I'm scared too.

I don't want to hurt her.

To make this worse for her.

I have an idea but, fuck, I'm not sure if she's going to go for it.

"You want me to eat first—" I scoop another forkful of pasta. "Or you want me to serenade you."

"I'll give you a few minutes to think."

"Thank fuck. It takes me awhile."

"I know." Her smile spreads a little wider.

It's pure Emma.

That smile that means *I love you.*

She hasn't said it.

But it's there.

It's in her heart.

She's as in this as I am.

She's as vulnerable as I am.

Sure, her life is a lot more put together. There are a lot more people who want the best for her.

But that only makes her devotion more meaningful.

It would be easy to say I'm only in love with her because I'm lonely and desperate.

It wouldn't be true.

But I can see how this looks from the outside.

This is still so fucked from the outside.

I take another bite. Chew. Swallow.

Gather all the courage I have.

It's not that I'm embarrassed to sing.

I know I'm terrible.

I'm willing to share that with her.

But—"I have to warn you." I pick up a napkin. Wipe my lips. "What's the worst singing you've ever heard?"

"There's been a lot of karaoke over the years. But a technically terrible performance can still be great. It's all about the showmanship."

"Don't have that."

"You do too."

I shake my head.

"Well… If it's not going well, take your shirt off."

"Dean get through to you?"

"No. I just think it's a good look for you."

"Yeah?" I tug my t-shirt a few inches up my stomach.

Her teeth sink into her lip.

Desire spreads over her face.

It's beautiful.

And it's pure.

There's no fear or nerves or apprehension in her eyes.

She's free.

I want that for her.

Even if takes three years and a million make out sessions.

I move to her laptop. Wake it from sleep. Go straight to her streaming service. "You sure you're prepared?"

"A hundred percent."

"One minute." I look up the lyrics. Scan them to make sure I won't stumble. Not that it helps. My abilities as a performer are… lacking.

I made a fool of myself plenty when I was drunk.

I was the life of the fucking party.

Now…

I don't miss many things about that guy.

But I miss his charisma.

That was inside me somewhere.

I just have to find it.

I pull up the song. Take a deep breath. Click play.

Closer by Nine Inch Nails flows through the speakers.

Emma's pupils dilate.

Her blush spreads to her chest.

She recognizes it immediately.

I move into the middle of the room.

I close my eyes.

And I sing about wanting to fuck her like an animal.

It's not exactly what I want to say to her.

Yeah, I do want to fuck her hard and fast.

But I also want it soft and slow.

I want it dirty.

And sweet.

I don't care.

As long as it brings me closer to her.

As long as it's what she wants.

As long as I get to watch pleasure spread over her expression.

Yeah, it's torture kissing her, touching her, making her come without being inside her.

But it's beautiful fucking torture.

I can live with waiting forever if that's what it takes.

It's not like I'm living in a state of blue balls.

She's plenty good at getting me off.

My cock stirs at the thought of her soft red lips.

Her long legs.

Her tight dress.

She's wearing one of those black dresses of hers. It's casual enough for work. Sexy enough to drive me out of my mind.

High hem. Low neckline. Snug waist.

She claps when I finish.

I take a bow.

Then I go straight to her.

I wrap my arms around her, lift her into the air, spin her.

She squeals as she wraps her arms around my neck.

"You forgive me?"

She nods. "This time."

Her fingers dig into my hair.

Slowly, she presses her lips to mine.

It starts softly.

Then it's harder.

Deeper.

Needier.

She doesn't have to say it.

We're done with dinner.

With karaoke.

With pretense.

It's time.

I pull back with a sigh. "You're sure you're ready?" She doesn't have to say it, but I do. I need to hear the words on her lips. To be sure I'm not pushing her.

"I think so."

"I brought something."

"Yeah?" Her eyes light up. With desire. And apprehension.

"I'm not sure you'll like it."

"Try me."

I set her down. "Hold on." This is better as a show, not a tell.

I go to my backpack.

Pull out what I need.

Her eyes go wide as I set the restraints on the table. "Those are…"

"Yeah."

"You want to tie—"

"No. I think you should tie me up."

"Those were just jokes—"

"Yeah, but it's a good idea." I move closer. Bring my hand to her cheek. Stare into her gorgeous dark eyes. "That way, you'll be in control."

"What do I even do?"

"Whatever you want."

She presses her lips together. "I guess I could tie you up and use you like a sex toy?"

"That sounds hot."

"Yeah." She nods. "It kinda does."

EMMA

For the third time, I take a deep breath.

It does nothing to calm me.

I'm not getting ready for a job interview or a test or an interrogation.

I'm preparing to fuck my boyfriend.

To prove I'm capable of fucking my boyfriend.

To prove I'm capable of fucking, period.

He's already in my bedroom.

He's already tied to the bed.

It ruins the illusion that he's completely under my control, if he's able to tie himself to the bed.

But still.

This really does put me in the driver's seat.

That's a good thing.

In theory.

But it's scarier too.

If I can't do this, it's not because he tugged at my hair too hard or moved too fast.

It's me.

My inability to handle my shit.

I take another deep breath.

Let out another steady exhale.

The apartment is buzzing with sexy slow jams.

It's empty.

Kaylee is at Brendon's for the night.

The place is ours.

No distractions. No interruptions. No hiccups.

For the ten millionth time, I check my reflection.

My hair is in loose waves.

My makeup is perfect.

My black chemise is gorgeous.

But it's not right.

The lingerie, the lipstick, the R&B—this isn't me.

I toss the chemise on the ground. Pull on my everyday bra and panties. They're comfortable, but they're sexy enough.

I go to my computer. Switch the playlist to one that's right.

There.

A thrashing guitar riff fills the space.

Then a laugh.

Hunter finds me amusing.

He loves mocking my taste in music.

Which is… sweet, actually.

There's something about it. Something that says *I love you*.

He knows me.

Trusts me.

Wants me.

This…

I can do this.

I can do this as me.

I wipe off my subtle mauve lipstick. Find my favorite crimson red.

There.

Now, I'm Emma Kane.

Maybe I'm not a sex goddess.

Maybe I'm still a scared, vulnerable girl.

But I'm not running from that.

Deep breath.

Steady exhale.

I step into the hallway.

Push the bedroom door open.

The curtains are down. The only illumination comes from the string lights lining the walls. The same ones that used to adorn my old room. Tiny paper stars that glow against the darkness.

They're beautiful, soft, perfect.

And there's Hunter, sprawled over the bed in nothing but his jeans, his arms pulled over his head, his wrists bound.

I've never had fantasies of tying guys up.

But there is something appealing about him waiting and ready for me.

At my mercy.

I'm in control.

I can do this.

We've done so much.

Touched so much.

I've heard him come so many times.

Thought about him coming as I fucked myself.

It's just this one bridge I haven't crossed.

He scoots up the bed enough to push himself up.

Then he tugs at the restraints until they kick.

To show me they work.

That I can trust him.

I already do trust him.

It's that voice in the back of my head that always ruins this.

"You look gorgeous, baby." He gives me a long, slow once over.

"I was wearing this all day."

407

"Wanted to fuck you all day." An edge drops into his voice. He's not playing anymore. He's not flirting for the sake of it.

He wants me.

Badly.

I want him too.

I just…

No, I'm not going there.

I'm not getting lost in my head.

I'm staying tuned into this moment. The one happening right now.

I used to be good at that.

I miss it.

My eyes meet Hunter's. "How about this?" I place my foot on the bed. Peel my dress up my thigh. All the way to the edge of my panties.

His pupils dilate.

His tongue slides over his lips.

His breath gets low and growly. "Show me."

I shake my head. "I'm in control here."

He nods slowly. Like he's barely managing to remember that.

"You do what I say."

"I like the music." He motions to the Bluetooth speaker on my desk. "This is going to be my new favorite song."

"Yeah?"

"Yeah." There's no pretense in his voice. He's not teasing. He means it.

"Your next tattoo?"

"Yeah." His eyes trace a line down my leg. "It's perfect."

"Is it?"

"It's you."

"You want me on your body forever?"

"Can't think of anything I want more."

"Really?" I pull my dress to my waist. Flash him my panties. "Nothing?"

"Fuck, Em." His voice drops back to that growly tone. "You drive me out of my mind."

"You do too."

"I want to see you."

"How?"

"Naked."

The need in his voice makes my sex clench.

"Coming."

I want more of that.

I really, really do.

Slowly, I pull my dress over my head.

His eyes go wide as I shift onto the bed.

I place my body next to his. So I'm kneeling, my knees brushing his hips.

His jeans are rough against my skin.

He's so close.

I can feel the warmth of his skin.

I can smell his shampoo.

And that faint hint of sweat.

It's never been appealing before.

But it is.

I want to work him hard.

Until we're both panting and dripping.

That's not happening today.

But one day…

Maybe I can get there.

Maybe it really is possible.

I take another deep breath.

This time, my exhale doesn't feel quite so heavy.

It's more… free.

I lean back on my heels as I bring my hand to Hunter's stomach.

My fingers trace the lines of his muscles.

Then his tattoos.

His eyelids flutter together as I drag my fingertips up his torso.

I make my touch featherlight.

Up his stomach, chest, neck.

Down the same path.

Past his belly button and that soft tuft of hairs beneath it.

All the way to the waistband of his jeans.

It feels good, touching him.

Watching need spread over his expression.

Bit by bit, I push my other thoughts aside.

Until there's only one thing in my head:

Must drive Hunter wild.

I undo the button of his jeans. The zipper.

My palm finds his cock.

The soft cotton of his boxers is in the way, but he's hard under that.

I rub him with my palm.

His lips part with a groan. "Em." He tries to reach for me, but the restraints catch him.

His arms fall back to the bed.

His eyes blink open.

He stares up at me as I rub him.

His eyes fill with the deepest, purest desire.

I need more of that.

To really, truly feel like he's under my spell.

Like I'm in control.

I push his jeans off his hips.

Then the boxers.

Mmm.

He looks good halfway out of his clothes.

Like he wants me so badly he can't bother to lose them completely.

I guess it's the other way.

I want him too badly to do away with his jeans completely.

I sling my legs around his thighs. Shift myself into position. Rest one hand on his stomach.

Wrap the other around his cock.

Slowly, I lean down.

Brush my lips against his tip.

Then it's my tongue.

He tastes good.

He always does.

We've done this a lot.

Fuck, I can't remember the last time I did this so much.

But I'm not getting tired of it.

The more I suck him off, the more I want to.

It's fucking thrilling, driving him to the edge, watching pleasure spread over his expression.

I pump him as I take him deeper.

He bucks his hips.

Groans my name.

He's egging me on.

He wants more.

He wants everything.

But, right now, I'm in control of exactly how this goes.

For once, I actually feel in control.

I reach my free hand up his torso. Brush my fingers against his chest.

Take him deeper.

"Em…" His wrists tug against the restraints. "Fuck me, baby."

My sex clenches.

My nipples pang.

My knees go weak.

God, I want that.

I want that so fucking badly.

I push myself up.

Then I climb up his body until my sex is against his cock.

There's a thin layer of fabric between us.

That's it.

There's only this tiny layer of cotton separating our bodies.

Fuck, he feels good against me.

He's so close.

So close to being mine.

To us being exactly where we're supposed to be.

I grind against him as I unhook my bra and slide it off my shoulders.

His eyes go wide.

Again, he tries to reach for me.

Groans as the restrains stop him.

There's something about Hunter denying himself.

Or me denying him.

It's hot.

Not as hot as him touching me.

But still fucking hot.

I stare into his eyes as I grind against him.

His cock presses the soft fabric of my panties against my clit.

It's just enough friction to drive me out of my mind.

I shift my hips, rubbing against him.

My nipples pang.

My sex aches.

My breath catches.

Fuck, I'm close.

This is already so much.

So good.

But I need to come with him inside me.

I need him inside me.

Period.

I dig my fingers into his stomach.

Force my thoughts to steady.

This isn't going to work if I rush myself.

I can't convince myself I'm ready.

I have to be ready.

My body is screaming *Need Hunter Now*.

Am I ready?

Or am I just that close to the edge?

I shift my hips to grind my crotch against his again.

He reaches for my hips.

Catches on the restrains. "You're gonna make me come, baby."

Yes, I want that.

I really, really want that.

I shift off him. Onto the bed.

Then I lift my hips, push my panties to my ankles, kick them off.

Hunter watches with rapt attention as I climb onto him.

As I wrap my hand around his cock.

I can do this.

I can really fucking do this.

I stare into his eyes as I lower my body onto his.

His tip strains against me.

Fuck, that feels good.

And not like with Vinnie.

I take him one inch at a time.

Until I have all of him.

Until I'm so full I think I might burst.

It's different.

Good different.

He looks up at me with hazy eyes. "Condom."

"Oh." Fuck, he's right.

There's nothing between us.

Only his skin against mine.

God, it's intimate.

And the lack of rubber—it makes it easier to push that night further away.

But I can't be stupid.

I don't need any other complications.

I force myself to pull back. Then I climb up the bed, grab the condom from the bedside table, rip the wrapper.

He stares down at me as I roll it over his cock.

I'm far from smooth.

I'm incredibly awkward.

But I don't care.

As long as I get him inside me again.

It clicks in my head.

My first thought isn't that I need to prove I can do this.

Only that I need it.

My thoughts fell so far away I forgot protection.

Even if this isn't perfect, that's a fucking win.

I'm getting there.

I sling my leg over his hip and shift into position.

His cock strains against me.

He's hard.

And warm.

But the tug of rubber.

Fuck, it's familiar.

I suck a breath through my nose.

Exhale slowly.

It happened.

I'm not running from it. Or putting it in a box. Or pushing it into the corner.

I'm acknowledging it and moving aside.

Vinnie hurt me.

But Hunter isn't Vinnie.

I trust him.

I really fucking trust him.

Concern streaks his blue eyes as he stares up at me.

He's worried.

Scared for me.

I'm not okay yet.

There's a long way to go.

But I'm getting there.
And I'm here.
I spread my thighs.
Take him deeper.
Fuck.
That's intense.
Good intense.
So fucking good.
The moment washes over me.
The growling vocals pouring from the speakers.
The soft string lights.
The sigh falling from Hunter's lips.
He groans as I press my hands against his shoulders.
I start slow.
Shift my hips forward and backward.
A little.
Then more.
Then just enough he hits me where I need him.
Fuck.
My eyelids press together.
But that's no good.
I need to stay here, in this room, with him.
I force my eyes open.
Force my gaze to him.
"Fuck, Em." He bucks his hips, shifting deeper.
He's close.
I need that.
But I also need to come like this.
With him inside me.
I press one hand to his chest. "Watch me."
I bring the other to my clit.
I rock against him as I stroke myself.
The tension in my sex winds.
He hits me just right.

And the pressure of my fingertips—
Being in control of this, of when I come—
It's exactly what I need.
I don't draw it out.
I barely even savor it.
My fingers work hard and fast.
A few strokes and I'm at the edge.
A few more and I tumble over it.
"Hunter." I groan his name as I come.
I rub myself through my orgasm.
Then he's shifting his hips.
Driving into me.
Deeper.
Harder.
Fuck.
"Em." His head falls backward.
His fingers curl into his palms.
With his next thrust, he comes.
His cock pulses inside me.
Even with the condom, I can feel it.
And it's everything.
Once he's finished, I untangle our bodies.
I untie Hunter.
He does away with the condom.
Then he wraps his arms around me and he pulls me closer.
I nestle into his chest.
"You're too good at this, baby." He presses his lips to my chest. "I need to make you come again."
I shake my head. That was good. Perfect. But it was all I can take. "Tomorrow."
"That a promise?"
"Yeah."
"Perfect."

HUNTER

Emma pokes her eggs with her fork. She looks from them to me then back to the eggs. "You tried."

"Cruel."

"It's just…" She stabs them again. "Well…"

"Yeah?"

"They're disgusting."

I can't help but laugh. That's her. No sugar coating. No easing me into it. No bullshit. "I haven't improved?"

"Well…" She grabs the Sriracha from the table and drowns her eggs in it. "Yeah, but, honestly, Hunter, you were hopeless then."

"Then?"

"You're still pretty bad."

"Fuck, Em."

"You're great at coffee." She wraps her fingers around her mug. The one that says *Sarcasm Loading....* "And sex." Her cheeks flush. "Tattoos."

"Is my ego that fragile."

She motions *a little* then she scoops eggs and brings them to her lips. She chews and swallows slowly. "Almost edible."

"Almost?"

"I mean, if I was starving and they were my only option…"

"You'd still toss them?"

She laughs. "Better than last time."

"You spit those out."

"Not everyone is good at everything." She stands, brings the plate of eggs to the sink, slides them into the garbage disposal. "Want me to make some?"

"If I haven't scarred you from ever eating eggs again."

She laughs. "No. But I wouldn't mind chocolate oatmeal instead."

"Go for it."

She grabs the oatmeal from the fridge and scoops it into a bowl. "What are you going to eat?"

"How about this legendary chocolate oatmeal?"

"You mock it every time you see it."

True, but—"I'll mock you for whatever you do."

"You're cruel that way."

"I know."

She fills the bowl with water, puts it in the microwave, hits the two minute button, gets to work on the next. "You're going to hate it."

"Not with how much you love it."

"This isn't emo music."

"It's not?"

She laughs. "You're lucky you're so handsome."

"Most of what I've got going for me."

Her eyes find mine. She shoots me that look. The one that means *I love you*. "Yeah." She leaves the bowl on the counter. Moves back to the breakfast table.

My fingers brush her wrist.

I wrap my hand around it.

Pull her into my lap.

She giggles as she slides her arm around my neck. "Hey."

"Hey." I look up at her. Brush her long hair behind her ear. Rest my palm on her cheek. She's gorgeous, but that's not why I love staring into her eyes. It's that she's Emma. That she's mine. "I have to make this up to you." I motion to my plate of eggs.

"I don't know. It's my fault too. I am your teacher."

She is. She's been teaching me to cook for almost two months now. I've learned a lot, but I'm still terrible. "Maybe I'm unteachable."

"I'm considering that." Her fingers dig into my hair. "At least you're good at following orders."

"You're good at issuing them."

"Don't even."

"You didn't enjoy that?"

Her cheeks flush. "Well, I, uh…"

"You were hot."

"Thank you." She turns her head away from me. "It was fun, but I think this time we shouldn't—"

"You're ready for that?"

"Yeah. I think so." She turns back to me. "Stop asking."

"I have to."

"Do you?"

I nod. I have to know she's okay. To be sure I'm not pushing her. I don't trust myself. Not with all that blood in my cock.

She's too fucking sexy.

It's too easy to let my *other* brain take over.

"How about we… don't talk about that?" The microwave beeps. She slides from my waist, goes to the kitchen, finishes fixing the first bowl of oatmeal.

It's a process. Cocoa powder. Sliced strawberries. Cinnamon.

She slides the second bowl into the microwave, brings the first to the table, sets it in front of me. "You first."

"Thanks." I pick up my spoon. Take a bite.

It's a lot. As rich as the eighty-five percent chocolate she favors. The oatmeal itself is bitter, but the sweetness of the strawberries balances it.

It's too much for me.

Too rich.

Too chocolaty.

Too bitter.

But fuck knows I'm not admitting that.

Not after how hard I've teased her for her love of sugar.

"You hate it." She laughs as she slides into her seat. "It's okay."

"Not hate."

"Hate."

"It's just…" I break for a sip of coffee, but that doesn't help. The sweetness of the milk and sugar only makes the oatmeal more bitter by comparison. "It's a lot."

"I'm a lot."

"Yeah, but that's why I love you."

Her cheeks flush.

"You think about Ryan's offer?"

"Which offer?"

"To make you assistant manager?"

"Over the summer. It's sweet, but…"

"You'd rather keep your lingerie discount?"

"I don't know. I prefer working at Inked Hearts, but there's not exactly a lot of upward mobility."

My lips curl into a smile.

"What?" Her cheeks flush. That same blush. That *omg, why are you giving me that look* blush.

"You sound so corporate."

"You're the one who taught me half this stuff."

I shake my head. I helped her with our books, explained a few things to her, but she learned most of it in school. Or from experience.

Emma is smarter than I am.

Smarter than she gives herself credit for.

She's good at what she does.

She could manage the shop if she wanted.

Or she could start her own.

Hell, she can take the world by storm.

I want that for her.

I really do.

"You're looking at me funny." She yelps as the microwave beeps.

"Funny how."

"You know how." She slides out of her seat, moves into the kitchen, fixes the second bowl of oatmeal. "Ryan might take it back. Once we tell him."

"Dean and Chloe work together."

"Yeah, but—"

"They're wildly inappropriate."

"True. I just…" She drops strawberries in the bowl. "What happens when we tell everyone?"

I wish I had a good answer for her, but I don't.

"What if Brendon kicks you out?"

"I can deal with that." I've found a place. But not the right moment to tell everyone.

Or schedule my move out.

It's a big deal, being on my own.

As much as I hate having to hide this from Brendon, it's nice staying at his place.

Knowing someone is around if I get lonely or scared or desperate for a drink.

Knowing someone is going to hold me accountable.

My own place—that's a lot of freedom.

Freedom to fuck Emma.

And freedom to fuck up.

"What if he lobbies to get you fired?" she asks.

"He won't."

"You're sure?"

No. Brendon is usually reasonable. But he is protective of Emma.

And he knows all the ugly stuff I've done.

He knows what a piece of shit I can be.

He knows better than anyone.

But he's seen me claw my way out of shit too.

If Brendon really thinks I'm not good enough for his sister—

Maybe he's right.

I swallow hard.

I don't want to acknowledge the possibility.

But it's there.

It's possible I'm not what's best for Em.

And, whatever happens, I'm not getting in the way of Em blossoming.

She has a big, beautiful life ahead of her.

I want to be a part of it.

But not if I'm holding her back.

"Where are you going?" she asks.

"Your brother is more reasonable than you think."

She sticks her tongue out. "He's a caveman."

"He's looking out for you."

"So you think he'll be okay with this?"

"Yeah." Mostly.

"You want to tell him?"

"Soon."

"How soon?"

"By the end of the month," I say.

"That's soon."

"I know."

"Maybe we can do it at the shop. Or a party. Tell him then. When other people are around. So he can't throw a fit."

"Strategic."

She nods. "You have to be." She brings a scoop of cocoa

oatmeal to her mouth. Chews. Swallows. Sighs. "How can you not love this?"

"I do." I love that sigh.

Her cheeks flush.

It never gets old.

"Okay, I'll agree to this on one condition." She takes another bite. Licks the cocoa from her lips.

"Yeah?"

"You don't bring it up until then."

"Fair. But I have my own condition."

"Yeah?" she asks.

"You go back to your bedroom and take all your clothes off."

"Right now?"

"After this," I say.

"That's kind of manipulative."

"We can play Bayside."

Her lips curl into a smile. "That was never up for negotiation."

"You're training me."

"Oh?"

"I hear that emo—"

"Watch it."

"And I think about tearing your clothes off."

"I don't have a problem with that."

"You will."

"No." She shakes her head. "I'll always want you tearing my clothes off."

"At work?"

"Yeah."

"In front of your brother?"

"I'll stop playing it in front of him."

"He'll be glad."

"Yeah." She laughs. "But it's worth it." Her eyes spark. There's no fear or apprehension. Just joy. "You're ridiculous."

"Yeah, but you love it."

"I do." She takes another bite. Chews. Swallows. "I have a counter-proposal."

"I'm listening."

"You go to my room and take all your clothes off."

"We go together?" I offer my hand.

"Take each other's clothes off." She offers her hand.

"It's a deal."

We shake.

HUNTER

I press the door closed.

Emma sits on the bed. She presses her palms into her quads. Spreads her legs.

"You're nervous?" I move to the bedside table. Get a condom from the box.

"No." She presses her knees together. "A little."

"That's okay."

"Yeah." She bites her lip. "You're not going to stop asking, are you?"

I shake my head.

"That's sweet." Her eyes find mine. "But annoying."

"Sums me up in a nutshell."

She laughs. "Yeah." Her eyes flit to the foil wrapper. "Do we have to?"

"Em—"

"It's just… it's easier without it. Not going there."

"Baby, I'd love to fuck you bareback."

Her pupils dilate.

"But not until we're safe."

Her nod is slow. "I... um... I'll make an appointment next week."

"Sure."

"I was thinking I'd try an IUD."

I nod.

"Since, um... well, I think we'll be together for a while. I hope. And they're really best if you're with someone. Because they can increase your risk of STDs." Her eyes find mine. "Unless you um—"

"I want to be with you a long time."

"Me too." Her eyes go to her laptop, currently sitting on her desk. "We're not playing music."

"Do I have permission?"

She laughs. "Only to hit play."

"What if I want to curate something?"

"Hmm." She tilts her head to one side, assessing my ability to choose music. Her brow softens. Then her shoulders. Her jaw.

It's pushing everything else out of her mind.

I know she wants to be over this.

For it to not matter.

It's going to take time.

But that doesn't mean it needs to hang over us.

I know how to relax her.

I sit at her desk. Wake her computer. Pull a few albums into a playlist.

There.

She lets out a sigh of contentment as a familiar guitar riff fills the room.

"This is my favorite song now." I turn back to her.

"Good taste."

"I think about you every time I hear it."

"Since last night?"

"Since always."

"Oh. Well, good."

"It's not on your desk."

"Add it."

I pick up a silver sharpie. "I'm not sure I can."

She nods. "It's tradition. People I care about write on the desk."

"I see your handwriting and Kaylee's."

"There aren't many people I care about."

"Just sounds like a made up tradition."

She laughs. "That's how all traditions start." She motions to the desk. "Pick your favorite part and write it."

I do. I scribble the lyrics that make me think of her.

Of us.

Of what I want to say to her.

"Read it to me," she says.

"I'll do you one better." I play the song. Skip to the lyrics I wrote for her. Adorn them with the perfect design as they play.

An ornate key next to a locked heart.

It's obvious.

But it's right.

She stands and moves toward me.

Her fingers brush the desk. Her lips part with one of those sighs of contentment. "Hunter..." She looks down at me.

I look up at her. "Yeah?"

"I... That's perfect." She leans down to press her lips to mine.

I stand and wrap my arms around her.

She groans as I pick her up and bring her to the bed.

She falls onto her back.

I climb on top of her.

She wraps her legs around my waist.

Her hand goes to the back of my head. She pulls me closer.

Grinds against me.

Fuck, that feels good.

She's wearing almost nothing today.

This tiny tank top and shorts.

But it's still too much fabric.

These jeans are too thick.

I need all this gone.

I need nothing between us.

It's so tempting, fucking her bareback.

I want to feel all of her again.

To let that soft cunt envelop me.

But fuck knows there's no way I'll have enough control to pull out.

She breaks our kiss to pull my t-shirt over my head.

I roll her tank top up her chest.

She arches her back and unhooks her bra.

Her hands go to my shoulders.

She flips me over and climbs on top of me.

Her eyes bore into mine as she slides her bra off her shoulders.

My hands go to her chest. I palm her breasts. Bring my thumbs to her nipples.

She groans as I toy with her.

Fuck, she looks so beautiful with pleasure spreading over her expression.

"Hunter." Her eyelids flutter together.

She rocks her hips to grind against me.

I should take my time warming her up.

But, fuck, if she keeps doing this, I'm gonna come in my jeans.

And that's fucking unacceptable.

I bring one hand to her back to pull her closer.

Then I kiss her hard.

My tongue dances with hers.

She groans against my lips as I toy with her.

Then her hands are digging into my hair. And she's pushing her shorts off her hips.

Flipping onto her back.

Pulling me on top of her.

I press my lips to her chest.

Kiss a line down her torso.

She groans as I pull her panties to her ankles.

I should tease her.

Torture her.

But I need to taste her.

I bring my lips to her cunt.

Lick her up and down.

Her hand knots in my hair.

My fingers dig into the flesh of her ass.

I pull her closer.

Bring my mouth to her clit.

Lick her exactly how she needs me.

"Fuck." Her hand tugs at my hair. "Hunter… Fuck."

Her groan fills the room.

She bucks against my lips.

I keep my pressure steady.

Move a little faster.

Faster.

There—

"Hunter—" Her breath catches in her throat.

I pull her closer.

Hold her against me as I push her to the edge.

Then over it.

She pulses against my lips.

Groans my name as she comes.

"Hunter." She tugs at my hair. "Fuck me."

My balls tighten.

Fuck yes.

I shimmy out of my jeans. Reach for the condom. Tear the wrapper with my teeth.

Her eyes fill with need.

Nothing but deep, pure, perfect need.

It's fucking everything.

I bring my hand to her cheek. Rub her temple with my thumb. Whisper, "You ready?"

She nods.

It's all there in her eyes.

She's not scared or nervous or apprehensive.

She's not drifting off to some ugly memory.

She's here.

She's mine.

She's everything.

Slowly, I lower my body onto hers.

She groans as my tip strains against her.

Her fingers dig into my hair. "Fuck, Hunter." Her breath is low. Deep. Heavy with desire.

She lifts her hips. Wraps her legs around my waist.

Pulls me deeper.

Fuck.

She feels good.

Warm. Soft. Slick.

I wrap my arms around her as I drive into her.

Emma's fingers dig into the back of my head.

She pulls my lips to hers.

Kisses me hard.

And deep.

We stay locked like that, moving and breathing together, until she pulls back to groan my name.

With my next thrust, she comes.

Her pulsing pushes me over the edge.

I rock through my orgasm.

Groan her name into her neck.

When I'm finished, I pull back.

I take care of the condom.

Then I climb into bed with her.

She nestles into my chest.

And dissolves between my arms.

IT'S STILL HARD KEEPING THIS A SECRET.

But it's easier, knowing there's an end date.

Knowing I'll be able to kiss her in front of everyone.

That I'll be able to lead her into the shop and yell *I fucking love this girl* to everyone who's there.

I start getting my shit together.

Fill my schedule with new clients.

Find my own place.

Think long and hard about how to break this to Brendon.

About what it means if he doesn't believe I'm good enough for Emma.

I don't want it to matter.

But it does.

It really fucking does.

HUNTER

Between her shiny necklace and her intense eyes, Emma catches every spec of light in the room.

She's dressed to the nines.

Long hair in careful waves.

Red lips.

Dark makeup highlighting her gorgeous eyes.

For a second, I forget I'm sitting next to her brother.

I forget I'm here to announce the next phase in my life.

I forget everything except how badly I want to hold her.

I stand. Watch her cross the room. Wrap my arms around her.

"Hunter." Her cheeks flush. She pulls back. Plays off our embrace.

"You look gorgeous." My gaze refuses to budge from her eyes.

She's radiant.

A vision.

Everything.

Fuck, I'm so in love with this girl.

It consumes every thought in my head.

Every minute of the day.

I want the world with her.

And for her.

"You don't clean up so bad, yourself." Her red lips curl into a smile.

She pulls out her chair before I can.

Does the same with Kaylee's.

Kaylee giggles as she takes her seat. She looks gorgeous in her powder blue dress, long blond hair swept halfway up, shiny silver makeup bringing out her green eyes.

She's a knockout, no doubt about it.

But Emma has all my interest.

Kaylee and Brendon exchange *fuck me* glances. They're both quiet. Coy about how much they want each other.

But I've stayed with him for long enough to know—

Let's just say they aren't quiet in private.

The walls at the Kane place are thin.

I can't complain. It's not every day I get free audio porn. Especially of the kinky variety.

"This place really your vibe?" Emma's gaze shifts around the dark restaurant.

It's a fancy place in Santa Monica. Complete with high ceilings, candles, soft music.

Not at all my vibe.

Or hers.

But it fits the occasion.

"You know I aspire to be a banker." I motion to my suit and tie.

Emma laughs. "Nailed it, as usual."

"Yeah." Kaylee tilts her head to one side. "I could see it." She looks to Emma. "He is really good with the numbers."

Emma nods. "He's taught me a lot."

"Only what I know," I say.

"Really?" Emma teases. "I thought you were teaching me stuff you didn't know."

"You're already better than I am," I say.

Her cheeks flush. "I'm just—"

"Your business final is next week, right?" I ask.

Emma nods. "Almost done with my project."

"What is it?" Brendon's gaze shifts from Emma to me then back to Emma.

There's something in his dark eyes.

His normal curiosity.

I think.

We talk a lot. Watch action movies. Trade notes on mock-ups. We're friends.

Close.

But we're not exactly trading secrets.

He never asks where I'm spending my nights. Only if I'm spending them sober. And even then, he's casual about it. So it never seems like a big deal.

Sometimes I forget what a big deal it is.

Emma does that to me.

She makes me believe I can do anything.

"It's a business plan for a small chain. A clothing line with three retail stores. There are a ton of moving parts. Inventory, designs, employees, rent, locations." Her eyes light up. "I always thought there were answers with business. That it was simple math. But it's all judgment calls."

Brendon nods.

"Don't even." She shoots him a knowing look.

He shrugs.

"You're going to start about how it's so good I'm in school." She folds her arms. "Kay, please—"

"You know I agree with him," Kaylee says.

Emma looks to me.

I nod. "You belong in school."

She shakes her head. "Et tu, brute?"

I can't help but chuckle. Her voice is bouncy. Her eyes are bright. Her posture is relaxed.

Easy.

This is where she belongs.

With her family.

With all this love in her life.

All this passion surrounding her.

I want that for her.

I want that more than anything.

"Be honest. I convinced you to love art history," I say.

She sticks her tongue out in distaste.

"What about those wood block paintings from the Edo era." There's a ton of erotic stuff. With full on penetration.

"Everything that's wrong about art history." Emma shakes her head. "It's porn for guys. Where is the—"

"They're ladies and dudes getting down. How is that for men specifically?" I ask.

Kaylee laughs. "He kinda has you there."

Brendon shoots her a look.

Kaylee blushes. "Not that I... I don't look at porn. Not that there's anything wrong with porn. I just prefer—"

"Dirty books," Emma offers.

"I read them for the story," Kaylee says.

"Some of them. Others..." Emma raises a brow.

Kaylee's blush deepens.

"Fuck, angel, I'm gonna have to drag you back to the car at this rate." Brendon's voice drops.

Emma's expression twists with exaggerated disgust. "I swear, they can't go five minutes without getting dirty."

"Can you really blame her?" I tease. "Kanes are irresistible."

"Well, that is true." Emma's eyes meet mine. "Everyone knows that."

"You know every single guy I tattooed this week asked if you were single," I say.

"What did you say?" Emma asks.

"Over my dead body." Brendon chuckles like he's teasing.

"Oooh, maybe we should find an especially annoying one," Emma says. "I'll grab him. Start making out. Brendon will kill him. Get sent to jail. I'll have the house all to myself."

"Flawless plan," I say.

"I'll visit you in prison." Kaylee blows her boyfriend a kiss.

"I'll have to break out. Go on the lam." He reaches across the table. Runs his fingers over her palm. "I wouldn't last a week without you."

Kaylee lets out a dreamy sigh.

Emma shakes her head. "God, they're so cute. It's like... disgusting, but it's so adorable that I can't even hate it."

"I love you too." Kaylee hugs her friend.

A server stops by to take our drink order. She frowns when I insist on sparkling water for the group, but she still returns with a bottle of Pellegrino.

"Oh my." Emma laughs as I fill her glass. "Is this really such a formal occasion?"

"I hate to break it to you, Em, but I'm not here so you can mock my attire," I say.

"You sure? I had more to say about your tie." Her red lips curl into a smile.

"This?" I tug at my tie. It's crimson. Same color as her bed spread. And her nails. And her lips.

Emma nods. "Wes was right. A brighter red would be better. You really are a spring."

"Oh my God, this again?" Kaylee laughs. "If I have to hear the words 'soft summer' one more time."

"But you're such a soft summer!" Emma protests. "Look how gorgeous she looks in that medium toned blue."

"You're a vision, angel," Brendon says.

Kaylee blushes, no longer concerned with Emma's color describing system. "What were you..."

437

"Hunter, please. You have to ignore the gaga eyes. They never stop," Emma says.

"I'm getting that vibe," I say.

"Fuck, how long have you suffered from her crashing at his place?" Emma asks.

"Too long," I say.

"He's only home half the time," Brendon says. "Won't admit that he's seeing someone."

"I see people every day, all day," I say.

"What a Dean line." Emma laughs.

Kaylee nods. "He and Chloe took forever to admit it."

Emma whispers something in her ear.

Kaylee whispers back.

There's no sign Brendon knows.

Kaylee's kept our secret.

But then...

He's not a fucking idiot.

He must have an inkling.

We're going to tell him.

Soon.

But not tonight.

I already have one life changing announcement tonight.

I uncap the Pellegrino. Fill our glasses one at a time. "That's what I want to talk about?"

"Can't take any more of their dirty sex?" Emma asks. "It's not hot at all? It's actually disgusting?"

"Hate to break it to you, Em, but it's hot as fuck," I say.

Kaylee's face goes white. "You can, um... We're not that loud."

"You are," I say.

Kaylee looks to Brendon *really?*

He nods.

"But we... I..." She looks to me. "Really?"

"Yeah. You could give a few professional performers a run for their money," I say.

"Oh my God." Kaylee's blush spreads to her chest. "I... you should have said something! I would have toned it down."

"No way in hell," Brendon says.

Emma shakes her head. "See. They're already back at it."

"Think you started it this time," I say.

"Nuh uh. You did." Emma's smile spreads over her cheeks. She wraps her fingers around her glass. Holds it up. "Tell me why I'm toasting."

Because I'm four months sober.

Because I have a job that fulfills me.

Because I remember what it means to be an artist.

Because I'm crazy fucking in love with her.

Fuck, there's so much right.

But none of that is the reason why I'm here.

"I found an apartment." I hold up my glass. "Already started moving in."

"Yeah?" Emma's eyes light up with a mix of pride and desire.

It will be a hell of a lot easier fucking her with my own place.

And we're going to christen every fucking inch of that place.

My balls tighten.

She looks too divine in that dress.

I need it on the floor.

I need her under me.

I need her groaning my name.

"That's awesome, Hunter." Emma holds up her glass. "To the end of your free audio porn."

Kaylee blushes. "Um... how about, to this new phase of your life?"

"I like mine better. But it's your call, Hunter." Emma's eyes meet mine.

"To everything going right in my life," I say.

"I'll drink to that," Brendon says.

The four of us clink glasses.

And for the entire fucking dinner, I feel it.

439

I have a place.

A family.

A life.

WE MEET AT BRENDON'S PLACE.

After a long conversation and too much herbal tea, the party breaks up.

Kaylee insists on a walk on the beach. Before she drags her boyfriend away, she whispers something in Emma's ear.

Emma comes to me with a smile. "We have time."

"How much?" I ask.

"Not enough." She waits until the sliding glass door closes, until Brendon and Kaylee are gone, then she intertwines her fingers with mine.

I lead her up the stairs.

Neither of us has to say it.

It's so obvious.

I need to be inside her.

I need her groaning my name.

I need her coming so hard she can't stand it.

HUNTER

I strip Emma slowly. Take my time laying her on the bed. Tasting every inch of her sweet cunt.

Driving her to the edge.

Pushing her over it.

She groans my name as she comes.

Then she tears off my clothes, climbs on top of me, and rides me hard.

I come too quickly.

But she's there right after me.

And, fuck, it really is beautiful watching pleasure spread over her expression.

After we're finished, she collapses next to me.

I pull her comforter over us. Wrap my arms around her. Hold her close.

My breath slows.

My heart steadies.

My eyes get heavy.

I don't mean to fall asleep in her bed.

But I do.

I don't wake to the sliding glass door.

Or footsteps.

Or Kaylee's voice.

No.

I wake to Emma shrieking as she pulls the blanket to her chest.

To horror streaking Kaylee's eyes.

Brendon staring at me like I'm pure scum.

"Brendon." Kaylee's fingers curl around his wrist. "Maybe we should…"

He pulls his hand back.

His fingers curl into fists. But he just stands there. Still. Angry. Patient.

It would be easier if he was hitting me.

If he was calling me an asshole.

This…

Fuck, the disappointment is worse.

"Brendon—" I try to reach for an explanation, but there's nothing I can say. I've been lying to the guy for weeks. I've had time. I've had chances. I've had nothing but bullshit excuses.

"Don't." He turns and slams the door shut behind him.

Emma's eyes turn down. Her lips curl into a frown. Her fingers skim my chest. "You don't have to go."

"Em—"

"Please."

She sees it in my eyes.

How much this changes everything.

It shouldn't.

But it does.

It's so fucking clear from the way he looked at me.

I'm still a piece of shit.

I'm fucking up her family. Her job. Her friends.

She presses her lips to mine. It's short. Fast. Needy.

I want to stay.

To give her every ounce of my affection.

But I can't.

Not right now.

I shift off the bed and into my clothes.

"Hunter, please."

"I'll see you soon."

"When?"

"A couple days." I grab my wallet. My cell. My watch.

"But—"

"We need to let this blow over."

She shakes her head. "He needs to get over himself."

"Maybe. But he's the only brother you're ever going to have."

"Fuck him."

"Em—"

"Don't say it like that."

"Like what."

"Like you're breaking up with me."

I can't.

She gathers the blanket in her hand. Holds it to her chest as she slides off the bed. "Really?"

"We can do this later."

"Fuck you."

"Em—"

She pulls the door open and motions for me to leave. "Go to hell."

I could say I'm already there.

But I don't have the snappy response in me today.

EMMA

I shower until I'm raw, but it does nothing to soothe me.
Righteous anger runs through my veins.
Fails to keep me warm.

This stupid raspberry towel just makes me think of Hunter and the hurt in his gorgeous blue eyes.

Fuck him for that.

I change. Disregard our *knock first* rule. Barrel straight into Brendon's bedroom.

He's sitting at his desk with his sketchbook.

Kaylee is sitting on the bed, her legs curled into her chest, her fingers around her Kindle.

Fuck, I don't know what I want to say to my best friend.

She should have stopped him.

Or talked sense into him.

Or something…

Why is every man in my life a hypocritical idiot?

"You don't get a say in who I date." My fingers curl into my jeans. I need to be home. I need to be somewhere else. I need to be in a world that isn't bullshit.

"Em—" Brendon's eyes narrow.

"No. Only people who respect me call me Em." I suck a breath through my teeth. "You don't get to—"

"Maybe we should go." Kaylee slides off the bed. Her lips curl into a frown. Her green eyes fill with concern.

She's worried about me.

About him too.

About being in the middle, probably.

But this isn't her fault.

"You don't get a say in who I fuck." I exhale slowly. Fail to find calm in it. "You don't get a say in my life. Period."

"This isn't about you," Brendon says.

"You warning your friend not to fuck me is about me." I take a step backward. "You can sell yourself whatever bullshit story you have about your noble intentions. I'm not buying it."

"I didn't," he says.

I stare at my brother.

He stares back at me.

"You fucked my best friend behind my back for months," I say.

He says nothing.

"She's younger than I am. You're older than he is. Where the fuck do you get off telling me that this is wrong when it's exactly what you're doing?"

"Have I?" he asks.

"What?"

"When did I say it was wrong?" he asks.

"Fuck you." I see red. The entire world is red. The entire world is bullshit. "He's gone because of you."

"He's gone because of him," Brendon says.

"Em. Let's go. Please." Kaylee hugs her Kindle to her chest.

I shake my head.

Stare down my brother.

God, he's so calm and sure and superior.

"Do you have any fucking clue what's going on?" I ask.

"I saw enough," he says.

"No. You don't know. I care about him. And you're fucking ruining that." My heart thuds against my chest.

"Em—"

"Save it for someone who can tolerate your bullshit." I turn and run down the stairs.

Tears well in my eyes. Then I blink, and my lashes are heavy, and I can barely see.

This is unfair.

This is bullshit.

How can he open me up then leave?

How can he promise to stay then leave?

How can he love me then leave?

After a few minutes, Kaylee climbs into the car. She gets me into the passenger seat, turns the key, drives us home.

I crumble on the couch a blubbering mess.

She hugs me and puts on Disney movies and plies me with chocolate.

But it's not enough.

As long as he's gone, nothing is ever going to be enough.

53

HUNTER

All night, I toss and turn.

My head buzzes.

The betrayal streaking Emma's expression.

The disgust in Brendon's eyes.

The same as Chase's stare.

The same as the day he caught me drinking and kicked me out of his life.

I'm still a piece of shit.

I'm still fucking up everything.

Yeah, maybe I'm sober now.

Maybe I'm staying away from the bottle.

But I'm as toxic as ever.

After a few hours, I give up on sleep. Find a spot on the couch. Stare at my cell.

Think of something to text Emma.

Come up empty.

Sometime around six thirty, the sun streaks the curtains. It falls over the empty apartment—I've got a mattress, a frame, and a suitcase full of clothes.

That's it.

I'm due at work in a few hours.

I can't ditch my appointments.

I can't face everyone I've hurt.

Not until I fix this.

I rack my brain for solutions.

The one that hits me is obvious.

It's awful.

But it's the only way.

54

EMMA

After four cups of coffee and too many chocolate chip pancakes, I'm semi-coherent.

Kaylee offers to call in sick. To stay with me all day.

But we both know she'll lose her serving job if she doesn't find a replacement.

I don't want that on my conscience.

I have enough on my conscience.

Despite the anger buzzing through my veins, my heart refuses to climb aboard the *I hate Hunter* train.

It's still screaming for him.

It's still begging me to fix this.

It will get the message eventually.

For now...

I don't want to be at Inked Hearts.

I don't want to watch my brother work.

I certainly don't want to see that hurt look in Hunter's eyes and feel his pain in my soul.

Sometimes, it's awful caring about someone.

I stop for an Americano on my way to work, but it's no comfort.

The taste makes me think of him.

His fingers on my skin.

His lips on my cheek.

His moan as he finishes a cup of coffee.

I finish the drink, but I don't enjoy it.

I don't enjoy the big yellow sun, or the bright blue sky, or the girly string lights lining the walls at Inked Hearts.

I hate everything.

Especially Hunter.

I'm ready to tell him to go fuck himself.

But he isn't there.

He's supposed to work today.

He's booked from morning to night.

I...

He...

What?

My asshole brother is standing behind the counter.

His eyes fill with apology as they meet mine.

That's nothing.

Worse than nothing.

I...

He...

Fuck, I can't find a cutting remark. This is too heavy. I'm too heavy.

"Em..." His eyes turn down.

"What?"

He pushes something toward me. A piece of paper, typed and signed.

Hunter's resignation.

"What did you...?" My fingers curl into the paper. It's... He... "Why?"

"I didn't."

"But…"

"He called Ryan first. Made sure we're still on board with hiring Chase and Griffin."

"But they said… they want nothing to do with him."

"Yeah. But if he isn't here…"

Fuck.

I want to hate him for this.

For leaving.

But he's doing exactly what I would.

Sacrificing for his family.

For what he thinks is right.

He's so fucking stupid, thinking this is right.

But, God…

I guess my heart is just as stupid.

Because I don't hate him more.

I want to hate him.

But I don't.

I really don't.

55

EMMA

It's easy, finding the info I need.

Tattoo artists are always sharing their work. Tagging their shops. Leaving hints to their exact location.

After work, I drive straight to the shop.

He's standing there, behind the counter, checking out a customer.

He has this stern look on his face.

That paternal *I know best.*

That bullshit *I know everything.*

The same as Brendon's expression.

Figures Hunter and I suffer from equally overbearing older brothers.

I watch Chase chuckle with his customer. Watch a smile light up his blue eyes—a little darker than Hunter's, but just as deep and beautiful.

He's hot. Smart. Quiet.

The type of guy I'd normally go for.

But I can't see any of that.

Only the hurt he's causing Hunter.

I wait until the customer leaves, then I suck a breath through my nose, and storm into the shop.

Chase's eyes go right to me.

They light up with recognition. "If you're here to beg me to come to Inked Hearts, you can forget it."

"Excuse me?"

"I told Hunter no. I told Ryan no. I'm going to tell you the same thing."

What? He... he doesn't want the job.

I exhale slowly. Try to get the gears in my brain to turn.

It doesn't happen.

I'm too tired. Everything is blurring together.

Hurt and caffeine are a powerful combination, but they aren't doing shit for my concentration.

Hunter is leaving in some attempt to repay his debts.

Of course his brother wants nothing to do with that.

They're all just...

UGH.

"Get the fuck over yourself, Chase." I press my palms into the counter. "Your brother screwed up, sure. He lied to you. He hurt you. Are you going to hold that against him forever?"

He stares back at me.

"You have any idea how much it kills him that you won't forgive him?"

He just stares.

"Do you even care or are you so stuck on this idea of cutting him off?"

"I'm doing what's best for him."

"Obviously not. Or he'd be at work right now. He'd be with me right now."

"You're better off."

"No. I'm not. That's what you don't get. Maybe he made mistakes. Maybe he really was a piece of shit when he drank. I don't know that guy. I never did, not really. But the Hunter I know now? The sober one? He's patient. He's sweet. He's funny. Supportive. Talented. Loyal."

"You're a sweet kid."

"I'm not a kid."

"Yeah, you are."

"I'm an adult. I have a job. I have my own apartment. I have my own desires and ambitions and dreams. I don't need another man telling me how I feel or what's best for me. Maybe I'm not the most objective source. Maybe I'm too in love to be objective. But the guy I know wouldn't hurt someone on purpose."

Fuck.

I'm in love with Hunter.

I'm so fucking in love with Hunter.

Of course it's hitting me now.

Feelings are cruel.

"You love him that much?" he asks.

"Yeah." My next breath is steadier. "I do."

"He ask you to—"

"No. He broke up with me."

His brow furrows with confusion.

"He's an idiot."

"We can agree about that."

"But he… he is a good person."

Something in his expression changes. Relents. Like he's accepting my words.

"You don't know me. Or owe me anything. But your brother loves you. He deserves another chance. And even if you do hate him, why not take a job at the best shop in Southern California instead of staying at this shit hole?"

"Maybe I like this shit hole?"

"Do you?"

He says nothing.

"I make the schedule. I can make sure you're never working the same shift."

"I'll think about it."

"No. You'll do it. Today. Or that's it. Job offer is gone."

"You don't have a lot of bargaining power."

"Yeah, but I'm pissed and hurt. I don't care."

He chuckles. "You want some coffee?"

"Are you taking the job?"

"Sit down. I'll make a pot."

"Yes or no?"

"I'm offering coffee. Take it or leave it."

Fucking asshole.

No wonder Hunter is such a mess.

I want to tell Chase to fuck off.

But I'm not turning down coffee.

I'm not completely senseless. "Fine. But it better be good."

"I can see why he likes you."

"Go fuck yourself."

He smiles. "You really are perfect for him."

56

HUNTER

I wake to my buzzing cell.
Three missed calls.
A dozen new texts.
All from Chase.
What the fuck?

Chase: Your girlfriend is here. I'm pretty sure she needs you. But she might kick the shit out of you too.

That sounds like her.
I don't think.
I reply immediately.

Hunter: Where is here?

He sends an address.
A shitty shop in Mar Vista.
One that doesn't deserve his talent.
Hell, the place shouldn't even be open.
But one thing at a time.

Emma is sitting in a chair in the lobby, fingers curled around her purse, head resting against the back of her chair.

She's sleeping like a baby.

The picture of serenity.

No doubt she's dreaming about murdering me in cold blood, but it still feels good, seeing her like this.

Chase moves out from his suite.

His eyes meet mine.

They fill with a tiny hint of hope.

There's a part of him that believes I'm not a worthless piece of shit.

It shouldn't mean everything.

But it does.

"She fell asleep about an hour ago." His eyes flit to Emma. "Can't believe she's comfortable here."

Fuck, it's the most he's said to me in six months.

"She probably hasn't slept," I say.

"Heard you dumped her."

"I ended things."

"You always had a way of losing a good thing."

"It's my signature."

He chuckles. "This time, you really fucked-up."

"Yeah?"

"Yeah." His gaze shifts to Emma. "She came here to defend you. Tore me a new one."

"She did?"

He nods. "Said I need to get the fuck over myself and accept your apology."

I can't help but smile. After everything, she's here.

Hell, she's defending me.

"She's in love with you," Chase says.

She is?

"You love her too?"

"Yeah."

"Fuck, I guess I'm a sucker for romance." He shakes his head. "Always have been."

He laughs at himself. "Yeah. But... fuck, Hunter, you broke my heart."

"I know."

"I don't fucking care if you know."

"I'm sorry."

He nods. Not accepting the apology but acknowledging it. "It's gonna take me a long time to forgive you."

I nod.

"And I'm gonna take Emma up on her offer to keep us on different shifts."

"You're—"

"Yeah. Called Ryan twenty minutes ago."

"Fuck."

"Guy's moodier than you are."

I chuckle. "It's close."

He laughs too.

For a second, everything is normal.

My brother loves me.

Wants the best for me.

Wants me in his life.

The moment passes, but it doesn't drift into hell.

Chase doesn't forgive me yet, but he does love me. He does want the best for me.

Right now, I can see that.

He's doing all this because he cares.

Not in spite of it.

He continues, "Ryan has a lot of good shit to say about you."

My cheeks flush. It's weird hearing secondhand compliments. Hearing Chase say anything good about me.

"I have a condition."

"Yeah?"

"Don't hurt her again."

"Didn't mean to—"

"I don't care. You hurt her again, that's it. I'm out."

"You don't know her."

"What can I say? I'm a romantic."

Behind us, Emma stirs.

Slowly, her eyes blink open.

"Hunter…" She looks around the room, slowly taking in her surroundings. "Shit."

"I'll drive you home," I say.

"No, I…" She bites her lip.

"You're not driving right now." I move closer. Until I can offer my hand. "So it's either me or Chase."

"You're talking?" she asks.

"Yeah. And if you want the details—" I hold out my hand.

She takes it. "And coffee."

"And coffee." I help her up.

Chase nods a goodbye. "Give him hell, kid."

She smiles *oh, I will.*

I'm going to make him work for this.

HUNTER

E mma falls asleep on the drive home.
I carry her to her apartment.
She stirs as I lay her on the crimson comforter.
Her eyes fix on mine.

For a second, she stares at me like I'm everything she wants.

Then she blinks and hurt fills her dark eyes.

"You sleep last night?" I ask.

"Sleep is for losers."

I sit on the bed next to her.

She rolls onto her back and unzips her jeans. "I am tired." She pushes her pants off her hips. "But mostly of your bullshit."

Fuck, she's adorable.

She's hurt and angry, but she's adorable too.

"That delivery was pretty good," I say.

"Thanks."

I brush a hair behind her ear. "I am sorry."

"Fuck you." She turns her head, breaking our touch. "I'm not accepting your apology. Not until you fix it."

I want to.

But this isn't my strong suit.

"If you don't want to be with me because you don't want to be with me, fine. If you need more time or space, if you can't handle the intimacy, if you're sick of me, fine. But fuck you if you think you're doing this for me." She wraps her arms around her pillow. "I don't care how good your intentions are. I get to decide what I want. You don't get a fucking say."

It's fair.

I don't like it.

I'm not sure I can accept it.

But it's fair.

"So… go… think about it. Lift weights or drink coffee or draw something moody. Whatever it is that helps you figure out your shit. Go. Figure it out. And come back. But this it, Hunter. If you're in, I need you to be all in." Her eyelids flutter together. She lets out a soft yawn. Stretches then curls into a tiny ball.

"Go to sleep."

"Are you…"

"I'll stay until Kaylee gets home."

"Thanks."

"Of course." I slide off the bed.

"Hunter?"

"Yeah?"

"I still hate you."

I chuckle. "I wouldn't expect anything less."

EMMA

I wake to darkness and Ariel singing about how desperately she wants to be part of the human world.

Kaylee's home.

Which means Hunter's gone.

My heart twists.

I want him here.

I want him a million miles away.

I want some magic apology that will earn my forgiveness.

Hell, I want to hate him as much as I keep telling myself I do.

But I can't see him as a traitor who betrayed me.

Only as a hurt guy who keeps sabotaging himself.

He warned me about his self-destructive streak.

I guess it's like that saying goes.

When someone tells you who they are, believe them.

I slip into the bathroom. Brush my teeth. Wash my face. Join Kaylee on the couch.

She rests her head on my shoulder. "You okay?"

"No." I wrap my arm around her. "But I'll get there."

"Even if he decides he'd rather be friends—"

"Maybe. But, God, I hope he doesn't."

"Me too." She grabs a bar of chocolate from the table. Breaks off a square. Hands it to me. "Brendon is sorry. He just—"

"I know. We'll talk. I'll get over it."

"Yeah?"

"Don't tell him though. I want him to sweat this for a few days."

She laughs. "You know I can't—"

"I know. But let me believe he's suffering."

"He is. He hates that—"

"No apologizing for him. Just informing on suffering."

"He's wracked with guilt. He can't eat or sleep."

"Or fuck?"

"Well, if you really want those details."

"I don't."

"It would distract you."

"Yeah. It would." I let the chocolate melt on my tongue. "But this is good too."

AFTER TWO MORE MOVIES, KAYLEE GOES TO SLEEP.

I stay up. Pore over the design Hunter drew on my desk.

My fingers trace the lines again and again.

Until my fingers are numb and my eyelids are heavy.

Somehow, I crawl into bed. Shut my eyes. Find sleep.

I dream about Hunter and apologies and a big, beautiful world where I can trust someone with my heart.

I wake to a heavy guitar riff.

It's still comforting.

It's still my favorite song.

And that—the smell of coffee.

And—shit—is something burning?

I jump out of bed. Into the main room.

Hunter is in the kitchen, flipping a pancake. Though that's putting it charitably. That thing is a charred mess.

He shoots me an apologetic look. "This is outside my skill set."

"Turn the burner down."

He does.

"Everything on a plate."

He stacks the charred, pancake-like discs of flour, eggs, and canola oil on a plate.

"Give me five minutes."

He nods.

"Don't burn the place down."

"I'll try."

"You'll do."

He chuckles.

"What?"

"You sound so nerdy now."

"How?"

"That's what Yoda says."

"You barely like *Star Wars*."

"Didn't say you got it from me."

"Shut up and make more batter."

"Yes, Mistress."

I fight my chuckle. God, it's good to see him. And hear his voice. And smell his shampoo.

I have to drag myself to the bathroom.

And, yeah, okay, I do make a point of fixing my hair, applying concealer and lipstick, changing into a cute dress.

If he's here to fix us, I want to remember it like this.

If he's here to end us, I want to make him feel the loss.

Deep breath.

Steady exhale.

I step into the main room.

His eyes fix on me.

Fill with appreciation.

Need. Affection. Love.

God, there's so much in those gorgeous blue eyes.

I want all of it.

I want to shoulder his pain.

To share mine.

To hold him up when he needs that.

And lean on him when I need that.

He's here, playing my favorite band and fixing my coffee and hopelessly trying to make pancakes.

God, I hope he figures his shit out better than he makes pancakes.

"You look gorgeous." His voice is soft. Sweet. Loving.

God, I need that. All of it. "Thank you." I step into the kitchen. Focus on our task.

Oil. Burner. Batter. Spatula.

He stays close as I fix a round of pancakes.

Then a second.

The room fills with the smell of chocolate and flour.

He pours a cup of coffee for me.

My fingers brush his as I take it. "You really make a girl wait."

"Need to improve my chances."

My lips curl into a smile. I can't help it. He's just so… Hunter.

And, fuck, this is good coffee. Smooth and clear with hints of grapefruit and almond.

I let out a heavy sigh.

His pupils dilate. "Fuck, Em. You have no idea what that sound does to me."

"So tell me." *Explain this. Justify it. Convince me to forgive you.*

He brushes my hair behind my ear. Rests his palm on my cheek. Rubs my temple with his thumb.

Fuck, that feels good.

I want to soak up the comfort of it.

But I can't.

Not if it's some sort of shitty consolation prize.

God, this whole thing could be some shitty consolation prize.

I don't love you. I can't be with you. But I can do breakfast. That helps, right?

My stomach twists.

My heart pounds.

My balance falters.

Waiting is impossible.

But, somehow, I manage to sip my coffee.

To stare into his gorgeous blue eyes.

To wait.

It feels like it takes a million years.

Finally, he moves closer.

"I thought about what you said." He sets his mug on the counter. Brushes my side with his free hand.

"Which part?"

"Mostly about me being an idiot."

"You are."

He nods. "Thoroughly."

I suck a breath through my teeth. That sounds good. But it… I… "And?"

"You were right. You're sharp as hell. You're certainly smarter than I am."

"Obviously."

His lips curl into a half-smile. "You know what you need."

I nod.

"I'm not used to that. I'm not used to people who really do know best. Fuck, Em… I can't remember a time when I had my best interests at heart. When I knew enough about who I was to know if I was good for someone."

"You… your brother really hates you."

"Yeah. He will for a long time. I deserve that. I'm the one who fucked that up. I was an asshole for years. I still am sometimes."

"Yeah. A lot."

He chuckles. "I'm getting there. I'm trying. But, fuck, it's hard seeing myself as this guy who deserves to be in your life."

I swallow hard.

"I want to believe I'm making your life better."

"You are."

"I know. I get it, intellectually, but it's hard to feel it." His voice drops. "I'm getting there. Learning how to see things as they are. But it's hard. It's going to take me awhile."

"Okay."

"If you don't want a damaged guy—"

"I would have kicked you to the curb a long time ago."

His lips curl into a smile. "I got you something."

"Yeah?"

"Close your eyes."

I study his expression, but it doesn't give me a clue to his intentions.

I'm not sure where he's going.

Only that I want to find out.

I close my eyes.

He unpeels my fingers from my coffee cup and sets it on the counter.

He takes my hand. Brings it to his stomach. The soft fabric of his shirt.

Something slick underneath it.

Plastic wrap stretched over muscle.

I don't wait for instructions.

I open my eyes.

There it is.

Just above his hip bone.

Above the waistline of his jeans.

The design he drew on my desk.

The one that's ours.

"You..." My eyes go wide. My fingers press into his skin. I.. He... What...

"I'm all in."

"But…"

"I love you, baby. More than I've ever loved anyone. I'm yours if you'll have me."

"Yeah. Of course." I stare into those gorgeous blue eyes.

He loves me.

He's all in.

He…

I rise to my tiptoes to press my lips to his. "I love you too."

"Fuck, I missed you."

"It was a day."

"I still missed you."

"Then don't fuck shit up again."

"I'll try."

"We just talked about this."

"Okay." His lips curl into a smile. "I'll do."

"Yeah." I take his hand and motion to the bedroom. "You will."

"Baby, that was terrible."

"Yeah, maybe. But that doesn't change the facts." I step into my bedroom and motion for him to follow.

He does.

And it really is fucking perfect.

EPILOGUE

HUNTER

Emma presses her palms to the black plastic to lift herself up. Her ass hits the slick surface. Then her legs.

She slides over the counter.

To me.

My hand goes to her hair. I cup the back of her head. Tilt her so she's staring up at me.

Her dark eyes are wide with enthusiasm.

Let's get out of here so we can fuck properly.

I see that look every day.

I never get tired of it.

Ever.

I lean down to press my lips to hers.

Her tongue swirls around mine. Her fingers dig into my hair. Her legs wrap around my hips.

I groan against her mouth.

She groans back.

Someone launches into a slow clap.

Someone else yells. "Come on, take it off. I want full penetra-ion this time."

That's Wes.

I think.

Everything is a blur of breathy vocals, laughter, Emma's groan.

I warned Emma she'd train me to associate her favorite music genre with stripping her naked.

She did.

It gets worse every day.

I start panting the second I hear that thrashing guitar riff.

Right now, with her favorite album pouring from the speakers, her hands in my hair, her body pressed against mine—

Fuck, I'm not sure I can contain myself.

I pull back with a deep groan.

It's the only way to make sure I don't deliver on Wes's demand for full penetration.

I want her now.

Here.

Anywhere.

It doesn't matter as long as I get all of her.

Emma lets out a heady sigh.

Her dark eyes get dreamy.

Her expression is the perfect mix of affection and desire.

She wants me.

My body.

My heart.

My soul.

She has all of it—all of me—but it never hurts to remind her.

I wrap my fingers around her wrist. Bring her hand under my t-shirt. To the raised lines of the tattoo I got for her.

She stares up at me as she wraps her fingers around my wrist.

Brings my hand to the tattoo she got for me.

My fingertips skim the soft fabric of her dress.

I can't see or feel the ink, but I know it's there.

Our design.

Our love, on her body, forever.

She surprised me with the tattoo at our one year anniversary. She played it down, said it was more about needing to mark her body than to proclaim our love for the world to see.

But I don't care if the world sees it.

Only that I see it.

The ink isn't exactly in a *show this off every day spot*.

It's on her right side.

Fuck, she's tough, getting her first tattoo on her ribs.

But that was never a doubt.

Emma has always been an adorable badass.

"Hey, lovebirds. You gonna deliver that show or not?" Wes calls.

Griffin laughs. "You love their love."

"No, I love hot naked chicks." Wes motions *go on*.

"Admit it. You cried when she did her ink," Griffin says.

Wes clams up. "I did not." He shrugs *whatever*. "Go home if you're gonna get mushy. We got enough of that all day."

"Aw, you and your girl in a fight?" Griffin reaches over and musses Wes's hair.

Wes slaps his hand away. "Watch it."

"She get mad at you?" Griffin asks.

Wes mutters something and storms off.

We thought falling in love would ease his obnoxious tendencies, but it hasn't.

He's less high strung (though he'd never admit it), but he's even more Wes.

"He does have a point." Emma runs her fingers through my hair. "We could be at your place."

"Yeah?" I rest my palm on her cheek. Rub her temple with my thumb.

Her eyelids flutter together as she leans into the gesture. "Hunter…"

"Yeah, baby?"

"Don't make me say it here."

"Say what?" This is the only time I see Emma shy.

It doesn't happen as often as it used to.

She's at home with her body now.

She's past what happened with that asshole.

But she's not the same as she was either.

Those scars made her stronger.

I lobbied for her to press charges. Make it official.

But she wanted to move on.

To close that chapter.

At the time, I was pissed he wouldn't hurt for what he did. I wanted to go to his place and kick his ass.

I wanted to kill him.

But I knew that would only poke her bruise.

I'm still not sure it was the right call—her deciding to keep the assault a secret, something that only me and Kaylee knew—but I trust Emma.

She knows what's best for her.

And I—

Fuck, I'm still over the moon that she believes I'm what's best for her.

"I want to fuck you senseless." Her voice pulls me back to the moment.

It's soft. Breathy. Needy.

The Emma only I get.

"Hunter." Her eyes flutter open. "Don't make me do it here."

"Yeah?"

"I don't want to give Wes the satisfaction."

"That's the only reason?"

Her nod is heavy.

It's there, in her eyes.

Right now, she doesn't care about anything but getting me naked.

I pull back and offer Emma my hand.

She takes it as she slides off the counter. "Your place is still a fifteen minute walk?"

I nod.

"You're cruel."

"You prefer the back room?"

Her eyes dart to the door. For a long moment, she considers it. Then she shakes her head. "No. Your place." Her fingers intertwine with mine as she takes a step toward the door. "But walk fast."

———

THE SECOND I CLOSE THE APARTMENT DOOR, EMMA POUNCES.

She hooks her first two fingers through my belt loop and leads me straight to the bedroom.

She doesn't even glance at the closed office door.

Thank fuck.

This needs to stay a surprise.

No. It doesn't matter how I tell her.

As long as she says yes.

But what I have planned for after—

I'm pretty sure that shit is going to help my chances.

She kicks the bedroom door open and steps backward. "Clothes off."

"You first."

She shakes her head. "You first."

"Baby, you know I love it when you get bossy."

"If you loved it, you'd obey orders."

"Yeah?" I raise a brow.

She laughs and falls back onto the bed. "Clothes. Off." She places her palms on the crimson comforter. Then she lifts one and motions *off*.

Fuck she looks good surrounded in crimson.

She belongs here.

In this bed.

Our bed.

It's practically ours—she spends every weekend here, her clothes take up half my dresser and most of my closet, her *Sarcasm Loading* mug is sitting on my counter—but that technical difference between practically ours and actually ours—

I can't take it anymore.

I need our lives intertwined.

I need to make it official.

Hell, if I thought her brother would accept it, I'd already have a ring.

As it is…

Brendon and I are close now.

Hell, he's one of my best friends.

He knows I love Emma more than anything.

We both want the best for her.

But he still sees her as his baby sister.

I can't wait for him.

I'm going to ask her one day.

Soon even.

But first things first.

"You're getting hazy." Her dark eyes fill with curiosity. "You okay?"

"Yeah." Nervous as hell. But okay. No, better. "I'm fucking fantastic."

"You know what would be fantastic?"

I shake my head.

"If you were naked."

"Baby, you're insatiable."

"Always."

"Always?" I raise a brow.

She nods. "When am I not?"

It's a fair point. There hasn't been a single point in our relationship where we've been able to keep our hands off each other.

It was equal points lust and affection at first.

I needed her perky tits in my hand, her apple ass against my pelvis, her cunt pulsing around me.

I still need her body.

But I need so much more.

I need her unfurling for me.

Offering herself to me.

Inviting me into her body.

Fuck, the trust that flows between us—

It still takes my breath away.

She clears her throat, calling me back to the room. "You're already—" She points to my hardening dick without a hint of coyness.

"Thinking about being inside you."

"You think too much." She lifts her leg and motions to her black wedges. "More stripping. Less thinking."

I nod. "Yes, Mistress."

"No Mistress shit."

"You sure?" I drop to my knees to peel her shoes from her feet. The right. Then the left.

They're so Emma.

Soft black suede with four inches of height.

She's not shy about wearing tall shoes.

She loves it when she towers over me.

I can't exactly complain.

These things make her legs look a million miles long.

Not that she needs them.

Right now—

Fuck, this is exactly where I need to be.

My fingers curl around her ankles. The right. Then the left.

Slowly, I peel her legs apart.

She climbs up the bed. Reaches for my hair and tugs *come here*.

I do.

I place myself between her legs.

CRYSTAL KASWELL

Drag my lips up her calf, over her knee, up her inner thigh.
Over her panties.
She squirms as I pull the soft fabric aside.
I lick her up and down.
Once, for me.
To savor the taste of her.
Then for her.
Again.
And again.
And again.
I lick her softly.
Then faster.
Harder.
Right.
Left.
Up.
Down.
Zigzags.
Circles.
Higher.
And higher.
And higher.
She gasps. "Fuck, Hunter." Her fingers dig into my hair. "Don't stop."
I focus on the spot where she needs me most.
Start soft.
Then get harder.
Harder.
There—
Her breath hitches in her throat.
Her back arches.
Her hips buck.
I keep my pace until she's at the edge.
Her toes dig into the crimson comforter.

480

Her moans bounces around the room.

Her thighs hug my cheeks.

There.

I push her over the edge.

She groans my name as she comes.

I lick her through her orgasm.

Savor the way she gets wetter. Sweeter.

She's so fucking beautiful like this.

I could stay here forever.

I really could.

But Em has other plans.

She reaches for me with her free hand. "Fuck me."

I nod as I climb up her body.

She pushes her panties to her ankles.

I undo my belt.

She tugs her dress over her head.

Then the bra.

She stares up at me as she does away with my t-shirt. My jeans. My boxers.

We're naked together.

It's far from the first time.

But it's every bit as thrilling.

It's different now. Not a rush of novelty. Something deeper and purer.

An intimacy that goes all the way to my soul.

Fuck, I'm so cheesy now.

I'm a walking, talking cliché, spouting slogans about sobriety and love and connection.

But I don't care.

She wraps her arms around me as she spreads her legs.

I stare into her eyes.

Lower my body onto hers.

My tip strains against her.

Then it's one inch at a time.

Fuck, she feels good.

It's so fucking right, her skin against mine, nothing between us.

I thank the genius who invented the IUD.

Then I let my conscious thoughts fade.

I bury myself in Emma.

She pulls me closer.

I drive deeper.

We move together until she's groaning my name.

Then she flips over. Grabs her vibrator—the one I bought her for her birthday, the first birthday of hers we shared—off the bedside table.

She brings it to her clit as she arches her back to beckon me.

I bring my hands to her hips. Hold her in place as I drive into her.

She turns her head back to stare into my eyes.

Then she's kissing me.

And I'm kissing back.

And the world is a perfect blur of her groan and her lips and her soft, slick cunt.

Fuck, the way that toy buzzes—

She comes again and again.

I rock her through every orgasm.

Until I'm there.

And we're groaning together, breathing together, coming together.

I wait until I've spilled every drop, then I collapse behind her, pull her body into mine.

Take her sex toy.

Bring it to her clit.

Make her come again.

I make her come until she's dizzy.

AFTER, WE SHOWER TOGETHER.

She helps me soap and shampoo.

Runs her fingers over the lyrics above my hip.

Then over the sobriety chip on my other hip—the one that marked two years clean.

Fuck, it's still hard to believe.

I've been sober for two years. Almost three.

She's been mine for nearly as long.

It was weird, at first, when we announced our relationship to our friends.

Most of them knew. Or suspected.

A few got overly involved.

Asked about us constantly. Offered unnecessary advice. Generally failed to mind their own business.

At first, it annoyed me.

But the more it went on, the more it felt like love.

I've always had a family. But this is the first time I've really felt it.

Chase and I aren't best friends, but we're okay.

I know he's going to be there.

As long as I devote myself to sobriety, as long as I keep trying, he'll be there.

Everyone will.

I see it all the time now.

There's so much love in my life.

Just Emma would be enough.

But this—

Fuck.

"You're going off someplace again." Her words dissolve in the running water.

She looks so fucking delicious sopping wet.

I'm tempted to have her again.

But this first. "Thinking about how much I love you."

"You are not."

I nod *am too.*

She shakes her head *are not.*

I nod back. "Thinking about how lucky I am."

"Yeah?"

I nod. "Fucking my gorgeous boss."

She giggles. "That is lucky." She rises to her tiptoes to press her lips to me. "You should enjoy it while it lasts."

She took that assistant manager gig Ryan offered after our first Christmas together.

Now that she's done with school, she has the manager gig waiting.

She says it's only for now, while she builds plans for her boutique, but I'm not so sure.

She belongs at Inked Hearts.

It's brighter with her there.

The entire world is brighter with her there.

"What are you really thinking about?" She kisses me again.

"How I want to fuck you again."

Her eyes fill with surprise. "Uh-uh. I'm too sore."

"Yeah?"

She nods. "How is that a surprise?"

"Go on."

"You made this happen."

"How?"

"You know what you did."

"Tell me."

She shakes her head *you're ridiculous.* "I don't think I have any more orgasms in me after that." She pulls the curtain and reaches for a towel. "But I'm happy to watch if you want to put on a show."

"Yeah?" I raise a brow.

She nods *hell yeah.*

"Not sure I'm up for it yet."

"Tease."

I nod. "You love it."

"Maybe." Her lips curl into a smile.

"A lot."

She holds up her thumb and forefinger *a little*. "I'm going to get dressed. What do you want for dinner? I'm starved."

After two and a half years under her tutelage, I'm a better cook, but I'm far from skilled. "Let's order in."

"Something spicy, yeah?"

I nod. "You pick."

She steps out of the shower and wraps herself in a raspberry towel.

I turn the water off.

She moves to the sink. Runs a comb through her hair. Washes her face. Turns back to me with that look. That *why are you staring at me like that* look.

"Sorry, baby, I can't help it."

"But what?"

"You're so Emma." And I'm so scared to do this. But I want it too badly to back out. "Do me a favor?"

"Sure."

I reach for a towel. Wrap it around my hips.

She pouts. "You could do me a favor and lose that."

"I'll think about it."

She shakes her head. "Less thinking. More doing."

I chuckle. She's perfect. She really is. "Put on some music for me. In the office."

"Yeah, sure." She looks at me funny—*why are you telling me where the speakers are*—but she still moves into the hallway.

Then the office.

Her gasp echoes through the space.

Then a squeal.

"Hunter!" She rushes into the hallway.

I meet her there.

She holds up the tiny box.

Points to the key sitting on the white stuffing.

Her fingers wrap around my wrist. She pulls me into the office.

Sits on the new desk.

The clean white one.

Bare except for a single design—the one we share.

"You... you... you want me to move in?" Her eyes bore into mine. She's wearing this perfect mix of confidence and vulnerability.

It's pure Emma.

"More than anything," I say.

"Really?"

"Really."

She wraps her arms around me. "Of course." She pulls my body into hers. Looks up at me. Kisses me.

Fuck, she tastes good.

Like home.

Because she is.

That's what I've figured out.

I still get lost sometimes.

But then I find her.

And I'm exactly where I'm supposed to be.

She's my heart, my soul, my home.

She's everything.

WANT MORE INKED HEARTS?

Sign up for <u>my mailing list</u> for an exclusive extended epilogue of *Breaking the Rules*.

Wes's book, *Losing It*, is coming in early 2019. Until then, keep your Inked Hearts fix going with Brendon and Kaylee's book, *Tempting*, a smoking hot forbidden romance.

ALSO BY CRYSTAL KASWELL

Sinful Serenade

Sing Your Heart Out - Miles

Strum Your Heart Out - Drew

Rock Your Heart Out - Tom

Play Your Heart Out - Pete

Sinful Ever After – series sequel

Dangerous Noise

Dangerous Kiss - Ethan

Dangerous Crush – Kit

Dangerous Rock – Joel

Dangerous Fling – Mal

Dangerous Encore - series sequel

Inked Hearts

Tempting - Brendon

Playing - Walker

Pretend You're Mine - Ryan

Hating You, Loving You - Dean

Breaking the Rules - Hunter

Losing It - Wes - coming early 2019

More coming in 2019

Standalones

Broken - Trent & Delilah

Dirty Rich

Dirty Deal - Blake

Dirty Boss - Nick

Sign up for the Crystal Kaswell mailing list

Made in the USA
Middletown, DE
06 June 2019